Beyond All Dreams

Books by Elizabeth Camden

The Lady of Bolton Hill

The Rose of Winslow Street

Against the Tide

Into the Whirlwind

With Every Breath

Beyond All Dreams

Beyond All Dreams

ELIZABETH CAMDEN

BETHANYHOUSE
a division of Baker Publishing Group
Minneapolis, Minnesota

Published by Bethany House Publishers
11400 Hampshire Avenue South
Bloomington, Minnesota 55438
www.bethanyhouse.com

Bethany House Publishers is a division of
Baker Publishing Group, Grand Rapids, Michigan

Printed in the United States of America

Library of Congress Cataloging-in-Publication Data
Camden, Elizabeth.
Beyond all dreams / Elizabeth Camden.
pages ; cm
Summary: "In 1897 Washington, D.C., Anna O'Brien, a librarian at the Library of Congress, assists charismatic young congressman Luke Callahan, but the more political secrets they uncover the more their growing trust is strained"— Provided by publisher.
ISBN 978-0-7642-1175-1 (softcover)
1. Women librarians—Fiction. 2. Legislators—United States—Fiction. 3. Washington (D.C.)—History—19th century—Fiction. I. Title.
PS3553.A429B49 2015
813′.54—dc23 2014031986

Scripture quotations are from the King James Version of the Bible.

This is a work of historical reconstruction; the appearances of certain historical figures are therefore inevitable. All other characters, however, are products of the author's imagination, and any resemblance to actual persons, living or dead, is coincidental.

Cover design by Jennifer Parker
Cover photography by Mike Habermann Photography, LLC

15 16 17 18 19 20 21 7 6 5 4 3 2 1

1

Washington, D.C.
October 1897

"I'm begging you, please stop looking at naughty pictures in the library." It was a sentence Anna never thought she would utter, and with a straight face no less. But these boys were on the verge of getting kicked out of the Library of Congress unless she intervened for them.

"They're medical pictures," Jack Wilkerson said from his position at the library worktable. "Please, Miss O'Brien, we just want to learn."

Was there anything more frustrating than a rowdy fifteen-year-old boy? The government hired hundreds of orphaned boys to serve as congressional pages at the US Capitol, where they performed odd jobs and ran errands for congressmen but rarely had much supervision. Lately, a group of them had been causing trouble in the library, and they'd just been caught flipping through anatomy books in the hunt for drawings of naked bodies.

Anna had an instinctive urge to protect these fatherless children. After all, she was an orphan herself, and a library could be a wonderful escape from the troubles of the world. She gathered the boys around the single worktable in the map room, which was crammed with atlases, map bins, and floor globes.

"You sounded like a pack of laughing hyenas as you ogled those books," she said. "I don't need a groveling show of contrition with sackcloth and ashes. A simple apology to the library's director will be fine."

"What are sackcloth and ashes for?" Jack asked.

"It's a metaphor," she said pointedly. "Metaphors are something grown-ups use when they can't set troublesome boys on fire."

Several of the boys giggled. "You're funny, Miss O'Brien."

"I'm also serious." She hoped she didn't sound too much like a schoolmarm, but working at the Library of Congress was the greatest privilege of her life. Even after six years, there were times Anna loved to stand in the aisles, awed by the immensity of the books towering above her. It was magical and magnificent. Amazing and inspiring. These books contained the wisdom of the ages, some of them outlasting the countries in which they had first been written. Caring for books and helping others unlock the mysteries inside them was what she'd been put on this earth to do.

She was going to miss this old library when they moved into their grand new building next month. The Library of Congress had been located in the US Capitol since 1810, when it was designed to hold a hundred thousand books. Now the collection had swelled to almost a million volumes, and they'd outgrown their space.

"The rules will be even tighter when we move into our new building," Anna said. "The light fixtures are plated with real gold. The floors have mosaics and precious metals in them. You can't hold footraces in the halls or slide down the banisters in the new building. You understand that, don't you?"

Jack smirked as he gave an antique globe a mighty twist to send it spinning. The ancient globe squeaked and wobbled, and Anna lunged to stop its dangerous spinning.

"Jack, you don't have cloven hooves and a pitchfork, do you? Because that would explain so much."

Honestly, she ought to give up and let Jack be banished for good. His necktie was lopsided, he'd tracked mud in that morning, and his reckless grin was entirely unrepentant. But the sight of that sloppily knotted tie . . . well, it got to her. Learning to knot a necktie was the kind of thing a father would have taught him.

Anna sighed. "Stand up and let me show you how to tie a proper Windsor knot."

She undid her own tie and tugged it flat to demonstrate the procedure. With her starchy white blouse and dark skirt, Anna tried to look as professional as all the men who worked in the Capitol.

Jack pretended not to care, but he scrutinized every movement as she demonstrated the technique for tying a Windsor knot. The other boys shifted in their seats to get a better view. This might be the most important lesson they learned all day.

A bell rang over the door as a man in a naval uniform entered, his ramrod posture and commanding presence making the map room seem smaller and more crowded.

"Miss Anna O'Brien?" the officer said.

Anna's heart sped up, and she let go of her partially knotted tie. This could only be about one thing. "Yes, sir?"

The officer handed her an envelope, its wax seal bearing the hallmark of the United States Navy.

"You are wanted downstairs in the naval affairs room. Immediately." He gave a slight bow and left the room, leaving them all a little stunned and amazed.

"I want a uniform like that," one of the boys said.

"Did you see his shoes? They were polished like mirrors!"

As the boys chattered, Anna wrestled with conflicting emotions. This had to be about the message she'd sent to the navy last week. There was no other reason she'd have come to their attention.

"What does it say?" Jack asked.

Anna popped the seal and scanned the message, a small smile curving her mouth. It was as she'd suspected.

"I found a mistake in an old naval report," she said softly. "I thought they'd want to know, so I sent them a message about it."

It was thrilling that the navy had taken her message seriously, for overlooking an error in the historical record was unthinkable for someone like Anna. Ever since becoming a librarian, she'd been feeling the vibrant golden chain that reached back centuries to other librarians, archivists, and historians, all of whom had chosen the same quest: the collection and preservation of the world's knowledge. Was there any more noble pursuit in all of human history? Future generations would depend on the diligence of librarians like her to ensure accuracy in the record of human knowledge. When she spotted that mistake in the old naval report, she knew it needed to be corrected.

"What kind of mistake was it?" one of the boys asked.

"A big one," she said, but didn't elaborate. It was too personal to discuss in front of a group of rambunctious boys. She wished the navy had sent her a simple thank-you note instead of demanding her presence. Meeting with strangers was always such torture.

"I don't even know where the naval affairs room is," she confessed as she fumbled to knot her tie again.

"I can show you," Jack said, springing to attention.

Anna rarely ventured outside the safety of the shabby old map room, where she was cocooned in a world of well-worn books, maps, and atlases. Everything was different downstairs in the main part of the Capitol, where the gilt and marble grandeur was like somewhere royalty gathered, because, well, royalty actually *did* gather there—along with senators, diplomats, prime ministers, and presidents. Pint-sized librarians didn't fit in down there, but given the formality of the summons, it didn't look like she had much choice.

She finished knotting her tie and wished she'd taken more care with her appearance that morning. Not that she could have improved it much. All her clothes were simple and plain because she hated anything that might draw attention to herself. Each morning she twisted her long brown hair into a tidy bun atop her head and fastened it with a modest onyx clip, the only piece of jewelry she owned.

She looked at Jack, wishing she had one tenth of the boy's bravado. "Let's go," she said.

It didn't take Anna long to realize the navy had no intention of thanking her for noticing an error in the fifteen-year-old report.

Oddly, it seemed they wanted her head on a platter.

"You've got a lot of gall," Lieutenant Gerald Rowland snapped from behind his mahogany desk. The bullnecked man began scolding Anna the moment she arrived.

Required to stand on the carpet before his desk while the seated officer snarled at her, Anna felt like a little brown sparrow quivering before a firing squad. She cleared her throat and tried to defend herself.

"When fifty-six men disappear in the middle of an ocean,

a complete and accurate investigation should be conducted," she said quietly.

"That investigation was done fifteen years ago." Lieutenant Rowland banged his fist on the table, making the pens and ink bottles jump. "The USS *Culpeper* sank during a late season hurricane, all hands lost. Case closed."

Anna was well aware of what had happened to the *Culpeper*. After all, her father had been one of the men who'd disappeared with the ship.

"That's the problem," she said, trying not to wilt under the blast of the man's glare. "The ship couldn't have sunk where the report claims. I'd like the case reopened so it can be corrected."

"Copies of that report were sent to the deceased sailors' families, and they were given a three-month period to file questions with the navy. That time is over."

"I wasn't in a position to ask questions. I was only twelve when the ship disappeared."

"When the ship *sank*," Lieutenant Rowland continued, "all the families received the sailor's wages plus six months of salary, just as the law allows. If you're trying to reopen the case to qualify for a pension, you can forget it."

Anna raised her chin a notch. "As you can see, I am gainfully employed and have no need for an orphan's pension. All I want is to know what happened to my father, and in light of this newly discovered error, I'd like the navy to correct its report."

"And you think you're smart enough to question the team of experts who wrote that report? What exactly does a map librarian do, anyway? Stack maps in alphabetical order?"

"Something like that."

Anna knew the nautical features of every bay, inlet, and harbor on the Eastern Seaboard, as well as the depth and navigability for every port from Maine to the Florida Keys. She could calculate longitude and latitude coordinates in her sleep. After all, she was a cartographer's daughter, and the skill came naturally to her.

Last week, Anna came across a new map from the weather bureau that tracked the historic paths of long-ago hurricanes. Her attention was drawn to the path of the storm that sank the *Culpeper*, and that was when she realized that the details in the navy's report on the *Culpeper* didn't correspond with this new information.

"The problem with the *Culpeper* was that it was crammed with scientists and bookworms instead of real sailors," Lieutenant Rowland said. "They could have ridden out that storm if there weren't so many useless scientists getting in the way."

Anna's father had been one of those navy scientists, dedicating years of his life to mapping the floor of the ocean. Using specially designed trawls, dredges, and thermometers, he lowered the equipment to measure the depth of the water and collect vials of sediment from the ocean floor. There had always been tension between warriors like Lieutenant Rowland and science officers like her father, but the navy owed it to the men of the *Culpeper* to ensure the report of their demise was accurate.

Lieutenant Rowland hadn't finished his rant. "Those scientists put decent sailors' lives in jeopardy, all so they could play with their test tubes in the middle of the ocean. We're not reopening the case, and you need to quit pestering the navy with ancient history. This incident is over. Is that clear?"

"I hear you, sir."

The lieutenant leaned forward. "What's the matter with your voice? You're muttering like you've got cotton in your throat. Speak up!"

Anna stiffened. She'd been teased about her voice since childhood, but at least now she had the ability to speak. As a child her throat had been so badly damaged she was completely mute. When she was fourteen, she had an operation that helped restore her voice, though she still spoke with a low throaty tone that made her the target of schoolyard bullies.

She cleared her throat and tried to speak a little louder. "I've heard everything you said, but I'd still like the case reopened."

Lieutenant Rowland's eyes iced over. "*Women*," he said contemptuously. "The government made a mistake ever letting women work in the Capitol. They're nosy, meddlesome, and don't know how to follow orders. I heard that the Library of Congress only employed female librarians on a probationary status. When is that up for review?"

Anna's knees went weak, and she was tempted to grab the desk for support. What he said was true. The library hired women for a trial period almost a decade ago, but their probationary status had never been officially rescinded.

"Well?" Lieutenant Rowland barked. "When are the women going to be reviewed for permanent appointments? Because if you keep meddling, I want to be at the hearing for the reconsideration of employing females at the Library of Congress."

"Don't!" Anna burst out, her voice finally loud enough to get Lieutenant Rowland's attention. Eight of the forty librarians were women, and all of their jobs would be in jeopardy if she couldn't placate this man. "There's no hearing scheduled," she said in a calmer voice. "Our appointment seems to have become permanent without formal acknowledgment."

"Is that so? Let's make sure you don't call undue attention to yourself by prying into military affairs that don't concern you. Is that clear?"

Horrifyingly clear. It wasn't only Anna's job he was threatening, but the livelihoods of all eight women who worked at the Library of Congress.

"Yes, sir, it's clear," she said softly.

Her limbs felt heavy as she climbed the stairs back to the top floor. She'd become complacent over the years, since the library's director treated the women with the same respect he gave the male librarians. Mr. Spofford was like a grandfather to them, but he had never actually made their appointment permanent. Instead, his career had been spent haggling for the funding, design, and construction of the new library being built across the street from the Capitol. It had taken decades, but the palatial new library building was nearly complete. Next month the Herculean task of moving the entire library into its lavish new home would begin.

By the time Anna returned to the map room, the congressional pages were gone, but she was surprised to see Mr. Spofford at the single worktable. With his narrow frame bent by age, Ainsworth Spofford looked even older than his seventy-three years.

"There you are," Mr. Spofford said, looking relieved. "I've been called to a meeting with the engineers about the new building. I need you to attend the hearing of the Committee on Fisheries for me."

Anna winced. Mr. Spofford was good at providing support at congressional hearings, but they were torture for Anna.

The library director noticed her anxiety. "This will be an easy meeting," he assured her. "The Committee on Fisheries is a paltry group. No one bothers to attend their hearings, so you'll be fine. Just be on hand in case someone needs to consult these maps."

He filled her outstretched arms with a stack of atlases and maps. It was doubtful she'd be called on to speak, but she loathed anything that dragged her out of the library. And congressmen could be so difficult. She prayed everyone would ignore her while she quietly blended into the woodwork.

Anna's skirts made it awkward to navigate down the staircases while lugging bulky atlases and map tubes, but the elevators were reserved for members of Congress. For a nation founded on the principles of democracy, the hierarchy in the Capitol was astounding. Congressmen walked the gilded halls like royal princes, while staffers like Anna scurried after them with maps or anything else they needed. After reaching the first floor, Anna walked through an acre of marble corridors until she arrived at the designated room.

Mr. Spofford was wrong; the meeting room was swarming with onlookers. They clustered in the doorway and trailed down the hall, anxious to get inside. She wiggled through the crush of people and headed to the chairs along the back wall that were reserved for staff, grabbing the last open seat. Like all the committee meeting rooms, the vaulted ceiling was covered with elaborate paintings and hand-carved cornices. A long table dominated the center of the room, already filled with congressmen from across the nation.

"What's going on?" Anna whispered to the congressional aide sitting beside her.

"It's Lucas Callahan's first meeting since he got demoted to Fisheries," the man replied. "Everyone wants to see if he'll show up and submit to the humiliation."

That explained it. Anna had heard about the Callahan affair. Literally. Last week the shouting from the House floor carried all the way up to the top story of the Capitol. Luke Callahan was one of the most charismatic men in Congress, but he was also a thorn in the side of the Speaker of the House. The animosity between the men boiled over, and rumor had it that Mr. Callahan tried to throw a punch at the Speaker, stopped only because the sergeant at arms intervened. Speaker Jones had had enough of Mr. Callahan's temper and removed him from the prestigious committee that controlled the budget of the United States and demoted him to the Committee on Fisheries.

Anna was secretly pleased by Luke Callahan's demotion, for he was an outspoken critic of the Library of Congress. Anyone who voted against libraries was someone she distrusted. She looked at the center table, scanning the wooden nameplates before each congressman, until she landed on Mr. Callahan's sign.

His chair was still empty. Was he going to appear? Rumor claimed Luke Callahan had a hot temper and wouldn't take the Speaker's humiliation lying down. She'd never seen the library's nemesis, but she imagined he'd probably be some stodgy old man without a trace of compassion or intellectual curiosity. What kind of barbarian voted against libraries?

Anna fidgeted, realizing she was the only woman in the room, and she always hated that. Anything that called attention to herself was to be avoided, but there was no help for it today.

"Make way, make way!" a boy shouted, his young voice cutting through the din. The crowd parted as a congressional page elbowed his way into the room, banging a ceremonial mace on the floor. "Make way for the esteemed congressman from Maine!"

Behind the boy, two pages carried a leather satchel and a folder of papers. And behind them . . .

Oh my.

Mr. Callahan was no stodgy old man. The young congressman strode into the room with the easy confidence of a man born to power. His chestnut hair was tousled with streaks of gold. He had sparkling blue eyes and the sun-chapped complexion of a man who loved the outdoors. Yet it was his smile that caught Anna's attention. It was effortless—confident and self-assured with gleaming white teeth.

"Look who is slumming with the peasants on Fisheries," a congressman from the table taunted.

"Slumming? On the contrary." Mr. Callahan flashed a broad smile and stretched his arms wide. "It's an honor to be of service to this nation's world-famous fisheries and oyster beds. The privilege is entirely mine."

His good cheer was greeted with a rumble of laughter and foot stamping. Mr. Callahan circled the table, clapping men on their backs and trading quips with enviable sophistication. He had an indomitable sense of energy as he made his way to the benches where the journalists sat, continuing to shake hands and exchange greetings with the newspaper reporters. Amethyst cuff links winked from his wrists as he reached across to the back row to personally greet each of the journalists.

It was the flashy cuff links that gave him away. Anna's eyes widened as the jolt of recognition hit her. She'd seen this man often, but always from the third-floor balcony looking down into the first-floor reading room of the Library of Congress. He was a frequent visitor to the library, always occupying the same spot at a table near a window as he quietly read each day during the lunch hour. From the balcony two stories above, all Anna could see was the top of his head, but he always wore those amethyst cuff links that glinted in the sunlight as he turned the pages of his book. She'd never known who he was until just now.

That was the man who had voted against every library bill ever brought before Congress? Whose blistering diatribes against their new building could peel paint from the wall? How strange that the library's chief critic was one of their most frequent patrons.

Against her will, a tiny bit of resentment softened, even though Luke Callahan was the embodiment of the type of person she always avoided. A man with that sort of blinding confidence and popularity wouldn't know what it was like to be teased or be on the outside. He never had to worry if he'd be allowed to attend school like a normal student, or if today was the day a pack of vicious children would circle around to see what it sounded like when a mute girl cried.

Anna pushed the memories away as the meeting began. Committee meetings were usually lethally dull, and the hours dragged by while a congressman from New York tried to protect his state's struggling oyster industry. "We refuse to pay taxes on beds suffering from New Jersey's smelting runoff. It is poisoning our oyster beds and degrading our waterfront."

"It's impossible for those smelting plants to pollute New York waters," another congressman said. "The currents don't flow that way."

Mr. Callahan raised an arm and snapped his fingers. "Someone get a map so we can settle this."

That was her cue. Anna fumbled with the map tubes beside her, searching for one that charted ocean currents.

"Map!" Mr. Callahan demanded in an obnoxious outburst. His eyes met hers across the crowded room. Unbelievably, he looked directly at her and snapped his fingers again. *Snap, snap, snap*. Did he really expect her to spring across the room like a dog summoned to heel?

Of course he did. Most congressmen were accustomed to people bowing and scraping, and Anna clenched her teeth as she approached. She laid the map on the conference table before Mr. Callahan and was close enough to smell his pine-scented cologne. Before pulling away, she whispered in his ear, "Snapping your fingers works better if you wear a crown and use a scepter to point out where I should scurry."

Without waiting for a reply, she returned to her chair, holding her breath the entire way back across the room. Had she really just reprimanded a congressman? She slid back into her seat, and then risked a glance at Mr. Callahan.

He was staring at her with a stunned expression, as if the natural order of his world had just been upended. A mouse had reached up to bat the snout of a fearsome lion. She tried not to smile, but her mouth twisted in an effort to suppress the grin.

The astonishment faded from Mr. Callahan's face, replaced by a dazzling smile that could slay a maiden at a hundred yards. He tipped his head in a tiny bow, new respect in his eyes.

Then, to Anna's horror, he rose to his feet and held an arm aloft, amethyst cuff links flashing as he gestured to her. "My thanks to the committee's research assistant, Miss . . ."

As his sentence dangled, anxiety flooded her. She'd rather face a public stoning than speak in front of strangers. But he was still waiting, and every congressman and journalist in the room turned their attention to her. Chairs creaked, men shifted in their seats, every eye in the room staring at her. She wanted to melt into the floor.

"Anna O'Brien," she mumbled, the words barely clearing her scratchy throat.

"What was that?" Mr. Callahan asked.

She cleared her throat and tried again. Her second attempt still sounded like the croak of a bullfrog.

The congressional aide next to her spared her further misery. "Miss Anna O'Brien, of the Library of Congress," he called out in a voice as loud and clear as a bell.

"Miss O'Brien," Mr. Callahan purred in a delicious voice. "I offer apologies for my caustic and inexcusable impatience. The uncouth savages from the north have much to learn from the gentle lady from Washington. She is the epitome of grace in the face of boorishness. Her wit and efficiency are a shaft of sunlight on the dreariest of afternoons. Miss O'Brien, the Congress stands in gratitude."

A low murmur and a little foot stamping greeted his statement, but all the congressmen immediately returned to their work.

Except for Mr. Callahan, who still watched her with that curious glint in his eyes. Anna glanced away in mortification, heat flushing her body. She would happily go to her grave without this sort of attention.

The meeting stretched on for hours, but against her will her attention kept straying to the congressman from Maine. For the most part he was an active participant in the meeting, though every few minutes he glanced back to smile at her again. They were always fleeting smiles, but they made energy race across her skin. Did he just *wink* at her?

He did!

Anna looked away and fumed. Women could get fired for flirting with members of Congress, and the last thing she wanted was some arrogant congressman she'd never met winking at her in public. Winking! That was how rumors got started.

The moment the gavel banged to end the meeting, she bolted from the room.

2

The weight of every eye was pinned on Luke as he left the committee room. Reporters crowded around, shouting questions and demanding answers. There was nothing better than watching the mighty fall, and Luke Callahan had plummeted a long way in the past week, but all he wanted was to escape this swarm of reporters and find that librarian before she disappeared.

He'd been stunned when she'd whispered that reprimand in his ear. Was snapping his fingers really so offensive? Everyone snapped fingers like that back home. Bangor was far from the marble halls of Washington, and Luke grew up in a rowdy world of sailors and lumberjacks, where people didn't take offense at such things. Yet he liked that Miss O'Brien had the backbone to call him on the carpet over it. When she returned to her seat and looked at him with a combination of intelligent humor and good-natured challenge, he was poleaxed.

She was a fetching little thing, with a winsome face and sparkling brown eyes. He wanted to catch her before she escaped, except there was a crush of journalists shouting questions in his face.

"Sir, would you care to comment on Speaker Jones's new legislation regarding the tariff?"

He didn't care. All he wanted was to find the librarian.

A congressional page ducked beneath the reporters and held a card aloft. "You have a telegram from Bangor, sir."

Luke froze. He had plenty of constituents in Bangor, but only one who sent him telegrams. His mouth tightened, though he refused to let the tension show. Journalists were like bloodhounds. If they scented anything amiss in Bangor, they'd sink in their teeth and never let go.

Forget the librarian. For pity's sake, he knew better than to indulge these reckless impulses. Since getting elected to Congress eight years ago, he'd lived like a virtual monk to preserve his reputation, and his sister's telegram was probably heaven-sent to stop him from reverting to the wild behavior of his past.

He took the telegram and headed toward the congressional retiring rooms, where no journalists were allowed. Guards parted to allow Luke through, then closed ranks as soon as he entered the private corridor. Journalists still hollered questions as he strode down the hallway, their voices echoing off the vaulted ceiling, but he ignored them.

Because the Capitol had few private offices, congressmen like Luke used the retiring rooms to work, socialize, or sometimes sleep during the long hours between meetings. The rooms had the comfortable luxury of a gentleman's club, smelling of beeswax, old leather, and raw power. Floor-to-ceiling windows were flanked with maroon velvet panels, and Turkish rugs covered the parquet floors. Boston ferns in brass planters helped demarcate groupings of chairs and tables. There were curiosities as well, such as a suit of armor from a Spanish conquistador, and a floor globe the size of a small pony.

Luke moved to the far windows, where he could read in private whatever his sister had to say. His jaw tightened as he scanned the first line of her telegram.

His brother had been arrested. *Again.*

He shoved the telegram into his coat pocket without reading the rest. Could he ever get far enough from his family so that their scandal didn't reach out to follow? Gamblers. Drunkards. Wife-beaters. All he had to do was look at his family history to find a trail of self-destruction so blatant it was a miracle any of them were still alive. He would give his eyeteeth if he could turn his back on them forever, and yet that was impossible.

He loved them. Every lousy, drunken, loose-living one of them.

There was a dangerous beauty to his family. The Callahans were like comets streaking through the sky, burning brightly with a passion that lit the night, but destined to flame out quickly, leaving a cold path of destruction behind. His father had already drunk himself into the grave, and it looked like Jason wasn't far behind.

Steeling his resolve, Luke pulled out the telegram to finish reading it. Jason had been arrested yesterday after a brawl with a sheriff's deputy. His sister needed four hundred dollars to bail him out of jail and wanted Luke to arrange a telephone call the following morning to discuss a solution.

He headed to the basement, where a telephone switchboard had been installed for members of Congress. Arranging a telephone call to Maine would require the cooperation of a dozen switchboard operators to patch the call through a network of connections all along the East Coast and up to Bangor. It was complicated, but people made allowances for members of Congress. Aside from the White House, telephone calls placed from the US Capitol got the highest level of service anywhere in the country. Even if the subject of all the trouble was some hothead from Maine.

A rush of heat flooded Luke's face. He hadn't exactly cured himself of that hotheaded impulse. Wasn't he about to dash upstairs in search of a fetching librarian, who had sparked his interest merely because she dared to whisper a clever, well-deserved setdown in his ear?

Even worse than his momentary slip with the librarian was his loss of temper last week. Why had he let himself get drawn into a shouting match on the floor of Congress? He knew better than to let the Speaker of the House goad his temper, and now he was paying the price for it.

He couldn't afford to give in to these impulses. He wanted to keep his seat in Congress, because quite frankly it was *fun* to be there, but he also needed to provide a stable home for Philip. One of the benefits of life in Washington was getting his nephew away from Maine, where on any given day his family home swung between the poles of exuberant joy and alcohol-fueled rages. His nephew was flourishing in Washington, but if Luke lost the next election, they'd both be plunged back into that chaotic household.

Luke dragged his nephew down to breakfast early the next morning so they could be on time for the telephone call to Julia. For a man born into a three-room house with no running water and oiled parchment for windows, the opulent breakfast room of the Willard Hotel was a palace. With a wall of arched windows, white table linens, and a high ceiling to accommodate the palms imported from Florida, it was the height of elegance and a little uncomfortable for a fourteen-year-old boy.

But anything was better than leaving Philip in Maine. Schoolyard taunts could leave wounds that lingered for years, and as the illegitimate son of an unmarried woman, Philip had endured his share of teasing.

A waiter brought their breakfast, setting down two platters of eggs, cubes of melon, and piping hot bacon.

"You can have my bacon," Luke said after the waiter had left. He passed his plate to Philip, averting his face so he wouldn't have to smell it.

Philip pounced. "I can't believe you don't like bacon," he said as he wolfed down a slice. "Everyone loves bacon."

"Don't talk with your mouth full."

Luke loathed everything about bacon, especially the smell of it. All it took was the scent of bacon to stir an avalanche of bitter memories. Luke was fifteen and had been helping his mother smoke bacon the day his life changed forever.

They were in their brand-new house, the one his father began building after a fortune in gemstones had been found on their land. The kitchen had polished hardwood floors and real glass in the windows. A fireplace dominated one side of the kitchen, where they smoked the bacon that filled the house with the scent of hickory.

"Where's that no-good son of mine?" his father had roared, striding into the kitchen and waving a stack of papers above his head. "What's this, boy? Am I raising a sissy in this household?"

Luke wanted to throw up at the sight of his poems clutched in his father's fist. In a world of logging, dirt, and sweat, Luke found salvation in the passages of Byron, Keats, and Coleridge. Poetry triggered fires of his imagination, and he'd been compelled to mimic the soaring verse of his heroes by trying to write his own poems.

"Give me those," he demanded.

Rather than being angry, it seemed Edgar Callahan was amused by his fifteen-year-old son's attempt to write poetry. Edgar sprang to the far side of the kitchen, tilting the pages to the light streaming through the window. "'Oh noble sun, cleanse my sorrows with the sweet kiss of morning dew,'" he mocked.

The jeering rendition made Luke's fledgling efforts sound overwrought and trite. He tried to grab the pages, but his father danced away, hooting with laughter as he read more of Luke's poetry in that obscene tone. His brothers and sister gathered to listen, their faces somber.

Edgar finally came to the end of the first poem, and the sneer fell from his face, replaced by rage. "Am I raising a sissy?" he bellowed. "Have you got so much free time on your hands that you spend it writing love poems?"

His father wouldn't know a love poem from a sonnet, elegy, or epic. Luke had spent months emulating the epic style, and he was proud of his work. "They're epic poems, sir."

"*Epic*, are they? I say they're epic trash, and there is only one thing to do with trash."

Edgar strode to the fireplace. Luke lunged after him, but the thick stack of poems was already on the fire, filling the room with a hickory-laden stench as the pages blackened and curled. Luke kicked them out of the fire, some of the kindling spilling onto the floor as well. He stomped on the burning pages, scattering bright orange sparks across the floor.

Edgar's fist caught Luke in the mouth and sent him sprawling, his head smacking against the wall. He rolled into a ball and covered his head.

"You want to stomp cinders on my new floor?" Edgar kicked the burning kindling at him. Luke covered his face, but cinders scorched the back of his hands, and flecks of ash stung his eyes. He curled tighter, grunting from the swift kicks into his ribs.

"Back off!" his brother said. Two thuds sounded as Gabriel's booted feet landed on either side of Luke, daring their father to continue. Gabe was the oldest and almost as big as their father. Luke remained frozen on the floor, holding his breath and praying Gabe wouldn't take a beating for defending him.

Edgar shoved Gabe aside and squatted down to grab Luke's shirt, hauling him up until they were nose to nose.

"Promise you will quit writing that flowery garbage," he ordered. "You're a fine lad, but I won't tolerate that girly rubbish in my house."

Luke's ribs hurt with each breath, but he looked squarely at his father. "I'm not quitting," he said, a rush of salty blood filling his mouth.

"Oh, yes you will. I want your word you'll quit wasting time with that rubbish and grow up to be a man I can be proud of."

He emphasized each word with a shake, causing fresh waves of pain in his ribs. It would be so easy to lie and make this problem go away. When his father was this drunk, he rarely remembered anything afterward.

But he wouldn't lie. Not about something this important. "I won't quit writing poetry—"

"Careful, lad," his father warned, drawing a fist back and holding it poised above Luke's head.

"I won't quit. You can beat me to a pulp, I don't care. I'm not quitting."

"Come on, Dad," Gabe said. "Let's go finish cutting down that elm tree by the creek." Gabe tugged at Edgar's raised fist, trying to pull him off Luke. Edgar let Gabe pull him up.

"Why don't you ask your mother to sew you a dress if you want to write poetry like a girl," Edgar said before storming out of the kitchen alone. They waited until the front door slammed before any of them moved.

Gabe helped Luke into a sitting position, his ribs hurting too much to stand. He stayed propped against the kitchen wall, blood streaming from his mouth. A few moments later, his mother brought a damp rag as Julia went to pick up the bits of paper that hadn't burned. Their little brother, Jason, wept in the corner.

Julia brought him the fragments of paper, only a few words visible in the center of the blackened pages. The stench of bacon filled the room, and Luke couldn't bear to look at the remnants of his poems. He'd spent over a year writing those poems. They had meant the world to him. The ashes Edgar had kicked in his face made tears stream from his eyes. He scrubbed them away with his cuff, hoping no one thought he was crying because of the poems. It was just the ash in his eyes.

Ignoring the ache in his side, he struggled to rise. "I'm all right," he said when his mother tried to keep him sitting. The room tilted and swayed, but he clenched his teeth, determined not to let the pain show on his face.

"Don't be foolish," his mother said. "You're dripping blood everywhere."

"I'm all right," he repeated.

And he was. He smothered the turbulent emotions, locking them away until the anger would wither and die if he didn't think about it. All he had to do was stuff the anger down until everything quit hurting. Learning to master his temper was his salvation in a world of chaos and brutality. Tomorrow wouldn't be the first time he'd gone to school with a black eye and a swollen lip, but he'd walk in with his head held high and dare anyone to ask why he'd taken a beating.

Luke pushed the memories away. His father was long dead, and reliving old memories was a pointless waste of time. He gave a sad smile as Philip wolfed down the remaining slices of bacon with relish. Luke had abandoned his dream of becoming a great poet long ago, but he still hated the scent of bacon.

"Finish quickly," he said. "Your mother will be waiting for us to call."

~~~

The telephone office was tucked into a corner of the immense mail room in the Capitol's basement. Maybe someday the Capitol would have telephone service with more privacy, but for now, anyone wishing to make use of the telephone needed to place their call alongside the hundreds of clerks who sat at long, narrow tables as they sorted bags of mail sent from all over the country.

"Let me speak with your mother first, then you can have the line," Luke told Philip as they walked toward the switchboard.

He loathed telephones, which he saw as annoying and soulless machines. Talking to someone you couldn't see was awkward and impersonal, whereas letters gave him the luxury of choosing the perfect phrase to communicate exactly how he felt.

The switchboard operator patched the final connection and gestured Luke over. He pressed the polished wood receiver to his ear and grasped the mouthpiece close to his lips. "Julia?"

"Yes, I'm here." Even from seven hundred miles away, the anxiety was plain in her voice.

"Tell me what happened."

Luke closed his eyes, bracing himself for the news. Apparently, Jason's debts had gotten so great that his creditors tried to seize two of his prized horses. He put up a fuss, and deputies were called, something that further riled Jason, who managed to land a solid right hook on the jaw of a Bangor deputy. And it would cost four hundred dollars to get Jason released from jail.

"Is there anything you can do?" Julia pleaded.

"No."

He wasn't going to pay this time. If giving money could solve
~~~

Jason's problem, Luke would gladly take out his wallet. Four hundred, four thousand, whatever it took. But money couldn't cure Jason; it would only add more fuel to the fire destroying his brother's life.

"Please, Luke, if you could have seen him. His right eye is swollen shut, and he's so ashamed of what he did. He started crying when he saw me. I think he may be ready to change this time."

Luke flinched at the image, but he couldn't be soft about this. Jason had always been the kindest of them all. He rescued injured birds and set the fish he caught free. He was gentle and loving, except for when he drank. Then he turned into their father.

"Let him change from inside a jail cell." It hurt to say it, but jail might be the only way for Jason to get thoroughly dried out. The biggest mystery was how both Jason and Julia could have turned to drinking after witnessing what it did to their father. Gabriel drank too, yet never to excess. While Luke was revolted by the smell of rum, Jason and Julia were captivated by it. It was one of the reasons she couldn't be trusted to raise Philip.

"Where's Gabriel?" Luke asked.

"He finished building that racing skiff and is trying to sail it to Canada. I've sent men out looking for him, but it will be days before he gets back, and even then . . ."

Julia didn't need to finish her sentence. Gabe had the raw talent to be an architect, a shipbuilder, or anything else he wanted, but he craved the life of a gypsy. Even if he could be found and hauled back to Bangor, Gabe wouldn't be much help taming the dragon that was destroying their youngest brother.

Perhaps it was the curse of sudden wealth. For generations the Callahans had been simple yeoman loggers, but then a large deposit of gemstones was discovered on their land. Luke's family was a classic case of what can happen when a fortune got dumped into the hands of those not expecting it, who were naïve about what wealth could do to a person.

"Philip is here," Luke said. "He wishes to speak with you."

Julia's quick indrawn breath could be heard from seven hundred miles away. As hard as the separation had been on Philip, it was even harder for Julia.

"Hi, Ma," Philip said into the mouthpiece. "Uncle Luke got into a fight with the Speaker of the House. Did you hear about it?"

"It wasn't a fight," Luke said, leaning again toward the mouthpiece. "It was only a war of words."

Although it was true he'd been charging toward the rostrum to confront the Speaker when the sergeant at arms rushed to intervene and separate the men. Who could say what might have happened had it not been for that.

He wandered farther into the mail room to give Philip some privacy. While Luke had inherited a hot temper from his father, he'd always been able to control it. Why was it becoming so difficult these past few months? He was starting to snap at insults and frustrations he'd always been able to tamp down and ignore before.

Which was terrifying. The long chain of drunkenness and aggression that polluted his family was going to stop now. Someday he would find a wife, then settle down and create the perfect family. It would be ruled by reason, order, and Christian compassion. His children would know he loved them. His wife would never cower or flinch when she heard him coming home. At all costs, he would hold the line against the curse of alcoholism tainting the next generation.

He could tell by Philip's face that the conversation with his mother wasn't going well. Luke walked over, and Philip eagerly gave the receiver back. Julia was weeping on the other end.

"We're doing the right thing," he said. "You know that, right?"

Julia's sigh was ragged. "I know. It's just so hard."

This was another reason he hated telephones. They were nothing but a torture device for his beautiful sister's already-punished soul.

"I love you," he added. "And you're doing the right thing by giving Philip a decent shot in this world. I won't let you down."

He turned the receiver back to the telephone operator and envisioned his ties to Bangor lengthen and snap. Bangor was the past. His future lay in Washington—with rules, reason, and order. The scandal of his fight with the Speaker of the House was going to make him vulnerable in the next election. He needed to begin rebuilding his reputation, and it was going to take work. And information. If he could find proof of the Speaker's corruption, it would help Luke regain his footing in Congress.

The image of a lively, sharp-witted librarian popped into his mind. He suspected Miss O'Brien had the mettle to wade through the quagmire of data in search of what he needed to knock the Speaker off his perch.

A smile curved his mouth. He would control the reckless impulse that temporarily blinded him yesterday and from now on behave like the perfect gentleman. But he needed Miss O'Brien's help, and he intended to get it.

3

It was a chilly morning, and Anna was still freezing from the streetcar ride to work. As soon as she stepped inside the map room, she tugged off her gloves and reached for the small oak box near the door. Her hands were numb as she skimmed the questions printed on the stack of cards that had been funneled to her. This was her favorite part of the morning. These questions would dictate how she'd spend her day, and she pondered various angles to solve each of the problems.

"Hello, Miss O'Brien," a voice said from the far side of the map room.

Anna was so startled she dropped the cards. The last thing she expected to see was a man casually sitting in her chair, his booted feet propped on her desk.

It was that obnoxious congressman from yesterday. With sunlight flooding in from the window, his hair looked more gold than brown. She blushed furiously and reached down to collect the scattered cards.

"What are you doing here?" It didn't sit well to have her

sanctuary invaded this way, and she hid her unease by shuffling the cards back into order.

"The clerk at the front of the library let me in."

He was breaking the rules by asking for the map room to be opened early, but it was hard to decline requests from members of Congress. She replaced the cards in the box and forced a polite smile.

"What can I do for you, sir? If you need the maps of the oyster beds, I'll be happy to bring them to you."

He simply stared at her, the oddest expression on his face as he rose from behind her desk and sauntered toward her.

"You have a very unusual voice," he said. "It reminds me of . . . well, I'm not sure *what* it reminds me of. I've never heard a voice like yours. Keep talking. I want to hear more."

Every muscle stiffened. "Which maps do you need, sir?"

She spoke as few words as possible. It was petty, but she didn't want to feed his morbid curiosity for how an esophagus with third-degree burns sounded. The day her throat was burned was the most awful memory of her life, and she tried never to dwell on it. Even so, Mr. Callahan cocked his ear and closed his eyes in a great show of studying her speech.

"You could go on the stage with a voice like that. Rich and throaty, like woodsmoke on a chilly autumn day. All the mysteries of Eve and Guinevere and Venus in one magnificent voice."

Her voice sounded like gravel. She turned her back on him and stalked to the case holding estuary maps, kneeling down beside a drawer a few inches from the floor. The drawer clattered on metal wheels as she pulled it open, jerking out charts of New England oyster beds. He wandered across the room until he was standing above her.

"Apparently I've said something to offend you, and that wasn't my intention."

Maybe she was a little thin-skinned. She *did* have a peculiar voice, and perhaps she shouldn't take offense just because he'd commented on it. Then again, the last time she saw him, he'd summoned her by snapping his fingers. Maybe peasants in Maine came to heel at such a gesture, but she didn't appreciate it. She stood and set the charts on the broad surface of the map case.

"I think these are the maps you need." What was he doing in here? Usually members of Congress submitted requests on note cards at the front desk, and then they were given to the appropriate librarian. But he obviously felt entitled to bypass the system.

He made no move to touch the maps. "The committee needs a written report on the delineation of offshore oysters, mussels, and clams inhabiting brackish waters. As the junior member of the committee, that happy task has fallen to me."

"Ah." She tried to hide the guilty pleasure at seeing him assigned to such a menial chore.

"I'm delegating it to you."

"No you're not."

His brows rose in surprise. "What exactly is your role if not to perform research for members of Congress?"

Honestly, the arrogance. She maintained a calm expression while she enlightened him about the realities of life. "Sir, although you may consider yourself to be the blazing center of the universe, for me you are merely one of over four hundred people I serve. We have limited time for research requests during the move to the new library."

"You mean that monstrosity next door?"

"Yes. The one you've repeatedly voted against. The most beautiful library in the world. A tribute to the human endeavor against darkness, savagery, and ignorance."

"A spectacular gold-plated waste of taxpayer funds."

She tried not to smile. He wasn't the only person to criticize the extravagance of the new library, but he was the most vocal member of Congress to complain about it.

"Like any other member of Congress, you may file a research request with my supervisor, and he will let you know when to expect an answer. Mr. Spofford is in the front office, although I'll warn you that he is a distinguished old gentleman and probably won't appreciate it if you snap your fingers to summon him."

"You mean like this?" The congressman raised his arm, flicked his wrist, and *snap, snap, snap*.

"Yes, like that."

"I gathered from your response yesterday that you took it amiss. I shall do my best never to . . ." He held his fingers out—*snap, snap*. "Never to do *that* again in your presence."

When he snapped his fingers, emerald cuff links flashed in the bright light streaming from the window. He was laughing, and it was contagious. With a smile like that, she could see why he was one of the most popular men in Congress. *She* was even starting to like him, despite herself. She glanced down at the gems on his cuff links.

"Emeralds? Usually you wear amethysts."

"Nonsense. I only wear the finest Maine tourmalines. Anything else would be gaudy in a government office."

She looked with new curiosity at the gems. "Tourmalines?"

"Pulled from the Callahan mine in the rocky soil outside Bangor. They come in purple, green, red, even black. Sometimes we find stones that are green on the outside and pink on the inside. We call those watermelons. See?"

He pulled a key ring from his pocket. A stone the size of a robin's egg dangled from the brass ring, and sure enough it had a cutaway section that revealed a pink center surrounded by a layer of green crystal. He tossed it to her, and she caught the set of keys in her hands, still warm from his body.

"How is this possible?" she asked, turning the gemstone in the light. It seemed as dazzling and outrageous as the man himself.

"The color depends on the ratio of iron and magnesium in the stone. I promote the tourmaline industry wherever I go, as the best tourmalines in the world are found in Maine. My family owns a fine tourmaline mine, if you'd like to acquire a few pieces."

Anna would be more likely to sprout wings and fly than to wear sparkly gemstones. She returned the key ring and directed the conversation back to the business at hand.

"Sir, if you wish assistance, this card needs to be filled out and put on file." She handed him a card and a pen.

"What's this? Don't you have anything decent to write with?"

"It's a pen with a roller ball to dispense the ink. They're new."

"I'm not writing with that newfangled nonsense. Don't you have a decent fountain pen?"

Many people were leery of new technology, but Anna's best friend worked at the Patent Office, and she had access to the amazing flood of inventions even before they reached the popular market. These new ink pens were still a little globby, but Anna loved the chance to use prototypes of new inventions.

"I can bring you a chisel and a clay tablet if you'd prefer. I believe they have some in the museum."

He set the pen down and fastened that enigmatic gaze on her. "Yes, please."

"Yes please . . . what?"

"I'd prefer a chisel and a clay tablet. You see, Miss O'Brien, I like old things. I prefer the challenge of a time when men went out and killed something when they were hungry, rather than opening a tin of processed meat. I don't want perfumed soap and a trickle of water from a copper pipe. I want a healthy blast from a frigid New England waterfall. I don't want the tinny noise from a gramophone. I want the thunder and vibrations of a real orchestra pounding out a Beethoven symphony. Technology has made us soft. I like hard muscle and loud voices and the satisfaction of a sweaty day of labor."

"You wear sparkly jewelry," she countered.

"I wear rocks hauled out of the land I own. Trophies, if you will." His eyes gleamed, and he looked flushed with health and vigor. Standing this close to him, she barely reached his shoulder, and his enthusiasm was palpable.

She held up the slim pen. "This is a trophy of modern times. If you'd like to fill out a research request, it is the device you will need to use."

"Miss O'Brien," he said in a long, slow drawl. "You don't think I intend to fill out that ridiculous slip of paper, do you?"

"I'm going to assume that was a rhetorical question and you aren't really expecting an answer."

"Very bright, you are. I wish I had you on my staff. Oh, wait . . . that's exactly what I intend to arrange. Don't get too comfortable. I'm on my way to file the proper requests to get you reassigned to the fascinating world of oyster taxation."

"Please don't plan on it," she said sweetly. "We are very busy with moving to the new library, and the director is quite stingy in assigning research assistants. You can't get your way all the time."

He leaned in with a devilish smile and a conspiratorial gleam in his eye. "Actually, Miss O'Brien, I usually do."

He whistled as he left the room.

Luke strode to the library director's office with renewed determination to usurp Miss O'Brien's time. She was as smart as he'd suspected. She'd have to be to land a position in this place. She had an alluring voice and a winsome face, with a sharp chin and a slim little nose. Yet it was her eyes that had captured his attention. Lovely, almond-shaped eyes that sparkled with wit and intelligence.

Not that it mattered what Miss O'Brien looked like. He'd happily work with a three-eyed troll if it meant getting enough information to launch his attack against the Speaker of the House. He suspected Speaker Jones was guilty of corruption, and it was going to be a challenge to wade through decades of budget data to find the necessary proof. In the meantime, he wouldn't neglect his new position on the Fisheries committee. He would perform every task flawlessly. Submit every report on time and in detail.

Or rather, Miss O'Brien would do it for him. He'd merely sign his name on each report and consider the mission accomplished. The Speaker had an army of research assistants, so why shouldn't Luke?

He followed directions to the office of the library director. What a mess it was up here, with crates of books stacked along the walls and dust heavy in the air. The director looked old enough to have been there when the Declaration was signed, with a gray beard and a tall frame bent with age. Luke ought to feel guilty pestering a man so ancient, but he needed the research help and was determined to get it.

"Miss O'Brien?" Mr. Spofford asked in response to Luke's request. "Certainly she can help you with the offshore fishing boundaries." The old librarian fumbled around on his desk, littered with mounds of paper that threatened to topple over, until he found a small card. "Fill out this form and I'll have Miss O'Brien begin work immediately. Whatever you need."

"I'm afraid my request won't fit on a five-inch card," he said smoothly. He needed a lot more research than fishing boundaries. Preparing to wage a war against the Speaker of the House would require an entire notebook. "I have a rather lengthy list of research needs. I would like to commandeer the majority of Miss O'Brien's time for the better part of the next few weeks."

That set Mr. Spofford back on his heels. "All the librarians are very busy with the move to the new building. Their time is scarce."

Luke glanced out the window, where the extravagant new Library of Congress could be seen through a break in the trees, its copper dome gleaming in the sunlight. Congress had appropriated a fortune to build a gaudy palace unlike anything the world had ever seen. Luke had voted against the additional funding. No library needed imported marble or engraved bronze doors. His arguments had fallen on deaf ears. The library was fully funded, and the public's excitement to see the new building was mounting by the day. That didn't mean Luke couldn't try to curtail their operating expenses in future years.

"Such a shame if the business of the people is neglected while we turn the new building into a gaudy showpiece rather than a legitimate research facility. Remind me again how much we've spent on that palace so far? Because the vote for the library's operating budget is coming up and I'd like to know."

"Heavens, I did not mean to imply we could not handle your research. No, no . . . my, no. Close the door and tell me what you need. I am certain we can be accommodating."

Luke closed the door. As he'd told Miss O'Brien, he had always been good at getting exactly what he wanted.

Anna was pulling maps to document water rights in the Dakotas when the bell over the door announced a visitor. She smiled when she recognized Mr. Spofford. Was there ever a more kindly man than Ainsworth Spofford? Despite his decades struggling to fund, engineer, and build their new library, at heart he was a scholar, and Anna sensed he would like nothing better than to curl up with a stack of good books. He almost never mentioned the female librarians' probationary status, and she suspected it had long since slipped from his concerns. Anna, though, couldn't afford to forget it—not after Lieutenant Rowland's threat yesterday.

"Miss O'Brien," the elderly director said as he tottered into the room, "I gather a member of Congress asked for assistance this morning and you refused to provide it."

She gasped. "I asked him to fill out a request card," she sputtered. "He refused to use the pen!"

"I understand," Mr. Spofford said, holding up a hand. "He refused to fill out the card for me as well. I spent a great deal of time with Mr. Callahan and have a complete list of his requests. They are extensive. I am assigning you entirely to Mr. Callahan until these requests have been met to his satisfaction." He set a stack of pages down on a map case. There must have been at least ten pages of handwritten notes!

"All my time? But there is so much to do with the move."

Mr. Spofford stepped forward and spoke in a firm voice. "Just do it. These questions are outside of map research, but you are a good generalist and I want you to look up whatever he needs. We can't afford to alienate Mr. Callahan. He's down on his luck right now, but I've been in this town long enough to know how quickly fortunes can change, and we don't need an enemy like him. I've screened his requests, and they are all legitimate. No more arguing, is that understood, Miss O'Brien?"

Anna swallowed hard. She wasn't used to being reprimanded at work, especially by Mr. Spofford.

"I'll get right on it, sir."

"And whatever you did to annoy the navy, stop that as well."

She sucked in a quick breath. Had Lieutenant Rowland already started the wheels moving to revoke her employment? "I didn't mean to cause any trouble," she stammered.

"Well, you did." The steel in Mr. Spofford's voice took her aback. "They were in here yesterday, complaining you've overstepped your bounds. I don't like being threatened by rude navy officers, so I'm not going to reconsider the probationary status of women, but I also won't overlook my librarians' poking into the navy's business. Is that understood?"

"Yes, sir," she whispered. Her fingers trembled as she picked up the pages of research requests.

She was still upset later that evening while she waited for the streetcar to take her home. Boarding the electric streetcars was always a struggle when thousands of people left work at the same time each day. She'd already failed to squeeze aboard the first two streetcars, but another was heading this way, trundling along on the electric conduits sunk into the pavement.

Surely Washington was the prettiest city in the entire nation, for while other cities were building trolleys with ugly overhead wires to power their streetcars, Washington had taken the extra time and expense to submerge their conduits in the roads, which made the horseless trolleys seem to move along the streets like magic. Already dozens of people surged forward in anticipation of the streetcar's arrival.

"Stick close to me," Gertrude Pomeroy said to Anna. "I'll see that you get aboard."

Anna smiled gratefully and lined up behind the older woman. Gertrude was a music librarian, and they lived at the same boardinghouse. More important, she was built like a plow horse and could help Anna get aboard the crowded streetcars. With her hand braced on Gertrude's mighty shoulder, Anna was swept along in her wake as they moved onto the streetcar. They even managed to snatch the last two seats.

"Now," Gertrude said as soon as they were seated, "tell me what's got you so upset, and don't bother denying it because I've known you too long not to recognize the anxiety radiating off you."

"I may have done something really foolish," Anna admitted, shame flooding her. After all, it wasn't only her job she'd put in jeopardy by locking horns with the navy. Gertrude looked at her curiously, but Anna was hesitant to share the details about Lieutenant Rowland's threat to the women's employment. They lived in a boardinghouse full of women, all of whom worked at various government agencies, and if word of the threat leaked out, it could fly through the entire city of Washington by the end of the week. The less said to Gertrude or anyone else about it, the better. Besides, at least half of her frustration was with that obnoxious congressman from Maine.

"Mr. Spofford reprimanded me because a congressman complained about my service," she hedged.

Gertrude pursed her lips and nodded. Everyone who worked for Congress knew what it was like to kowtow for the royal princes, each of whom was secretly convinced he was destined to be the next president and expected to be treated accordingly.

"Those men can be a challenge," Gertrude said. "Just hold your breath, brace yourself, and do it. I once held a two-hundred-pound hog during a delousing. It's not pleasant, but it has to be done."

They arrived home just before the kitchen closed for the evening. Dinner was included in her rent at O'Grady's Boardinghouse, and Anna couldn't afford to miss meals for which she'd already paid.

She almost bumped into Mary-Margaret as they hurried inside. "Best hurry before Mrs. O'Grady closes the kitchen," Mary-Margaret said with a fleeting smile. "I hear it's beef stew tonight."

The scent of beef with simmered vegetables filled the narrow, dimly lit hallway to the dining room. All the rooms upstairs were leased by women who worked for government agencies. The government had a tradition of employing women in clerical positions throughout the city, and almost all of the women were either spinsters or widows. If a woman married, she was swiftly nudged out of her position to make room for a needier woman.

Mary-Margaret burst into the dining room, her hands outstretched and her eyes closed as she pretended to fumble toward the long oak table in the center of the room.

"Somebody bring me a bowl of stew. I've gone blind from feeding the punch cards into those horrid machines." It was a typical complaint. Mary-Margaret worked alongside hundreds of women employed at the Census Bureau, whining incessantly about the monotony of her job. Girls moved aside on the bench to make space for Mary-Margaret, but no one rushed to get her dinner.

Anna approached the sideboard, relieved to see there was still plenty of stew in the iron kettle. She had been living there for six years, ever since graduating from the Mount Vernon College for Women right here in Washington. The quarters were tight, the food merely adequate, and there was no privacy, but she'd happily live in a cardboard box if it meant keeping her position at the Library of Congress.

"Can I get you another serving?" Anna asked Mrs. Horton as she approached the dining table. The elderly widow was always exhausted at the end of her day, performing clerical duties for the Agriculture Department. Anna was happy to fetch food for Mrs. Horton. Mary-Margaret, not so much.

Mrs. Horton scooted aside on the bench to make room for Anna. "I'm fine, dear."

"If you hate working at the Census Bureau, why don't you quit and move back home?" Gertrude barked at Mary-Margaret.

"Because if I move back home, I'd have to share a room with my two little sisters. No thanks! I'd swallow a dose of strychnine first."

Anna said nothing while she ate her stew. She'd been sharing a room with Mrs. Horton for six years, and it wasn't so bad. Most of the women who lived here paid extra to have a private room, but Anna had responsibilities. The upkeep of Aunt Ruth was a bottomless well that drained Anna's paltry bank account each month. Sharing a room with Mrs. Horton meant that Anna could afford to keep Aunt Ruth in comfort, and it soothed the guilt that weighed on Anna's conscience every day of her life.

As usual, the volume of twenty chattering women in the dining room was deafening. Anna rarely joined in. It wasn't that she was shy; she simply didn't have much in common with these women.

Mary-Margaret had just bought a jar of cream labeled *Bust Food* at the pharmacy and was eagerly passing it around the table to the delighted women. Gertrude's large hand snatched the jar to read the label aloud.

"'Designed by a French chemist to provide the right food for starved skin and wasted tissues of the bust,'" Gertrude stated in her loud, blunt voice. "'Unrivaled for developing the flesh of the bosom.'"

"I'm trying it tonight!" Mary-Margaret said.

Gertrude handed it over. "Use a lot. Your bust looks like it's been malnourished for a decade."

"I'm trying it too," another girl added. "If I get a husband, I can quit addressing envelopes for the rest of my life."

Anna locked eyes with Gertrude across the table. They both loved their jobs, but not all the women here did. Another wave of guilt surged through Anna. The crowning achievement of Gertrude Pomeroy's life was being appointed the head music librarian at the Library of Congress. Gertrude's parents warned her that girls who looked like a russet potato shouldn't aspire to marriage and encouraged her love of music as a means of earning a living. It was cruel to convince a child she wasn't worthy of romantic love simply because she was homely, but at least Gertrude had a genuine love for her work. If the navy had its way, female librarians like Gertrude would be shoved out of their jobs, all because Anna dared to ask the navy to correct that old report.

Later that evening, Mrs. Horton sighed as she peeled the sheets back from her bed. "That woman is fooling herself if she thinks 'bust food' is going to land her a husband."

"Mary-Margaret?"

Mrs. Horton nodded. "A bit of human decency goes a lot further," she said as she sank onto the mattress.

It was too early to sleep, so Anna propped herself up against the headboard, wiggling to find a comfortable spot on the lumpy mattress. Their room was humble, with a single window and a dressing table between two narrow beds.

Lieutenant Rowland's sneering words kept prodding at the back of her mind. *"The problem with the* Culpeper *was that it was stuffed with scientists and bookworms instead of real sailors."*

Her father had been a cartographer, but he'd been a good sailor as well. The box of letters beneath Anna's bed proved the strength of her father's commitment to the navy. Even better than her father's letters were his sketches. He'd been a fine artist and had sketched charcoal pictures of Anna playing at whatever exotic ports of call the *Culpeper* visited. He drew fanciful pictures of Anna swinging from a coconut tree, swimming in the surf with a dolphin, or climbing on the rigging of the *Culpeper*. The sketches gave her a glimpse into her father's daring life as he was traveling the world.

It was Friday evening, and there was no need for her to rise early the following morning. "Do you mind if I read?" she asked Mrs. Horton.

The older lady smiled gently as she reached for her sleeping mask. After sharing a room together for so long, they'd developed a routine. All Mrs. Horton cared about was tidiness and quiet, and Anna could provide both. So long as she had access to enough light to read, Anna could entertain herself for years. Anna twisted the dial on the kerosene lamp to brighten the room.

Thoughts of the *Culpeper* had been nagging her all day, and she had a craving to revisit her father's old letters. It had been years since she'd read them. She sneezed from the dust when she dragged the box from its hiding place beneath her bed.

Sitting on the floor, her back against the bed frame, she began skimming the letters. Most were brief, written in simple language a child could understand. Aside from the whimsical sketches, her father's letters were very ordinary, usually consisting of gentle admonitions to study hard and behave for Aunt Ruth.

All except his last letter. She pulled the final letter from the stack. It had been posted only a week before the *Culpeper* disappeared and was different from all the others. Anna unfolded it, and for the first time in her life she read her father's last letter with adult eyes.

With each line she read, the constriction in her chest grew tighter. Something was very wrong with this letter.

As an expert cartographer, her father had been meticulous; his attention to detail was flawless. But it seemed that each line of this letter contained contradictory information. She read it over and over, her confusion growing as the implications sank in. Her father was trying to tell her something with this letter, but he was careful to disguise his words and she couldn't make sense of what he was trying to say.

One thing was certain, though. The *Culpeper* did not sink in that hurricane, and this letter could prove it.

4

The following morning, Anna was still mulling over her father's confusing letter. She needed help putting this puzzle together and knew exactly to whom she could turn. Neville Bernhard had been Anna's best friend since childhood, and he would help her now.

The seafaring neighborhood of Alexandria, tucked just outside of Washington, wasn't the easiest place for quiet, introverted children, which guaranteed both Anna and Neville were destined to be ridiculed by the confident, well-groomed children of naval officers and shipping magnates. Neville suffered from strange jerks and tics that never left him in peace. He blinked his eyes rapidly and hard, and the muscles of his face twitched. Sometimes the spasms were so bad it was difficult for him to speak clearly, but at least he could speak. For two years, Anna's throat was so badly damaged she was unable to speak at all.

When she was fourteen, she had an operation to remove the scar tissue that lined her esophagus in hopes it would restore her voice. It worked . . . sort of. In the months following her surgery, all she could do was croak like a bullfrog, but Neville was kind to her as she learned to speak again, while the other children teased and made fun of her.

Often after school, she and Neville would escape to the small public library where they would sit together in silent companionship, a haven where they could open a book and slip into another century, another continent, another world. Those long-ago afternoons with Neville by her side would always be among her fondest memories.

People tended to underestimate Neville because of the twitching, yet his mind functioned with the precision and sharpness of a surgeon's blade, which made him a valuable asset to the US Patent Office. As thousands of patent applications flooded the office each year, Neville could study the design for a new mechanical invention and recall the details of similar inventions or spot anomalies.

It was Neville's eye for detail that Anna needed to search her father's letter for clues she might have missed. She set off to visit him the first thing on Saturday. It was a blustery October morning, the wind sending fallen leaves swirling through the air. Neville lived at a boardinghouse on F Street and had the world's surliest landlady. Mrs. Norquist always looked at Anna as though she were a scarlet woman come to lead Neville into temptation. Which was ridiculous. She and Neville were like two peas from the same pod. If ever she had a brother, she imagined he would be exactly like Neville Bernhard.

She sent a note up to his room: *Want to break into the Library of Congress with me?*

Neville appeared two minutes later, his lanky frame bounding down the staircase. He was so tall and skinny, he looked like all elbows and knees, with straw-colored hair flopping down to obscure his eyes. But nothing could cover his wide grin. She held up the prized key ring that opened the door to the Library of Congress, rattling it with a satisfying jiggle.

"Are we on a mission or just prowling the world's greatest treasure trove?" Neville asked.

The letter burned in her pocket. "A mission. I need your help solving a puzzle."

On normal days, over three thousand people streamed into the US Capitol, but it was nearly empty on Saturday, which made the building eerily quiet. Their footsteps echoed across the marble halls and vaulted ceiling, until they arrived at the main floor of the library.

Tucked into the west wing of the Capitol, the library had a formal reading room on the main floor, filled with tables and surrounded by ornate bookshelves. The room was surrounded by two floors of book stacks that soared all the way to skylights cut into the ceiling. Balconies lined the second and third stories and were open to the bookshelves. Was there anything more inspiring than being able to look up and see oneself surrounded by thousands of books all the way to the ceiling three stories above?

The library was empty except for a dozen workmen, who arrived on the weekends to box up thousands of books to be moved to the new library. Anna could hear them thumping around in the floors above as she laid her father's letter on the table at the center of the grand room.

"I need to find out what happened to the USS *Culpeper*," she said in a whisper, her voice echoing in the cavernous space. "I've noticed details in this letter that don't line up with the navy's official report. The navy says the *Culpeper* sank off the coast of Bermuda in a late season hurricane, but I don't think the ship was anywhere near the islands when it sank."

Pointing to the final drawing her father sent to her, she said,

"Look at this sketch." It showed Anna leaning against a palm tree, a row of simple houses in the background. "My father's letter says he's writing from Bermuda, but Bermuda was a British colony, and those houses look like Spanish architecture."

Neville listened as Anna recounted other details that had struck her as odd. His brows lowered as he took the letter from Anna and read silently. "I see what you're getting at," he said. His intelligent eyes scanned the letter and sketch.

It seemed as if every line they pulled apart revealed something odd. Her father mentioned listening to the native people singing in the Arawak language. It took some hunting, but Anna found a book about the native tribes of the Americas, which told her the Arawaks were indigenous to Cuba.

Her father mentioned eating tropical fruit that couldn't be grown in Bermuda's temperate climate. He included a drawing of a starfish that lived only in the Caribbean. She didn't want to follow where the evidence was leading. Despite the heading at the top of the letter declaring he was writing from Bermuda, everything else in the letter pointed to Cuba, located more than a thousand miles from where the navy insisted the *Culpeper* had sunk. The hurricane that battered Bermuda in 1882 never came anywhere near Cuba.

"The *Culpeper* didn't sink off the coast of Bermuda," she said quietly. "Something else happened to that ship, and the navy is covering it up."

It hurt to open up these old memories. As a child, she had been miserable living with her aunt and uncle, and for years she prayed that one day her father would come striding through the front door after his long adventure, his arms open wide and his sack full of presents. She'd clung to that fantasy for years, until it became too painful to keep manufacturing implausible explanations for the *Culpeper*'s long absence. Anna accepted that her father was dead, but she still wanted—needed—to know what really happened.

"Why are you digging this all up?" Neville asked. "Ripping the scab off the wound again."

"Because I *can*," Anna asserted. Knowing how to find answers was the only thing Anna was really good at, and she loved the hunt.

"Anna, do you remember the summer you were convinced that Shakespeare's plays were actually written by Francis Bacon?"

She smiled at the memory. They were sixteen when Anna read an article suggesting Shakespeare couldn't have been the author of his plays, triggering her imagination and launching them both on a quest, scouring the public library for corroborating evidence. They spent months searching for clues buried in Shakespeare's plays and tracing the history of aristocratic rivals in Tudor England, until they were finally satisfied that the exotic theory attributing authorship of Shakespeare's plays to someone else was hogwash and they needed to accept the plain, boring truth.

"You have to admit," Anna said, "that was still a fun summer."

"It was glorious," Neville agreed. "But it's proof you've got an overactive imagination eager to pounce on farfetched ideas. The truth is probably something as mundane as your father writing that letter in Cuba, but he didn't get around to posting it until he reached Bermuda. Maybe you should let this one go," he said gently. "No matter what we find, it won't bring your father back."

Neville's words were meant to be kind. Neither one of them had had an easy childhood, but this letter was seeping into her blood, resurrecting memories of a bold, daring cartographer who had traveled the oceans to better understand the world around them. Her father had been a hero, and she wanted to be worthy of his legacy.

"All my life I've ducked and hidden and avoided, but I don't want to run from this. I think my father was trying to communicate something in this letter, and I need to know what that was."

Anna leaned back in her chair and stared up at the skylight in frustration. On the floor directly above them, a worker leaned against the railing with his ear cocked toward them. His face was in shadow, and there was something sinister about the way he hovered directly above them.

"Is that man watching us?" she whispered to Neville.

He followed her gaze. When the man noticed, he pushed away from the railing and went back to packing up books. Anna kept her eyes trained on him. Over a dozen men came to the library every weekend to crate the books, but she couldn't recall ever seeing this one before.

"He was probably just taking a break," Neville said. "Your imagination is running away with you again."

She forced her muscles to relax. Neville was probably right that these little clues didn't hint at some grand conspiracy about the disappearance of the *Culpeper*. The truth was surely far more mundane. But just like she had to investigate the farfetched claim that someone else wrote Shakespeare's plays, she was going to need proof before she would abandon her quest to find out what really happened to the *Culpeper*.

~~~

On Monday morning, Anna went back to slogging away at Luke Callahan's immense stack of research. No congressman ought to get special treatment merely because he'd barged into Mr. Spofford's office and demanded it. But some people felt entitled to special privileges, and it appeared Mr. Callahan was one of them. It was especially galling since he'd always been the
~~~

library's harshest critic. Why did he need all this information that wasn't even related to fish?

Anna pushed her frustrations aside as she delved into the research. He wanted decades of taxation rates compiled for all states, broken out by industry and municipal zone. After three hours of poring over minuscule text, her back ached, her hand was cramped from writing, and her vision was cross-eyed. She'd be useless unless she had a break.

She wandered out of the stacks to the balcony, where she could rest her eyes on the most glorious sight in Washington—three floors of books circling a scholars' reading room on the first floor. There was a certain shabbiness to this library she would miss when they moved into their new building. Resting her forearms on the balcony railing, she breathed in the comforting scent of leather bindings and old paper.

Then the vision was ruined.

There he was, ensconced in his customary alcove near the west window. Mr. Callahan was engrossed in a book, his head bent a little, completely oblivious to the world around him. The tourmaline cuff link winked as he fiddled with a page and . . . she gasped.

No, he couldn't possibly be doing what she suspected. Scurrying to the far side of the balcony to get a better angle, she leaned over the railing and narrowed her eyes to see more clearly.

He was writing in their book!

She raced to the stairwell, the soles of her shoes barely touching the treads as she flew downstairs. Those books were for posterity. They were to be protected from thoughtless people who scribbled in the margins like barbarians. It was bad enough when the congressional pages misbehaved in the library, but Mr. Callahan was a grown man who ought to know better.

Her skirts swished as she marched down the center aisle of

the reading room, approaching him from behind to catch him in the act. Standing over his shoulder, she had a perfect view. The book was practically mutilated. He had cracked the spine so that the book lay flat on the table, and there were notes scribbled in the margins. He was unaware of her presence as he continued writing in their book, his pencil making a scratching sound like an insect gnawing on wood pulp.

"Ahem," she said primly.

Without turning his head, he held a hand up to silence her and had the gall to finish writing his sentence before folding down the corner of the page, closing the book, and turning his attention to her.

"Miss O'Brien. Don't you look peevish this afternoon. If I were a normal man, I might wilt under the heat of that glare."

"You were writing in our book. That is prohibited, as I am sure you know."

He raised a brow. "You don't believe in writing in books?"

"Of course not. Nor do I dog-ear the pages, crack book spines, underline passages, or otherwise mistreat government property."

"Easy there, O'Brien. It's my personal copy." He tucked the book into the crook of his arm to obscure her view of it.

"May I see the book?" This could be resolved if he simply showed her the book, but his hand completely covered the title, and a hint of annoyance simmered on his face.

"First of all, it's none of your business what I choose to read. Secondly, I've fought hard for my reputation as an honest man, and I'm not going to lose it over a fifty-cent book."

"Look, I know you don't have respect for libraries, but—"

"Where did you get that notion?" He was getting angry now, his voice taking on an edge that cut through the quiet of the reading room. A man at the next table frowned at them, but this was her opportunity to tell Mr. Callahan exactly what she thought of a person who didn't believe in supporting libraries or the preservation of knowledge.

"Your long record of voting against funding for the Library of Congress was my first clue of your dislike of us."

"That's it? Just because I don't believe a library needs gold-plated chandeliers and acres of imported marble? Keep going, Miss O'Brien."

"Your penchant for writing in books. It's disrespectful. And I still think that book you're hiding belongs to us."

He lowered his head and glowered, his hand still protectively covering the spine of the book. "It's my personal copy," he repeated between clenched teeth.

"Prove it."

Without warning he tossed the book at her, its pages splayed as she caught it in midair. The book was littered with handwritten notes and underlined passages. She flipped to the back cover, looking for the card pocket that would proclaim the book their property. There was none. Nor was there a call number printed on the spine.

The book was his. Her face flushed with embarrassment, and she was about to return the book but couldn't resist the temptation to peek at what he had been reading with such rapt fascination. "Elizabeth Barrett Browning?"

He flushed. "Now you know my secret."

A glance at the other books stacked beside him revealed an explosion of poetry: Wordsworth, Coleridge, Byron, and Keats.

"You don't strike me as the sort to read romantic poetry," she said.

He snatched his book back, and a little heat faded from his glare. "Poetry captures the immensity and radiance of the human soul. There is *nothing* I'd rather be doing than getting lost in stacks of poetry."

"Oh."

A chink of her armor cracked, and she clutched the back of a chair for support. Why did a shared love of literature spark an immediate sense of camaraderie? It made no sense, but denying it would be like trying to stop the sun from rising. Maybe he hated libraries, but he loved reading, and that counted for a lot.

"I can't figure you out," she said. "You love poetry and I see you here all the time, but you never miss a chance to insult the library or curtail our funding."

"Just because I believe our tax dollars can be put to better use than building more libraries doesn't mean I don't admire them."

"But you complain about everything. Money spent on libraries, on the military, on building projects. What would *you* do if you were in charge of the budget?"

His response was immediate. "I'd put an American embassy in every nation in the world. It is through knowing one another that nations are more likely to establish trade and avoid war, and how can we do that when we have only six embassies? We live in a world where war is considered merely a continuation of politics, and that is unacceptable to me. I grew up among people for whom violence was always a first resort, and it seems that sometimes nations behave in the same way."

His shift into such a sobering topic was surprising, yet she was fascinated as his attention drifted out the window, becoming softer and pensive. "It doesn't have to be like that. I believe the most perfect speech in human history was the Sermon on the Mount, especially the part where Jesus said, 'Blessed are the peacemakers: for they shall be called the children of God.' That simple passage has been the guiding principle for my entire political career. I want our nation to strive for peace and never again sink into the misery of war." He turned back to face her, a bit of humor lightening his expression. "And foreign embassies are more likely than gold-plated libraries to achieve that goal."

It was annoying how persuasive he was, but she wasn't ready to surrender just yet. "It wouldn't hurt you to say something nice about libraries now and again."

He looked amused rather than offended at her statement. "Do you know how I got elected to Congress when I was only twenty-eight years old and had no political experience?"

"You may find this shocking, but I didn't rush out to read your political biography the moment I made your acquaintance."

He smiled. "Pity. If you had, you would know that I came to public attention because I provided the people of rural Maine with a library I built and paid for out of my own pocket."

She caught her breath, stunned that a solitary man could build a library entirely on his own.

"It wasn't the sort of library you would recognize," he continued. "There are no marble halls or rare manuscripts. There aren't even any librarians. I bought an old railway car, fitted it out with bookshelves, and paid for it to be stocked with two thousand books. It's attached to the train that makes the route to the logging camps of Maine, supplying people with books free of charge. The men trapped in those camps usually have nothing to do with their downtime but drink or play cards. Or *read*."

Anna's heart picked up a notch, suspecting where this was leading.

"The men fell on those books like hungry wolves. I doubt if you could find a library anywhere in the country that is more appreciated than the monthly route of that railway car."

"How did you set up a circulation system? Or track usage?"

"I didn't bother," he said. "When the train comes through, the doors are thrown open, and the men return their borrowed books and are welcome to take more. And I don't care whether or not the books come back. Those camps are raw. The tents leak, and mudslides are common. I'm not going to punish a man who damages or loses a book. Everything operates on the honor system. Honesty is important to me. I've vowed never to lie to my constituents, and I think that means something to them. If they say they lost the book in a mudslide, I'm not going to quibble about it."

"Some of them are probably stealing those books, taking advantage of you."

He shrugged. "I figure if a man wants a book badly enough to steal, I'm not going to interfere."

Anna's mouth dropped open. Keeping track of books and protecting them, be it from insect damage, humid air, or pilfering fingers, was her duty. Mr. Callahan was speaking heresy, but his position had merit.

"When I was growing up, books were my only escape," he added. "I was born into a family of swinging fists and bellowing voices, but when I opened the pages of a book I found men of valor. To anyone watching, it probably looked like I was reading a book in the front room of my father's house, but I was really in Paris, fighting alongside the three musketeers. Or twenty thousand leagues under the sea, or racing around the world in eighty days. They led me to the Holy Grail and to the Sermon on the Mount. Reading was my liberation, my Magna Carta, from hopelessness and tyranny."

His eloquence was moving, and she latched on to his reference to England's most historic document. "Did you know we have a copy of the Magna Carta on loan from the British Museum? We've got it in the archives."

That seized his attention. He shot to his feet, eyes gleaming with a flare of excitement. "Show me," he said.

He followed her out of the reading room and into the private hallways leading to the rare manuscript room. The clutter of excess books was dense back here. Two decades of overflow books were stacked to shoulder height in the hallway, leaving only a narrow passageway down the middle.

"Be careful of the books," she cautioned. "If you bump a stack over, we'll both be buried alive."

"Keep walking, O'Brien. I want to see that document." She hid a grin at the barely leashed anticipation in his tone.

"Let's hope Mr. Ferris isn't in the manuscript room," she said over her shoulder. "He watches over the rare documents like a gargoyle. His sole joy in life is fending off as many people as possible from getting their vulgar hands near his treasures."

The hallway grew wider, and Mr. Callahan pulled up alongside her. "You had a whiff of gargoyle when you swooped down on me a minute ago. Rather terrifying. Like a bunny with fangs."

She tried not to laugh and it came out like a snort, which made them both laugh harder.

Mr. Ferris loomed into view. "What's going on here?" he demanded.

Mr. Ferris was the sort of fussy librarian who washed his hands incessantly. He refused to eat anything that had not been boiled into limp submission and wore a pinched, pained expression whenever he was required to interact with one of the women hired to work in the library.

"Mr. Callahan is a member of the House from Maine," she answered. "He would like to see the Magna Carta."

"Stay and look at it with me." The casual way Mr. Callahan threw the invitation out startled her. She hadn't yet had the chance to see the famous document. The Library of Congress was a treasure trove brimming with priceless delights, and temptation clawed at her. Before she could reply, Mr. Ferris's reedy voice interrupted her.

"It seems someone has forgotten the sad tale of Miss Sarah Starling," he said pointedly, and Anna's enjoyment of the moment evaporated.

"Who is Sarah Starling?" Mr. Callahan asked.

Anna took a step back from both men. What happened to Sarah Starling was a warning to every woman who worked in the Capitol. "She used to work in the telegraph office on the first floor," Anna said. "She . . . umm, she was let go a while back."

Sarah Starling had had the poor judgment to indulge in a brief flirtation with a newly elected member of Congress. When she was caught kissing him in the cloakroom, she was fired that same day. Three months of training to learn telegraphy, and then poof! Without references, Sarah was unable to land another professional position and finally settled for a job cleaning shrimp. And the congressman she was caught kissing? He was now the governor of Montana.

Anna took another step back from Mr. Callahan. She didn't have the luxury to spend time admiring rare manuscripts or indulge in a friendship with a member of Congress.

"I'd better get back to the map room," she said hastily.

"Please, stay and look at the Magna Carta with me," Mr. Callahan pressed. "I can see by that hungry glint in your eye that you're salivating over the prospect."

Mr. Ferris wrinkled his nose as if he smelled something foul. What he smelled was a librarian skating on thin ice. Any implication of a flirtation between her and Mr. Callahan was ridiculous. They were as different as chalk and cheese, but she still couldn't risk a hint of impropriety.

"I'll have the taxation schedules for mollusks completed for you by tomorrow morning," she said, turning to leave.

She had no intention of following in Sarah Starling's footsteps.

It didn't take long for Mr. Ferris to come slinking into the map room later that day. Anna was standing over a stack of nautical maps that contained the fishing territories of New England.

"I gather you are quite friendly with the congressman from Maine," Mr. Ferris said.

"Mr. Spofford assigned me to be Mr. Callahan's research assistant for a spell. I hope you don't mind?"

"I do, actually."

She dropped her map and put her hands on her hips. "If you have any smutty accusations about my behavior, I'd like to hear them." There was a time when she'd allowed people to bully her, but those days were over.

"It seems you are performing research for him that falls outside your duties as a map librarian," he pointed out. "I find that odd."

"I am perfectly capable of researching general information requests, and Mr. Spofford has asked me to do so. Most of the generalists are over at the new building, getting ready for the move."

Mr. Ferris cleared his throat delicately. "I also thought you'd like to know that others noticed your tête-à-tête with Mr. Callahan in the reading room earlier today. I'm sure you don't need to be reminded how that appears to outsiders."

"Correct. You don't need to remind me."

He retreated after that, leaving Anna feeling annoyed as she paged through the maps, looking for historic taxation boundaries in the fishing beds.

Her annoyance didn't last long. It was too easy to become engrossed as she searched the oversized maps of the estuary bays along the rugged New England coastline. Home to some of the most important shipping channels in the nation, the coastline had been well documented over the years, and she carefully peeled back each map, the paper warping and crinkling as she flipped to one portraying Narragansett Bay.

Her heart squeezed. It was a map drawn by her father.

In the course of her work, she often stumbled across maps her father had made, and the bittersweet rush was always the same. She smiled as she traced the coastline, noting the pale-blue hash marks that indicated brackish water. In her mind's eye she could see the thick brush of sea grass and smell the salty air.

Nevertheless, this map didn't contain the information she needed, and she stood to grasp one side of the oversized map and peeled it to the side, the paper rustling loudly in the silence of the map room.

"Nice seeing you again, Papa," she whispered.

It was hard to concentrate after seeing that map. She didn't want to provoke Lieutenant Rowland's ire, but neither was she going to ignore the inaccuracies in the navy's report about the *Culpeper*. Her father had been trying to tell her something in his final letter, but for the life of her, she could make no sense of it.

Was it possible he had written a similar letter to Aunt Ruth? He always enclosed separate messages to her aunt and uncle, and if those letters still existed, there might be more clues to begin piecing this puzzle together.

Anna's monthly dinner with Aunt Ruth was due this weekend. The visits were a halfhearted attempt to preserve the only familial relationship Anna had left in the world, although she suspected her aunt only welcomed them because Anna handed over a portion of her salary during those visits. Aunt Ruth had countless techniques to make Anna feel guilty for Uncle Henry's death, but she tended to keep her claws sheathed in front of others, which was why Anna dragged Neville along for the visits.

Anna always used some excuse for Neville's presence, like checking to be sure Ruth's stove was in good working order. Since it was October, they could say he'd come to clear the gutters in preparation for winter.

With any luck, this week's visit would reveal another letter from her father that Neville could later help her decipher.

5

Aunt Ruth's town house was nestled into the close-knit seafaring community just a few blocks from the Potomac River. Elm and oak trees sheltered cobblestone streets worn from a century of foot traffic. The cold air smelled of autumn and woodsmoke as she and Neville walked toward Ruth's house, their feet crunching over scattered acorns and leaves.

"I'll have to be careful asking about my father's letters," Anna said. "Aunt Ruth blamed him for my mother's death. He's never been her favorite subject."

"Your mother died in childbirth. How was that your father's fault?"

Anna tried not to laugh. "Do you really need me to explain it to you?"

"Maybe we can skip that part," he said with a grin, but then he sobered quickly. "Anna, why are you doing this? Maybe the *Culpeper* was farther south when it sank, but it's not such an important detail, is it?"

Anna paused. Overlooking *any* error in the historical record was aggravating to her, but it was much more than a fussy need for accuracy. "My father explained it to me once. He said that in 1707, a tiny navigational error steered an entire fleet of ships off course as they approached the English Channel. In the middle of the night, the HMS *Association* smashed into the rocks because of that tiny error, and eight hundred sailors died. Our maps and reports can't merely be good, they need to be flawless. And I think the *Culpeper* report is full of errors."

"Yes, but we're not talking about a map sailors rely on for navigation. That old naval report is only a historical curiosity—"

"Stop right there," Anna said, turning to block Neville from walking any farther on the cobblestone path. "We don't know how people in the future will use that report, but because it was written by the navy within a few months of the disaster, it will *always* be the most important record people will rely on. Who knows how people in the future might use that report. I know it is full of errors, and they must be fixed. If Aunt Ruth still has any of my father's old letters, I need to see them."

"Okay, I get it," Neville conceded.

They had arrived at Ruth's house, a two-story Colonial of ruddy brick with shiny black shutters that had once belonged to her father. After her mother died, Aunt Ruth and Uncle Henry moved in so they could look after Anna while her father was at sea. The house now belonged to Anna since inheriting it after her father died. It contained terrible memories, though, and Anna never wanted to live here again. Still, she could hardly evict her widowed aunt just so she could sell the home.

Aunt Ruth opened the front door wearing a threadbare work smock, her faded hair twisted into a loose bun. "Oh, you've brought your friend," she said flatly. "I hope the meal will stretch."

"Don't worry, I brought a shank of smoked ham," Anna said.

Ruth's eyes lit up. "Meat! Oh, I haven't been able to afford meat in weeks." She accepted the wrapped cut of ham.

Anna was pleased to see Ruth's mood brighten, especially since discussing her father was always a delicate topic between them. She followed her aunt back to the kitchen, where a small pot of lentils sat simmering on the stove. A loaf of brown bread was the only other food in sight. Anna always brought extra food when Neville came, but Ruth put the ham inside the icebox, clearly not intending to share.

"I'll step outside and have a look at your gutters, shall I?" Neville asked.

It would give Anna a few moments to bring up the subject of the letters. Her father had always posted two letters at a time—one for her and another discussing "grown-up business" addressed to her aunt.

Anna grabbed a knife and began dragging it through the loaf of bread, careful to cut uniform slices. "Do you remember the letters father sent us?"

"How could I forget? Always full of instructions and worrying over you."

"Do you still have any of them?"

"I'm not a librarian who thinks every piece of paper with a word scribbled on it needs to be saved for posterity."

The glimmer of hope inside Anna grew smaller. "You don't have them anymore?"

"Of course not. I usually tossed them out with the next batch of trash."

Anna set the knife down and drew a careful breath. Whenever she delved into the past, she was liable to touch raw nerves and awaken the firestorm of bitterness and regret that simmered between her and Ruth. After all, Uncle Henry's winter coat still hung from the hook on the back of the kitchen door, as though he might return any moment, when the man had been dead for fourteen years. All because of Anna.

"Were Papa's letters to you only about instructions for my care? Or did he sometimes . . ." How could she frame this question? She didn't know what her father had been trying to communicate in that final letter, so it was difficult to probe Aunt Ruth's memory. "The last letter I received from Papa, dated just a week before the *Culpeper* sank, seemed very strange. Do you remember if his final letter to you was also strange? Did he go into unusual detail about anything?"

The pot banged as Aunt Ruth moved the lentils to the far side of the stove. "All his letters were the same: rules, instructions, and nonstop worrying over his precious Anna. You'd think he didn't trust us, the way he worried over you."

It wasn't an entirely misplaced fear. Ruth and Henry had never had children of their own and weren't particularly affectionate people. It had been a lonely household to grow up in.

Anna's shoulders sagged. It seemed that as her curiosity about the *Culpeper* grew, the likelihood of finding more information dwindled. Feeling deflated, she walked over to the small jar tucked amid the tins of flour and tea. Lifting the lid, she tilted the jar to peek inside. Only two dollars and a few coins rattled in the bottom. Without a word she reached into her pocket and slipped a small wad of bills into the jar—the unspoken routine they'd been practicing for years. While there was little familial affection between the two of them, Aunt Ruth took it for granted that Anna would support her.

There were so many things Anna could do with the money that went to Ruth each month. All her adult life she'd wished to buy herself a typewriter. Or perhaps a private room in O'Grady's. Not that she needed a typewriter or her own room, but it was fun to dream all the same.

"Let me help set the table," Anna said. She began removing bowls from the cupboard. If there were any other clues left by her father, she would not find them in this house.

As usual, the meager food at Aunt Ruth's could not be comfortably stretched to feed three people, which meant Anna and Neville paid a visit later to a cozy pub overlooking the waterfront. The excellent Maryland clam chowder, with spicy stewed tomatoes and lumps of fresh crabmeat, was the only thing either of them missed about this town.

Neville started in on the chowder the second the bowls were set before them. For being so slim, the amount of food that disappeared down his throat was remarkable. Anna, meanwhile, toyed with her spoon, drawing swirls in the chowder as she recalled the sight of Uncle Henry's coat hanging on the back of her aunt's kitchen door. Perhaps someday she'd visit the house to see that Aunt Ruth had finally put the past behind her, but she doubted it. She sighed.

"You need to quit feeling sorry for your aunt," Neville said as he polished off the last of his chowder and pushed the bowl aside. "After I finished cleaning her gutters, I took the leaves to her dustbin, where I saw the bones of a fine rib roast. A chicken carcass as well. For a widow who hasn't been able to afford meat for weeks, it has a strange way of getting into her rubbish."

Anna rocked back on the bench. She could barely afford the shared room with Mrs. Horton, all so she could keep funneling money to her aunt. She had suspected Ruth sometimes exaggerated her poverty, but a rib roast and a chicken all in one week? She slid her untouched bowl of chowder toward Neville.

"Here, you can have this. I'm too annoyed to get it down."

Neville smiled and grabbed his spoon again. "Wow. I wish you got angry more often. This is really good chowder."

Anna had to smile. Neville could always make her laugh, even when she didn't want to. She was so amused watching Neville devour the chowder that she missed the entrance of a nattily dressed couple into the pub.

"Why, look who it is," a silky voice called from across the room. "'Romeo, Romeo, wherefore art thou.'" Neville stiffened at the old taunt as a blond woman in a canary-yellow walking suit approached their table. It was Eliza Sharpe, an old classmate from their school days.

In a school with students who ranged from harmless to downright vicious, Eliza always floated along the spectrum depending on shifting schoolyard alliances. During one year, Neville developed an unrequited crush on Eliza. It faded, but not before Neville had been dubbed with a nickname he despised to this day.

The moment Neville saw Eliza waving at them, his affliction got worse, blinking so hard his whole face twitched with the spasms he was helpless to stop. Beneath the table, Anna reached for his hand. He clasped it like a lifeline.

Neville was able to calm a bit by the time Eliza ambled to their table, leading a portly gentleman alongside her. A cap with a dazzling display of white feathers perched atop Eliza's coifed hair.

"Hello, Eliza," Anna said. "What's that, a snowy egret on your head?"

The snowy egret had been driven almost to extinction by the popularity of its milky-white feathers and was the subject of a hotly contested bill before Congress to outlaw the slaughter of endangered birds for their plumage. Eliza preened as she touched the feathers with dainty fingers.

"Yes, aren't they pretty?"

"At least they aren't bald eagle," Neville muttered.

The comment flew past Eliza. "Are the two of you married yet? I always thought you would be perfect for each other." She glanced down at Anna's ringless hand. "Oops! Guess not," she said, then leaned over to pat Anna on the shoulder. "Don't worry. You'll probably find someone soon."

Why did the whole world think she and Neville ought to get married? She adored Neville, but he was like a brother to her. Even the thought of kissing him made her fight back laughter.

Eliza prodded the portly gentleman beside her to step closer. "Have you met my husband? Walter works at the Postal Department, and someday I expect he'll be the postmaster general. Walter, these are my two old friends from school, Anna O'Brien and Neville Bernhard. Except we always called him Romeo. It was the funniest thing. He used to let me peek at his paper during math tests. Do you remember?"

Neville's infatuation with Eliza began when Anna had been absent from school for a month to have the operation on her throat. That left a vacant seat beside Neville, which was eagerly filled by Eliza Sharpe, who was extremely kind to him. Neville, being neither stupid nor blind, knew Eliza's sudden need for his friendship was entirely dependent on the help he gave her in mathematics, but he didn't mind. Without Anna, he was friendless, and there was no worse torment for a fourteen-year-old boy than to be alone amid a throng of meanspirited schoolmates.

When Anna returned to school, she had to admit to a smidgeon of jealousy over the attention Neville lavished on Eliza. It came crashing to an end the afternoon their teacher caught Neville tilting his test paper so that Eliza could see it. Mr. McLaren lurched across the room to snatch Neville's test. "For pity's sake, Romeo, don't sell your self-respect over this girl. Move to the other side of the room immediately."

Mortified at being caught cheating, Neville scooted to an empty chair well away from Eliza's wandering eyes.

Mr. McLaren wasn't finished with his humiliation. "Now, let's see if she stabs herself in the heart after Romeo is torn from her side." The rest of the class giggled behind their hands while Neville twitched in misery.

The teacher walked over to Neville and returned his test, then swiveled to pierce Eliza with his gaze across the classroom. "No attempted suicide from the lovely Miss Sharpe? What a surprise. So you see, Romeo, she's really not worth your trouble. Finish the test and don't let me catch you cheating again."

Neville would have liked nothing better than to have the entire incident scrubbed from his memory, but Eliza enjoyed recounting that day for her husband.

"Everyone called us Romeo and Juliet after that," Eliza said. "It was the funniest thing! Of course, I always thought of Neville as 'Blinky-Blinky.'"

Neville blanched, and even the future postmaster general looked embarrassed at his wife's remark.

Anna painted on a tight smile. "It's always such a treat to see you again, Eliza. Just when I think there are no more arrows in your quiver, you always manage to find one."

"Come along now," her husband said, leading his wife to the other side of the pub.

Neville's twitching had gotten worse, his condition always aggravated when under stress. He set his spoon down, leaving the remainder of the spicy chowder in the bowl. They both knew it would be a sloppy and embarrassing mess if he tried to eat with his twitching this severe. Neville had been to countless physicians over the years, but no one could figure out how to calm the spasms that made his life miserable.

Both she and Neville came to terms with their weaknesses

long ago. Neville would forever twitch with involuntary spasms, and she'd never feel comfortable among the beautiful people like Eliza Sharpe. But that was okay with her, because she'd built a good life for herself at the library, where she didn't need to depend on anyone for companionship or financial support. And if her world was a little lonely . . . well, loneliness never killed anybody. There was a time when she had hoped for marriage and a family, but that was beginning to fade as she grew older. Besides, if she remained single she could continue being a librarian, which wasn't merely a means of support but a calling she cherished.

To this day she still missed her father, and yet she felt comforted in knowing he would have been proud of her. They shared a similar mission, both dedicated to the collection and preservation of the world's knowledge.

Today she had tried and failed to glean more insight into the truth behind the *Culpeper*'s disappearance, but that didn't mean she would stop the quest. After all, the only thing Anna was truly confident about in her life was that she was very good at finding answers to questions that wanted to remain hidden.

6

Walking down the street with Caesar Trammel was like walking alongside a celebrity. Though Luke was well known in Congress, few people recognized him on the street. That wasn't the case with Caesar Trammel, the oldest veteran of the Civil War still serving in Congress. Having been in the path of cannon shrapnel at Gettysburg, Caesar was missing his left eye and left leg, and his tiny, shrunken frame was easily recognizable as they proceeded down the tree-lined street full of shops and people enjoying the unexpectedly warm Saturday morning. Luke slowed his stride to match Caesar's uncertain gait as the old veteran hobbled along with the aid of a cane. A patch covered Caesar's eye, yet the old man saw more with his one good eye than most men saw with two.

"We'll need to plan this carefully," Caesar said. "Speaker Jones has enough votes to pass that revolting new tariff, but if we can convince enough members to be absent for the vote, Jones won't have his quorum and the vote will be scuttled. He'll have to wait until next term to bring it back to the floor."

It was a brilliant plan no one would see coming. Caesar

Trammel might be the only man in Congress craftier and better connected than the Speaker of the House. It was important to the workingmen in Luke's district for the tariff to be defeated, and Caesar's plan would stop the vote from ever taking place. Then Luke could move in with the mountain of data he'd amassed from Anna O'Brien to begin dismantling the Speaker's reputation. Luke smiled, feeling the end of his political exile drawing nearer.

"Sir, may I shake your hand?" A man wearing a cab driver's uniform had recognized Caesar and sprang off the carriage to pay homage to the renowned veteran.

Luke stepped aside to let Caesar enjoy his moment of glory. It was often like this when he was with Caesar, who loved basking in the limelight. Luke never cared for that sort of fame. The only thing he envied about Caesar was the man's long and happy marriage. Unlike most politicians whose families remained living in their home districts, Caesar's wife insisted on living with him in Washington. "I spent three years apart from my wife during the war," he once groused. "As long as the two of us still draw breath, I will never spend another night without my wife by my side."

It was exactly what Luke craved. He'd fallen in love only once, a blazing few months that still lit the corners of his memory. At thirty-six, he'd never expected to remain a bachelor this long, and over the years the hollow ache of loneliness had grown and expanded. While he had many friends, a demanding career, and the satisfaction of raising his nephew Philip, still he longed for a wife.

Caesar shook hands with a few other bystanders, and afterward they continued walking along the shady street, passing by the shops and cafés. With the regular interruptions from people wanting to meet Caesar and the crush of morning shoppers, it was a strange place to hold a political meeting, but far safer than the Capitol, a place filled with eavesdroppers and the constant risk of being overheard.

"I expect to have the data to launch a corruption charge against the Speaker soon," Luke said as he leaned down to speak quietly into Caesar's ear. "I don't have clear-cut proof yet, but I'm still looking." Or rather, Anna O'Brien was still looking, and it was only a matter of time before she found something.

"All I care about is blocking the tariff vote," Caesar said. "Any other personal vendetta you have against the Speaker is on your own."

"But if I find evidence of corruption, I can count on your support. . . ." Luke let the sentence dangle. Caesar paused and cocked his head to scrutinize him through that single good eye.

"The hostility between you and the Speaker seems unusually bad. What's going on between the two of you?"

Luke didn't want to spill more scandalous stories about his family. He paused before the wide glass window of a general emporium and pretended to study the jars of imported tea in the display.

"Jones once asked me to lie," he began. "I refused. It was just a silly squabble."

"This is more than a minor squabble." Caesar's voice dripped with humor. "If there was a committee for scrubbing tobacco stains off the steps of the Capitol, Speaker Jones would put you in charge of it. Tell me, why do the two of you hate each other so much?"

Luke kept staring at the goods displayed in the window—anything rather than let himself get pinned down about the root of his conflict with Cornelius Jones.

"When I was a boy, I once saw a painting of a lion resting in a green pasture beside a lamb," he said slowly. "The lion was huge and powerful, while the lamb was tiny, but it wasn't afraid of the lion. They lay side by side in a peaceable kingdom. The image was so compelling that I wanted to believe it could be real. If a lion can lie beside a lamb, who knows what will happen between me and Cornelius Jones?"

"One of you will end up with a bloody carcass dangling from your jaws. The question is, which one."

Luke stiffened. That image of the lion and lamb had been his guiding light during a childhood ruled by brutality, and it wasn't a laughing matter for him. His commitment to pacifism was based on more than a tranquil painting of a peaceable kingdom. As the son of a man who'd served in the Civil War, Luke had witnessed the indelible scar that war had carved into his father's soul, and it strengthened his commitment to pacifism. *"Blessed are the peacemakers: for they shall be called the children of God."*

He wanted to be a peacemaker. He wanted to live in an age ruled by good judgment and Christian charity, not the savagery of swinging fists.

Caesar still waited for his answer, and Luke tried to reply honestly but avoid as many painful personal details as possible. "I learned a long time ago that sometimes it takes more courage to refuse a fight than to join the battle. I won't sink to Cornelius Jones's level, even if that means taking a punch now and then."

His political meeting with Caesar was concluded, and he looked about for an excuse to disengage. Behind the plate-glass window, the figure of a lady moved into view near the rear display table. There was something familiar about her. Her plain dress couldn't disguise her fetching figure. He smiled in recognition.

Seeing Anna O'Brien outside the library was like seeing a goldfish outside its bowl. It was simply something he'd never expected to see. Strange, but he'd never even considered that she had a life outside of the library, but here she was, shopping. Even from a distance he could see the yearning on her face as she leaned over a display table.

He excused himself from Caesar and headed into the shop. He winced at the rude jingling of a bell above the door when he stepped inside. Thankfully, Miss O'Brien was too engrossed to look up from the object of her fascination to notice. Hiding his grin, he sidled up to the store's manager to whisper a few instructions.

It was time for a little fun.

Anna ran her fingers over the gleaming keys of a new typewriter. It was a model from Remington, five dollars cheaper than she'd seen before. She glanced between the two typewriters on display, wondering why the new model was more affordable and wishing Neville were with her. He'd be able to spot the differences immediately, but when she'd stopped by his boardinghouse that morning, he wasn't home. She'd been a little miffed. They usually spent Saturdays together, and his insight would have been helpful just now.

She was about to ask the shopkeeper for a sheet of paper so she could experiment with both models, but just as she drew a breath, an obnoxious male voice shouted from the other side of the store.

"Service!" *Snap, snap, snap.*

She whirled around. Luke Callahan was snapping his fingers, his jeweled cuff links flashing.

"What's wrong with this store?" he shouted again with a few more snaps of his fingers. "I need service, and I need it now."

Rushing footsteps came from the back of the store as the

flustered manager stepped into view. "I'm sorry, sir. I was stacking chicken wire in the back room."

"Chicken wire! I am a congressman in the United States House of Representatives. I don't have time for chicken wire."

The arrogance of the man. Anna was stunned, watching in disbelief as the store manager rushed to placate him.

"It's very fine chicken wire, sir," the man stammered. He turned away to cough, his hand covering his face.

It was impossible to tolerate this any longer. Anna stepped forward. "Do you really think the world should stop rotating so the peasants can bow down and kiss your ring?" she demanded. If he was surprised to see her, it didn't show as he raised his chin.

"I certainly expect to come before chicken wire." His mouth twitched, and a hint of mirth lurked in his eyes. Then the shopkeeper snorted with laughter.

"Are you making fun of me?" she asked, glancing between the both of them.

"Mr. Callahan is a loyal customer here, ma'am," the shopkeeper rushed to explain. "He buys his nephew's art supplies from us. We consider him a friend." And given the way they grinned and shared in the laugh at her expense, she could see it was true.

She was still irked and refused to join in their hilarity. "I consider him the most annoying man in Congress."

"Come on, O'Brien. It was funny."

It was, but she didn't feel like admitting it. Aside from his terse commands to her in the Fisheries meeting, he'd always treated her with respect, even when she accused him of writing in their book. Perhaps Mr. Callahan was exactly as he appeared—a blunt man who didn't conform to the stilted manners of Washington, but not a bad one.

She ignored him and looked at the shopkeeper. "Can you

tell me why this new model of typewriter is less expensive than the other?"

"Certainly, ma'am. The slimmer design requires less metal and a shorter ribbon of ink, but it has all the features of the larger model."

"Don't tell me you're tempted by those clickety-clack machines," Mr. Callahan said. "No typed document will ever rival the beauty of fine penmanship."

Though he was probably right, she lifted her chin and hid a smile. "I don't care. I want one."

"Why?"

She'd never in a million years confess the reason. She hadn't even told Neville why she wanted a typewriter, and she certainly wouldn't be spilling her dreams to this charmingly obnoxious congressman. "Because they are modern."

"Heaven save us," he muttered.

"Can I practice on it a bit?" she asked the manager.

A few moments later, she sat before the table and fed a sheet of paper beneath the typewriter's rubber roller. It was awkward yet exciting as the machine made a satisfying thud with each keystroke. She didn't know the keyboard well enough to move with any speed, and it took some time to type out her own name.

"Look how slow you are," Mr. Callahan taunted. "This is hardly an improvement over a pencil and paper."

"All I need is a little practice."

"They've got dozens of the horrid machines in the Capitol. They echo all over the building. Can't you practice there?"

She wrinkled her nose. "I don't want to get caught. Using a typewriter isn't part of my responsibilities. I have a friend in the Patent Office who says the government has a technology where they can see fingerprints and trace them to the exact person. It's safer not even to touch the machines."

He looked amused. "Miss O'Brien, do you honestly believe the government is so fascinated by your daily activities that they'd bother to monitor your fingerprints?"

Maybe he never needed to fear for the security of his job, but she didn't have that luxury. "They might."

He made good-natured jibes the entire time she practiced with the typewriter, but she didn't care. This was too much fun. When the shopkeeper moved to close up the store for the lunch hour, she reluctantly surrendered her spot at the machine and headed outside.

Mr. Callahan followed. "All right, O'Brien," he said as he strode alongside her on a path crowded with Saturday shoppers. "Time to confess. Why do you want the typewriter? And don't give me that silliness about admiring technology. It's more than that. You were drooling over that machine like it was your firstborn child."

A flush heated her cheeks. Was she so obvious? She stopped to pretend interest in the pumpkins mounded on a street vendor's cart. "Haven't you ever wanted something for no good reason? Just to have it?"

"Me? Of course, but I expect the world to bow down and kiss my ring, so I'm entitled to whatever I want. You're far too practical for such indulgences."

His good humor was contagious. Maybe she could tell him why she really wanted that typewriter. For as soon as she completed his research requests, they would go their separate ways and never see each other again. He wouldn't be there to witness her humiliation if she failed in the lofty goal she had set for herself.

"Do you like reading biographies?" she asked.

He picked up a gourd from the vendor's stand and tossed it from palm to palm. "In the past year I've read biographies of

Lafayette, John Milton, and Ferdinand Magellan, so yes, I enjoy reading biographies. Why?"

"I've noticed that only famous people have biographies written about them. Warriors and kings and princes. Not that they don't deserve to have their stories told, but there are other people who get overlooked." The waxy skin of the pumpkin was cool as she pressed her fingers into its ridges . . . anything to avoid looking at him.

"Who do you want to write about?"

No, she couldn't tell him. She set the pumpkin back down and brushed the grit from her palms. "I don't know, just a biography. Maybe about an ordinary person who made the world a better place, but who would never be remembered otherwise."

"So what's stopping you? And don't say it's because you don't have a typewriter. John Milton wrote *Paradise Lost* without a typewriter, and he was blind."

"It would be a big gamble," she said with a frustrated breath. She turned to walk toward the streetcar stop on the corner. She'd never been one to take risks, and the odds of her realizing success were small. Minuscule, really.

"Life is a gamble. What other excuse have you got?" he said, then fell into step beside her.

"My idea isn't a practical one," she admitted.

Soon they arrived at McPherson Square, one of the dozens of small parks dotting the city. This one was dominated by the imposing statue of a Civil War general atop his mighty horse.

Anna sat on the low stone wall encircling the statue. "The odds are good I would pour my heart and soul and every minute of my free time into writing a book and then no one would publish it. It would probably be a colossal mistake even to try."

"There are worse things in life than a few mistakes, O'Brien." He braced a foot on the space beside her, smiling down at her.

"If you don't ever make mistakes, it means you aren't dreaming big enough, and something tells me that behind those prim clothes you've got the mind of a dreamer." She ought to take offense, but he wasn't teasing. He was smiling gently, and the tenderness in his eyes felt strangely comforting.

"Making mistakes means you're learning, growing, pushing . . . that you yearn for something and aren't afraid to chase after it. You're being creative and contributing to this world, even if it doesn't work out as you hoped. Go ahead and make mistakes. For once in your life, quit playing it safe and make some spectacular mistakes," he said with relish. His voice rose to a pitch that started attracting attention. "Make glorious mistakes that will echo through the ages. Make mistakes that no one has ever *thought* of! Don't limit yourself, no matter how outlandish. Reach out and strive for something beyond all dreams."

Pedestrians turned to stare at him, but oh, what she wouldn't give to be the sort of confident person who could stand on a street corner and shout to the world. To be the kind of person who chased the wildest of dreams, no matter how improbable.

"Be brave, O'Brien!" he went on. "Write your book. Write it even if no one will ever publish it and you have to roll it up in a bottle and throw it in the sea so someone will find it on the other side of the world."

"You're insane," she said with a giggle.

He calmed down and took a seat beside her on the wall. "You're only saying that because you don't believe me yet. There's no shame in making mistakes or failing. Heaven knows, I've done both."

It was hard to believe this brash, self-assured man could have failed at anything, and it aroused her curiosity. "Tell me when you've failed."

"I'm a failed poet. I have a stack of atrocious poetry six inches thick back home in Bangor."

"Really? I don't believe it."

"Don't believe I am a poet or that my poetry is bad? Come on, don't spare my feelings."

"I don't believe someone like you would waste time scribbling bad poetry."

"Miss O'Brien," he said in a low, purring voice. "If you read my poems, your eyes would bleed in pity and despair."

"That bad?"

"That bad." He nudged her foot with his boot. "Come on, I've told you my secret. What kind of biography do you want to write?"

Why did she feel so comfortable with this man? She couldn't afford to relax around him in the Capitol, but out here everything seemed different. A sense of affinity was blossoming between them, and it felt as though there was nothing she couldn't tell him.

"You read a biography of Ferdinand Magellan," she began hesitantly, "but did you know that a cartographer named Estêvão Gomes sailed with him to the Far East? He risked his life right alongside Magellan on those dangerous voyages, but no one remembers him because all he did was make maps. I'd like to change that. I'd like to write a big, fat book documenting the lives of the great mapmakers. I know it sounds foolish, because no one ever thinks about the people who draw maps."

A streetcar headed toward them. She glanced at him. "Do you need to catch that streetcar?"

He shook his head. "I'll wait for the next. I'd rather hear about your book."

She gathered her thoughts while the streetcar stopped and passengers boarded. She didn't like talking about her sad childhood as an orphan. It inevitably brought looks of pity, and she didn't want that from him. But it was impossible to discuss her dreams unless he understood about her father. When the streetcar departed, she drew a breath and outlined her plan.

"My father was a mapmaker," she said proudly. "His ship went down at sea when I was twelve, but I would love to include a chapter about him in the book. He was one of the first cartographers to start mapping the bottom of the ocean. He sank test tubes and measures down to the ocean floor, trying to figure out the mysteries of what no one could see. It was amazing work, and he deserves to be remembered."

She stared into the distance, trying to find the words to express why this was so important to her. "Maybe someday, a hundred years from now, someone will pull my dusty old book off a library shelf and read about my father and be amazed by all the things he did. I dream about that possibility all the time. I just don't want him to be forgotten."

"Is that why you became a map librarian? To be closer to your father?"

"Yes," she admitted quietly. "I used to stare at maps and trace his voyages, daydream about the places he'd seen. I know it sounds foolish, but when I study maps I hear my father's voice in my head, helping me interpret what I see. The love of maps is something we can share, even now. It's a way for me to be close to him."

She held her breath, praying he wouldn't laugh at her. It was risky to expose such deeply rooted longings and hard to guess how he would respond.

"I envy you."

She looked up to see if he was mocking her, but there was no meanness in his countenance, only a gentle sort of wistfulness. "It's clear you admired your father, but I feared mine." She blanched at the appalling statement, but he then explained, "Oh, I loved him too. It was complicated. Your admiration seems pure, and I envy that more than you can imagine. My father was a decent man at heart—loving and passionate, and his laughter could shake the rafters. But when he was under the influence of liquor, he was like Janus, the Roman god of two faces. War and peace. Hope and destruction. Even my mother was afraid of him. I think he would have respected her more if she stood up to him, but she always battened down the hatches and prayed for the storm to pass. The rest of us were left to fend for ourselves."

In that instant, Anna knew that she and Luke Callahan were more alike than she could have thought possible. On the surface he was outgoing and confident, while she was quiet and reserved, yet they both knew what it was like to feel abandoned in a world of uncertainty. How fascinating to feel this unexpected surge of communion with a person so different from herself. Thrilling, even.

"I need a wife who isn't afraid to stand up to me," he continued, "someone who can challenge and inspire me. I want a woman who can weep at the beauty of a splendid poem, but can also spot blarney when she sees it. I want an honest, God-fearing wife, but also a woman who can set my blood on fire and wouldn't be afraid to dash stark naked into the ocean with me."

"Mr. Callahan!"

"Don't turn into a schoolmarm on me," he teased. "You've read *Madame Bovary*, you know what I'm getting at. I'm not interested in a marriage without passion. I want a wife of good sense and sound values, but also a red-blooded woman who is eager for the end of the day and the sanctity of the marriage bed." He grinned.

She couldn't believe he was saying this. His tone wasn't the least bit lewd, only blunt and unashamed. "Madam Bovary came to a bad end," she pointed out.

"Why must you be such a stickler for details?" His voice was frustrated, but his eyes were laughing.

They stayed in the park for hours, discussing novels, music, and Mr. Callahan's irrational dread of technology. "No electric bulb will ever compete with the warmth and beauty of candle flame," he asserted.

He was wrong, of course, but so eloquent in his convictions that it was fun to listen to him. Four more streetcars came and went while they laughed and argued about everything under the sun.

Finally, the five o'clock streetcar approached. "I've enjoyed our afternoon, but I have responsibilities back home," Mr. Callahan said. "My ward is a fourteen-year-old boy who morphs into a rampaging monster when he isn't regularly fed."

He still didn't make any move to leave, but instead continued staring at her. The moment was broken when the streetcar slowed to a halt, startling them both with a loud rasp of escaping air as the pneumatic pump opened the levered doors.

A little warmth left as he went to stand in line for the streetcar. Had she really just spent an entire afternoon with a member of Congress without once being ordered about, spoken down to, or feeling even a tiny bit inferior?

Studying Mr. Callahan from a distance, he didn't look very different from the others waiting to board the streetcar. His boots were a little dusty, he could use a haircut, and his winter coat was rumpled from being in storage most of the year. He fumbled in his pocket for a coin and boarded right behind a woman carrying a caged chicken. He seemed like an entirely ordinary person.

The streetcar was already setting off down the street when Mr. Callahan stuck his head out one of the open windows to holler out a final command to her. "Write your book, O'Brien!" His shout echoed off the buildings, and she stood at the intersection, smiling like an idiot.

She watched the streetcar disappear down the street. Maybe he was right, and she should be brave enough to risk writing her book, but how could she write her father's story if she didn't know how it ended? If what she suspected was true, the *Culpeper* was nowhere near Bermuda when it went down, and for some reason the navy didn't want her to know the truth. It was merely a detail, but accuracy was important. If she was going to write a book, it would be flawless.

Sooner or later she would find the truth about the *Culpeper*, whether the navy cooperated with her or not.

Despite their temporary truce at the McPherson Square trolley stop, five days later the inspiring man who urged her to write an improbable biography was gone, replaced by the annoying congressman barking demands at her.

"O'Brien!" he yelled upon entering the map room. "I need the data on the mollusk harvest."

"I'm sitting ten feet away; you don't need to shout," she said from behind a mound of books. She no longer took offense at his abrupt demeanor. That would be like resenting a locomotive for barreling ahead at full steam. This dynamic, oversized personality was simply the way he was designed. "Here is your report."

He skimmed the document before tossing it back at her. "This is only last year's harvest. I need at least ten years' worth of data."

"Then why didn't you say so in the first place?" she asked in exasperation.

"Because I didn't realize I needed it until just now. These

numbers look low. I want to know if this is a trend or just a bad year. Please have it by tomorrow."

It rankled her the way he was so dismissive. "That's it? I bring you pearls from the East, and all you can do is toss the file on the table like it's rubbish?"

"You brought me the mollusk report, not pearls." A hint of laughter lurked in his eyes, and she suspected he was deliberately goading her. "Have you started on that biography of mapmakers yet?"

"I haven't had time. I've got ten years of mollusk data to scrounge up."

He winked at her. "Excuses, O'Brien."

"Don't *wink* at me," she whispered, but he was already striding out the door, whistling in that annoyingly charming manner.

The more Anna worked on Mr. Callahan's requests, the odder they seemed. It was understandable that he'd want information on oysters and mollusks. Even his request for twenty years of budget expenditures seemed legitimate. But why did he need information about cranberries, or corn? He wanted to know about the engineering of hydraulic sawmills and why the government was giving it preferential treatment.

The technical design of hydraulic sawmills was beyond her ability to analyze, so she brought the problem to Neville at the Patent Office.

As usual, Neville's work area looked like the laboratory of a madman. She ducked to avoid the model of a hot air balloon dangling from the office ceiling. Blueprints and charts covered the walls and the surface of his desk, stacked high with patent applications and models of mechanical contraptions. Anna drew up a chair so they could look at the designs of the hydraulic sawmills together.

"It's a brilliant design," Neville said, "but traction engines may start giving them competition. I can pull a few examples from the patent archives if it will help."

Anna stared at the papers spread out on the table before them. "I just wish I understood why Mr. Callahan needs this information. Most of it doesn't relate to his appointment on the Fisheries committee. Sawmills? Cheese? For heaven's sake, he wants to know everything about the cranberry industry for the past thirty years. And apparently he has quite the thing for Elizabeth Barrett Browning and romantic poetry."

"Did you know you start flushing whenever you speak of him?" Neville asked.

She grabbed the sheaf of papers to fan herself, wishing she had a bucket of ice water to plunge her head into. How could she explain this tangle of complicated feelings? Luke Callahan was the embodiment of the type of person she always avoided. Showy, brash, overconfident, someone who lorded over underlings like her and Neville while he paraded around the Capitol like a peacock. She decided to ignore Neville's question.

"There's no rhyme or reason to his research requests. I can't understand what he's really looking for."

Neville flipped through the ten pages of Mr. Callahan's research requests, his face tight with concentration. He was silent as he scanned them, scrutinizing Anna's carefully printed notes in the margins. As he neared the end, a small smile tugged at his mouth, finally breaking into a grin when he finished the last page.

"I see it," he said, triumph resonant in his voice.

"See what?"

"I see the pattern in his thinking. Come on, Anna! Don't you see what all this is driving at? Think! Who does Luke Callahan dislike more than anyone else in Congress?"

"The Speaker of the House."

"Correct. And where does Speaker Jones come from?"

Anna glanced at the research notes. Cheese, cranberries, timber, sawmills . . .

"Wisconsin?"

"Exactly!" Neville said. "I'm not sure what Callahan plans to do with this information, but you can bet it has something to do with undermining the Speaker of the House. Why else would he be so curious about how much funding has been directed to the industries important to Wisconsin?"

Anna closed her eyes to think as the pieces began falling into place. "I think it's a lot bigger than that," she said. "Next month the Speaker is going to try to raise the tariff. It's a hugely controversial vote, and Mr. Callahan is probably trying to tarnish the Speaker's name so that it won't pass."

It was worrisome. At a time when the library operated with a skeleton crew as the move to the new building was under way, to be used as a foot soldier in a congressman's private feud against the Speaker of the House could be a problem.

"I think I should tell Mr. Spofford," she said. "I don't know if it's right to let ourselves be drawn into this sort of vendetta."

"Careful," Neville warned. "Callahan is an influential congressman. He's been knocked down a peg, but don't underestimate him. He's got a lot of sway on Capitol Hill, and it doesn't pay to make enemies without good cause."

How could a man who loved romantic poetry be anyone's enemy? Against her better judgment, she was coming to like Luke Callahan. Maybe a little too much. And a woman in her situation couldn't afford to let such rumors take root.

"O'Brien, this is perfect!"

The voice shattered the silence in the map room and nearly

gave Anna a heart attack. She whirled around to glare at Mr. Callahan, who was holding aloft her latest batch of research.

"This is a library," she said, trying to calm her heart to a normal rate. "We generally try to avoid howling like banshees."

She braced herself, knowing that Luke Callahan's visits rarely happened without a slew of new demands on her time, but perhaps today would be different. He seemed pleased as he held her latest report. Perhaps he was there to thank her for the research and leave her in blessed peace.

"This is exactly what I hoped you'd find," he said. He propped his hip against her desk, invading her sense of privacy. "I need you to present this data before a special committee I've convened."

Every scrap of pleasure she had from his praise evaporated. "No."

"No?" He raised a brow and sent her a pointed look, as though if he waited long enough she'd change her mind.

"I don't speak in public," she said, her throat already starting to ache at the idea. "I can ask Mr. Spofford to make the presentation—"

"But you were the one who gathered the data. You'd be the best person."

"Mr. Spofford makes the formal presentations to Congress. I merely compile the data."

Mr. Callahan fiddled with one of his fancy cuff links while he pinned her down with a challenging stare. "That doesn't seem very logical. What if members of the committee have additional questions?"

She wished the rush of acid in her stomach would go away. She got hot and sweaty at the very thought of speaking before a group of strangers. She pushed away from her desk and paced the tight confines of the map room. "I can't speak in public," she said as she twisted her hands.

"Can't, or don't want to?"

"I physically *can't*. My throat will close up, and all I'll be able to do is croak like a frog."

"Why are you so sensitive about your voice?"

The question startled her. Her hand instinctively flew to protect her throat. She glanced around the map room, praying no one else had heard this mortifying conversation. There was no one else there, but it was still an embarrassing topic.

"Why would you ask such a thing?" she asked.

"Because you nearly bit my head off that first morning when I complimented your voice. And you cover your throat when anyone mentions it."

There was no point in evading the topic. It wasn't as if it were a big secret, for everything that happened to her was a matter of public record. He could even look it up if he was so inclined.

"My throat got badly burned when I was twelve years old. It's never been quite the same." She hoped he would let it go at that, but he leaned forward in curiosity.

"How did your throat get burned?"

Even thinking about it summoned the caustic scent of lye. She'd probably always be haunted by that stench whenever she remembered that night. "I lived with my aunt and uncle after my father's ship went down. I, uh . . . I wasn't the easiest child. I had a terrible habit of swearing when I got angry."

His brow quirked in surprise. True, she was a quiet person today, but as a child? She could curse a blue streak when she got angry, and she'd thrown some royal temper tantrums.

"My uncle was very strict about swearing and always washed my mouth out with soap if I said a bad word. One night he'd been drinking. I don't remember why I was so upset, but I sassed him and he reached for the soap. When he couldn't find it, he grabbed a bottle of lye instead. I saw him heading my way."

She knew what that bottle meant. Once she'd helped Aunt Ruth with the laundry and some lye splashed on the back of her hand. It took only a few seconds to burn painful red splotches into her skin. Anna dashed for the door, but her uncle caught her, hauling her off the ground and back to the washroom. She still remembered the smell of his hand over her face as he pried her lips open, the glass bottle clicking against her teeth, the wash of caustic liquid down her throat. The smell, the burn . . . she gagged and tried to throw it up, but he clamped a hand over her mouth, holding the liquid in until it slid back down her throat. White, searing pain . . .

She didn't remember much after that, except that her throat swelled up so much it was hard to breathe and she ended up in the hospital. It hurt to talk, but she still had a little bit of a scratchy voice left. Within a week scar tissue built up in her esophagus, gradually robbing her of the ability to speak at all.

"He made you drink *lye*?" Luke's voice was filled with horror. He shot up so quickly that his chair tipped over, clattering onto the floor. He paced the narrow space between the table and a stack of atlases like a lion in a cage. His eyes glittered with a fierce emotion she couldn't place. Rage? Revenge? Whatever it was, it was frightening. She averted her eyes.

"Yes," she said simply.

"There is nothing I despise more than a man who mistreats a woman. *A child*, no less. Did anything happen to your uncle because of this?"

"He was sentenced to three years in jail." Aunt Ruth had never been enthusiastic about taking Anna in, and after Uncle Henry was sentenced to jail, the atmosphere at home got even chillier. It was hard to stand still, and Anna went to set Luke's overturned chair back upright. She kept her hands braced against the chair for support.

"Anyway," she said, "I wasn't able to speak for a couple years because of the damage to my throat, but I had an operation and things got better. I still don't sound like I did before. The doctors say my voice will never get any better than it is right now. I sound awful, I know."

"You have a beautiful voice."

She scooped up an armful of atlases and began shelving them so she wouldn't have to look at his face. She didn't need pity or lies to make her feel better.

"You also use it as an excuse to hide up here and shirk the normal responsibilities of a librarian."

She dropped an atlas. "I do not!"

"I've seen other female librarians make presentations before committees. That music librarian, the one with the big shoulders . . ."

"Gertrude?"

"I don't know her name, but I heard a presentation she made on some Mozart manuscripts the library wanted to buy. Your voice functions perfectly well, but it is a convenient excuse to avoid work you don't want to do."

He could be really irritating. People like him had no conception of how hard it was to stand up before a group of intimidating men and speak with authority.

"Maybe some people crave the limelight, but I don't," she said as she slid a heavy atlas back onto the shelf so hard it banged into the back wall.

"Look, we've all had challenges in our lives," Mr. Callahan said. "If we lick our wounds and rehash old grievances, we'll never move forward. It's time for you to shake this off, O'Brien. I need a competent research assistant to attend an important meeting, and I'm not letting you off the hook."

"Why do I get the feeling this 'important meeting' of yours

all boils down to an attempt to undermine the Speaker of the House?"

He stilled at her words, his eyes narrowing. "What makes you say that?"

"Aside from a few paltry questions about mollusks, all the data you've asked me to gather relates to Wisconsin industries. It can also be used to undermine the upcoming vote about the tariff, and everyone knows Speaker Jones has invested a great deal in that issue."

A gleam of respect warmed his features. "What a keen observation. I knew there was a reason I liked you."

Anna snatched up another atlas to shelve. "I think it's unseemly the way you're using me to build a case against Speaker Jones."

"I prefer to call it clever," Mr. Callahan said. "A hundred years ago people would have launched a revolution over things like this upcoming tariff vote. Even now, it's causing riots in factories and mining camps all over the country, but I intend to use rationality to persuade people to my point of view." He held up her report. "And the information gathered in these pages will help me build my case. I need more congressmen who see things my way. That's why I want you to attend this meeting."

Her fingers curled around the atlas cradled in her arms. One of the reasons she was so proud to be working here was that she loved helping people find information. It was information that powered innovation. Progress. Maybe he was right in accusing her of hiding behind her damaged voice to avoid anything that might drag her out of the safety of this room.

The sound of running footsteps heralded a man wearing the uniform of a hotel valet, who barged into the room. "Mr. Callahan," he said breathlessly. "I've been looking everywhere for you. You are needed back at the Willard immediately. Something about your nephew, sir."

Mr. Callahan blanched. The hotel valet passed a note to him, and he tore it open, his fingers shaking as he read. She had never seen him so agitated.

"Is something wrong?" she asked.

"I don't know." But there was fear in his words. The valet had no additional insight into the terse message, except that his nephew had gotten into "mischief."

"I've got to go," he mumbled. He tucked the note into his coat pocket and hurried from the room.

Luke clenched the leather hand strap as he stood in the streetcar, agonizing over what kind of mischief could cause him to be summoned home in the middle of the day. Philip was supposed to be in school by now, so what happened? A fall down the stairs? A broken back? He nearly fainted with relief when he was shown into the hotel manager's office to see Philip alive and well, sitting in the corner like a truant child.

"Your nephew has caused considerable damage to the first-floor renovations," Mr. Gloster said. "Apparently, young Michelangelo here thought to grace our hotel with an original fresco on the storage room wall."

Luke was well aware of Philip's aspiration to become a great painter, as the boy spent every cent of his allowance on art supplies. He listened in slack-jawed amazement as the manager outlined the entire event. Last night, Philip broke into one of the newly renovated rooms to paint an anonymous mural. He had timed his scheme carefully, waiting until the wet plaster had been set on the walls of the storage closet. It was the perfect opportunity to try his hand at painting a fresco, using the ancient technique of laying paint on still-damp plaster to create the luminous murals of the old masters.

Philip had waited for Luke to retire before proceeding to gather his painting supplies and a lantern, and slipped out of their room. It was after midnight, the plaster in the closet having already begun to dry. Philip applied a liberal amount of water to refresh the plaster, then began painting a mural of Saint George slaying the dragon. It didn't take long to realize he'd added too much water to the plaster, as it all began to slide and thicken at the base.

"The entire wall will need to be demolished and replastered," Mr. Gloster said.

Luke swiveled his attention to Philip, who sat frozen in the chair, his face white with fear and his lower lip trembling. He looked ready to throw up.

"I'm sorry," Philip said. "I just wanted to surprise everyone with a great painting. It wasn't supposed to turn out like this."

Mr. Gloster waved a copy of the contract he had with the builders. "It's going to cost seventy-five dollars to knock down that wall and rebuild it."

If Luke opened his wallet and made the problem go away, Philip would learn nothing. "I'm not paying," he said bluntly.

"Do you propose we put the boy in debtors' prison?" Mr. Gloster asked incredulously.

"No, he needs to work it off," Luke said. "He needs to learn the value of a sweaty day's labor and a healthy dose of respect for other people's property."

It took a while to figure out a fair way to compensate the hotel. Philip was to work in the laundry every day after school for four hours, and the entire day on Saturdays. It would take a month of hard labor to work off the debt.

Luke maintained a stern expression throughout the negotiation, but it was hard. This was such a classic case of Callahan grandiosity that he knew someday this story would be funny, but for now he needed to apply a firm hand with his nephew.

He walked Philip back to their hotel room, their footsteps muffled by the thick carpet running down the fifth-floor hallway. "You know this means no more dabbling in art, not until your debt is fully paid."

Philip stopped, whirling to face him in the hall outside their room. Stained with paint and flecks of plaster, Philip looked out of place in the ornate hallway lit with crystal wall sconces and hand-painted wallpaper.

"That's not fair," he said. "I'll pay the debt to the hotel, but I need art. You don't understand what art means to me. I can't live without it. I *can't*."

Luke recognized the desperation in Philip's voice. Hadn't he been equally devastated when his father tried to force him to quit writing poetry? The passions of an adolescent were so raw and unrefined, so overwhelming it was hard to imagine life could function if severed from the source of that zeal.

"How are you going to keep your grades up at school and work in the laundry if you're still painting?"

"I'll find a way," Philip vowed, his voice trembling with urgency. "You've got to trust me on this."

There were worse things in life than an overabundance of youthful enthusiasm. When seized by the fires of creativity, what task couldn't be accomplished? Perhaps the only crime would be to try to stand in the way of that flood of passion.

Luke unlocked the door to their suite of rooms and held it wide for Philip. "If your grades don't slip and you don't shirk a single minute of the time you owe the hotel, you can continue your painting."

The relief on Philip's face would have been amusing were it not so poignant. To this day, Luke savored the memory of his failed quest to become the world's greatest poet. That quest had brought him both soaring joy and withering disappointment, but the journey had been priceless. It had taught him perseverance and accomplishment. It had given him a glimpse into a world of incomparable beauty, and even though he'd only walked along the perimeter of literary adventure, he'd loved every moment.

Those blistering memories of triumph and heartbreak had helped sculpt him into a man. If he was going to do the right thing by Philip, the boy needed the opportunity to explore that same path.

Anna wasn't going to let the navy's threats stop her from discovering what had happened to the *Culpeper*. She couldn't set foot in the navy's archives without setting off a firestorm, so looking for evidence elsewhere was her only option. For the past three weeks she'd used every scrap of her free time scouring old newspapers for references to the sunken vessel.

An isolated island like Bermuda celebrated whenever a ship pulled in to port, and the local newspapers reported the cargo and business of the arriving ship. If the *Culpeper* was anywhere near Bermuda in 1882, it would have been mentioned in the *Royal Gazette* of Bermuda. The Library of Congress had copies of those old newspapers, and Anna read through every issue from 1882 looking for any mention of the *Culpeper*. If she found such a reference, it meant the navy had been right all along and she was letting her imagination run wild.

She found nothing. So the next place to look was where she thought her father's ship really sank: Cuba.

She arrived at the library on Saturday and spent the entire day scrutinizing yellowing old newspapers from Cuba. Curled up by the window alcove in the library's reading room, she tipped the newspaper to catch the light. She didn't know a lick of Spanish, but she didn't need to in order to spot the word *Culpeper* in the text. Above her, workmen continued their weekend chore, noisily boxing up books for the upcoming move.

"I didn't realize you knew Spanish."

She jumped. Luke Callahan was standing directly behind her, a stack of poetry books in the crook of his arm. "You almost gave me a heart attack!"

"May I join you?" he asked. The books thumped on the table beside her, and he pulled out a chair to sit without waiting for her answer. "Spanish?" he prodded again.

The less she said about the *Culpeper* the better. "What are you doing here on a Saturday?" she asked, sidestepping the question.

"My nephew has been condemned to indentured servitude for the next few weeks, and I find my hotel room depressingly bleak. I thought I'd come here for a chance to read in peace, but I'd much rather talk to you. Why are you reading a Cuban newspaper?" He grabbed the issue, skimming it with curiosity. He let out a bark of laughter. Apparently his Spanish was better than hers.

"Look at this," he said. "You've got a fifteen-year-old newspaper and even then the Cubans were bellyaching over their lack of independence from Spain."

She scrambled for what little she knew of Cuban politics. "Don't you think the Cubans are entitled to their liberty? The Spanish have been exploiting them for almost three hundred years."

"Yes, I'm worried about Spain and Cuba. If Speaker Jones wasn't so obsessed with cramming a new tariff down our throats, he might have a little more time to consider the revolution brewing in our own backyard." He tossed the newspaper down in disgust.

Anna needed to get the topic off Cuba and why she was reading a newspaper in a language she couldn't understand. "Why do you and Speaker Jones dislike each other so much?"

"Don't you know?" he asked, a hint of amusement in his eyes. "There are clues scattered about . . . of course, that would require you to have actually read my political biography, and you've already told me you have no interest in doing so. Which is odd. Most women find me fascinating."

"I find you maddening. But go on, tell me why he hates you."

"Forget it, O'Brien. It's really no one's business."

"I told you about my voice, even though it's a horrible memory for me. The least you could do is reciprocate." Mr. Callahan glanced up at the men packing up books on the floors above them. "They can't hear us," she said. "Talk. Unless you're afraid, of course."

His eyes lit at the challenge. Mr. Callahan pulled his chair a little closer to hers and said in a low voice, "A few months after I was first elected to Congress, there was a huge scandal with my family back in Maine." Over the next several minutes he was surprisingly candid as he recounted the tale of his youngest brother, Jason, whose love for animals had prompted him to begin herding the wild goats that roamed the mountainside into the pens on Callahan land. A judge ruled that it was impermissible to seize hoofed animals from government-owned land and ordered the goats released.

"Jason was incensed," Mr. Callahan recounted. "He and my brother Gabriel vowed retribution. They painted their faces blue like the ancient Celtic warriors, snuck onto the judge's land in the middle of the night, and released all his livestock."

Anna gasped. "They did *what*?"

"They released more than two hundred sheep into the wilderness. Everyone knew who did it, and my brothers didn't bother to deny it. They were proud of what they'd done. Charges of theft were lodged, and the scandal carried down to Washington. Speaker Jones wanted me to publicly renounce my brothers and say I would have nothing more to do with them. I couldn't do it. He said he understood, but that I should lie and *say* I would cut ties with them. In a year or two, the scandal would die down and I could mend fences when the trouble blew over. I wouldn't do it."

Mr. Callahan spoke proudly, without flinching. What must it be like to have that level of support? Aside from Neville's friendship, Anna had been alone since she was twelve years old.

"Gabe and Jason are still paying off the judgment from that bit of foolishness," he continued. "It's why they never have a spare dime. My father was charged as well, and he was still paying the debt when he died."

"Your father participated in this?"

Luke grinned. "He wouldn't have missed it for the world. He was proud his boys were standing up to the judge, and he painted his face along with them. My dad and Gabriel are both wild forces of nature, but Jason is different. He's probably the kindest, most compassionate soul I've ever known. He's got a bit of my father's hotheaded streak in him—especially when he drinks—but I remember him as the boy who used to find wounded birds in the woods and bring them home to nurse back to health. I would no more turn my back on him than slice off my own arm."

Mr. Callahan's voice vibrated with tension, and she noticed his hands were clenched into fists. For whatever reason, this conversation was upsetting him.

"Honesty is very important to me," he said. "I grew up in a difficult household where lies were commonplace, and I vowed that when I became a man and had control of my life, I would never tell a lie again—no matter how difficult or what the personal price."

"I understand."

His smile turned skeptical. "I'm not sure you do. Most parents raise their children to be truthful. My parents taught me to lie. When my father was too drunk to attend an important meeting at the mine, we lied about where he was. I lied when I went to school and the teacher wanted to know how I got a black eye and a split lip. To the outside world, our family looked like the image of hard-won success, but inside? It was a rudderless ship, and we created a smoke screen to lie, deceive, and evade. If people really knew my father, no bank would loan us money to build the tourmaline mine. No jewelers would contract to sell our gems. Lying was essential to maintaining our way of life, and we were good at it."

Anna shifted in her seat. "I'm not sure why you're telling me all this."

"Because I like you, O'Brien."

Her corset suddenly felt tighter, and it was hard to breathe. Surely he'd meant that in a friendly fashion, not anything more.

"I like you, and I want you to understand why I'll always be honest, even when it's awkward or inconvenient. Politicians have a reputation for glossing over the truth to suit their needs, but my constituents know that if I look them in the eye, they can rest assured I'm telling them the truth. No matter what, I will *always* tell the truth."

Realizing she'd been holding her breath, Anna shook herself. The attraction she felt for him was growing, like a sponge expanding in water, and this sort of fascination was dangerous.

She stood and began stacking the Cuban newspapers, anything rather than to look at the dazzling man sitting next to her. The faster she could gather the newspapers, the faster she could get away from this dangerous attraction. She'd worked hard to get to where she was in her profession and wasn't about to let it be spoiled by a reckless flirtation with a man who was off-limits to her.

He snatched her hand. "Don't go. It's Saturday. Stay and spend the day wallowing with me in Shakespeare and Byron. A kingdom built by words and verse, an ocean of sentiment . . ."

She tried not to laugh. "Oh dear, you really are a terrible poet after all."

He grinned, but didn't let go of her hand. She tugged it away and scooped up the newspapers. She'd sign them out and spend the weekend reading them in the privacy of her boardinghouse, because lingering with this man was putting both her heart and her career teetering on the brink of disaster.

Luke set off for the hotel, wondering what to do about his fascination with Anna O'Brien. He wasn't accustomed to spilling mortifying stories of his family, but he felt comfortable with her. She was soothing merely to be around. Practical, level-headed, and priggish . . . but enchanting. He needed someone like her to steady him. His entire *family* needed someone like her. Ever since taking Philip under his wing, Luke had been trying to teach the boy what it meant to lead a sober, responsible life, but it seemed the streak of recklessness had already taken root in Philip's soul. His spoiled fresco was on par with Jason's and Gabe's stunt with the judge's sheep. Luke shouldn't be laughing about the incident, for Philip's stunt was just another example of the grandiosity typical in his family.

Luke tried not to smile as he dashed up the front steps of the Willard Hotel. The grandeur of the main floor was in stark contrast to the sweltering laundry room attached to the back of the hotel, where Philip had been working all day. As Luke headed toward the laundry, he pulled a battered copy of *Romeo and Juliet* from his coat pocket. There was no reason the boy couldn't soak up a bit of culture while working off his debt.

Heat engulfed Luke the moment he set foot inside the laundry room. A row of irons were balanced on a rack before the fire, keeping hot as Philip cycled through them.

Philip looked up, his shirt soaked and his face glistening with sweat. "Thank heavens," he said, sagging a little as he pushed a lock of dark hair back from his face. At fourteen, Philip was shooting up like a weed, but was still skinny and unaccustomed to manual labor.

"You've got another thirty minutes," Luke said. Though he could see that Philip was beyond exhausted, the boy couldn't shirk his obligation. Luke ambled over to the far corner to catch the faint breeze filtering through the single window.

"You could help with the ironing," Philip grumbled.

"Could. Won't." Philip shot him a glare, but Luke merely waved the worn copy of *Romeo and Juliet* in the air. "I've brought this so you won't fall behind on your schoolwork. Keep ironing while I read aloud."

Philip's feet dragged as he carried the iron to the heating rack, then plopped onto the hearth and hung his head. "Everyone at school heard about what happened. Senator Kobler's son lives here and saw me collecting the laundry from the lines and told everybody. I just feel so *stupid*. No real fresco painter would be so brainless. I'm a failure, and now everyone at school knows it too."

Luke's heart went out to the boy. "So what? All great men fail."

Philip tilted his head a little, confusion in his eyes.

"Failure is a necessary part of the journey," Luke added. "It takes a long time to develop mastery in anything, and there will be times when you doubt yourself and you'll start wondering if your critics are right. But your biggest critic right now is *you*, Philip. So what if your first attempt at a fresco was a disaster. You'll probably fail a dozen more times before seeing any success, but you've got what it takes to stand up, brush yourself off, and keep trudging forward until you become great at it."

And he did. Philip's artistic talent was raw, but unmistakable. A surge of energy blossomed inside, and he pushed away from the wall, passion filling his voice.

"You have so much potential bursting inside that it compelled you to get up in the middle of the night to resurrect the frescos of the grand masters. Do you think I'm embarrassed about that? I love you for it!" Luke could hear his voice echoing down the hall, but he didn't care. "I *love* your passion and commitment and the fact that you weren't scared to make mistakes."

Philip started laughing, and it was good to see a smile on his face for the first time in over a week. "I want to see you soar, Philip," he continued. "You're going to stumble and fall at times, but that's all right. You've got what it takes to learn from your failures and keep pushing forward. You are unstoppable, and that's what makes the difference."

He leaned back against the wall, folded his arms, and looked Philip straight in the face. "But I'm still not going to help you with the ironing. Get moving, boy."

Philip grinned as he picked up the next iron on the rack and attacked the bed sheet. Luke took a chair by the window and began reading from *Romeo and Juliet*. The room was sweltering, yet there were few things he enjoyed more than Shakespeare. Would there ever come a time when Shakespeare would lose the power to make the earth shift beneath his feet? He savored the splendor of the verses, the pure distillation of longing and joy.

Across from him, Philip seemed equally mesmerized as he listened to Romeo's impassioned soliloquy. It was ten minutes past the time the boy was due to stop work, but Luke was reading the balcony scene and he could no more stop before the end of the act than he could stop his next breath of air.

At last Luke came to the end of act two. Philip set the iron aside as Luke closed the book. "This is a really good play," Philip said in an awestruck voice.

"You know love at first sight is for fools and idiots," Luke said. He stood, welcoming the chance to stretch his legs.

"Uncle Gabe said you fell in love at first sight once," Philip said with a knowing look.

"That's how I know it's for fools and idiots," he said lightly. It was easy to laugh about it now, but Luke had been hit hard by his infatuation for Violet Desjardins. At first it was a purely physical attraction. Luke was eighteen years old, and Violet was stunning, with dark red hair and a figure that would put an hourglass to shame. The moment they locked eyes, the air sparked with electricity. Violet seemed as spellbound as he.

At the time, he thought it was love at first sight. Now he knew it to be infatuation mixed with lust, but nothing in this world had been quite as glorious as those reckless, hazy days of summer when every ounce in his body felt alive. It was impossible to adore a woman so passionately, so completely, and not have it leave a scar that would last until his dying day. In all honesty, Luke didn't want that scar to fade. The memory of that blazing, ruined paradise would forever hold a cherished place in his memory.

He vowed long ago never to marry until he found a woman who sparked his passion the way Violet had. And although Anna O'Brien was the complete opposite of Violet, he was feeling the same impulsive attraction, the same blissful ache. He'd been trying to ignore it, but she was getting harder to dismiss.

And why should he? There was no impediment between them. He and Violet were a hopeless combination . . . but Anna? The more he thought about it, the more he realized she could be exactly what he'd always hoped to find in a wife.

Nonetheless, he would be sensible about this. No shouting on the rooftops like he'd done in Bangor. No endless stanzas of overwrought poetry or pleas to elope in the middle of the night. No, Anna O'Brien was a very different sort of woman, and he would need to court her carefully.

"Come on," he said. "It's getting late."

"I'd rather hear about the woman you fell in love with at first sight," Philip said.

Luke picked up the boy's jacket and held the door, savoring the rush of cool air in the hall. "Brace yourself for disappointment."

Philip pestered him the entire way up to their room, yet he didn't want to think about Violet. He wanted Anna.

Perhaps he would send her something. Not something boring and predictable like flowers or chocolate. Or anything that could be mistaken as a token of appreciation for all the work she'd been doing for him. He needed to come up with something truly unique.

He knew three things about Anna. She liked maps, she had a vivid imagination, and she was going to be hard to win.

Two days later, he walked into an antiquarian shop near Georgetown and found exactly what he was looking for. It was so perfect it was as if providence had guided his footsteps to the quaint shop. Satisfaction rolled through him as he carried it to the counter and paid for the charming, whimsical piece of nonsense.

It was time to start storming Anna O'Brien's fortress walls.

When a congressional page delivered the package from Luke Callahan, Anna assumed it contained more research requests. Snipping the string and carefully peeling the brown paper aside, she caught her breath, stunned to see the colorful antique map inside.

It was fantastic! The map was undated, but judging from the ragged outlines of the western part of the Americas, it probably dated from the late eighteenth century. An artist had painted a frost monster hovering over the North Pole, and a dragon in the Caribbean blew a mighty bellow to symbolize the Gulf Stream. An angry sea god lurked off Cape Horn, stirring up turbulent waters.

Her heart raced and she caught her breath. It was the most unique and personal gift she'd ever been given. And so thoughtful. To imagine that Mr. Callahan had spotted this map and thought of her! It was . . .

She stopped herself. It was a donation to the map room, nothing more.

Congressmen and wealthy people often made gifts to the library, and it was embarrassing that she'd mistook the map as a personal gift, even for a second. She would arrange for it to be prominently displayed on the wall of the map room with a proper acknowledgment on an inscribed nameplate beneath the map. The catalog record would cite Mr. Callahan's name as the donor, and Mr. Spofford would send a note of confirmation.

Still, it was a thrilling donation, and she was sure it wouldn't have happened but for the relationship she and Mr. Callahan had formed over the previous weeks. The map was a magnificent work of art. The characters were whimsical but accurate nevertheless. Cape Horn was called "the sailors' graveyard" because it was notorious for treacherous waters, and the angry sea god looked perfectly at home in the dangerous stretch of ocean. The depiction of the dragon bellowing a mighty wind was an accurate portrayal of the Gulf Stream, one of the strongest ocean currents in the world.

The smile froze on her face.

Staring at that ferocious dragon, another detail clicked into place. How blind she had been! For a mapmaker's daughter, how could she have overlooked such a huge, obvious clue about what had happened to the *Culpeper*?

The navy's report claimed that wreckage from the ship washed ashore on the east coast of Bermuda. She was no oceanographer, but given the strength of the Gulf Stream, it was unlikely the wreckage from the ship could have drifted backward in the current to end up in Bermuda.

She knew exactly where to go to confirm her suspicions.

A leading expert on ocean cartography, Howard Clover worked in the navy's Hydrographic Office and had known her father. He'd even mentored Anna in the basics of map librarianship. She used her lunch hour to escape to the War Building, where the Hydrographic Office was located in the basement.

The War Building was as imposing as its name. The building's granite exterior featured hooded windows, carved mantles, and was topped with a mansard roof. Inside, ornate gaslight chandeliers lit the spiraling staircases and tunnels of vaulted sandstone.

Anna hurried down the staircase as it curved into the basement. Going to see Howard wasn't violating the navy's demand that she steer clear of the *Culpeper*. All she wanted was the answer to a scientific question, and Howard would be the perfect source to confirm Anna's suspicion about that old hurricane.

Howard's office was crammed with map cases, the walls covered by nautical maps. He stood over a table-sized map of the Pacific Ocean, leaning over to study it through a magnifying glass as she stepped through the open door.

"Have you got time for a question?" she asked. Howard's thin frame straightened.

"Of course I've got time for you, my girl." Anna had always

longed for grandparents, and Howard Clover embodied every quality she could hope for in a grandfather. His narrow, careworn face always had a gentle smile, and every sentence he spoke seemed laden with wisdom and insight.

"I'm trying to figure out the strength of the Gulf Stream," she began.

"Easy. One of the strongest in the world."

"Is that true near the Bermuda islands?"

He nodded.

"What about during a hurricane?"

Howard paused, setting down the magnifying glass. His brows lowered. "Would this have anything to do with the sinking of a certain ship about fifteen years ago?"

Anna moved farther into the room, resting her hands on the cold metal map case. "A new map of historic hurricanes has just been issued from the weather bureau. They say the hurricane that sank the *Culpeper* tracked east of Bermuda, not west like we always thought. The navy's official report claims wreckage from the *Culpeper* washed ashore in Bermuda. That would mean the wreckage drifted *backward* in the Gulf Stream. I can't imagine such a thing is possible."

Howard folded his arms across his chest and stared into the distance while he thought. He scrubbed a hand across his jaw. "You're right," he finally said. "It would be more likely for the wreckage to end up in England rather than Bermuda. No one has been able to get accurate measurements on ocean currents during a storm that bad, but I'll pull together what we know. It will take a few hours. Can you come back later this afternoon?"

"I'll be here," she replied.

If Howard could back up her assertions about the implausibility of wreckage drifting backward in the Gulf Stream, it would be one more detail convincing her that the navy was wrong. Anticipation tingled through her, and it was hard to concentrate for the next couple of hours.

But when she returned, Howard was locking up early for the day. "We're closed," he said as he pulled the door shut. His keys jangled while he fumbled with the lock.

"Oh," she said. Was he angry with her? How strange that he wouldn't meet her eyes as he worked the lock. "Can you at least tell me if you found anything about the effect of hurricane winds on the Gulf Stream?"

Howard froze, then glanced up and down the hallway. A few men were leaving for the day, but no one was paying them any mind. A moment later, the clatter of the keys resumed and he unlocked the door.

"Come inside," he muttered impatiently. "We need to speak quickly."

She followed him, surprised when he pulled the door shut again, the snick sounding loud in the silence of the darkened office.

"You need to let this go," Howard said.

"Let it go? But either the weather bureau's research is wrong or the navy's report of the *Culpeper* needs to be corrected. One of them is clearly wrong, and I'm not the type to let things go."

Howard stepped closer and lowered his voice. "Admiral Channing came by the office less than an hour after you left. He got word you'd been here and reminded me that I answer to the navy, not librarians from the Capitol."

The breath froze in her lungs. If others in the navy were angry at her for poking into their report of the shipwreck, perhaps Lieutenant Rowland hadn't been issuing idle threats. And if word of this got to Mr. Spofford . . .

"All I asked was a simple research question," Anna stammered. "Government offices help each other all the time. Why should this be any different?"

Howard's expression didn't waver. "In my thirty years working for the government, I've never had an admiral in my office directing my work. Whatever you're doing, stop. Just stop."

"Maybe I could come in and do some research while you're at lunch someday?"

Howard sighed and looked away. "Anna, I'm three months away from drawing my pension. It will be the only form of support for my wife and me. Do you understand what I'm saying?"

He was saying he couldn't help her. His face was regretful, but firm. "Okay, I understand," she answered.

She walked back to the Capitol alone. It would have been faster to take the streetcar, but she needed time to organize her thoughts. The navy was trying to browbeat her. When she'd been teased and bullied as a child, she'd hunkered down and endured it. She wouldn't tolerate that anymore. There was something wrong in the navy's report about the *Culpeper* and they knew it. She didn't want to stir up trouble; all she wanted was to ensure that the story of the *Culpeper* would be remembered accurately. But it seemed she'd turned over a rock and exposed something that wanted to remain safely hidden in darkness.

As she began climbing the dozens of white granite steps leading up to the Capitol, a sense of resolve gathered inside her. She was a librarian. It was her job to know how to seek out and uncover information. If one avenue closed, she'd keep searching until she found another.

"I will find a way, Papa," she whispered. "I'm not sure how I'll do it, but this won't end here."

Luke shifted in his seat, trying to find a more comfortable position in the hard-backed chair. Packed onto the floor of the House of Representatives, this small oak desk and chair was the closest thing he had to an office. There had been talk for years of adding a building beside the Capitol where ordinary congressmen like him could have a proper office, but that funding had gone to the construction of a palatial new library that made Luke's thrifty Yankee soul cringe. He tried to ignore the congressman from Kentucky rambling from the podium about the growing hostility between Spain and Cuba while he scanned Anna's latest batch of budget reports.

Had she gotten that whimsical dragon map yet? A reluctant smile curled his mouth as he imagined her delight upon opening the brown paper wrapping. The map would appeal to her outlandish daydreams, and he'd buy dozens more silly trinkets if it would help soften her toward him.

A congressional page entered the chamber, sidling behind the wide semicircle of desks to deliver the mail. When Luke first arrived in Congress, he was shocked at the amount of business that occurred while the House was in session. Congressmen answered their mail, vendors delivered sandwiches, and others dabbled in card games during boring debates.

Luke was dismayed at the short stack of envelopes the boy delivered to him. When he'd been a member of the powerful Budget Committee, he was flooded with letters from all over the country. Now he had three measly letters, one of which was from his sister.

He opened Julia's letter first. A slow burn began as he read the letter. His jaw clenched, his skin prickled with heat.

Julia reported that a challenge from within his own party was being mounted against him for the next election. She enclosed a political cartoon from a Bangor newspaper, showing him frolicking in the ocean with dolphins while the shoreline was filled with doleful Maine loggers consoling their hungry children.

Luke's jaw tightened, wishing he could get his hands on that cartoonist. Didn't anyone understand how impressive it was to arrive in Washington and land a coveted position on the Budget Committee? Luke sat on it for six solid years while that arrogant cartoonist scribbled pictures like a two-year-old.

And then Julia had the audacity to include a postscript. *When may I expect the $400 to secure our brother's freedom?*

Luke balled the letter into a wad. Jason could sit in jail until the next century as far as Luke was concerned. What he needed to worry about was winning the next election. He glared at the Speaker of the House, shrouded in a haze of cigarette smoke as he sat at the center of the rostrum. Cornelius Jones looked like a withered autumn leaf clinging to life as he rolled another cigarette the moment he snubbed out the previous one.

His temper ratcheted higher. He was mad at Jason, mad at Julia, and mad at the Speaker of the House. He was mad at the congressman from Kentucky who kept droning on and on. Most of all, he was mad at himself for losing his temper and getting booted off the most powerful committee in Washington, all because he picked a reckless fight with the Speaker of the House.

There was only one person who could calm him down when he was in a foul mood like this. The instant the gavel banged to call the meeting to a close, Luke shot out of his chair. He plowed around congressmen lingering at their desks and darted out the door, dashing down the hallway and vaulting up the west staircase to the library.

"O'Brien!" he shouted as he rounded the stairwell onto the third floor. The door to the map room was open, and he charged inside. Anna didn't even look up from her paper work when he entered the room.

"Is the building on fire?" she asked dryly. "Otherwise I'm not speaking to you until you lower your voice."

"I need you to find me a recipe for poison," he snapped. "Something that can kill the varmints that riddle this town."

"Animal varmints, or the human variety?"

She was so prim when she said it, earning a reluctant twist of his lips as he tried not to smile. "The Cornelius Jones brand of varmint. I've had it up to here with that desiccated husk of a human."

Anna cocked her head to one side. "Is he really that bad? The people of Wisconsin seem to like him well enough to keep him in office for the past twenty-five years. How bad can he be?"

"He's ruining our country! *That's* how bad he is."

Anna's face remained passive as she rolled up a map. "Mr. Callahan, what did your constituents expect of you when they elected you to office?"

His answer was swift and unequivocal. "To vote to keep the tariff rates low and protect the industries of Maine."

"And have you been doing that?"

"Yes, but Speaker Jones has been blocking me at every turn!"

Anna rose, looking him directly in the eyes. "Don't you see?" she asked, her beautiful, velvety voice full of encouragement. "You're doing exactly what the people of Maine elected you to do, so why are you so upset? Shaking your fist won't change anything. Letting that man get beneath your skin is counter-productive, Congressman."

Luke crossed his arms, forcing his breathing to return to normal. He rocked back and forth on his feet, the remnants of frustration still echoing in his blood. "Keep talking," he ordered. "The sound of your voice calms me down."

Anna rolled her eyes as she began filing map tubes in the bin. "You were pretty scary when you barged in here just now."

"Scary?"

"Yes. The cords on your neck were standing out, and your voice could send lesser mortals scurrying."

His father used to look like that. When Edgar Callahan was in a rage, the cords on his neck bulged, and a vein in his forehead throbbed. Luke looked away. His deepest fear, so deep that he could barely even acknowledge it, was becoming like his father. The seed of rage was within him, and he didn't need alcohol to bring it to life. He'd fled from Bangor to live in the marble halls of Washington precisely so he could work alongside other accomplished, rational men.

Now he was having shouting matches on the floor of Congress. Yelling at a perfectly charming librarian all because he was angry with his sister.

The heat drained from his body, his muscles sagging. "I'm sorry, Anna. Truly. It's been a lousy morning, but I shouldn't have barged in here to shout at you." He glanced at the wall. His dragon map hung there beside a map of the mining districts in the Dakota Territory. She noticed his gaze.

"Thank you for the map," she said. "Antiques like that are

wonderful for a library, but we can never afford them unless they're gifts from donors. A formal acknowledgment from Mr. Spofford will be sent to you shortly."

"It was a gift for you . . . not the library."

She looked confused. "Why would you give me a gift? Especially such an expensive one?"

He sighed. For an intelligent woman, Anna seemed remarkably dense when it came to reading the traditional signs of courtship. He needed to quit making excuses for coming here and be honest with her. He peered out the window toward the botanical garden that bordered the Capitol. "Will you go for a walk with me?"

"Not unless you calm down. I generally don't walk alongside men with homicidal interests in poison."

She was doing it again—calming him with her cool wit and steady logic. She was like a balm on inflamed skin, soothing his frustration and making him think of wild, improbable things like autumn walks in sun-kissed gardens. He wanted to wallow in the sound of her voice, soft but with a fascinating patina of warmth and depth. He wanted to plop a book in her hands and coax her to read to him . . . he didn't care what. She could read the telephone directory to him for all he cared.

"Please," he whispered, leaning closer. "Come for a walk with me."

"It isn't the lunch hour yet."

"The greenhouses in the garden will be packed at noon. Walk with me now, and I'll show you a new orchid that just arrived from South America. It's orange."

"Orange?" She didn't sound impressed, but he didn't care.

"I'll bet you've never seen one of those before. Please, Anna."

He breathed a sigh of relief when she rose to fetch her coat.

Anna was careful to maintain a respectable distance from Mr. Callahan as they walked to the greenhouse maintained by the Department of Agriculture on the opposite side of the Mall. Originally designed to showcase the variety of botanical life in the Americas, it had evolved to include exotic specimens from all over the world.

The orange orchid had dropped its petals and proven a disappointment, but Anna happily followed Mr. Callahan as they wandered the greenhouse. The warm air was perfumed by scents of verbena, oakmoss, and the memory of summer.

"Don't ever let me get away with shouting at you," Mr. Callahan said, his voice uncharacteristically somber. "I hate it when I lash out like that. I know better, but sometimes it builds up inside and just . . . explodes. Like steam blowing off a valve. I hate myself when I feel it rising inside."

The frustration in his voice reminded Anna of Neville when they were growing up. Neville had been helpless against the incessant twitches that seized his body. Sometimes he actually hit himself or lunged against a wall to stop the twitching. It never helped. He went through years of self-loathing before finally accepting his affliction.

"Mr. Callahan, you must learn to accept who you are. You're both a saint and a sinner. Beautiful, but broken. Aren't we all? God has endowed you with the intelligence and ambition to get out of rural Maine and into the halls of Congress, but that won't magically transform you into someone else. The anger you inherited from your father is there for a reason. It can alert you that something is wrong, a signal of righteous indignation that spurs you to fight for a noble cause. But the flip side is that it can corrupt you. I don't think you'll ever be able to extinguish that hot flame that burns inside you. All you can do is learn to control it. Didn't you once say your favorite passage from the

Bible was 'Blessed are the peacemakers'? Perhaps there's a reason God has made that passage resonate with you."

Mr. Callahan scrutinized her as though she were as rare and exotic as the orchids surrounding them. "Where have you been all these years?" he asked in a voice tinged with admiration.

She smiled and turned away. It was flattering, the way he looked at her, but she mustn't let it go to her head. A man like him probably had a dozen of Washington's socialites trailing after him, waiting for whatever scraps of affection he tossed their way. She had no desire to compete in a game she could never win.

"Let's step outside," he said. "There are too many people in here."

While the greenhouse didn't seem all that crowded to her, she followed him outside into the crisp autumn day. The breeze was chilly, and she drew her coat tighter.

"Let's head over to the chestnut trees," he suggested, gesturing toward the Mall, where few people wandered. There were plans to tear out all these trees someday and build a huge grassy lawn, where visitors could see all the way from the Capitol to the Washington Monument, but Anna couldn't imagine how they would accomplish it. The Potomac Train Depot sat as an ugly blot in the middle of the Mall, and it would surely take decades to rip out the station and reroute the tracks. For now, though, there were clusters of leafy trees where a person could find some privacy. Mr. Callahan was silent as he guided her to an iron bench beneath the spreading limbs of a chestnut tree. The corners of his mouth were drawn down in an unusually somber expression. She sat, wondering at his strange silence.

"Why did you ask me out here?" she asked. "I gather it wasn't to see an orange orchid or these chestnut trees."

For the first time since she'd met him, he seemed nervous. He

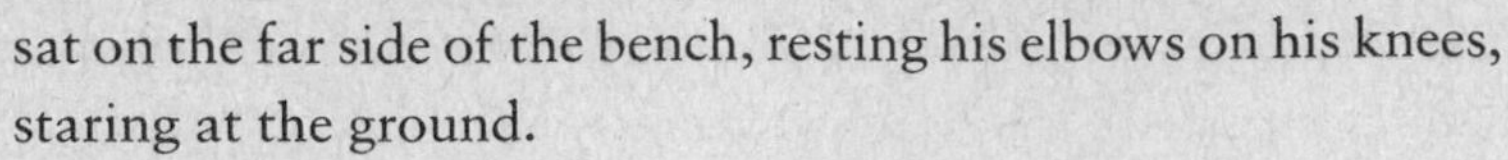

sat on the far side of the bench, resting his elbows on his knees, staring at the ground.

"The French have an expression called *coup de foudre*," he finally said. "Are you familiar with the term?"

Lessons in foreign languages were hardly something Aunt Ruth had been willing to fund. "Never heard of it."

"The literal translation is 'stroke of lightning,'" he said. "It's the moment when lightning strikes and transforms you. When an indelible impression is made and you want to hold on to it so it lasts forever." He turned to look at her. "The English are much more straightforward. They call it 'love at first sight.'"

He looked at her with a blend of caution and hopefulness, as though waiting for her to respond, but what on earth was she supposed to say? She had no idea where this conversation was heading, yet how strange he looked . . . vulnerable and ill at ease as the wind tugged at his hair.

"Love at first sight is an instinctive, compulsive feeling," he said. "It makes you feel unbelievably alive. Like the world will never be quite right unless you leap across the room and claim the object of your affection. Of course, love at first sight has no basis in the logical world and is likely only a figment of a hopeful imagination. Only poets and irrational fools believe in it."

"I agree."

He laughed a little at that. His eyes warmed, and the tension broke as he leaned back against the bench, studying her. "The problem is," he said slowly, "despite all my efforts to deny it and then ignore it—and listen carefully, because this part involves you—I was struck hard with that bolt of lightning the moment I first laid eyes on you."

She shot up from the bench, unwilling to believe she'd heard him correctly. Her mouth went dry, and she began pacing around the bench, casting her eyes everywhere but at him.

"This is when I need to look around for hecklers lurking behind the trees," Anna said, "to see if you've got friends eavesdropping and waiting to burst out into riotous laughter. Come on, where are they?"

"There's no one here but us." His face flushed, and he sat a little straighter on the bench, rubbing his palms against his thighs as he resumed speaking in a clipped voice. "I keep waiting for the feeling to fade, but it's not going anywhere. I've spent most of my adult life alone. I was like an unlit match, and then suddenly *you* were there and everything flared to life. Nothing's been the same since."

"Oh, for pity's sake . . ." He had to be teasing her. She kept waiting for that reckless grin to appear and his confession that this was all a jest, but the earnest, hungry look remained on his face.

"This has happened to me before—"

She whirled around to look at him. "It has?"

"Once. Only once before in my entire life have I felt this uncontrollable—" he searched the sky as if looking for the proper word—"this *unquenchable* obsession that knocked me flat."

"Who was she?" It was none of her business, but she was curious all the same.

"Violet Desjardins. She was an opera singer whose company came through Bangor on tour. I took one look at her and fell hard. We liked the same poets, the same music. We'd escape from the city and spend hours wandering in the woods, doing little but staring at each other in stupid wonder. At the time, it felt like magic. Even now the memory still feels a little magical."

The longing on his face, the wistfulness . . . Anna didn't know if she'd ever seen that level of pain and joy mingled at the same time. "What happened?" she asked.

He took a deep breath as he snapped back to the present.

"Well, Violet and I had a huge fundamental stumbling block in our path. I was only eighteen, and she was twenty-nine."

Anna gasped.

"That was my mother's reaction as well," he said, humor lightening his expression. "Bangor was still very much a small town, and it didn't take long for that juicy bit of gossip to spread like wildfire. My father threatened to cut me out of my share of the tourmaline mine. He was convinced Violet was a gold digger, but she wasn't. Besides, I didn't care about the money. I didn't care about the difference in our ages. She was beautiful, she loved me, and I was quite certain I would love her until my dying breath, so who cared about a few years? I asked her to marry me, and I think it was my proposal that brought her to her senses. She left me two days later."

He plucked a blade of grass from the ground, rubbing it between his palms. "The people of Bangor treated it like a big joke, although it wasn't a joke to me. There was a real beauty to our relationship. After she told me it was over, I staggered up to my bedroom, locked the door, and sobbed so hard I could barely breathe." He tossed the blade of grass to the ground and sent her a smile. "You know I'll be forced to have you executed if you ever breathe a word of this to anyone."

"Believe me, I won't be sharing this conversation."

"Violet was very decent about it when she left, saying I'd thank her someday. She was right, of course. The rush of infatuation eventually faded. I fully expected that to happen with you."

She stilled. "And?"

"Not yet. I'm still bowled over by you, but I'm working on it. I figure it's bound to get better soon."

She stifled a laugh. "Are you looking for some kind of cure? Trust me, I'm no prize. You'd learn that about me if you got to know me a little better."

"That's what I'm banking on."

She rolled her eyes heavenward. She couldn't believe this conversation was actually happening. It was embarrassing and uncomfortable. "So this is why you arranged for me to handle all those research questions? Hoping that the constant exposure would render you immune to my astonishing charm?"

He shook his head. "I needed the research done and knew you would be up for the task. I thought the infatuation would pass quickly, but it hasn't. In fact, it's getting worse."

"Oh dear." So she hadn't been imagining the electricity that hummed in the air whenever he was near. She'd been stifling her own instinctive attraction, and now it was going to be impossible to ignore. A squirrel ran across the path in front of them, burrowing through the leaves and hunting for some hidden treasure. It was easier to watch the squirrel's nervous movements than focus on the powerful, charming man sitting only a few feet away, spilling out his innermost feelings.

"Anna," he began slowly, rising to step closer to her. She backed up until she bumped against the trunk of the tree. "Is there some small chance that my feelings might be reciprocated? I don't believe in love at first sight, and I fully accept that this infatuation is going to fade. But now that I know you better, I think you might be exactly what I've always been looking for. I want more time with you to see if this strike of lightning could turn into something real, something lasting."

"It can't. It would be a disaster." She turned to face the trunk of the chestnut tree, deeply furrowed with coarse gray bark. She pressed her fingers into the rough grooves, running her thumb up and down in one of them, picking at the bark—anything rather than to look at Luke Callahan, who was laying his heart at her feet.

"Why? Is there someone else?"

There was no one else, but she'd already resigned herself to living alone. She'd have to quit her job if she ever married. Not that it was inconceivable for her to trade in librarianship for life as a wife and mother, but she could never marry a politician. The expectations of a political wife were beyond what she could handle. Hosting parties, mingling with senators and diplomats, maybe even, heaven help her, making speeches at election campaigns. If Anna had to imagine what the inner rings of Dante's *Inferno* looked like, it would be life as a politician's wife.

Not that Luke Callahan was asking for her hand in marriage, but she'd be a fool to overlook where this path could lead, for there were only two outcomes. It would either be a courtship that ended badly with hurt feelings and the possibility of losing her job for dallying with a member of Congress, or marriage and the ghastly duties as a congressman's wife. Those were the only possibilities, and neither one appealed to her.

"We're too different, Mr. Callahan."

"Luke."

"We're too different, Luke. If I were to ever have a serious suitor, he'd be someone like me. Bookish. Private. Ordinary."

"There's nothing ordinary about you."

A chunk of bark broke off in her hands. She tossed it aside and began picking at another groove. "I don't believe in love at first sight either."

"Actually, it wasn't so much the sight of you as the sound of your voice," Luke said, and Anna remembered leaning close to his ear to whisper that setdown in the Fisheries meeting.

"Love at first insult?" she asked.

He broke into a laugh, but sobered quickly. "I think it really hit me the first time I met you in the map room and saw the way you handled those books as if they were holy relics. I felt like a piece of my soul recognized you. I don't know any better words for it than that."

This couldn't be happening. Luke Callahan couldn't possibly have any serious intentions toward her, and anything short of marriage would put her at risk of losing her job. Rumors about the two of them could leave her unemployed, with no income and no way to support her aunt Ruth.

"My feelings aren't going to change," she said, still facing the tree. "I don't share your interest."

"Ah." It was only a single syllable, but the weight of disappointment in his voice was unmistakable. A rustling of fabric behind her signaled his approach. His hand braced on the tree above her head, his voice a whisper. "Are you sure about that? I can be a patient man if you'd like to think about it for a while."

It was safer to continue living her life exactly as it was. She had a job she loved and an abiding friendship with Neville to help assuage her loneliest days. Still Luke remained, not moving his hand, and the silence became awkward as he waited for her reply.

"I don't need time to think about it," she said quickly, hoping to squelch the seeds of temptation beginning to take root.

He pushed away from the tree, and finally the tension eased a bit. She risked a glance at him. The corners of his mouth were turned down as he tugged his jacket straight.

"Well, I expect the infatuation will fade soon enough," Luke said. "I have no intention of withdrawing my research requests, as you've been shockingly efficient. And since absence tends to make the heart grow fonder, I'd like to continue working with you. It's impossible to sustain this level of infatuation for someone you know well. So, feel free to show me your worst. Although why you'd want to pass on a man of my stunning qualities is beyond me."

"You must be the most arrogant man ever born."

"See? Already a bit of your appeal is fading. Thank you, O'Brien." He opened his pocket watch, then snapped it closed. "I am due back at the Capitol. Another scintillating meeting on mollusks."

He set off at a brisk pace, and she stared at his straight back as he walked away from her. She rubbed her throat and wished she had a lozenge to soothe the ache. She'd done the right thing, of course. If Luke Callahan really understood who she was, he'd be embarrassed to be seen with her. She was a short, ordinary girl who had a voice like sandpaper and the habits of a hermit crab.

She also had a job at the most prestigious library in the country, and it would be foolish to ignore the realities of her position. Sarah Starling had been fired for kissing a congressman in the cloakroom. They would be no kinder to Anna if she was caught kissing a congressman beneath a chestnut tree or anywhere else in the city.

Anna's rejection hurt a lot more than he let on, and as Luke walked home that evening, the crushing weight of it became a physical ache. How could he have misread Anna's signals so badly? She seemed to brighten every time he walked into the map room. That wasn't arrogance; it was a fact. He'd hoped his long days of bachelorhood were finally drawing to a close, but Anna had flicked him away like an insect that dared to scale the high walls she hid behind.

Maybe he was just lonely, but his gloom felt so heavy it was an effort to slog up the four flights of stairs to his hotel room. Which felt dark, barren, and cold. Someday Luke wanted to stride through his front door after a long day at work and be greeted by a radiant wife. By the laughter of little children as they hurled themselves across the room at him.

At least he had Philip. On evenings like these, Luke wished he'd simply opened his wallet and paid off the debt the boy owed to the hotel. It would have spared Luke a month of lonely evenings in this cramped suite of rooms. Philip wasn't released from bondage in the laundry room until eight o'clock. Five minutes after eight the boy dragged himself into their suite, and Luke pounced.

"Let's go for a walk," Luke said. Anything to get out of this dreary room and dwelling on Anna's rejection.

Philip wilted. "Now? I'm so tired the bones in my face hurt, and I've got an astronomy test tomorrow."

"We'll study for it outside. The night is clear, and we can study beneath the laboratory of the open sky."

A glint of excitement broke through Philip's fatigue, and ten minutes later they were flat on their backs on the soft grass of the park across from the hotel, looking up at a spray of stars scattered across the sky.

"What's that one?" Luke asked, pointing to a cluster of stars in the western sky.

"Centaurus . . . the centaur. Although those Greeks must have had overwrought imaginations if they saw a centaur in that."

Luke smiled but added no commentary on the subject of overwrought imaginations, for he'd been suffering from one most of his life. "And what makes the Centaurus constellation unique?" he prodded.

"It has Alpha Centauri. The closest star to Earth."

"Very good."

"How do you know all this?" Philip asked.

"Anyone who reads the poetry of Samuel Taylor Coleridge will get quite an education in astronomy."

They lay like that for hours, studying the stars and the myths fueled by Greek imagination. It was nearing midnight, but the fires of youth had given Philip a second wind. The boy seemed to be enjoying this starlit night as much as he.

"What did you want to be when you were my age?" Philip asked as he stared at the stars.

"A great poet."

"What happened?"

"I realized I wasn't very good at it."

Philip sighed. "If I can't become a great painter . . ." His face darkened, and he swallowed hard. "Well, I guess I'll be okay," he said in a voice heavy with skepticism.

"Always be honest," Luke cautioned. "Even when you're only talking to yourself."

Philip brightened. "Okay, then I'll be honest. I want to be a painter so badly I think I'll die if I fail. Like my purpose for living will be over."

Luke rolled onto his side to look Philip in the eye. He framed his next words carefully.

"If you don't make it as a painter, funnel that passion into something else, but it doesn't have to die. Do you think I would have turned that old boxcar into a traveling library if I hadn't been in love with poetry? My love of poetry was a gift from God. So is your passion for art, even though we don't know yet what form it will take. If you don't make it as a painter, perhaps you'll be a great teacher. Or a museum curator. Maybe you'll become a rich industrialist and fund a museum. Just don't limit yourself by thinking you already know God's purpose for you."

It was a privilege to help raise Philip and guide him through these treacherous adolescent years. Someday he hoped to have a son he'd love as much as Philip. There were days he wanted a wife so badly his entire soul ached, and he wondered how much longer he was destined to wait. He still couldn't believe he had misread Anna O'Brien's feelings for him, but he wasn't quite ready to give up yet.

Anna was his opposite. She never did anything impulsively and liked the safety of her map room in the attic of the Capitol. She hid up in that room like a princess in a castle tower, surrounded by a fortress of books and maps.

A slow smile lit his face. He'd never been the type to give up easily, and more than anything he wanted to climb those walls and sweep Anna O'Brien into his life.

And he'd always been good at getting what he wanted.

9

It was mortifying, but Anna was helpless to resist the temptation. Ever since learning of Luke's long-ago obsession with an opera singer, she was consumed with curiosity about the woman. And to make matters worse, Anna knew exactly how she could learn all about Violet Desjardins. With the nation's finest music library just down the hall, all it would take was a quick visit to begin unearthing the information she was desperate to see.

"Name?" Gertrude asked as she withdrew a card and prepared to jot down Anna's request. Anna glanced around the music room, afraid of being overheard by the half-dozen patrons sitting at the worktables nearby.

"Violet Desjardins," Anna whispered. "She was an opera singer. Anything you can find on her would be much appreciated."

"Spelling?" Gertrude demanded.

"I'm not sure. I know she toured New England around twenty years ago. That's all I know for certain."

And that Luke Callahan had adored the woman. What did she look like? Anna wondered. Had she been a good woman, or was she a fortune hunter and Luke's besotted brain never accepted the fact?

Anna still couldn't quite grasp the bewildering conversation she'd had with Luke only yesterday. It was flattering—thrilling, really—but impossible for her to even toy with the idea. He would be utterly disillusioned when he finally got to know the real Anna. How could she measure up to his charm and prominence?

She returned to the map room and tried to concentrate on her work, wondering what it would be like if she had a normal imagination that didn't start spinning fantasies at the least provocation. Maybe she wouldn't entertain foolish daydreams about a relationship with an attractive congressman. Or lose sleep over strange fantasies that the navy was out to get her for questioning the validity of a fifteen-year-old report.

The door banged open, the sound echoing through the room like a gunshot.

"There you are," Lieutenant Rowland snapped. "I've been looking everywhere for you."

Anna clenched her fists, vowing not to be cowed by this man. "Map rooms are usually a logical place to start looking for map librarians."

The twinge of anxiety ratcheted higher as the surly lieutenant stalked into the room, striding down the narrow aisle and bumping over a stack of atlases. The books toppled over with a heavy thud, their pages splaying open. Anna dashed over and knelt down to correct the damage. Atlases were expensive! Lieutenant Rowland looked down at her as if she were a serf as she scrambled to stack them again.

"Then why don't you stay in the map room?" he demanded. "Why are you pestering Howard Clover about ocean currents?"

Anna whirled around to stare up at the man towering above her. "Librarians at government offices consult with each other all the time. There's no crime in it."

"You were stirring up trouble." He squatted down and shoved

his face close to hers. His taunting glare reminded Anna of every schoolyard bully she'd ever encountered, and she'd met a lot of them.

"Is it time for me to have that chat with old Mr. Spofford? It seems this library has a problem with nattering, nosy, and insubordinate females." Lieutenant Rowland leaned in so close she could see the pores on his nose. "Why were you poking into ancient history and bothering Howard Clover with your nonsense?"

The atlases were heavy as she scooped them up and turned away. He followed, his feet knocking against her skirts as she mounded the atlases on the table. "You haven't answered me, girl. Is there something wrong with your hearing?"

She didn't want to turn around and face him. It felt like she was back in the schoolyard with the bullies closing in, and all she wanted to do was disappear.

Luke climbed the stairs to the map room, feeling like a condemned man walking to the scaffold. After the embarrassment under the chestnut tree yesterday, he'd like nothing better than to hibernate and lick his wounds in private, but Anna had the tariff data he needed and it was too important to ignore.

He was surprised by the angry male voice coming from inside the map room. He paused outside the open door, cocking his head to listen. It seemed Anna was getting royally scolded for something. Had she been neglecting other duties while he commandeered her time?

". . . poking your nose in where it doesn't belong. What makes you think you're smart enough to question us?" the voice snarled.

Luke's jaw clenched. There was nothing he despised more than bullies. The last time he'd backed down from a bully was when his father was on a bender and shouting at his mother over some spoiled cheese. The next morning his mother had two black eyes. Luke hadn't backed down from a bully since.

That didn't mean he was going to handle it with his fists either. Locking down all traces of anger, he strolled into the map room. A man shaped like a brick towered over Anna, his face red with anger. Anna looked like a daisy wilting under the scorching blast.

"Why don't you drag out the thumbscrews?" Luke said tightly, startling both Anna and the naval officer. "Or perhaps the cat-o'-nine-tails. Or better yet, I saw a group of schoolchildren downstairs lining up to tour the Capitol. Perhaps it would be more fun to go gang up on them?"

The officer straightened, but the scowl remained. "This is private business," he snapped.

"Then don't conduct it in a public building." Luke stepped closer, lowering his voice. "And if you ever comport yourself like a foulmouthed savage again while wearing the uniform of a US military officer, I will see you drummed out of the navy so fast your head will spin."

Indecision flickered across the officer's face as he scrutinized Luke. He was clearly trying to figure out if Luke might be a higher-ranking officer out of uniform, an elected official, or just an ordinary government bureaucrat. Luke had no intention of enlightening him.

The lieutenant glanced back at Anna. "This isn't over," he warned before storming out of the room.

Luke turned to Anna. "Someone who wasn't happy with your maps?"

She was trembling. She shook her head and dragged out a chair, lowering herself as though too weak to keep standing.

"I don't know why he's so hostile," she said. "All I wanted

was for the navy to verify the details of a shipwreck. It seems my request was not well received."

She tried to laugh a little, but her distress was obvious. It aroused every protective instinct in his body, and he wanted to draw her into his arms until she quit shaking, which was impossible. For now, she was off-limits to him, that much had been made clear yesterday afternoon under the chestnut tree. He walked to the far side of the table to avoid getting too close, pulled out a chair, and sat opposite her.

"What ship?" he asked softly.

"My father's ship was lost at sea in 1882. Fifty-six men died on that ship. I don't believe the navy's official report about the *Culpeper* is accurate, but they refuse to discuss it. They've been very aggressive about discouraging any steps I make to correct the report."

"What do you mean?"

She gave an exasperated sigh. "You just saw a taste of it. I feel like they are spying on me. Each time I try to get more information about the storm that sank the *Culpeper*, they find out about it and shut me down."

"They won't shut *me* down."

She sucked in a quick breath. "You'd help me with this?"

"Of course! Why do you sound so surprised?" His job as a congressman was to be an advocate for the people. If government agencies were throwing obstacles in Anna's way, he'd clear the path.

"It's just . . . people usually come to *me* for help," she said. "I'm not used to it working the other way around."

"I'd be happy to ask a few questions. Get people moving."

The way she looked at him, like he had just slain a dragon for her, made him feel like a conquering hero. She was breathless as she explained a newly released report from the weather bureau that tracked the paths of historic hurricanes. The report contradicted what the navy wrote about the sinking of the *Culpeper*. She seemed a little irrational in her conviction that this warranted a new full-scale investigation, but weren't librarians supposed to be sticklers for accuracy? Her passion was one of the things he found so attractive about her. He jotted down all the information she could provide.

"I don't know how I can thank you," Anna said. "I've been so frustrated, and if you could use a little of your influence . . ."

"O'Brien, shut up," he said with a smile. "I said I would work on it, and you can count on me. Now, show me that tariff data."

It didn't matter how much work it would take to fulfill Anna's request, Luke was going to find the answer even if he had to pester every navy official and plow through stacks of old files in the War Department's archives. Anna's mistrust of the navy seemed somewhat irrational, but regardless he'd do what he could to help her.

Over the next few days, Luke knocked on doors and tracked down rumors. Normally, his position as a congressman guaranteed that doors were flung wide open for him, but he'd started encountering the same resistance Anna had run up against. When he tried to verify her information about the 1882 hurricane, he found the well of information had already dried up. He went to the weather bureau to locate their newly released report, but they'd retracted the new map showing the path of the hurricane, claiming it needed additional study to verify the course. Luke asked who'd ordered the retraction, and he got back a two-word response: "the navy."

Maybe Anna wasn't so irrational after all. Frustrated by the bureaucratic quagmire, Luke requested an appointment with the secretary of the navy. John Davis Long was a politician with no military experience who once boasted he "wouldn't know the stem from the stern of a ship." All Secretary Long wanted was to return to his family's farm in Buckfield, Maine, to put up fences and watch his cattle graze. He only accepted the appointment to be secretary of the navy at President McKinley's request. The president needed men he could trust surrounding him, and he'd found one in the plainspoken John Davis Long.

It was that connection to Maine that Luke hoped would buy him a little goodwill. He made an appointment to meet with the secretary at his home. Upon arriving at the leafy neighborhood in Georgetown, Luke was surprised to be led into the backyard, where Secretary Long was wearing a battered old coat, mud-encrusted boots, and a pair of work gloves.

"You're from a logging family," the secretary said. "Prove it by helping me fix this fence." He handed Luke a splitting maul, and the two of them worked to knock the rails free of the post to begin the repairs.

"I can't stand anything that smacks of navy rigmarole and hidebound rules," Secretary Long groused as he rocked the post free of the soil. "They only bother me if they need something signed, but I hear you've been asking about an old shipwreck. What's that about?"

Luke explained Anna's concern over the validity of the old government report on the sinking of the *Culpeper*. Secretary Long grunted as he hefted the post from the ground.

"Look, Callahan, here's the thing," the secretary said. "Admiral Channing signed off on that report back when he was still a junior officer wet behind his ears. They know it's full of errors, but it would be an embarrassment to admit it. Admiral Channing is the best thing this navy has seen in decades. We can't risk damaging his reputation. So tell this young lady to stand down. She's probably right that the *Culpeper* was a lot farther south when it sank, but we won't be revising that report just to make her happy."

Luke thanked Secretary Long, careful to verify what he had learned. A few well-placed questions confirmed Admiral Channing's burgeoning reputation, and from what Luke knew of Washington politics, it made perfect sense. He had firsthand experience with the way people could close ranks around favored politicians, while draining the life from ones who'd been deemed troublesome.

It wasn't until he knocked on the door of a retired diplomat that he got an answer he'd never expected to hear. Jeremiah Hammond was ninety years old, and he could remember the main courses served at White House dinners almost half a century ago. He'd served in diplomatic posts all over the world and had seen the *Culpeper* many times over the years.

And what he had to say about the ship was astounding. Luke was so baffled, he asked the old diplomat to repeat the story before he could accept that he was hearing correctly.

"Are you certain?" Luke pressed. It would be cruel to bring this kind of information to Anna unless it could be verified.

"I know what I saw," Jeremiah replied. "The *Culpeper* was docked in the bay of Manila two years after it supposedly sank off the coast of Bermuda. It had been freshly painted and had a new name, but it had a big metal sounding machine bolted to its stern, the kind exploring ships use. That kind of ship costs a fortune, and the *Culpeper* was unique. I know it was the same ship."

Luke was flabbergasted. "What did you do?"

"I asked the navy about it, and they insisted I was mistaken. I didn't have any proof, and the navy was adamant the ship sank, so I dropped it. Very clannish folks, those navy fellows. That was back in 1884. I remember because it was the same year I had dinner with Thomas Jefferson."

"Thomas Jefferson? The one who wrote the Declaration of Independence?"

Jeremiah nodded. "Did you know he had red hair? Very clever, that young man."

Relief trickled through Luke. Jeremiah Hammond was ancient, but not old enough to have dined with Thomas Jefferson. The man's mind was clearly failing, and it called into question everything he'd just said about the *Culpeper*.

Luke thanked the old diplomat and headed back to the Capitol, mulling over the strange new information about the *Culpeper*. What was he supposed to do with it? He couldn't tell Anna. He needed more proof of the ship's survival than the sketchy memory of a ninety-year-old man. The diplomat could have had his dates wrong. Or the ship's sighting could be a figment of his imagination, just like his dinner with Thomas Jefferson.

Besides, if he told this to Anna, it would stir her suspicions like a tornado. It didn't take much to stoke Anna's overactive imagination, and it would be cruel to tell her unless he had real proof.

Later that evening, Luke sat sprawled in a club chair in the congressional retiring room, an oversized globe on the floor beside him. He idly tapped his shoe on the globe, setting it into a slow rotation as he watched the continents and oceans of the world rotate. Fifty-six men disappeared along with that ship. Anna's request aside, what obligation did he have to those men? They were American sailors, and it appeared the navy's official story about their fate had been covered up to protect the reputation of the officer who signed off on a shoddy report.

He drew a deep breath, massaging the skin between his eyes. He wouldn't lie to protect anyone, but withholding Jeremiah's ramblings wasn't precisely a lie, was it? Everything he knew about politics told him that Secretary Long was correct, and the old diplomat was confused.

But Luke still didn't know what to do.

It didn't take long to find a treasure trove of information about Violet Desjardins. Gertrude discovered that the opera singer had left the stage a decade ago, married an Italian aristocrat, and now lived in a villa overlooking Italy's Lake Como.

Anna sat in the map room and stared at Violet's photograph. When Luke told her of the singer who traveled through Bangor long ago, she suspected Violet had been a washed-up vaudeville performer.

That wasn't the case. She was a wealthy woman of stunning beauty. The black-and-white photograph showed a middle-aged woman still hauntingly beautiful, draped in jewelry and diaphanous silk. Violet's posture was self-assured, her skin perfect as she gave a half smile at the camera, lovingly fingering a long rope of gemstones draped around her neck.

Gertrude also brought articles about the famous opera singer. Anna devoured every word of them. Violet's answers to the questions were confident, witty, and elegant. In one interview she was asked about the collection of jewelry she'd acquired on her travels through Russia, France, and the Mediterranean islands. She had a brooch from a Russian prince and a torque excavated from an Etruscan dig in Crete. When asked what her favorite piece of jewelry was, she laughed and dismissed her famous collection of jewelry.

"I've always been quite fond of tourmalines," Violet was reported to have said.

Anna grabbed the black-and-white photograph of Violet, studying each detail. It was impossible to know for certain, but she'd bet her bottom dollar the long rope of gems around her neck were tourmalines. It set off a surge of jealousy. Had they been a gift from Luke?

"Hello, Anna."

She dropped the picture. Luke stood in the doorway, a rolled-up report in his hand. As he crossed the room toward her, she tried to shuffle the photograph beneath a stack of papers, but he'd already spotted it.

"Is that . . . ?" He pulled the photograph from beneath the papers, his face going very still as he recognized the woman in the picture. She wanted to sink into the floor and disappear, especially given the way he seemed hypnotized by the image of the woman he'd once loved.

"Why do you have this?" he finally asked.

Her mouth went dry and the room felt unaccountably hot. "I was curious," she admitted.

The fondness in Luke's eyes as he looked at Violet's photograph was unmistakable. Was he still in love with her? Did he know she had married? Luke seemed too mesmerized to drag his eyes away from the photograph and articulate a coherent sentence. Or issue a normal greeting. Or even breathe.

"She's still beautiful," he said. "It's hard to look at a picture like this and not wonder about what might have been if only . . ."

His sentence trailed off as he stared at the picture, a faint smile on his lips. "Violet Desjardins," he murmured, almost like a prayer. "That woman could hold a room of people spellbound merely by talking about the weather."

The jealousy festering in Anna grew and expanded. She had no business getting jealous over Violet, but what would it be like to be the recipient of the unabashed adoration she saw glowing on his face. Literally *glowing*! His thumb traced the edge of the picture, and his deep poet's expression turned wistful.

He tossed the photograph down. "Violet and I would have been a disaster," he said with a note of humor creeping into his voice.

"You would?"

"We were too much alike. Impulsive. Hotheaded. It was an exhilarating ride, but a dangerous one. I've always needed someone to reel me in, and she couldn't do that. I wanted the two of us to run off, get married, and shoot straight for the stars. It would have been spectacular, until we killed each other competing for center stage." He looked at her, a half smile on his face. "You'd be a much better choice in that respect."

She moved back a half step. "Why are you here?" she asked, eager to change the subject.

"I thought you might like to know what I found out about the *Culpeper*."

"You found something?" She forgot about the pictures and gestured for him to sit. "Tell me."

Luke took a seat, looking stiff and uncomfortable. "Anna, I've spoken with people from the navy, the War Department, and the State Department. There's no grand conspiracy or mystery; it's all just an attempt to save Admiral Channing's reputation."

Her spirits sank as Luke outlined the coordinated campaign to protect Admiral Channing's sterling reputation. The man's military prowess rivaled Napoleon, but as a young officer he'd been sloppy with the paper work, and that was why the navy was so adamant in their refusal to reopen the case.

Luke's news ought to have been comforting. She didn't want to imagine there was some dark plot behind the disappearance of the *Culpeper*, but something still didn't sit right.

"It still seems strange," she said, "the way everyone was so hostile to me."

"Now you know why."

"Are you sure?" she pressed. "Are you positive that's all there is?

"I'm certain of it, Anna."

She could trust him. Of all the men in Washington, Luke had vowed he would never lie or varnish the truth. And why should she be disappointed by this news? She didn't really believe her father had somehow miraculously survived, and yet it irked her to leave that final report on the *Culpeper* uncorrected. Her entire life had been devoted to cultivating and protecting the world of information. So was her father's. How could she stay silent about such an inaccurate report?

It was almost as if Luke could read her mind. "Buy the typewriter and write your father's story," he suggested, a conspiratorial glint in his eye. "Set the record straight. If Admiral Channing needs to hide behind the skirts of a map librarian to protect his reputation, he isn't worthy of his rank."

When he talked like that, she felt as if she actually had the power to make a mark in the world. She was trapped in his gaze, savoring the energy that flowed between them simply by looking into his eyes.

"Anna . . . would you join me for dinner tonight?"

She jerked back in her chair. It was one thing to dream about a man like Luke, but stepping into the real world beside him was quite another.

"I'm not the sort of woman who can hold a room of people spellbound by talking about the weather. You don't know who I really am." The girl who'd been teased on the playground, who clammed up in front of crowds, who got nervous even venturing into unexplored hallways of the Capitol.

He stared at her for the longest time, and she fought the temptation to fidget in her seat. Finally he rose, adjusted his vest, and headed for the door. Relief gusted out of her lungs. She gathered the articles about Violet Desjardins into a stack with the photograph on top. They'd need to be returned to Gertrude before . . .

Luke strode back into the room, and she dropped the pages, startled by the intensity on his face.

"I don't know why you are so distrustful of me," he said. There was no accusation in his voice, only frustrated bewilderment. "If it's the last thing I do, I intend to earn your trust and convince you I know *exactly* who you are, and I adore you anyway. Maybe then you won't be so intimidated by a happily married woman who lives five thousand miles away."

He glanced both ways, scanning the room and finding it empty of onlookers. He leaned down and planted a long, deep kiss directly on her mouth. He pulled back, his face flushed with determination. "Or afraid of a man who wants to lay his heart at your feet."

This time he left for good. She stared at his back in stunned disbelief as he walked out the door, her lips tingling and her heart pounding.

Luke wended his way through the crowd on the staircase, angling around staffers and clerks as he made his way to the ground floor of the Capitol. Seeing that photograph of Violet took him by surprise. He knew about her marriage, of course. Over the years he and Violet had exchanged occasional letters, and she was delightfully happy with her Italian count, who was a much better match for her than Luke could have been.

But the fact that Anna felt curious enough to seek out information on Violet was a good sign. He hid his smile as he reached the basement level, noise and the scent of grilled meat drifting from the restaurant. The lunchroom was packed, with hundreds of clerks and secretaries lining up to get their food quickly before heading back to work. There were fancier dining rooms set aside for members of Congress, but he didn't have time today for table service. He just needed to grab a sandwich and—

"Luke!"

He'd recognize that beautiful voice anywhere. Turning around, he caught sight of Anna O'Brien, her petite figure dwarfed by the dozens of other employees bustling toward the lunch counter.

She looked flushed with embarrassment as she approached him. "I mean, Mr. Callahan," she amended, drawing near.

"Don't apologize," he said with a grin. "I like it better when you call me Luke."

Her mouth tightened, and she looked nervously around the lunchroom. "Mr. Callahan, I need to explain something. I need for you to understand—"

Her sentence was cut off by a gang of congressional pages, who bumped into her from behind as they plowed toward the sandwich counter. The pages received lunch as part of their wage, and boys in their teens were never too considerate of anyone who stood between them and a meal.

"Let's go to the congressional dining room," he said. "It's quieter."

"No!" she said, then cast a glance at the hundreds of people crammed into the lunchroom. She leaned closer and lowered her voice. "I have to be careful. I can't let rumors get started."

The way she spoke under her breath with averted eyes made it seem as if she were passing him state secrets, and he struggled to hide the mirth from his face. With almost three thousand people working in the Capitol, finding a bit of privacy was almost impossible. He nodded to the terrace off the lunchroom. It had been sleeting all morning and no one was dining outside. The flagstone terrace was surrounded by a six-foot hedge and contained dozens of empty tables. They were alone, but freezing. The icy wind cut through his jacket within seconds, and Anna looked even colder given the way she hugged her arms around her body.

"Should we go back inside?" he asked.

"No, this will only take a moment," Anna said. She looked ill at ease in a way that had nothing to do with the frigid temperature. "Have you ever heard of a woman named Sarah Starling?"

He searched his memory, but came up blank. "Tell me," he said.

It didn't take long for Anna to recount the story of a perfectly nice young lady who was caught kissing a congressman in the cloakroom. Sarah had been fired on the spot. The pieces started falling into place, and Luke realized it was more than the memory of Violet Desjardins that kept Anna at arm's length.

"All the women who work here are in a tricky position," she said. "We need to be friendly and approachable, but can't ever get too close with any of the congressmen. I love my job and can't risk it just because a handsome man has a passing fancy for me."

"So you think I'm handsome?"

She huddled against the wall to keep out of the wind. "Yes, until you open your mouth and your astounding ego slips out. Then the effect is spoiled." Even shivering against a wall with her lips tinged blue, she looked delightful as she peeked up at him. Now that he understood her reluctance, he could battle it properly.

"You don't need to fear getting fired. I won't let rumors get started. And if they do, you won't be left destitute on the streets. I'd marry you before I let that happen."

"I could never marry you!" She looked appalled, and if he weren't so taken aback, it would have been funny.

"Careful, O'Brien. For a moment my self-respect was about to recover, but then you had to go kick it in the teeth again."

She winced and reached out to lay a hand on his arm. "It's just that I've seen what political wives need to do. They host parties and have tea with other fancy ladies. The happiest day of my life was when I graduated from school and could escape those kind of girls and do exactly what I wanted."

"Which was what? Hide in a library?"

"I prefer to think of it as gainful employment in a career I love."

He loved that he couldn't push her around, that she tilted up her chin and matched him barb for barb. He could stand out here in the sleet for hours and get lost in her flashing dark eyes and never grow bored. All he had to do was convince her how perfect they were for each other.

"Perhaps you'd love being a wife and mother. Most women seem to like it."

She skewered him with a razor-sharp glare. "Most women aren't married to congressmen. There are a lot of drawbacks to a husband like that."

"Have you ever met the president's wife?" Luke asked.

"We obviously move in different social circles. No, I've never met President McKinley's wife."

"Neither have I," he said. "That's because Ida McKinley is a recluse who rarely shows her face in public. And you know what? President McKinley is perfectly content with his wife's preferences. Rumor has it she knits booties all day. Booties! If the president's wife can withdraw from political life in favor of knitting booties, I expect the nation will survive if my wife chooses to abstain from political duties."

She stared at him as though stunned by such a revelation. Did she think so little of herself that all he wanted was someone to host parties for him? Anna opened her mouth to say something, but sneezed instead.

"You're freezing," he said. "Let's go through the congressional dining room instead. There will be fewer prying eyes."

He guided her to the French doors farther down the terrace. They were locked, so he tapped on the glass until someone at a table near the window noticed and rose to let them in. It was Karl Winstead, the other congressman from Maine.

"Thanks, Karl," Luke said, guiding Anna inside, savoring the warmth of the room. With luck, he might persuade Anna to join him for lunch. Congressmen invited visitors to dine in their private lunchroom all the time, but now that he knew of Anna's reluctance to trigger rumors, it would be hard to convince her to join him. He scanned the room, spotting a vacant table near the back.

"You might find the atmosphere a little chilly over yonder," Karl said, humor in his eyes. Luke followed the man's gaze.

House Speaker Cornelius Jones was holding court just a few yards away, sitting like a king at the largest table in the room, surrounded by a haze of cigarette smoke. With thinning gray hair and a bloodless complexion, Speaker Jones always reminded Luke of a shriveled old scarecrow. Luke noted the other men sitting at the table, those gathering around to curry Jones's favor today.

Jones noticed, setting his cigarette down. "What's that I smell?" Speaker Jones asked as he sniffed the air. "Clams? Catfish? Or another bottom-feeder altogether?"

There was a rumble of laughter from the sycophants next to Jones, but then a hush fell over the dining room as others cast nervous glances Luke's way. Ever since being demoted to the Fisheries committee, Luke was accustomed to the teasing barbs and maintained a tight smile.

Beside him, Anna stiffened and seemed to shrink a few inches. He walked toward Jones with his head held high.

"I suppose there are plenty of bottom-feeders in Washington," Luke said, eyeing the fawning admirers at Jones's table. He waved his hand to clear away the cigarette smoke. "I miss the clean, untainted air of Maine."

"God willing, it won't be long before you can enjoy the Maine air permanently," Jones said in a silky voice.

The implication was unmistakable. The next election was a year away, but Luke's political reputation was plummeting fast.

"It's always such a pleasure seeing you," Luke said. "Each time we meet I discover entire new wonders of hot air. I keep waiting for the laws of gravity to take effect so that your house of cards will collapse along with you."

The Speaker's only reply was to pull a long draw on his cigarette, the tip glowing in the dim light. Luke gestured for Anna to follow him from the room.

"I don't know how you can stand politics," Anna muttered as they moved into the cooler atmosphere of the hallway outside.

"Are you trembling?" he asked. Luke enjoyed a little healthy confrontation, especially with a man who deserved it as much as Speaker Jones. Someday soon he would have enough information to sink Jones, but until he did, he would never turn tail and run from a confrontation.

"That man was the Speaker of the House!" Anna said, still wringing her hands. "You were hurling insults like Zeus with his thunderbolt, and I thought the room would combust at any moment. I hate this sort of thing."

"Anna, it's just a little bluster. Look, I escaped with no scars. Come on, let me buy you lunch."

She shook her head. "I need to get back to the library. We are officially moving into the new building over the weekend, and I have to pack up my desk."

"This weekend?" He was surprised at the hitch in his voice.

If he and Anna no longer worked in the same building, it would be harder to see her, and that would be . . . He swallowed. How strange that just knowing she worked beneath the same roof as he had helped to brighten his day. It would be harder to court her if he couldn't dart upstairs at a moment's notice. The new library was only across the street, but it felt like she was slipping away and he hadn't made much headway in softening her resistance to him.

"Let me walk you back upstairs," he said, his mind scrambling to find a way to continue seeing her after the library moved. Anna had almost completed the stack of research for him, and after that? He tried to reach for her hand, but she slid a few feet over, maintaining a proper distance between them.

"In the future we will have congressional pages deliver requests back and forth," she said. "You need never come to the new library to—"

"I'll still come," he said.

"It would be better if you didn't."

He kept his expression neutral as he walked beside her up the grand staircase. With each floor the staircases got less formal, until they'd made it to the attic, where the map room was located. "And why is that?" he finally asked.

"We don't have to keep discussing this, do we? I would be a terrible wife for a congressman. You really ought to know how unsuitable I would be."

She unlocked the door to the map room, but when she tried to open it he stepped in front, blocking her access. She froze, and he had a perfect view of her glossy hair, smoothed into a perfect coil only a few inches beneath his nose. She smelled of lemon and sunshine and a thousand summer days filled with laughter. If he moved even a fraction of an inch, his entire body would be flush against hers. He held his breath, careful not to frighten her away.

"Anna," he whispered, and was pleased at the way she stilled. She tipped her head up to look at him. He leaned down to murmur in her ear.

"Booties," he whispered gently. "The president's wife knits booties all day."

He kept his face pressed to her hair while he reached behind his back to twist the knob and push the door open. He then slipped around her, leaving her staring, openmouthed, as he waltzed back downstairs.

10

Luke deliberately stayed away from the library for the next three days. Anna was well aware of his intentions toward her, but he didn't intend to moon about like a lovesick idiot while she got over her fears.

The problem was—and this annoyed him to no end—he missed her. And he *was* a lovesick idiot. He couldn't concentrate because he kept wondering how the move to the new library was progressing, if she was going to be happier in that gilded monstrosity across the street, and if she was thinking about him at all.

The library had closed during the week while movers packed the last of the books into crates and lugged the furniture to the first floor of the Capitol, where it cluttered the floor of the rotunda until it could be carted across the street.

On the day of the move itself, Luke surrendered to the whims of his infatuation, put on his heavy coat, and headed to the new library. The space between the two buildings was choked with carts and wagons. The Army Corp of Engineers had built the new library, and their soldiers were overseeing the move as well.

Desks, filing cabinets, and tables filled the terrace, waiting to be hauled inside. Little white tags with room designations had been tied to each piece of furniture, and dozens of soldiers scrambled amid the disorder, hoisting chairs and desks onto rolling carts.

An army officer directed the operation, checking items off a chart. "Sir, the library is closed to the public," the officer said when he noticed Luke. "You'll need to move along."

"I'd like to help," Luke offered.

"Absolutely not. The Capitol police are removing people who've gotten too curious, so I'll ask you one more time before I summon the police."

It was the army's efficiency that had brought this monumental project to completion on time and under budget, and the move appeared to be progressing like a well-oiled clock. They didn't need his help, but this was a big day for Anna and he wanted to share it with her.

He stepped forward and extended his hand. "We haven't been introduced. Representative Luke Callahan, second congressional district of Maine." Luke rarely flaunted his credentials, yet he wasn't going to be turned away. Not today.

The officer stood a little straighter. "What can I do for you, sir?"

"I'd like to help," Luke repeated. He nodded toward the oversized map cases on the far side of the terrace. "I'm particularly anxious to see the map room back in operation."

The officer consented and appointed two soldiers to help Luke hoist the first of the map cases onto a cart. Its wheels squeaked under the weight as he guided the cart toward the building. Solemn sculptures of Benjamin Franklin and Sir Walter Scott stared down on him from the entablature above the entrance. The massive bronze doors featured carvings of slinky nymphs reading from scrolls. Inside, the interior of the great hall swarmed with workers using pulleys to hoist furniture over the ornate banisters and lugging crates up the stairs. The air hummed with excitement. Voices echoed and bounced off the marble floors and vaulted ceilings embellished with breathtaking murals.

Given the weight of the map case, the elevator was the only way to get it upstairs. The map case barely fit inside the compartment, and all three men had to hold their breath as the doors closed and the floor lifted beneath them. It wasn't that he was afraid of technology, but elevators seemed silly to him . . . until it was time to carry a five-hundred-pound map case to the third floor.

The top floor was as impressive as the first, with the hallway walls covered by murals of people reading, writing, and telling stories around a fire. The women in the murals were idealized personifications of memory, imagination, truth, and research. Luke had a stupid smile on his face as he wheeled the map case down the hall. He'd voted against the funding for this palace, but it was impossible not to gape at the wonder of it all. He wheeled the cart down an acre of floors that gleamed with polished metal and stone mosaics until they finally arrived at the map room.

He let the two men roll the huge case into the room while he lingered in the doorway to drink in the sight of Anna O'Brien. Dressed in a simple brown skirt and white shirt, she looked dusty, sweaty, and quite possibly the most beautiful woman he'd ever seen. Her face glowed as she directed a gangly man to position a topographical map of Antarctica on the far wall.

"Here?" the gangly man asked. "Make sure you like it, because I'm not moving it again."

"It's perfect," Anna said. "Absolutely perfect. Let me get a hammer." She hurried to a desk in the corner, piled high with unpacked crates. She looked over, then under the desk. Luke grabbed the hammer from the stepladder in front of him.

"Looking for this?"

Anna whirled around. "Luke! Can you believe it? Have you ever seen anything so grand?"

He considered the question for a moment. Washington was full of spectacular buildings, but nothing rivaled what he had seen today. "I agree," he said. "It's magnificent."

"What are you doing here?" she asked. "I thought the army had everything under control. Don't tell me they've recruited members of Congress for the heavy lifting."

She was doing it again, drawing him in with that velvety voice that melded excitement and curiosity. He had no excuse for being here and would rather be skinned alive than admit the real reason he'd come. He kept his face neutral, but couldn't resist a bit of teasing.

"I figure I'd better help get this library back in operation or I'll be destined to go to my grave with unfulfilled daydreams about the effect of cranberries on the American economy."

"Can you two compare notes later?" the gangly man said, his hands still bracing a map high above his head. "This thing is heavy!"

"Sorry!" Anna gasped, racing forward with the hammer. "Luke, this is my best friend, Neville Bernhard, from the Patent Office. He's been helping me all day."

After the map was properly displayed, Anna gave Luke an impromptu tour of the room. A window overlooked First Street and had a view of the Capitol. It was infinitely more spacious than the old map room, with a librarian's desk, three worktables, and five aisles of bookshelves on the far side of the room. The other side was reserved for the map cases.

"We'll have space for more atlases," Anna said excitedly, "but some of my maps are going to be dispersed to the Africa and Asia rooms. Can you believe it? We'll have an entire reading room devoted to Africa. We've got special collections for folklore and business and religion. And the blind!" She reached out to lay both hands on his arm, squeezing. "There's an entire room dedicated to blind people that has Braille books and globes with raised features, and we'll be hosting daily readings for blind people. . . ."

Her voice choked off as tears pooled in her eyes. He remembered feeling like that when he was younger. There were days when he would open the pages of a book and be struck dumb by the wellspring of emotions the book could conjure. Anna's bottom lip started to wobble, and she tried again, talking through happy tears in a way that made Luke want to weep along with her.

"I know you think this library is a spectacular waste of money, but it says something about this country, that we would lavish such a fortune on books and learning. This building is a celebration. An unabashed, glorious hymn to the human endeavor to collect knowledge. . . ." Her voice choked off again, and a fat tear plopped down the side of her face.

"She's been weepy all morning," Neville said. "All it took was one look at the statue in the great hall of the goddess holding up the Torch of Knowledge, and she started getting all misty-eyed."

Anna threw a crumpled-up ball of paper at Neville, who caught it and pitched it back at her.

Luke narrowed his eyes. These two seemed very friendly with one another. Too friendly.

Perhaps this was the reason Anna had been holding him at arm's length. Neville Bernhard didn't look like a romantic rival. He was as skinny as a bean pole and had a body that jerked and twitched, but it was impossible to overlook the camaraderie between the two. He didn't like it.

Anna scampered after the ball of paper and launched it back

at Neville, then dove for cover behind a map case. They seemed as delighted as two children on a playground. He needed to get out of there.

"I'll go get the next map case," he grumbled.

By the time he wheeled the next map case upstairs, he arrived at the map room to the appalling sight of Anna sitting on Neville's shoulders as she placed a globe atop a tall bookshelf. Her skirts were hiked up, with both legs draped over his shoulders as she reached to position the globe. Leather boots covered her ankles, but her calves were plainly visible beneath her skirts.

"Just what I always wanted to know," he said in a stiff voice. "The color of Miss O'Brien's stockings." He hadn't meant to sound so blunt, but her stockings were showing all the way to her knees! Luke hadn't seen such a shocking display since he visited a lumber camp when a wagonload of dancing girls came to spend the weekend with the loggers. And this was a *library*, for pity's sake.

Anna blushed. "Oops! I'd better get down." Luke held his breath as Neville sank to his knees, Anna swaying like a ship's mast in a choppy sea. She rolled off his shoulders, tugging her skirt down and sending an embarrassed smile his way.

"Regained our dignity, have we? The world can breathe a little easier."

"I'll help you with the next map case," Neville said, casually following Luke out the door and down the steps.

Luke stared straight ahead, an unfamiliar curl of jealousy unfolding and expanding in his gut. What did Anna see in this gawky, twitchy man? He was about to stride through the door onto the terrace when a hand clamped around his arm and pulled him aside. Neville propelled Luke toward the empty coat closet on the first floor. The goofy, affable look was gone from Neville's face.

"Lay off Anna," the younger man ordered in a low voice. "You have no idea how fragile she is. She's good at pretending to be tough, but she heard the scorn in your voice. I won't let you throw stones at her."

Luke pulled back a step. "What's between the two of you anyway? It's more than a simple friendship."

"True. She's my sister."

Luke sucked in a breath, but Neville rushed to clarify. "There's no blood relationship, but we share the same spirit, the same heart. That's been true since we were eight years old." The man's twitches grew worse. His neck and shoulders seized with repeated jerks, though they didn't take away from the quiet intensity in his face.

"It wasn't a lot of fun growing up," Neville continued quietly. "Anna didn't have an easy time either, and we formed a friendship that will last until the final breath leaves my body. I'm not sure why you've been showing so much interest in Anna, but I'll figure it out eventually. Let me be blunt. I may look skinny and weak, but if you hurt Anna, I will metaphorically kill you, burn your village, and sow your fields with salt. Is that clear?"

Neville stepped closer until they were nose to nose. Since arriving in Washington, Luke had taken on political rivals, labor leaders, and overbearing military officers, but the resolve in Neville Bernhard's steely eyes was unlike anything Luke had experienced.

"I'm glad to hear it," Luke said calmly.

"You are?"

Luke owed the younger man an explanation. He'd been hostile and rude, deliberately so, because the sight of Anna atop another man had set off a flare of irrational jealousy Luke had no business feeling. He intended to change that.

"You say you can't figure out my interest in Anna O'Brien, so allow me to clarify it. I want to put Anna on a pedestal, drape her with tourmalines, and write endless streams of extravagant poetry for her. I want to shower her with books and typewriters and whatever else she needs to keep her overactive imagination fueled. But she won't let me get close to her. If I fail, I'd like to know she has someone by her side to look out for her."

The intensity faded from Neville's face, replaced by a smile. "Very well. My mission is accomplished."

By the time they returned to the map room with the final map case, Luke felt as though he'd made a new friend.

The new library had been wired for electricity, and lamps with frosted glass shades illuminated the chaos inside the map room. The tables, card catalog, maps, and books had all been delivered. The sun had gone down hours ago, but Anna was too giddy to leave. Tired, grimy, and with muscles drained from exertion, this had been the very best day of her life. Moving into the new library was a thrill unlike anything she'd ever experienced.

Neville went home with the other workers, while Luke stayed to help her refill the map drawers, put books in call-number order, and move her desk three times, until it was in the perfect place for her to survey her kingdom. Ever since he and Neville brought up that final map case, Luke had been in an excessively good mood, losing his earlier surly attitude and eagerly helping her arrange furniture and hang maps. He even went downstairs and stood in line for the delivery of potted ferns that were distributed to the public rooms. When he returned with a Boston fern in a simple brass pot, he beamed with the pride of a man bearing gold, frankincense, and myrrh.

It was amazing how quickly the map room was falling into

place. Finally, the only thing left to do was refill the catalog drawers with thousands of individual cards.

"I wouldn't ask my worst enemy to file the cards," she said. "It's the most tedious of chores."

Luke eyed the cards, carefully arranged according to their call numbers. "It seems criminal to make you file those cards on your own. Like Psyche confronted by a mound of seeds that must be sorted by dawn. Show me what to do."

Was there anything more attractive than a man who knew his Greek mythology? Anna could scarcely believe it, but she was sitting at a worktable with the most eligible bachelor in all of Congress, showing him how to release the metal rod and tension springs from inside each card-catalog drawer. He teased her for the precision with which she numbered every batch of cards prior to packing. Yet she wouldn't let the taunt stand.

"If even a single card is misfiled, we will probably never find the map it belongs to. It could be decades before we see it again . . . if ever."

"And you worry about things like that?"

He was teasing, but she wasn't embarrassed by her diligence. "I take my job very seriously. Once something is lost in a library, the odds of finding it again are minuscule. I know most people think this obsession with order is silly. After all, everything in here is just pieces of paper with words and lines on them. They're not even very valuable."

"Pieces of paper with words and lines on them have the ability to change the world," Luke said softly. "They always have." His eyes gleamed in the dim light, and his words sent a thrill through her. She swallowed hard.

"I really love it when you talk like that."

Who would have guessed that this flashy, arrogant man had the exact same values as she? But this was a man who bought a railway car and then filled it with books to transform it into a traveling library. He set the metal catalog rod down and touched the back of her hand. Just a tiny fingertip, but it triggered a ripple of excitement that raced up her arm.

"We're not so different, O'Brien. You want a cathedral for your books, while I'll put my money on a railcar heading up to the mountains. The outside packaging looks different, but we both cherish the same thing. The incomparable magic of words written on pieces of paper."

From a distance, the sound of running footsteps echoed down the hallway. They pounded closer until a congressional page came careering into the room. "There you are, sir!" the boy said, breathless from his race down the hall. "We've been looking everywhere for you. A telegram arrived for you this afternoon. From Maine, sir."

The boy held out a small notecard. Luke merely stared at it, distaste twisting his handsome features.

"Aren't you going to take it?" she asked. The boy fidgeted, meeting Anna's eyes in confusion. When Luke still made no move to take the telegram, she crossed the room, took the message, and thanked the boy. She waited until the sound of the boy's steps faded before turning to Luke. How could he ignore a telegram like this?

"Please don't tell me your fear of technology extends to telegraphy. This might be important. Do you want me to read it to you?"

He snatched the note from her hands, turning away to read it. It suddenly seemed cold in the room. She wrapped her arms around her middle, wishing for a shawl. If the stiffening of his spine was any indication, the message didn't contain good news. Luke said nothing, his eyes turning stony as he stuffed the note into his pocket.

"Is something wrong? Is there anything I can do to help?"

She'd seen Luke on the warpath, keen on getting his own way. She'd seen him roiling with anger. But she'd never seen him behave this coldly.

"It's nothing I can't handle," he finally said.

Luke folded his arms and stared out the window, the street-lamps creating warm circles of light in the city below. Only a few moments ago, this room had felt like a cozy haven. Not anymore. He drew a ragged breath, and a little of the tension drained from his shoulders.

"Is there any way you can find information on the conditions within a specific prison?" he asked.

"A prison? What kind of information do you need?" If it was a federal prison, it would be easy to find data, but most prisons were operated by states or cities. That would be tricky, and she'd probably need some help.

"My sister is about to make the trip to Washington to twist my arm, and I don't want her here. I need to put her mind at ease about something, and in order to do so, I need more information about the county prison in Bangor. Just find me anything I can pass on to her that says the place isn't a foul pit of squalor."

"Most of them are."

He glared at her. "Look, my brother needs to sit for a spell in prison, and my entire family is ready to burn me in effigy unless I bail him out. I'm not going to do it. It would be the worst thing for him."

She sucked in a breath. "Your brother is in *prison*? And you aren't moving heaven and earth to get him out?"

"No, Anna, I'm not," he snapped.

She closed her eyes, an avalanche of ghastly memories closing in on her. She'd only been in a prison once, but the stench of it was branded on her soul forever. After her uncle served four months of his three-year term for forcing lye down Anna's throat, Aunt Ruth started the wheels in motion to get Henry released early. She wanted Anna to plead with the judge for leniency, and because Anna had lost her voice, Aunt Ruth put a pen in Anna's hand and dictated a letter. Anna was so terrified of her uncle's return, the pen froze in her hand. She couldn't write, couldn't put the words down on the page that might bring that man back into her world. Her aunt dragged her to the prison so that Anna could see what her foul mouth had caused.

The stench had been unbelievable, the sight of her uncle worse. She barely recognized the pale wraith of a man. It was impossible to look into his eyes that brimmed with remorse and not feel pity. Every drop of fear dissolved, and Anna rushed to hug her uncle through the iron bars. His ribs were bony beneath his shriveled skin, and they shuddered as he wept. She forgave him. Noiseless sobs tore from her throat as she cried against his chest and her fear was replaced with guilt. Her uncle cradled the back of her head with a trembling hand.

"I'm so sorry," he wept. "Anna, I'm so very sorry."

She believed him. She raced home to write the letter to the judge, saying she was sorry for misbehaving and please not to blame her uncle for the bad words she'd said. Her uncle had been punished enough and she wanted him out of that filthy place.

She never learned if the letter would have done any good. Within a month, her uncle was dead from tuberculosis he'd contracted while in prison. Instead of a three-year term, Uncle Henry got a death sentence for what he did to Anna. And she still blamed herself to this day.

Later, Anna learned that most prisoners caught tuberculosis within a year of incarceration. Very few people lived longer than five years in prison before they died from the disease.

"Prisons are notorious breeding grounds for tuberculosis," she said to Luke. "My uncle caught it and was dead within six months. How can you just sit there and ignore it?"

His eyes iced over. "You don't know anything about me," he said in a cutting tone. "You've got no grounds to question my decision. He's my brother, and I'll do what's best for him."

"And in all likelihood he will be clobbered with tuberculosis within a year. The longer he sits in there, the greater the chance he'll get it. He will *die*, Luke. Do you want that on your conscience? Because I can tell you what it's like. Every time I think about my uncle, I wish I had never learned those cusswords. If I hadn't, my uncle would be alive today."

"Your uncle was in prison because he abused a child. You can't blame yourself for his death."

"But I *do*."

"Then you're a weak-minded idiot. Your uncle chose to pick up that bottle of lye. Jason chose to pick up a bottle of rum and assault a sheriff's deputy. He knows rum is a poison for him, but he picks it up again and again and again."

"It doesn't matter. You've got to get him out. I could never respect a man who put his own brother at such risk."

Luke spun away from the window. "You have no idea what you're talking about. My brother has been coddled by irrational feelings of pity all his life. He is *exactly* where he needs to be."

"He could die—"

"And you don't think the rum could kill him?" Luke shouted. She flinched and took a step back, but he advanced. "It killed my father. It soaked into his blood and brain until he lost all semblance of humanity and became a foul, soulless animal. It's why I'll never touch a drop of it. It's why I want Jason to get dried out in prison, because nothing else we've tried has worked for him."

He stormed toward the door, but then froze before leaving. Without turning his head, he said through clenched teeth, "If you can find information about the county prison in Bangor, I'd appreciate it. But I don't want to hear another word of pity for Jason."

The door rattled in its frame when he slammed it behind him.

11

Luke spent the morning slumped in a leather chair in the congressional retiring room. With a newspaper held high, he hoped to avoid anyone trying to make chitchat with him. Today was the culmination of his plan to scuttle the tariff issue. Speaker Jones had enough votes to pass the radical new tariff, but only if he could summon a quorum, the minimum number of congressmen who must be present in order to hold the vote. Dozens of congressmen from both sides of the aisle feared the new tariff. Luke and Caesar had been quietly persuading members to boycott the meeting today. Without the necessary number of congressmen present, the Speaker could not proceed to a vote and the tariff would be defeated for at least another year.

Luke glanced out the window. It was a foul, rainy day, with steel-gray clouds scudding across the sky and tiny droplets of rain spattering the windows. A perfect reflection of his mood.

Anna's face floated before him. He cringed at the memory of calling her a weak-minded idiot. There was nothing wrong with Anna's mind, but how could she be so forgiving of her uncle? That man poured *lye* down her throat, and yet she blamed herself for his imprisonment. Anna was another casualty of the corrosive effects of alcohol.

But he shouldn't have flung those insults at her. She was a kind woman, capable of extending forgiveness where he could not. Everything in him wanted to leap out of his chair, dash across the few acres that separated them, and apologize to her, tell her how much he admired her.

Coup de foudre. A bolt of lightning. Love at first sight.

Shouldn't these irrational feelings have eased by now? This wild, impulsive instinct to be near her should have faded, and yet it was growing stronger.

He turned the page of the newspaper with an impatient jerk. He was stuck in this room until his sister replied to his telegram; he expected a reply within the hour. Afterward, he'd grab Philip and they'd catch a train out of town for the rest of the day. He didn't want to be anywhere near the Capitol when the boycott went into action.

From behind the newspaper, the distinctive tapping of Caesar Trammel's cane penetrated Luke's gloomy thoughts. He raised the newspaper higher, hoping to avoid the encounter, but the paper collapsed as the tip of Caesar's cane shot out and knocked the pages from Luke's hand.

"And good morning to you too, Mr. Trammel," Luke said, forcing an artificially pleasant tone.

"I'm surprised to see you here today," Caesar said.

To mention anything else in a room where they could be overheard would be foolish. It was hard to keep secrets on Capitol Hill, and the retiring rooms were notorious for eavesdroppers. Nevertheless, so far it appeared that Caesar's plan of coaxing dozens of members into boycotting this afternoon's vote on the tariff had been successful. For sixty-five members of Congress to maintain their silence and agree to the boycott had been a miracle. They only needed a few more hours before they would spring the trap on Speaker Jones.

"I'm waiting for a telegram," Luke said. He'd sent a message to Bangor late last night, advising Julia to stay in Bangor and authorize the family lawyer to pay the fine to get Jason out of jail. As soon as the telegraph operators in the basement received her reply, he could leave.

Caesar leaned down. "Leave now," he said. "I don't want you anywhere in the building today, and if the telegram comes, I'll keep it safe until I can pass it on."

Luke rose, tugging his vest and straightening his tie. "Agreed."

It was still bleak and drizzly outside, but the copper dome of the new Library of Congress gleamed in the damp morning. Was Anna upset over what he said last night? Shame flooded him for losing his temper, for how his shouting had caused her to flinch.

Soon he was striding up the steps of the library and barreling through the front doors. He needed to beg her forgiveness and expel the bitter note that soured their friendship yesterday. Washington was crammed full of ambitious men and social-climbing women, all jostling for position. Anna wasn't like that. She was an unassuming person who took pride in her job, not for prestige or for riches but for the sheer love of knowledge, and that fact alone slid beneath every one of his defenses and made him long for her.

Would she even see him? Apprehension trickled through him as he rounded the grand balcony and walked down the corridor to the map room. It was still disorganized, with empty boxes mounded in the hallways and the sound of banging hammers in the distance. The doorway to the map room was open. Anna sat at a worktable, feeding cards onto a skinny metal rod. He rapped on the door, and she looked up.

"Are we on speaking terms?" he asked.

She set the rod down. "You tell me. I'm not sure you want to be associated with a 'weak-minded idiot.'"

He sighed. Of all the times to lose control of his tightly wound anger, why did he have to lash out at the one woman who least deserved it? "Please forgive me," he began. "There's no excuse for my behavior. Jason is my problem, and I shouldn't have lashed out at you. I'm sorry for acting like a foul-tempered bear."

"You can at least make yourself useful." She extended the metal rod in his direction, an unconventional peace offering.

A rush of warmth expanded in his chest. Was she always going to have this effect on him? He took the metal rod and sat in the chair opposite her, resuming the easy rhythm of the previous evening when she handed him a batch of catalog cards to funnel onto the tension rod.

"I gather your brother is a sensitive topic for you," Anna said cautiously.

That was an understatement. "I fear Jason is following in my father's footsteps," he said slowly. "My father was a decent man when sober, but when he was drunk he turned into an animal who trampled on everyone and everything standing in his way. For the life of me I can't understand why Jason or Julia turned to drink after witnessing what it did to our father."

"Julia is your sister?"

Julia, his beautiful but tragically flawed sister. Her problem wasn't only alcohol; it was also her inability to control the deluge of emotions that blotted out every scrap of logic and reason. She was like a moth rushing toward a flame, heedless of the power of that burning temptation. Those unwieldy emotions had propelled her into an affair with a married man. *"You wouldn't understand,"* she'd cried. *"Our souls are one!"*

Their bodies had certainly become one, as evidenced by Philip's arrival when Julia was only seventeen. And her adoring married lover? He fled with his wife to Boston at the first sign of Julia's pregnancy. Julia turned to rum to soothe her depression, gradually losing her ability to take care of herself or her young son. It was Julia's dependency on rum that compelled Luke to take Philip with him to Washington.

"Yes, Julia is my sister. The only girl among three brothers."

Anna nodded and began funneling cards back onto the rod. "I've always been a little jealous of people who have big families. I don't have any experience with worrying over brothers and sisters, but I wish I did."

His family was a bottomless well of frustration, yet he loved every one of them. They were the framework by which he defined himself. They gave spice and laughter and color to his world. It was hard to imagine the isolation Anna must have felt as an only child who lost her parents so early. Was that why she'd been acting so obsessed with tracking down the details of her father's final voyage and correcting the navy's report of the sinking?

"Are you going to keep digging into what happened with the *Culpeper*?" he asked.

She gave a weary sigh. "I've nearly gone blind scanning old newspapers, looking for any mention of the ship in the summer of 1882. I've spotted three references to the ship in Cuban newspapers that summer, but they don't mention anything about why it was there. If I try looking into the navy's archives for more information, they'll likely fire me."

That was probably true. The navy and the government would close ranks to protect Admiral Channing's reputation, while the fate of a single librarian was of little consequence. They'd flick her away like a mosquito if she threatened to tarnish the good name of their prized admiral.

"It's like a sore tooth I can't ignore," Anna said. "That report is wrong, they know it's wrong, and I'm forced to sit here and let that error get calcified in the historical record. As more years go by, it will be harder and harder to correct."

Her rambling was cut short as she startled and stood up. "Can I help you, sir?"

Luke turned to see three uniformed members of the Capitol police clustered in the doorway. Jonathan West, the sergeant at arms for the House, stepped into the room, the insignia flashing on his uniform. Luke rose in concern. Such men rarely left the Capitol unless it was for good reason.

"Sir, you are under arrest," the sergeant at arms said. The two police officers behind him moved to stand on either side of Luke.

Luke let out a bark of laughter. "Is this a joke?"

"No, sir. You are to follow us to the Capitol immediately."

"What are the charges?" he sputtered.

"Illegally seeking to evade a House vote," the officer responded. "The Speaker of the House is authorized by the Constitution to compel your presence for the vote. He has chosen to do so. You and the other sixty-five members of Congress who have chosen to miss this afternoon's vote are all subject to immediate arrest."

Luke clenched his fists, so angry he couldn't speak. Everything the officer said about the Speaker's power to arrest him was true, but this sort of stunt hadn't happened in decades. And all his colleagues still in the city were most likely being simultaneously arrested as well. Obviously their secret had been exposed. Most of the conspiring congressmen had surely left the city, but it seemed a careful watch had been kept on those within the reach of the Capitol police. One of the officers moved closer, a pair of handcuffs dangling from one hand.

"Don't even think it," Luke snapped. He wouldn't put it past Speaker Jones to have Luke handcuffed and frog-marched all the way down Constitution Avenue, with journalists and photographers gathered around to memorialize the spectacle.

Luke swallowed hard, his mind working fast. He had to be smart about this. He wasn't going to be the only member of Congress arrested today, and they needed a unified strategy to snatch this victory out of Cornelius Jones's salivating jaws.

He glanced at Anna. Her face had gone white, and she was staring at him with wide eyes. He smiled and reached out to squeeze her icy hand. "Don't worry about this," he whispered. "It's just another salvo in a long-running war."

He left the map room with his head held high, shoulders back, determined to handle this with the same cool composure as when Cornelius Jones bumped him down to the Fisheries committee. He would smile, take it in stride, and keep working behind the scenes with all engines firing. The officers trailed behind him like serfs in the wake of royalty. Wending his way through the crowds in the great hall of the library, he nodded and smiled to the onlookers, who didn't know what to make of the uniformed men following a member of Congress through the building.

But inside, Luke was seething.

The floor of the House was crowded, but rather than return to his normal seat, the sergeant at arms directed Luke to a seat in the front of the room. Walking across the blue-and-gold carpet, Luke met the eyes of twelve of his compatriots who had already been rounded up to sit before the Speaker's rostrum like truant children, their expressions a blend of resignation and annoyance. The raked semicircle of chairs behind him was almost full, packed with men whispering and muttering behind their hands. No doubt by now the tale of what was happening had swept through the chamber with the speed of light.

"What can we expect?" Luke asked the nearest of his allies. "A tar and feathering?"

"Jones doesn't have a quorum yet," the congressman said. "We can still hope he won't be able to find enough of us."

Luke glared up at the rostrum, raised on three tiers to the Speaker of the House at the top. Behind Speaker Jones, a huge American flag hung on the wall, loaning the Speaker an aura of distinction. Cornelius Jones looked as thin and desiccated as a praying mantis as he scanned the crowd assembled before him, not even bothering to conceal his gloating.

Three more arrested congressmen were escorted into the chambers. Luke swung around to scrutinize the hundreds of people in the chairs behind him, mentally tallying the numbers. There still weren't enough members present for a quorum. Unless the Capitol police succeeded in producing four more of the wayward congressmen, the Speaker couldn't proceed to a vote on the new tariff. He glanced at the clock. Ten more minutes until the House would be called to order. There was still a slim chance the Speaker couldn't round up enough of them to hold the vote. There was talk of someday outlawing this clever technique for a minority of congressmen to scuttle a bill they disliked, but for now it was still legal, and Luke's only hope for delaying the tariff.

The door to the chamber opened again. Luke held his breath. Two members of the Capitol police stepped inside, followed by the slow, lopsided gait of Caesar Trammel. A murmur of disapproval rippled through the House. No one wanted to see the old warrior humiliated like this. Caesar kept his head high as he joined the others in the pit of the House floor.

"What do our numbers look like?" Caesar asked. He took the empty seat beside Luke.

Then four more arrested congressmen filed into the chambers. They were sunk.

"Jones has his numbers," Luke said in a grim voice.

The sergeant at arms moved to the floor of the House, carrying the ceremonial mace, a stylized ebony staff topped by a silver eagle. He proceeded to bang the staff on the floor, calling the House to order.

It took some time to settle the crowd, but Speaker Jones relished the moment as he surveyed the hundreds of men seated in a semicircle around the rostrum.

"Now then," the Speaker began, "the first order of business is to ascertain why our honorable colleagues failed to appear at the appointed hour. Wasn't the time publicized in all the appropriate places?"

General stamping of feet and voices of approval rose from the assembled crowd. It seemed the majority of the House was ready to enjoy the ritualized humiliation.

"Representative Simmons," said the Speaker, "please inform the House why you failed to appear at the designated time." It appeared that each man who dared to defy the Speaker was going to be singled out for a personal reprimand.

A few seats down from Luke, a congressman stood, his face flushed and his voice weak. "I overslept," he said.

"Overslept?" The Speaker shook his head. "At two o'clock in the afternoon?"

"Yes, sir. I overslept."

The next three men questioned by the Speaker also claimed to have overslept. Luke shifted in his chair. A little creativity wouldn't be amiss at this point—anything to draw attention away from the overwhelming disgrace that was about to pour down on them all.

Caesar Trammel seemed to understand. When the Speaker demanded Caesar account for his actions, the old man rose on his single leg, making sure to wobble in a commendable imitation of frailty.

"I was consulting with my physician," he answered. "War wounds."

"And you could not schedule this urgent appointment with your physician at a more appropriate time?" Speaker Jones pressed.

"Not if I wanted to get it in before the tariff is put in place," Caesar said. "I'll be too poor to pay the doctor's bill if this vote is passed."

The comment was greeted by a roar of laughter, and Caesar took his seat. There was simply nothing left to add. Speaker Jones banged his gavel.

The Speaker then turned to Luke. "And what accounts for your lack of punctuality this afternoon, Mr. Callahan? Did you oversleep as well?"

Caesar had done admirable work in pricking a hole in the Speaker's balloon, and Luke intended to do the same. He stood and said, "I was at the library."

"The library?" Speaker Jones said incredulously.

"Yes. The gold-plated, grossly overdecorated palace you voted for time and again. It turns out there's a very fetching librarian on the third floor." Hoots of laughter filled the room. This was exactly what was needed to ruin the Speaker's triumph. "I found myself enthralled and incapable of paying attention to mundane issue like votes for the destruction of the American economy. My apologies."

Speaker Jones smiled tightly. "Indeed. And does this enthralling librarian have a name?"

Luke froze. Silence descended on the chambers, broken only by the stenographer who tapped out a transcript of every word spoken. The stenographer looked up at Luke, waiting.

Soon everyone was looking at him. His mouth went dry. Anna was really going to hate him for this.

"Miss Anna O'Brien," someone from the back row hollered. "She was at the Fisheries meeting last month."

Speaker Jones appeared satisfied. "Well, now that you've torn yourself free of the enthralling clutches of Miss O'Brien, I look forward to your participation in the coming vote. Mr. Higgins, please explain your absence this afternoon."

The inquisition dragged on, and Luke knew all hope of defeating the tariff had been lost. Jones had his quorum, the vote would proceed, and the tariff would pass. Luke's reputation and the industries of Maine had just taken another hit.

After Luke's arrest, Anna sat dumbfounded at her desk, feeling useless and afraid. Her heart had been pounding like a freight train ever since he'd been marched out of the map room. She wasn't built for this kind of stress. That was why she'd become a librarian, so she could live a quiet life surrounded by books and maps and not worry about political enemies coming out of the woodwork to arrest you or demote you or turn you into a national laughingstock.

Rather than let her anxiety fester, she found a law dictionary and tried to piece together what kind of mischief Luke had gotten himself into.

"Miss O'Brien?" Standing in the doorway was a bald man with the widest mustache she'd ever seen. He held a camera before him.

"Yes?"

"I was wondering if I could get a photograph. No, no . . . you needn't get up. You looked very becoming poring over that book. This will only take a moment."

She supposed it would be all right. Photographers had been swarming all over the new library yesterday as they moved in, but they hadn't photographed the map room yet. She glanced around. Most of the books had been put away, though the map tubes were still in a messy heap along the back wall.

"I'll just stash these tubes out of sight, shall I?"

"No need," the man said. He had been fastening his camera to a tripod, but stopped to gesture her back to the center table. "Quickly now. Just a simple photograph of you next to that open book. Standing would be better. Just place your hand on the edge . . . yes, perfect."

He went back to adjusting the camera, looking down through the viewfinder. "Hold still, and . . . perfect! Exactly what I needed. Thank you, Miss O'Brien."

Before he could leave, another man pushed into the room, this one holding a notebook. "Are you Anna O'Brien? The map librarian?"

"Yes, can I help you?" It was rare to have such urgent needs for cartographic assistance, but more men followed.

"Would you like to comment on Representative Callahan's arrest? Were you here to witness the event?"

"Are you a reporter?" she asked. Good heavens, there seemed to be so many of them . . . four, plus the photographer. All these strangers crowding into the room set her teeth on edge. A wiry man with bushy red hair stepped farther into the room.

"Mr. Callahan had very flattering things to say about you, miss. He said he'd been too entranced to leave your side—"

"No, *enthralled* was the word he used," another reporter chimed in.

"Enthralled! Even better." The redheaded man scribbled in his notebook while others began filling the room. One of them stood over her desk, lifting her blotter and examining her belongings.

"Those are my things," she sputtered. "My personal things . . ."

She wanted to drag the man back from her desk, but she was distracted by another photographer, who was pushing a century-old globe aside in order to set up a tripod in the corner.

"Quit touching that globe! It has hand-painted panels imported from London—"

"Tell us, have you known Mr. Callahan long?" one of the men asked. "He seemed quite taken with you and was unstinting in his admiration."

The man plundering her desk looked up, awaiting her answer. All the others had their pencils at the ready. Her throat closed up, and she didn't even know if she could breathe. What on earth had Luke done?

"How about it, ma'am?" one called out. "How does a humble librarian bring a congressman to his knees?"

Her panic began to dissolve, replaced by anger as she replied between clenched teeth, "Apparently, all it takes is finding a little data on the mollusk harvest and he goes all aquiver."

"A spirited girl! How refreshing. And how did you first come into contact with Representative Callahan?"

This was a disaster. Mr. Spofford was the only person authorized to speak to reporters, so she needed to be careful. She skirted around the table, moving quickly so that the other photographer couldn't get a picture of her.

"What's all this about?" a surly voice cut through the din of the reporters clustered in the map room. Never had Anna been so grateful to see a security guard in her life. She sagged against the cool plaster wall in relief. The guard hustled the men out of the room, and then Anna closed the door behind them, still not sure exactly what Luke had done.

But she knew it wasn't good.

Anna was horrified to find reporters loitering on the stoop of O'Grady's Boardinghouse when she returned at the end of the day. They had to be reporters. Who else traveled with photographers and carried little notepads?

She pivoted and slinked away in the opposite direction. The circulation war between the Pulitzer and Hearst newspapers had taken journalism straight into the gutter, always on the hunt for shamed women, torrid love affairs, or grisly murders. She could only pray they wouldn't pounce on the little seed of Luke's infatuation and blow it up into an all-consuming love affair.

She could lose her job over this. She'd worked so hard to get here, and what library would hire a woman whose name had been smeared in the newspapers? It wouldn't matter what was true, only what those awful men wrote about her. She'd even posed for a photograph!

Neville would help her. He had a clear head at times like these, and surely he'd protect her. A blister rubbed on the side of her heel, worsening with each step until it was screaming for relief by the time she mounted the short flight of stairs leading up to Neville's boardinghouse. She knocked and braced herself to face the most ill-tempered landlady in the city.

"Oh, it's you," Mrs. Norquist said after she yanked the door open. The landlady was a strong-jawed woman who reminded Anna of the Statue of Liberty, only with a hostile stare. She might be an attractive woman if she could ever summon a smile instead of a scowl.

"Is Neville home yet? I need to see him."

"Why?" the landlady demanded.

Mrs. Norquist's disapproval always rubbed Anna the wrong way. For a split second, she wanted to say she intended to fling Neville down in the front hall of the boardinghouse to make passionate love to him for all to see. For pity's sake, what did the woman think?

"I just need to talk to him. It's private."

"Anna?" Neville came around the corner, eating a pretzel. "What brings you here?"

She beckoned him outside, feeling Mrs. Norquist's accusatory eyes boring into her back. Just wait until that woman saw tomorrow's newspapers. Whatever slender thread of respect Anna still had with the landlady would be blasted to pieces. She dragged Neville to a bench in the park across the street, but was too nervous to sit.

"I need a place to stay tonight. I can't go home." She told Neville of the bizarre events of the afternoon. Watching the horror cross Neville's face made her feel even worse.

"Have you talked to Mr. Spofford?"

She shook her head. "I tried, but the reporters were following me all the way out the hall. I finally asked one of the security guards to keep them away and escort me to the streetcar."

"Keep clear of the reporters," Neville said. "The story will blow over as soon as they can be distracted by a house fire or other gossip. If they can't find anything on you, they'll move on to the next bit of scandal."

"Can I sneak into your room for the night? I can't risk going home."

"Mrs. Norquist wouldn't like it."

"Don't tell me you're afraid of her too. I thought I was the only one who cringed at the sight of her witch's broomstick."

Neville rolled his eyes. "She's not that bad, Anna. Besides, it's for your own benefit. The last thing you need is to be seen sneaking into a man's room. Come on, I'll get you a hotel room."

She didn't relish another long walk, yet what choice did she have? "I'll pay you back," Anna promised as they set off down the street.

Neville shot her an exasperated look. "As if I'd take your money."

She almost wanted to weep. How comforting to have a solid friend she could always rely on. For a few silly weeks she'd thought she could trust Luke Callahan, but she should have known better than to fall under the spell of a politician.

12

The next morning's newspapers led with the startling arrest of twenty-three congressmen who had attempted to thwart the tariff vote by staging a boycott. While all the men were released after the tariff vote had been passed, most of the ink was spilled on the scandalous behavior of the wayward congressmen.

Anna sat huddled in the corner of a coffee shop, reading each of the three major Washington newspapers. She felt grubby from sleeping in her shift and wearing the same clothes from yesterday, but she didn't dare return home and dreaded having to report to work this morning. What if the reporters returned? She'd worked six years with a spotless reputation, and now it had been blown to smithereens on the pages of Washington's newspapers.

Luke's colorful excuse for missing the session was gleefully reported. None of the articles mentioned her name, but all described the petite, winsome librarian known for working in the map room and supplying personal service to Representative Callahan.

Personal service. That was the exact phrase used, and it was branded into the front of Anna's mind like a scarlet letter. Heat flooded her cheeks, and a prickly sensation covered her skin. This was going to be awful, but Mr. Spofford would protect her. It was under his orders that she'd been appointed to work with Luke.

She deposited the newspapers in the wastebasket as she left the café. Stepping into the blustery November morning, she smoothed the collar of her blouse and raised her chin. She'd done nothing to be ashamed of, and maybe no one at the library had seen the newspapers yet. With all the unpacking, who had time to waste reading Washington gossip?

She didn't sense any unusual attention as she entered the library and crossed the gleaming marble floors, her boots clicking and echoing in the chambers. She learned otherwise when she entered the workroom on the second floor. A group of librarians was clustered around the lunch table, a newspaper spread out before them. They were all men, and they swiveled to stare at her as she entered the room.

"Ah," Mr. Ferris said stiffly, "the Capitol's most enthralling librarian."

So much for wishful thinking. Mr. Ferris, the rare-manuscripts librarian, looked annoyed, while the law librarian and the two art librarians were laughing.

Anna smiled and dipped into a curtsy. "It's a burden, but I suppose someone must own the title." She hung her wool frock coat on a hook.

"Don't get too comfortable," Mr. Ferris said. "Mr. Spofford wants to see you."

Anna hoped the panic didn't show on her face. "Did he say what he wanted?"

Mr. Ferris shook his head. "No, but you need to go right away. He seemed unusually upset this morning."

Surely Mr. Spofford would protect her. It was under his direct orders that she'd been assigned to Luke in the first place.

Although most of the library had been moved to the new building, Mr. Spofford's office was still in the old library. Anna murmured a prayer as she crossed the street and entered the Capitol. Her footsteps echoed in the vacant rooms of the former library. How much larger it looked now that it had been emptied of its books, just a few scattered pieces of trash and abandoned furniture littering the floors. It seemed sad, the beloved old library now stripped of its treasures. She walked down a long corridor to Mr. Spofford's office. His door was closed, but he answered as soon as she knocked.

"Miss O'Brien," he said warmly, ushering her inside. He looked tired and careworn as he closed the door behind her. "Forgive me that I cannot offer you a place to sit, but this won't take long."

The office was crowded with packing boxes, and every available seat was stacked with books. She twisted her hands, trying to tamp down the fear building inside her.

"I am afraid I'm leaving the Library of Congress," he said.

Anna blinked in confusion. Ainsworth Spofford had been at the helm of the Library of Congress since before Anna was born. He'd been appointed to the position by Abraham Lincoln himself.

"You're leaving?" she asked.

"It's time. I have completed the great monumental task of my career. The new library has been funded, built, and opened to great acclaim. It now seems the government prefers a younger man to lead the library into the next century, and it's time for me to step aside."

"I don't understand," Anna said. "You love it here."

Mr. Spofford winced, and to her horror tears began pooling in his eyes. "I'm afraid I didn't have a lot of say in the matter."

Mr. Spofford had been fired! She was dizzy with the injustice of it. He deserved more credit than anyone in Washington for creating the vision of what this magnificent library should be, and now to be disposed of like yesterday's newspapers . . .

He settled his hands on Anna's shoulders. "Enough about me," he said. "I need to let you know that I've left a letter for my successor, taking full responsibility for assigning you to Mr. Callahan. I know you to be a woman of good character and don't believe anything unseemly has occurred between you and the congressman. I can only hope there are no negative repercussions."

Anna nodded, her mind reeling. She was depending on Mr. Spofford to shield her against the rumor mills. "I can't continue doing his research. Please don't ask it of me."

He nodded. "I'll reassign whatever remains to another librarian before I leave. You need have no further contact with Mr. Callahan."

Relief settled over her. Her business with Luke had gone on much too long. He'd been wildly inappropriate and was her complete opposite in temperament, comportment, and occupation.

But somehow she couldn't help feeling that she had just lost a very good friend.

Mr. Spofford asked Anna to keep silent about his news until he could make a formal announcement. Two hours later, he assembled the librarians in the lunchroom and made the stunning announcement. His tone was diplomatic, but there was no doubt that he'd been fired.

"I will be leaving this afternoon," Mr. Spofford continued. "My office in the old library has been packed and it seems an appropriate time to leave. I wish you all the very best."

The room was silent, everyone staring in disbelief as if unsure what to say. The saddest sight in the world was Mr. Spofford turning around and walking back to his office to finish packing up.

Why wasn't anyone protesting? All the librarians just stood there like docile sheep as though they'd been struck mute. Were they going to let this injustice pass and not do anything to prevent it? Anna looked at Mr. Ferris, the librarian most likely to throw fits at any insult delivered to the library. But he just shook his head and walked slowly out of the lunchroom. The others followed suit.

Anna wasn't the right person to organize a protest; timid girls like her made terrible leaders. Yet she'd gladly be a foot soldier if someone else would take action. She fumed all the way back to the map room. She wanted the earth to stop spinning and to take out an advertisement in the newspaper proclaiming the insult that had just been delivered to a great and honorable man. She glared out the window, across the street to the Capitol, wondering who was responsible for Mr. Spofford's termination.

She grabbed her coat. It didn't matter. She could hide up here in the safety of her cozy library, or she could use her God-given sense of outrage to do something about the situation.

Anxiety ratcheted higher as she crossed the street and headed to the Capitol, its dome looming larger and more intimidating than ever before. She had no illusions about her powers. She was a shy girl who could barely speak in public, but it was time to muster every ounce of her courage and take action.

She scurried down the staircase to the lunchroom, where the congressional pages often congregated when they had nothing to do. She spotted Jack Wilkerson immediately. Over the years, Jack had always frustrated Anna by making a nuisance of himself in the library, but for today's task he was the perfect choice.

After explaining what she wanted done, Jack's eyes gleamed in respect. "You can count on me, Miss O'Brien."

For once in her life she was grateful for Jack's sense of mischief as he led a group of the boys to the east wing. Next, she dashed upstairs where the Supreme Court shared office space above the Senate chambers. Like Congress, members of the Supreme Court had been hankering after their own building for decades, but they had to wait until the new library was complete before funding would be available for another massive building project.

Every instinct urged her to run and hide in the safety of the library, but she wasn't going to let her shyness get the better of her. Not today. It didn't matter how she felt; it only mattered how she acted. The door creaked as she opened it to the chamber where the court clerks worked, and two dozen grim lawyers turned their heads to stare at her. They didn't look very amused by the interruption.

Anna swallowed hard, then stepped forward with her request. Mr. Spofford had served in the Capitol longer than most of these men had been alive. He was well liked and a familiar sight to them all. To her relief, it appeared that even these lawyers felt outrage after hearing about Mr. Spofford's abrupt termination. They quickly agreed to her plan.

The House chambers were next. The last person on earth she wanted to see was Luke Callahan, but after the fiasco yesterday, he owed her a favor and she was ready to call it in. Hating the idea of setting foot inside the all-men's club, she gritted her teeth and marched toward the chambers.

The House wasn't in session and so the chamber was almost empty. A few members were playing cards while others were reading at their desks. Luke was nowhere to be seen.

She scanned the chamber once more, wondering what to do

next. Though she dreaded seeing Luke, he was her best chance at getting the cooperation of the other members of Congress.

Speaker Cornelius Jones sat at the top of the rostrum like an emperor, idly smoking a cigarette while reading. He glanced up at her. Unless he was the henchman who'd wielded the ax to bring about Mr. Spofford's termination, he was the best person to help.

The prospect of approaching such a powerful man, especially one with a ferocious reputation, was more than daunting. She clenched her fists, took a deep breath, and started heading up the rostrum steps.

Speaker Jones was a thin man, his skin tinged with a gray cast from the decades of smoking. He drew on the cigarette, curls of smoke surrounding him as he studied her, waiting for her to speak.

"Mr. Spofford has been fired," she said bluntly.

The Speaker looked astonished. It was exactly the response she'd hoped for. It meant that it wasn't Cornelius Jones who had ordered Mr. Spofford's dismissal, and perhaps she could count on his help. She leaned forward and whispered what she wanted.

The Speaker nodded. "It will be done," he said calmly as he tamped out his cigarette.

At five o'clock in the afternoon, Ainsworth Spofford closed the door to his office for the final time. Carrying the last of his personal effects in a small box, he headed toward the grand double staircases that descended toward the rotunda of the Capitol.

He froze when he saw the staircases filled on both sides with people, all standing solemnly. He glanced at them, uncertain what to make of the hundreds gathered all the way down to the first floor and filling the rotunda, but as he began descending the stairs, the applause was deafening.

Anna stood at the base of the stairs. Every senator in the building had agreed to stand in support of Mr. Spofford. All nine of the Supreme Court justices joined in, as did members of the House, military officers, and every employee with the Library of Congress. Hundreds of mail room clerks, telegraph operators, congressional pages, the secretarial staff, the cooks from the lunchroom, even the janitors were assembled. All of them applauding. Anna clapped so hard, the palms of her hands stung.

Mr. Spofford paused on the landing, looking around at the throng, and probably for the first time that day a smile graced Mr. Spofford's face as he nodded in acknowledgment. The applause continued as he finished descending the stairs, crossed the rotunda, and left the building for the final time. It didn't stop until the door had closed behind him.

Beside her, Gertrude, the music librarian, bawled like a baby. Anna had to blink back tears as well. Although she was glad she'd done what was needed to assemble this show of respect and appreciation for Mr. Spofford, it didn't change the fact that the man had lost his job. Tomorrow Anna would try to slink back into complete anonymity in the map room, but for today she was grateful that her voice had been heard.

When Anna reported to work the next morning, she was relieved to have a hearty backlog of cartographic questions awaiting her attention. It appeared Mr. Spofford had been true to his word, and Luke's few remaining questions had been reassigned to other librarians. At last, she could return to her safe world of maps, gazetteers, and atlases, never having to worry again about political infighting or audacious congressmen or what made the color of tourmalines so dazzling.

Would she ever see Luke Callahan again? Yesterday he'd sent

a note pleading for her to meet him at a streetcar stop, but she'd ignored it. They had nothing to say to each other, and since they no longer worked in the same building, there was no reason for their paths to cross again. That was for the best. Of course it was . . . and yet she couldn't help but regret it just a little.

A message from Neville arrived late in the afternoon, suggesting she visit his office after work to play with a new tabulating machine that had just been submitted for a patent. She loved toying with the new inventions that flooded the Patent Office, and Neville always helped her put things in perspective and reel her in from whatever doomsday scenario was taking shape in her mind.

When she arrived at the top floor of the Patent Office, the building looked deserted. Most of this floor was filled with the cavernous model room, where glass-fronted cases displayed thousands of models for new inventions. It had the look of a library, except the shelves were filled with mechanical models instead of books.

She headed toward Neville's office, where the low rumble of men's voices could be heard. She tipped her head forward so that Neville would know she'd arrived. From behind his desk, he sent her a guilty smile and shrugged his shoulders. She understood why when the man sitting opposite him turned around.

"Hello, O'Brien," Luke said.

She shot Neville a glare, but he took it in stride. "You need to bury the hatchet, Anna," Neville said.

"In his skull?" she asked.

Luke rose and faced her. "Anna, can we talk? I need to apologize. *I'm sorry*. I'm an idiot and a fool, and I deserve to be boiled in oil for dragging your name into this mess."

She didn't want to hear it. Turning on her heel, she stormed toward one of the aisles in the model display room. If she hurried, she could find cover among the display shelves. She hiked up her skirts and darted to the far side of the room, but his footsteps were right behind her.

A firm hand grasped her elbow and slowed her steps. "Anna, I'm sorry," he said again.

She whirled to face him. "Do you know what happens if I lose my job? I don't have any family. No one I can turn to for help."

"You're exaggerating again. You're not going to lose your job."

"You don't know that." Yesterday Anna might have believed she was safe, but no one was indispensable if Mr. Spofford could be fired.

"If you lose your job, I'll help you get another."

"There *is* no other job like the Library of Congress!" Her voice sounded loud in the normally silent model room. "I'm proud to be working for Congress. I was the girl who other children teased and laughed at behind their hands, the girl who never fit in. I wasn't supposed to amount to anything, yet now I work at the *Library of Congress*. Maybe most people don't understand what that means, but it's the whole world to me."

"I know what it means." The corners of Luke's mouth were turned down, his eyes deep pools of regret. Maybe he did understand. This was a man who'd escaped a chaotic childhood by fleeing into the world of poetry. Who'd bought a railway car so that he could bring books to the young men working in logging camps.

"All I can say is that I'm sorry," he continued. "From the moment the words left my mouth, I knew it was a mistake, and I've regretted it ever since. I'll use whatever political capital I have to ensure you don't suffer any consequences."

She sighed and strolled to a window seat cut into the alcove. It was a relief to sit and let some of the tension drain from her muscles. Luke followed, propping his boot on the window seat and peering down at her with somber eyes. The sadness radiating from him made it impossible to doubt his remorse.

"Okay, I forgive you," she said.

"You do? Just like that?" His confusion would have been comical if he didn't sound so upset.

"Do you want me to drag it out some more? I suppose I can, but I've never been very good at holding grudges."

It was dangerous to stew over insults and slights. That kind of bitterness usually turned into self-pity and resentment, poisoning her ability to simply be happy. The greatest irony was how she always found a sense of healing by extending forgiveness.

"I'm pretty good at nurturing grudges," Luke said wryly. "My father burned a stack of my wretched poems when I was fifteen years old, and I never forgave him for it. I *still* get angry when I think about it."

Luke had hinted at the stormy relationship with his father, but she had assumed it was the normal clash of two strong-willed people living within the same orbit, not this sort of malicious cruelty. "Did he ever say he was sorry?"

"Never."

Anna bowed her head. In the months after Uncle Henry forced the lye down her throat, she suffered a bewildering combination of fury mixed with guilt. A piece of her wanted to make Uncle Henry drink lye so he'd feel the scorch of pain with every swallow and the never-ending torment of being mute. That bitter piece of her grew and festered until it tainted all her thoughts, blotting out whatever glimpse of light tried to seep through the dark clouds of her life.

The bitterness vanished within a few seconds of seeing Uncle Henry in that prison cell. The remorse in his eyes washed her anger away, and she raced into his arms. Forgiveness swept away the bitterness that darkened her world. When she managed a smile for her uncle, he fell to his knees, sobbing, and for the first time she understood the gift of forgiveness. It wasn't for her uncle's benefit. By forgiving him, she was freed of the burden of bitterness and anger. There was no sin that could not be forgiven.

Her uncle had begged for forgiveness, but Luke's father had not. It was harder to extend the grace of forgiveness to someone who was resolute in their sin, but it had to be done all the same.

"My aunt never forgave me for putting Uncle Henry in prison," Anna said.

Luke's mouth tightened. "You didn't put that man in prison. He did it to himself."

"Maybe, but my aunt will never accept that. She will go to her grave believing I caused her husband's death. I found it easier to forgive Uncle Henry than Aunt Ruth, because at least Henry was sorry for what he did. Aunt Ruth will always blame me for what happened. Over time I came to accept that we're all imperfect humans. I didn't want to be trapped in a downward spiral of anger just because Aunt Ruth was so shortsighted. Your father was too weak to understand the destruction he brought to his children, but he was an imperfect man who deserves to be forgiven, even if he didn't ask for it. We are all beautiful but broken people. Jesus forgives us, even when we don't deserve it. That's a pretty good reason to be forgiving."

Luke tilted his head to look at her, a quizzical expression on his face. "It's humbling to be around you, O'Brien. I don't think I can follow your example. Here I am, the beneficiary of your unstinting forgiveness, and I'm still harboring a twenty-year grudge over the acts of a vicious drunk. Those poems weren't even any good."

"There's no statute of limitations on extending forgiveness. I think you'd feel better about it if you could."

"Maybe." He still looked skeptical, though. "I want you to know I took your advice about getting my brother out of jail."

"You did?" She'd been so immersed in her own problems, she had completely forgotten about Luke's family troubles. "What made you change your mind?"

"You."

He rolled his palms together, his knuckles cracking under the pressure. "I didn't know about the danger of disease inside a prison. I don't want to punish Jason. I just want . . ." His voice choked off, and he clenched his hands into fists. "I want so badly to save him, but I don't know how to do it." Luke scrubbed a hand across his face and drew a steadying breath.

"In any event, I've made arrangements for the transfer of funds, and my sister vows she'll keep him on the straight and narrow. I'm not sure this is the right thing to do, but Julia has been able to quit drinking, and she insists she can help Jason do the same. I'm just not sure . . ."

"I'll pray for them both," Anna said.

She reached out to touch him, then pulled back before she made contact. She needed to snuff out these inconvenient feelings. An awkward silence filled the air. She fiddled with her hands, wondering how to say goodbye to this man who had been her friend.

"Mr. Spofford has reassigned your research to another librarian," she said. If he understood her hint that this was probably the last time they'd be meeting, he gave no sign of it. Instead, he gave her one of his half smiles.

"I heard about that send-off you arranged for him. Very impressive, O'Brien."

"You wouldn't say that if you knew how hard I was shaking as I made those rounds. I thought I'd faint before it was all over."

"But you did it, and in the end that's what counts."

"Do you know who ordered Mr. Spofford's termination? No one seems to know."

He shrugged. "It's just politics, Anna. Sometimes these positions are used to reward a loyal supporter. Or to rig the way research will proceed. So much of what drives this city happens behind closed doors for reasons that don't make much sense to the outside world. The way they've circled the wagons to protect Admiral Channing is a perfect example."

Her shoulders sagged a little. She'd found the courage to speak out for Mr. Spofford, but had failed the fifty-six men of the *Culpeper.* By threatening the employment of the women at the library, the navy had her hog-tied. The eight women working at the Library of Congress were alive and depended on their jobs so as to keep a roof over their heads. The men of the *Culpeper* were long dead, and their families had moved on. . . .

Or had they?

Maybe she'd been too shortsighted by assuming she was the only one who cared about the accuracy of that old report. What if there were other family members like her who cared enough to get involved in what she was attempting to do?

Fifty-six men had disappeared with that ship, which meant there were fifty-six families out there that might be recruited to help. Just as she'd organized the Capitol's employees to stand up for Mr. Spofford, she could organize the surviving families of the *Culpeper* to demand a correction of the official report. And she knew exactly who to turn to for help.

13

Silas Zanetti had been her father's best friend and the chief petty officer of the *Culpeper*. His wife, Maria, had been like a loving aunt to Anna. Whenever the *Culpeper* was at sea, Mrs. Zanetti visited Anna at least once a week, descending on the house like a singing beam of sunshine. Mrs. Zanetti had an amazing operatic voice. Anna and Neville used to plead with her to show off her talent. They'd cover their ears as she warmed up her world-class soprano voice and sang a note so piercing that it could crack a crystal glass.

Mrs. Zanetti stopped singing after the *Culpeper* went down, plummeting into deep depression. Soon she was only a shadow of the laughing, vibrant woman Anna once knew. Only a year after the *Culpeper* was lost, Mrs. Zanetti stunned everyone when she made the abrupt decision to start her life over in the wilds of the Yukon Territory after seeing an advertisement for a mail-order wife placed by a Canadian trapper named John Smith.

Mrs. Zanetti's fate was another aching, unanswered question for Anna. She'd never heard from the woman after she abandoned the comforts of Washington, D.C., for a dubious life in the Canadian wilderness.

It would be a challenge to locate the family members of those lost with the *Culpeper*, who had probably scattered across the country after fifteen years, but she needed to start with Mrs. Zanetti. She was the only family member of the lost sailors Anna personally knew, and besides, she was desperately curious about whatever happened to Mrs. Zanetti. Or Mrs. Smith, as she was now probably known. How could a colorful woman like Maria Zanetti marry a man with such a pedestrian name?

Neville wasn't optimistic about their chances of tracking down Mrs. Zanetti. When Anna descended on his office the following day to plead for his help, he looked at her as if she'd gone insane.

"You want us to go looking for a man you know nothing about, who lives somewhere in northwest Canada, and is named John Smith? Could you have picked a more impossible challenge?"

"I work at the finest library on this continent," Anna replied. "I have access to records and archives. Yes, I think we can find him, and if we find him, we find Mrs. Zanetti. It's just going to take some legwork."

Neville tossed a half-read patent application on his desk. "Anna, don't you think you're taking this too far? I have no explanation for why your father's last letter was so strange, but what are the odds of your finding someone by the name of John Smith somewhere in Canada, and that his wife is going to be interested in your campaign to correct the report on what happened with the *Culpeper*? Even if we find her, Mrs. Zanetti has moved on. She probably won't care."

Anna shook her head. "Her love affair with Silas Zanetti was one for the ages. She will want to know what really happened to her husband. Her *real* husband, not the trapper she settled for in Canada. Mrs. Zanetti will help us, I know she will."

"Anna, you're crazy."

"Do you remember what happened when Aunt Ruth tried to abscond with that money set aside for my college education?"

Neville winced at the memory. "Mrs. Zanetti summoned a dozen members of the Bluestocking League to cause a ruckus in the banker's office."

"That's right, and she was arrested because of it. She's not the sort to tolerate an injustice, and she won't ignore the pack of lies in that old navy report." After storming the bank with the bluestockings, Mrs. Zanetti was released from prison with only a warning, but Anna would never forget that Mrs. Zanetti had been willing to risk incarceration on her behalf. Furthermore, her bold actions had saved Anna's college money from certain misuse by Aunt Ruth. Even from the remote Canadian wilderness, Mrs. Zanetti was her best ally to help blow away the veil of lies the navy had built around the loss of the *Culpeper*.

Neville sent her a reluctant smile. "I surrender. When do we start?"

Excitement surged through her. "How about first thing Saturday morning? We'll go to the library and spend the day prowling through every document about Canada."

Neville shifted in his chair and fiddled with a pencil. "Saturday won't work for me."

"Why not? You never do anything on Saturday."

"I just can't. Pick another time."

"How about Saturday afternoon?"

He shot her a pointed look. "Anna, you're going to have to pick another day. I have plans on Saturday."

She waited for him to provide an explanation—they held no secrets from each other, and Neville told her everything—but he locked eyes with her and refused to say another word about his mysterious plans for Saturday. It was maddening. Now that she was on the hunt again, her blood quickened and she wanted to tackle the problem immediately. It looked like she'd have to do the work on her own, since waiting until the following weekend was unthinkable.

"Don't worry about it," Anna mumbled. "I can handle it on my own."

As if sensing her annoyance, Neville offered an olive branch. "Do you want to come to my parents' house for Thanksgiving dinner?"

"Is your father going to be there?"

"Naturally."

Anna didn't have anywhere else to go for Thanksgiving, but she was tired of coping with the blatant pressure from Neville's father every time she walked through their door. *"There's little Anna O'Brien,"* he would coo. *"Maybe someday I'll be calling her Mrs. Anna Bernhard, hmm, Neville?"*

Why did everyone assume she and Neville ought to get married? It was embarrassing and awful and she was tired of it. "If I come for dinner, is your father going to have wedding bells ringing in the background?"

Neville winced again. "I'll tell him to knock it off."

"It's a deal then."

Although it still annoyed Anna that Neville wouldn't tell her where he was going on Saturday. It wasn't the first time either. Lately he'd been distracted and unreliable, not always where he was supposed to be. It was bothersome, but she had other issues to worry about at the moment.

Like how she was going to find out what happened to the *Culpeper* without getting fired.

On Saturday morning, Anna arrived at the library to begin searching for information connected with Mrs. Zanetti. She pulled every book the library had about Hudson's Bay Company, the largest employer of fur trappers in Canada. Perhaps she'd find a list of their trappers or points of contact where someone could write for more information.

She lugged the books to the reading room in the new library, a majestic space surrounded by tall marble arches, balconies, and artwork to rival the Louvre. Hours passed, and as Anna learned more about the Yukon Territory, she grew to dislike John Smith. What kind of man enticed a grieving widow to leave her family and friends to go live in the Canadian wilderness? The photographs she found of the Yukon showed primitive buildings and rugged trappers whose skin looked as weather-beaten as old shoe leather.

"Hello, O'Brien."

How could two words send her heart skittering? Luke Callahan stood beside her desk, a volume of Byron's poems tucked under his arm as he peered down at her. She supposed it was naïve to assume they would no longer see each other after his research had been assigned elsewhere. Luke often spent his free time in the library, and that wasn't going to change now that the new building was open.

He tilted his head to read the spine of her book. *The Directory of Beaver Pelt Traders of the Canadian Northwest Territories.* "Could you possibly have found a drearier book in the entire library?"

She set her pencil down. "Shockingly, I find it more interesting than mollusks or hydraulic sawmills."

He accepted the barb with grace. "What wretched member of Congress has set you to this mind-numbing task? Tell me, and I'll go scold him for you."

"I'm here of my own account. I'm trying to find an old friend."

He glanced at the photographs printed in the open books before her. "Not one of those hairy cavemen, I hope."

For all Anna knew, Mrs. Zanetti could indeed be married to one of these long-haired men with weather-beaten faces and hard eyes. Did Mrs. Zanetti know what she was getting into when she left for Canada to marry a complete stranger? It seemed inexplicable, although Anna knew better than anyone how loneliness could grind on a person.

She outlined the problem to Luke, filling him in on the lively woman who made the years living with Aunt Ruth bearable, and Mrs. Zanetti's abrupt decision to become a mail-order bride only a year after the *Culpeper* went down.

"I want to find other family members from the *Culpeper*, but I was so young when it sank, and the Zanettis are the only people I really knew. I'm certain Mrs. Zanetti will help me if I can find her."

Luke dragged out the chair next to her, its legs scraping against the tiled floor. "Show me how I can help. After all you've done for me, it's the least I can do."

She glanced at the tower of thick books. She and Neville were accustomed to the glorious monotony of research, but someone of Luke's caliber might not appreciate it.

"This promises to be a long and dull slog," she warned. As quickly as possible, she provided the scanty facts they had to work with. Maria Zanetti married John Smith in 1883. She was Catholic, but Anna had no idea if the marriage ceremony had been performed in a Catholic church. Because John Smith was a trapper, it was likely he did business with Hudson's Bay Company.

As the oldest surviving corporation anywhere in North America, the Library of Congress had collected and archived all documents relating to the company. This collection was constantly being updated with a steady stream of news clippings and financial reports. Anna dug through boxes of uncataloged stock reports and industry statistics, and countless grainy photographs of the trappers and trading posts scattered throughout Canada.

She thought Luke would be bored stiff by such a task, but he seemed to be enjoying himself. "Are you sure I'm not dragging you away from more important things?" she asked.

"And what would those be? Haranguing you to provide me with two decades of data on hydraulic sawmills?"

"You seemed pretty fascinated with it a few weeks ago."

A little of the light faded in his eyes. "Well, it seems all of our work was pointless. I never found definite proof of corruption coming from the Speaker's office."

Anna would have thought that to be a *good* thing, but apparently Luke had invested tremendous political capital into justifying a corruption charge against the Speaker of the House.

Luke clenched a pencil in his fist and looked away. "For the life of me, I don't understand that man's power. Cornelius Jones is surly and mean, and he stinks like an ashtray. I was sure he was using his control over the purse strings to buy himself votes. There's no other explanation for why such a frosty reptile could wield so much power."

She sighed and opened another box of documents tracking Hudson's Bay Company. Founded in 1670, the company was proud of their history and sent photographers all across Canada to document their far-flung empire. Many of the photographs showcased the spectacular beauty of the Canadian wilderness and the country's remote trading posts. Some of them depicted long-ago traders standing beside the indigenous people of the area, while others appeared to be newer photographs that included recently built trading posts.

She scanned a recent photograph of the Grey Wolf Trading

Post, with members of the local community lined up in rows before the clapboard building to have their photograph taken. Anna studied their faces, quickly spotting a lone woman in the crowd.

"I found her!" she cried. Her voice echoed and bounced off the high-domed ceiling, and Luke nearly fell off his chair at the sound. She slid the photograph across the table for him to see. "There she is! That's Mrs. Zanetti."

The date written on the back of the photograph indicated it'd been taken only three years ago. Going by Mrs. Zanetti's fine sealskin coat and beautiful gloves, it looked as if her husband supported her quite well. Anna glanced at the others in the photograph. Most of them appeared to be rugged, tough-looking men.

Her gaze then landed on the man standing next to Mrs. Zanetti, and her breath froze.

"What's wrong?" Luke asked. "You look like you've seen a ghost.

Because she had. For standing beside Mrs. Zanetti, staring directly at the camera, stood Silas Zanetti, the chief petty officer of the *Culpeper*. And he looked alive and well.

"Are you sure it's him?" Luke asked for the third time, his voice loud in the quiet of the map room.

Immediately after spotting Silas Zanetti in the picture, Anna grabbed the box of photographs and fled upstairs to the map room, where they could speak in private. Only the main part of the library was open on Saturday, and they had complete privacy in the map room. Maybe she was getting paranoid again, but she didn't want to be overheard by anyone.

"I'm almost certain of it," Anna said. "Silas had a huge nose with a dent right at the top. My father always teased him about it, saying Silas could hang a picture from the dent in his nose. That is the exact same nose."

"I don't see a dent," Luke said.

"Look closer."

Rather than examine the photograph more carefully, Luke looked at her, pity in his eyes. "Is it possible you're imagining it, Anna? That you want so badly to believe this man is this Silas Zanetti person, perhaps you're seeing things that aren't there? I don't see a dent on the man's nose."

The photograph was grainy, and maybe it was just a shadow or a smudge of dirt. Most of the men lined up for the photograph seemed rather grubby. The man in the picture looked much older than Silas, but it had been fifteen years since she'd last seen him. Of course his hair would be thinner, his face more gaunt. Besides, the moment she clapped eyes on that man, every instinct cried out that she was looking at Silas Zanetti. It also explained why Mrs. Zanetti had abandoned the comforts of Washington for the Canadian wilderness to marry a total stranger, as she knew John Smith was no stranger.

Forget the picture. There was something much bigger going on. "I need to know what happened to the *Culpeper*," she said in a voice vibrating with tension. "The navy knows, and they've been lying to the world for fifteen years. The story they told you about Admiral Channing is hogwash."

Luke's expression turned somber. "Anna, have you considered that it could have been a mutiny?"

It was a terrible thought, making her feel light-headed. Her corset pinched, and she sat straighter to drag more air into her lungs. It was hard to imagine her father being involved in such a scandal, but sometimes officers had little choice. The *Culpeper*'s captain had a reputation as a stern man, but a mutiny?

Yet a mutiny made the most sense when compared to any

other scenario she'd considered. In the interest of preserving discipline among the men, the navy might have suppressed any mention of a mutiny and used the coincidence of the hurricane to explain the disappearance of the ship. No crew member participating in a mutiny would return to the United States to face certain execution. Look at what the mutineers of the *Bounty* had done. They'd settled on a remote Polynesian island and scuttled their ship so they'd never be found again. If there was a mutiny on the *Culpeper*, her father might not be dead.

It was a stunning and exhilarating thought.

"What if my father is still alive?" Again her voice echoed in the silent map room. Now that she'd spoken the words aloud, hope began blossoming. At the time she'd been too young to leave Washington and follow her father into a rugged, unknown world. But what if he was still alive and hoped to one day see her again?

Luke's warm palm encircled her hand. "Anna, don't do this to yourself. If your father was alive, don't you think he would have contacted you by now?"

She closed her eyes. For so many years, the possibility that her father was still alive had been her dearest wish. Over the years she'd sent up thousands of prayers to heaven, begging for a miraculous explanation for his disappearance. A mutiny would explain everything.

Could her father have been a traitor? It sickened her to even think such a thing. She grabbed the photograph and scanned the face of every man lined up before the Grey Wolf Trading Post, looking for her father.

He wasn't there. No man participating in a mutiny would ever dare to return home. Silas never did, though somehow he made contact with his wife and got her to meet him in Canada. The fact that the Zanettis had changed their name to Smith indicated they were trying to cover their tracks. It gave further credence to the likelihood of a mutiny.

Maybe her father's last letter was intended to let Anna know he was headed to Cuba. He couldn't tell her directly, so he veiled his message in riddles and secrets, hoping she would one day solve the puzzle and go in search of him.

Could he really be alive? It seemed impossible, but no less farfetched than Silas Zanetti's inexplicable appearance in this photograph.

"Could you help me?" she asked Luke, who looked a little baffled. "The story about Admiral Channing is nonsense and you know it. I need help figuring out what really happened and don't know who else to turn to. Please . . ."

Luke's confusion was replaced by humor as he struggled to suppress a smile. "Anna, forgive me, but may I assume you're a literate person who has the ability to write a letter?"

She blinked. "What are you suggesting?"

He stood and picked up the photograph with Mrs. Zanetti's picture, holding it before her eyes. "This woman has all the answers you need!" he said, too loudly. "She's your Oracle of Delphi, your Rosetta Stone. The Alpha and Omega of every question you've got about the *Culpeper.* Pick up one of those newfangled pens you're so fond of and ask her about the large-nosed man standing beside her. Either he is Silas Zanetti and can explain exactly what happened to the *Culpeper*, or your imagination is running wild once again. Either way, the answer you need is right here."

His exuberance cracked through her knot of anxiety, and she started laughing, even though she ought to be appalled by the way he was practically shouting in a library. How could this man always coax her into laughter, even in the midst of such a stressful situation?

"I really do hate it when you are both obnoxious *and* right," she said.

"Do you? I rather thought this afternoon was the most fun I've had since coming to Washington."

He looked at her with that gleam in his eyes again. She looked away. When he was flushed and alive with such humor, it was like looking straight into the sun, dazzling but dangerous.

And he was right—it *had* been fun. The entire day had been exhilarating, and a bit frightening too. It appeared her suspicions about the *Culpeper* might be built on a solid foundation after all, and there was no one she'd rather have beside her on the hunt than Luke Callahan.

Which was odd. Normally she wanted Neville for companionship, but Neville had been so distracted and unreliable lately. Neville's scientific mind always worked along the lines of logic and proof, and those things had been failing in their search for the truth regarding the *Culpeper*. Luke trusted instinct. His wild, passionate nature seemed a perfect counterpart to her methodical outlook on life.

"Will you help me with the letter to Mrs. Zanetti?"

Luke cocked a brow at her. "You need help with your writing skills?"

It was embarrassing, but she explained to him the paranoia that had plagued her ever since noticing the flaw in the navy's report. "I feel like people are watching me. The other day I posted a telegram to an army outpost in Wyoming. It was for legitimate library research, but I noticed a young boy followed me all the way to the Capitol and back. It was the strangest thing. When I asked him why he was following me, he stammered and denied it, but I'm almost certain he was spying on me. If I post a letter to the Yukon Territory, it wouldn't surprise me if someone intercepted it and read it before it could be sent."

"Well, they won't intercept *my* mail," Luke said.

"You'd post it for me?"

"Of course. Now let's get down to business."

Too many people had seen her and Luke together that morning in the main part of the library for Anna to feel entirely safe spilling all her questions into a letter. She opted to keep the note brief and vague just in case the letter was intercepted, despite Luke's assurances. After a few pleasantries, she asked the one question most pressing on her mind: *I'm searching for your husband's good friend. Is Cuba the right place to look?*

Mrs. Zanetti would know exactly what Anna was asking with that veiled question. How long would she have to wait for a reply? The Grey Wolf Trading Post was hundreds of miles from the nearest city. It could be months before she heard anything back, and Anna wanted to shriek in frustration. But it had been fifteen years since the *Culpeper* disappeared. She could wait a few more months.

14

What was he going to do about Anna? Pinpricks of sleet fell from the gloomy December sky as Luke headed back to the Willard, tugging his collar higher in a vain attempt to block the icy air snaking down his neck. Watching Anna flail against the navy made him fear she was on the verge of getting smashed and broken. For the life of him, he couldn't see a dent on that man's nose in the photograph. But Anna so desperately wanted to believe there were survivors of the *Culpeper* disaster that she might have seen Silas Zanetti's image on a portrait of Napoleon or the czar of Russia.

He slipped Anna's letter into a mailbox on the way home, wondering if he should have told her about the suspicions of the old diplomat who claimed to have seen the *Culpeper* sailing into the bay of Manila two years after it supposedly sank, but it would have been a cruel thing to do. The best course of action would be to wait until Mrs. Zanetti replied to this letter. Telling Anna of the diplomat's ramblings would only upset her.

Besides, he had bigger problems to worry about.

Cornelius Jones was launching a full-scale retaliation against him for leading the attempted boycott. A week after the incident, Luke and the other renegade congressmen were formally censured by the Congress. It was a meaningless ritual in which the entire House was assembled to witness a verbal rebuke of the disgraced congressmen. It carried no penalties other than shame, but the Speaker of the House reserved special treatment for Luke, who was suspended from the Fisheries committee until further notice.

Now Luke was in complete political exile. He was a bird with no wings, a congressman with no voice. Stripped of all his responsibilities, he had nothing to do in Washington other than squander a few hours reading poetry in a grossly over-decorated library, or flirt with Anna while she indulged in a wild goose chase.

His hands and feet felt frozen by the time he arrived home. The hotel usually served hot coffee in the lobby on days like today, and he looked forward to holding a steaming mug between his icy fingers. The rousing scent of percolating coffee surrounded him as soon as he stepped inside. As was his custom, he stepped to the front desk to check for messages. Since being stripped of his responsibilities, his mailbox was empty and his social calendar vacant, yet some habits were hard to break.

"Any messages for me?" he asked the clerk at the walnut counter in the front of the lobby.

"A visitor, sir. She's waiting near the piano."

She? Luke's brow furrowed as he headed around a screen of potted ferns, wondering what woman would risk her reputation by meeting him in a hotel lobby. Against his better judgment, he hoped it might be Anna.

His sister rose from the satin-covered bench, and disappointment flashed through him. He forced a smile and took a step toward her, but froze when he noticed her clothing. She was dressed entirely in black, all the way from her ruffled collar to her shoes. Her complexion was chalky white, a stark contrast to her ebony hair and dark eyes. She remained motionless by the bench, staring at him as he approached.

"This isn't the kind of thing I could tell you in a telegram," Julia said in a halting voice.

He stiffened, his heart nearly stopping. "Please don't say it."

She closed her eyes and drew a ragged breath. "Jason is dead, Luke. He died the night after he was released from prison. He found a bottle I didn't know about. I'm so sorry."

The breath rushed from his body, and he curled over. This couldn't be happening. No, it wasn't happening. . . . Julia grabbed his shoulders, hauling him upright and trying to embrace him, but he shoved her away. He couldn't look at her, couldn't even breathe past the desperation that choked him. He wrote the order to get Jason out of prison. He let this happen.

He had to get out of there.

"Luke, please . . ."

"Back off," he growled.

She went to grab his arm, but again he shook her off. People gawked at them, craning their necks to watch as he strode toward the rear door. He would do anything to turn back time and hold firm against the temptation to set Jason free. He'd signed Jason's death warrant when he wrote that check.

"Luke, it's freezing out there. Stay and talk to me," Julia pleaded.

He spun around. "Was this what you wanted? Jason free so he could kill himself?"

Tears stained Julia's face, and she flinched. Just like their mother would flinch when their father raged. He turned and punched the wall. Pain exploded in his hand, a white flash clouding his vision as the sting shot up his arm and through his body.

He leaned against the wall and punched it again. Again and again and again until chips of plaster began flying and specks of blood dotted the white paint. Julia pressed against his back.

"Stop it!" she said. "Stop it right now. Don't you *dare* turn into an animal. Not you. Of all people, not you too."

The words penetrated the fog, but he still couldn't face her. Right now he hated her.

He sagged against the wall, heaving in breaths and trying to stop his head from whirling. *Jason*. His baby brother. He wanted to find something else to break, somewhere else to unleash the white-hot anger rolling through him. Footsteps rushed toward them, and from the corner of his eye, Luke saw the footman who provided security for the hotel.

"Is there anything you need?" the man asked, a note of warning heavy in his voice.

"I'm fine," Luke said.

"The wall doesn't look fine, sir."

"I'll pay for the damages," he snapped. He moved farther into the corner, anger and hatred coursing through him. Julia said pacifying words to the footman, ushering him away.

Luke closed his eyes. This wasn't her fault, but right now he was angry at the world.

It had been two days since Anna wrote the letter to Mrs. Zanetti, and already she was growing anxious while waiting for a reply. It was the first thing she thought about as she rose each morning. Would a reply take a month? Two months? She dressed quickly, her cold hands fumbling with her buttons as she hurried through her morning routine. The bedrooms in the boardinghouse weren't heated, so she was rushing to get down to the breakfast table.

Stepping into the dining room, warmth from the kitchen surrounded her. There was only one spot left at the table. She hiked her skirt up to step over the bench and sit beside Gertrude.

"Your congressman is getting into trouble again," Gertrude said.

"He's not *my* congressman," Anna said in a fierce whisper. "What's he done?"

Gertrude passed her a section of last night's *Washington Evening Star*, but before she could read the article, a young woman at the end of the table started giggling.

"Is he handsome?"

"I'll bet he's one of those stodgy old ones with muttonchop whiskers," Mary-Margaret said. "Come, tell us about your congressman."

All the women at the table paused to listen. Nothing here was more eagerly devoured than gossip, especially if it involved men.

"I don't have a congressman," she muttered, scanning the article about an unnamed congressman from Maine who had indulged in a shouting match with a mysterious woman dressed in black inside the grand lobby of the Willard Hotel. Apparently, his outrage was so great he slammed his fist into one of the hotel's fine walls, cracking the plaster and rattling the crystals of the chandelier above him.

"There are thirty-five unmarried congressmen, and three unmarried senators," a redheaded woman at the end of the table pronounced. "I wish I worked in the Capitol and had a shot at one of them."

"No woman in the Capitol hankers after the elected officials," Gertrude snapped. "It's against the rules."

"Maybe for someone like you," Mary-Margaret said with a pointed look at Gertrude's sacklike dress. "I'm only twenty-four, and there's no reason I can't aspire to one of those men.

I'm surprised Anna is on the hunt. I always figured you'd end up like Gertrude."

Gertrude ignored her and leaned over to take the newspaper back from Anna's numb fingers. "This morning's *Washington Post* has an almost identical story," she said.

The first thing Anna did after arriving at the library was to collect all the recent newspapers. All three Washington papers reported the story about Luke with glee. She felt sick as she read them. Newspapers sometimes exaggerated, but the details in these articles were all consistent.

Something was wrong. Luke was losing his hold on something that was very important to him. She'd heard the revulsion in his voice when he spoke of his father's uninhibited rage and knew he would never sink to that level unless something was terribly wrong.

Should she offer to help? It was impossible to know why Luke was slipping from his moorings, but if there was anything she could do to help, she'd offer it.

As soon as she arrived at the map room, she grabbed a research request card and flipped it over to write on the blank side: *Will you meet me? I'll be at the tidal basin at 6:00 today. Tell me how I can help, and I'll do it. Anna.*

People often went to the tidal basin at the end of the river to feed the ducks or watch the sunset, yet it always cleared out after dusk. She ought to be able to meet Luke without fear of prying eyes or eavesdropping staffers. After sealing the note inside an envelope, Anna slipped downstairs and gave it to a congressional page to take across the street to the Capitol.

Anna's note burned in his pocket as Luke walked toward the tidal basin on the west end of the Mall.

He didn't want to see her. He'd been in a foul mood ever since Julia's arrival two days ago and he didn't want Anna seeing him like this, but he couldn't ignore her note. She meant too much to him, and he couldn't bear to sever the thread of friendship that still tied them together.

He spotted her sitting on a bench at the far end of the basin, a lone figure in the gloomy night. Anna shouldn't be out alone after dark, but he didn't have the energy to grouse at her about it. Not tonight. Besides, he felt better just seeing her. Her profile looked so lovely and fragile against the last streaks of the sunset. But he knew better. Anna was tough. She'd endured and survived . . . thrived even. She'd been battered by life and yet hadn't become bitter and twisted.

"Hello, Anna."

She stood at the sound of his voice, looking a little hesitant and embarrassed. "Luke."

Just hearing his name in her throaty, velvety voice made his heart ache. It was torture being near her. If he'd never met her, Jason would be alive right now. Locked in a jail cell, but alive and with hope for a future. That was all gone now.

He held her note up between two fingers. "Care to explain?"

She took a step forward, her eyes on his hand. With gentle fingers she took hold of his wrist and lowered his hand, exposing his scraped knuckles. "Care to explain?" she countered. "The newspapers are having a field day over this."

There was a note of humor in her voice, and it rubbed him the wrong way. "Jason is dead," he said bluntly.

She sucked in a breath, her horrified eyes meeting his.

"He got intoxicated the night following his release." As quickly as possible, he relayed the story of what happened. After returning home from jail, Jason was pale, shaky, and nauseous. Julia had emptied the house of liquor, but in the middle of the night Jason found a bottle of cough medicine in the pantry and drank every drop of it. No one was sure what he did after that. He was found dead the next morning half a mile from town, facedown in a snowbank.

"We think he was trying to get to a pharmacy or a tavern when the cold and the opiates in the cough medicine overwhelmed him. In any event, he's dead."

"I'm sorry," Anna said. "I don't know what to say. . . ."

Her voice was aghast, and she looked so vulnerable in her shabby wool coat, standing there in the buffeting wind. Without thinking, he dragged her into his arms, tucking her head beneath his chin. She didn't resist him. Instead, she tightened her arms around his back.

"It's not your fault," he managed to say.

But it was. Jason would be safe in that jail cell if Anna hadn't planted the seed of doubt in Luke's mind. He hated himself for it, but he didn't think he would ever be able to look at her without remembering it was Anna who'd prompted him to order his brother's release.

"Jason was a good kid," he said in a hollow voice. It made no sense, but he didn't want Anna thinking badly of his baby brother. "When he was little, he used to worry about where butterflies went during the rain. Butterflies!" His voice choked, and his eyes brimmed with tears. "I loved him so much. I keep wishing I had done things differently, that I'd never left Maine, never let him out of my sight. That I'd never let him out of prison."

"I'm so sorry," Anna said again as she extricated herself from his arms. There was a void now where she'd been. He watched as she turned to stare out over the tidal basin.

He sighed. "Anna, it's not your fault. And the rational piece of my brain says it's not my fault or Julia's either. I just need to keep repeating that until I believe it."

"I sent you that note because I thought you might need my help, but I'm afraid there's nothing I can do for you. It would have been better if we'd never met."

She was probably right. There was a time when he'd wanted nothing more than to pounce on this thrilling fascination he had for her and follow wherever it led . . . hopefully to the altar. That was probably ruined now, although he knew a tiny chunk of his soul would be forever owned by Anna O'Brien, and that was exactly how he wanted it.

But he had to get away from her. Maybe someday they could move past this, but not today. For now, he needed to mourn. He had to pull together what was left of his family and find some sort of meaning in this senseless death. And he couldn't do that while his emotions were splintered by his complicated feelings for Anna.

He reached into his pocket and twisted the keys off his tourmaline key ring. He reached out to grasp her hand, pressing the walnut-sized stone into her hand.

"I want you to have this, Anna, a piece of Maine to remember me by."

She held up the gemstone, the weak light glinting off its surface. "I probably shouldn't accept it."

"Please. I want you to have it." If they never saw each other again, he needed her to remember him.

She clutched the stone, holding it to her chest. And when she looked up at him with those luminous eyes, he knew she felt the tug as well. It was mirrored on her face, the combination of longing and regret.

"I wish things had been different," she said wistfully.

"How so?"

She glanced over his shoulder at the last streaks of light in the sky. "If you were just an ordinary man, like a clerk at the corner store or a post office employee, I wonder if we would have been good together."

He leaned down and kissed her on the cheek. "Make no mistake, O'Brien. We've *always* been good together."

He left before she could give him back the tourmaline or he did something stupid like beg her to wait for him, to hang on until he could dig himself out from beneath this avalanche of dark thoughts.

Tomorrow he'd leave for Maine to bury his brother. Afterward, he would return to Washington and try to repair his crumbling career. Yet he didn't know if he'd ever be able to look at Anna again and not remember that it was her fault his brother was dead.

15

The funeral, held at the old stone chapel less than a mile from the Callahan estate, was a solemn affair, with Luke's mother silently weeping in the front pew. From the moment he arrived in Bangor, Luke was amazed at Julia's ability to steer the difficult funeral arrangements through to completion. She'd organized a small army of neighbors to coordinate food for after the wake, chosen the readings for the service, and met with the undertaker, all while comforting their mother and keeping Philip occupied. She even had their older brother, Gabriel, helping with the arrangements, not an easy feat.

When Luke left for Congress eight years ago, he fully expected Gabe to tame his reckless spirit and become the leader of the family in Maine, but it never happened. A self-taught architect with shaggy chestnut hair and a booming laugh, Gabe would disappear for months without warning. Once it was to live for a year with the Penobscot Indians in the mountains of the Northeast. Last month it was to sail the skiff he built all the way to Canada.

No one wanted to talk about the reason they were all there.

Jason had dug his own grave. Still, they could have done a better job stopping him. They should have handcuffed him to his bed. They should have set guards on him and paid a physician to be in attendance. They should have appealed to the sisters at Saint Agatha's to light candles and say prayers around the clock.

And they should never have bailed him out of jail.

Luke didn't want to blame Julia for it, but he did. He didn't want to blame Anna for it either, but he did.

Most of all, he blamed himself. Jason was his baby brother, who used to hide in Luke's room when their father stormed and raged. Luke always protected him. But later, when he left for Washington, he abandoned Jason to the demons that seemed to plague the Callahan family.

The damp air was freezing as Luke walked back from the funeral, but he let his coat hang open, refusing to protect himself against the icy chill. Jason must have felt far worse during his final minutes of life as he lay freezing in that snowbank. Luke's boots crunched through the thin sheet of ice crusted atop the snow as he trudged uphill toward their house. How many times had he and Jason sledded down this very hill together? How many endless summer days had they wrestled on this lawn or caught fireflies in the evening?

Fresh waves of pain rolled through him as he slogged toward the house, a rambling home of roughhewn timber and stone on the highest point of Callahan land. Over the years, Gabriel had expanded the house, tacking on rooms, towers, and balconies. The house had become a reflection of Gabe's impulses. Mismatched gables, a wing added diagonally from the house, a turret slapped on because their mother had mentioned she fancied one. After a brief fascination with the challenges of designing a spiral staircase, Gabe had built one in the corner of the great room. He'd always intended to add a loft and attach it to the staircase, but then he grew bored with the project and abandoned it. To this day, the winding stairs led to nowhere.

The house had become a metaphor of his family—spectacular, audacious, and impractical. And yet it had been a good place to grow up. The streams were packed with striped bass, and in the summer a thousand shades of green surrounded them from the pines, oaks, maples, and grassy fields. When the trees were bare, they could see all the way to the lights of Bangor.

Inside the house, everything was still in disarray from the wake the day before. Hundreds of people had tromped through the first floor as every logger, miner, tradesman, and merchant paid his respects. After expressing the obligatory words of grief, half the men wanted to talk politics with Luke. It was the last thing he'd wanted. No one here quite grasped how steep his political exile in Washington had become, and the less said the better.

The moment everyone arrived home from the funeral, Julia sprang into action. "Gabe, I need you to take the carpets outside for a beating. Luke, the tables in the parlor need to go back into the kitchen. Get Philip to help. I'll have Mother clean the silver and get it wrapped for storage."

Luke stepped closer and said quietly, "Can't someone else do that? She's about to collapse from grief."

"That's why I'm keeping her busy," Julia replied, opening the sideboard drawers to put away the china platters. She was probably right.

"Come on, Philip. Help me move the tables."

Philip followed Luke to the kitchen. Once the door closed behind them, Philip stunned him when he said, "I don't want to go back to Washington. I want to stay here."

"No." In all the years Luke had been Philip's guardian, there had never been any question that the wisest course of action was for the boy to live with him in Washington.

"I don't like living in a hotel," Philip said. "Mother doesn't drink anymore, and Uncle Gabe is here too. They can look after me."

Like they looked after Jason. "Absolutely not," Luke said.

"Why not? Uncle Gabe is older than you."

"I can give you opportunities in Washington most boys would sell their eyeteeth for. You can't get a decent education here."

"Uncle Gabe never finished school. He said he'll take me into the mountains, and I could learn from the school of nature. We could find things to paint, just like Winslow Homer did."

"Winslow Homer had a fine education in Europe and America before he became a great painter. Don't put your cart before your horses." Gabe always started projects with great enthusiasm, only to abandon them the moment something more interesting seized his attention. Raising a teenaged boy wouldn't be any different.

"Philip, this isn't the time," Julia said as she hustled into the kitchen, dumping a bucket of coal into the box by the stove. Luke looked from Julia to Philip, then back to Julia. Had they been speaking about this behind his back?

His mother sat at the kitchen table, listlessly polishing the silver. While it seemed cruel to be putting her to work just now, Julia was indeed right. Every few minutes his mother set the item down, her eyes staring vacantly into space. Julia noticed within a heartbeat. "I need those forks polished, Ma."

Could he return to Washington anytime soon if his mother was still like this, overwhelmed by grief? And since when had Philip become dissatisfied with their life in Washington? True, making him work off his debt in the hotel laundry had been a stern punishment, but it was fair. More important, it was *over.*

After the kitchen had been restored to order again, he escaped into the great room to read in solitude. It didn't last long.

"Hey, Luke!" Gabe bounded into the room, glancing around and seeing they were alone. "Come out back and help me chop wood. Quick, we've got a lot to do."

He threw on a coat and followed Gabe to the towering stack of timber laid in for the winter. Listening to Gabe's plan for the evening made him doubt his brother's sanity. "I just got word the ice cutters are heading in from the fields," Gabe said. "They couldn't make it for the funeral, but we'll hold a bonfire tonight that will light the skies all the way to Bangor."

Luke leaned against the handle of his ax. "Bonfires are a throwback to pagan Europe, a reckless show of male bravado and shameless waste of resources. Besides, it's a fire hazard."

"Of course it's a fire hazard. It's a blithering bonfire!" Gabe laughed. "It will be big enough for Jason to see from heaven. Those dreary ceremonies Julia has been subjecting us all to are about to drive *me* six feet under. Now pick up that ax and get to work."

There was some truth to Gabe's comment. Picking up the splitting maul, Luke took aim at the log propped on the chopping block and split the wood with a satisfying *crack*. The ice cutters were a rowdy lot, and if they were coming all the way from Big Bear Lake, they'd expect a proper bonfire.

Soon he and Gabe settled into a rhythm as they chopped in tandem. The scent of freshly split pine, the sound of chopping wood, even the ache in his muscles—all of it brought back memories. How much of his life had been spent on this exact spot, splitting wood alongside his father and brothers? Now only Gabriel was left. A sheen of tears made it hard for Luke to see, but he didn't break his rhythm.

Jason. If he closed his eyes, he could imagine Jason swinging a maul only a few feet away, cracking jokes and whistling a tune.

Luke's muscles quivered, and his lungs struggled to keep up

after an hour of splitting wood. He'd gotten soft in Washington, but the bonfire might not be such a bad idea. Julia came outside once to scowl at them, and he saw his mother look out with curiosity a few times as he and Gabe rolled stones into a big circle that would contain the bonfire. There would be a rousing send-off for Jason tonight.

The sun had just slipped below the horizon when the ice cutters began arriving. When Maine's logging season ended, the ice harvest began, and many of the lumberjacks took to the hills for another three months of labor. Maine's deep lakes and frigid winters produced a pure crystal-blue ice that was shipped down the East Coast and made a good living for the men willing to live in the frosty wilderness. It didn't take much to coax them down into civilization, even if it was to commemorate the death of someone they barely knew.

But they knew Luke Callahan, the man who sent books to their camps and fought to protect the logging industry. They were willing to come and pay homage to Luke's fallen brother. They even helped stack the timber into a tall column that climbed higher as more men arrived to help prepare the bonfire.

By nightfall it was ready. With wood chips and bark stuffed into its base, the bonfire was lit and began shooting up the column, the flames burning brightly against the dark sky, reflecting on the field of snow. The men circled the fire, staring into the glow with hypnotic fascination as the wood snapped and sparks swirled into the air above.

Gabriel hopped up on top of a stump, his eyes reflecting the fire, his face flushed and full of life. "We're here to pay homage to my brother," he shouted, his voice echoing over the field. "He was like the sun itself, bursting with light and warmth. A light that burned so fiercely it could not long survive. He will not vanish from this earth, but live on in our memories forever.

Jason Callahan was taken from us in the depths of winter, when snow and ice grips the land and freezes the blood in our bodies."

Gabe reached down, light glinting off a bottle he snatched from the ground. Holding the bottle of rum aloft, he shouted to the sky, "You're free now, brother! You're free of the shackles of this life. But your memory will echo across the hills and valleys and down into the deepest reaches of the tourmaline mines!" Gabe threw the bottle into the bonfire, the glass smashing into pieces and igniting in blue flames that leaped toward the sky.

"To Jason!" one of the ice cutters said. "He always loved this old carving knife. Now it's yours, lad!" The knife spun in a high arc before landing in the center of the fire. Another bottle of liquor followed, along with an old pair of snowshoes.

Everything about this firelit night was typical Callahan bluster, but against Luke's will, a surge of joy welled up inside. His heartbeat quickened, exuberance racing through his blood. Gabriel was magnificent, standing there and shouting his grief with the strength of a Viking. Jason had been magnificent too. He'd stumbled during his final years, yet Gabe's heartfelt tribute summoned only the good memories of Jason.

His face tilted upward. The clear night sky was spattered with countless stars, their beauty nearly driving him to his knees. He could only pray that somewhere up there, his brother's spirit soared with a peace he'd been unable to find in life.

A movement near the house caught his attention, and Philip slid behind one of the stone pillars that supported the wraparound porch. Luke's eyes narrowed. This was precisely the sort of wild behavior he wanted to protect the boy from. Pivoting on his heels, he strode to the house, his boots thudding as he sprang up the steps and crossed to where Philip stood staring at the bonfire.

"They're drunken idiots," Luke said.

Philip shook his head. "They're men, real men. I want to cut ice too. I want . . . I want something *more* in life. I'll cut ice during the day and paint at night."

Luke recoiled. Philip had no idea what he was talking about. He was just a fourteen-year-old boy responding to an outpouring of sentiment and camaraderie.

"Believe me, working out in the ice fields is lonely, grueling work. I can show you a better way."

But Philip couldn't tear his eyes away.

Luke leaned on the opposite side of the pillar, watching sparks ascend heavenward every time one of the revelers threw something else into the fire. Every muscle in his body ached as the surge of bittersweet joy summoned by Gabe's eulogy began to fade.

He didn't belong here anymore. There was a time when logging and mining were all Luke knew, but then he opened the pages of a book and the axis of his world shifted. He started longing for more. He learned to restrain his impulses, play by the rules, and work hard when other men abandoned the quest. He wanted more and he got it. He *earned* it.

Bangor no longer felt like home. Not that he fit in at Washington either, but he was working on it. He could adopt the charm and polish of a congressman with ease, attend formal galas, make conversation with diplomats and senators. But he wasn't one of them, not really.

With Anna O'Brien he felt like he belonged. For a brief few weeks he'd known someone he could show this piece of his soul to, without embarrassment or apology. She had the same wild dreams as he, yet she was grounded, sensible. Their strengths and weaknesses were mirror opposites, which combined to make them almost invincible. They would have been so good together.

He thought about rushing back to her, even though she'd

rejected him for a life of safe predictability. Would that ever change? *Could* it ever change? He stared at the fire and yearned to turn back the clock.

Anna represented a beautiful, perfect dream, like something out of an epic poem. A blight like Jason's death shouldn't have intruded to tarnish it. He prayed for the strength to triumph over the destructive thoughts and emotions roiling within, but he feared the tragedy of his brother's death would forever taint the perfect dream.

16

January 1898

Business in the city slowed as congressmen returned to their districts for the holidays and government employees stayed home with their families. Back in early December, a huge Christmas tree was erected in the great hall of the new library, filling the first floor with the crisp scent of pine.

The new director for the Library of Congress arrived to replace the aging Mr. Spofford, a man appropriately named John Russell Young. With a full head of dark hair and a brisk step, Mr. Young projected the modern era, the man qualified to lead the library into the twentieth century.

He was also a cold fish. Aloof and businesslike, he had none of Mr. Spofford's friendly demeanor or comforting love of books.

Anna had yet to hear back from Mrs. Zanetti, but that was to be expected. The village Mrs. Zanetti lived in was so isolated that their mail was probably delivered by dogsled. The weeks passed, and Anna held her breath each evening when she returned to the boardinghouse and checked her mailbox.

Nothing.

Neville was a little skeptical about a grand conspiracy too. When she'd shown him the photograph of Mrs. Zanetti, he'd studied the face of the gaunt man standing beside her. "He looks pretty different from the Silas Zanetti I knew," Neville said.

"Of course he looks different; he's fifteen years older. But is that not the same nose my father used to tease him about?"

Neville bit his lip. "Maybe," he said, but he didn't sound sure at all.

She'd heard nothing from Luke in the weeks since he'd left for Maine. Did he think of her at all? She ought to be relieved he hadn't contacted her. It meant his bizarre infatuation with her was surely gone by now. Even so, there was a void whenever she thought of him, which was almost constantly. For a while it felt so nice to have a man in her life. Neville was a brother, not a man to her. For the first time in her life, Anna knew what it felt like to come first with someone. She'd never been first with anyone, and it had been an exhilarating thrill while it lasted.

She shared Christmas dinner with Aunt Ruth. Knowing how difficult Anna found these dinners, Neville usually joined her. This year, though, he begged off without explanation. She wished he would have come but couldn't really blame him. It was awkward and stilted being around Aunt Ruth, whose eyes regularly strayed to Uncle Henry's coat still hanging on the peg beside the door.

Anna's Christmas gift to Ruth was a bolt of sprigged blue calico and a few yards of lace. Her aunt's face lit with genuine pleasure when she saw the lace. Anna opened her package from Ruth, a brand-new collection of short stories from Nathaniel Hawthorne.

"It's not nearly as fine a gift as your lace," Ruth conceded.

"Nonsense," Anna replied. "There's no better gift than a book."

But in the pocket of her skirt she felt the weight of a large tourmaline. With its spectacular layer of emerald-green crystal overlaying a deep pink center, she'd never be able to look at it without recalling the strange mingling of bittersweet sentiment on that tragic, chilly night.

The following week, Anna and Neville made their annual pilgrimage to the top floor of the War Department to watch the lavish celebrations at the White House directly across the street. The president always held a reception for Congress on New Year's Day, and Anna loved watching the pageantry as fancy lacquered carriages wheeled up to the circular drive in front of the White House. Even the horses were gussied up, with feathers on their bridles and bells on their reins. Senators and congressmen took over an hour to arrive, the carriages backed up all the way down Pennsylvania Avenue. Servants in their finest livery opened the carriage doors and helped the ladies alight. The wives wore furs and jewels, often with tiaras that glittered with real gemstones. Anna would be too shy to wear anything like that, even if she could afford them. Those women looked like royalty.

She didn't want to admit it, but she held her breath as each carriage arrived, wondering if Luke would appear. Neville had a pair of binoculars he let her use to study each carriage as it rolled to a stop. If Luke came, would he be escorting anyone? Most of the congressmen were married, but the few bachelors always had companionship for such events.

When the last of the carriages departed with no sign of Luke, she passed the binoculars back to Neville, uncertain if she was relieved or disappointed.

"Remember, I'm not letting you back down this afternoon," Neville said as he took the binoculars back.

Anna pursed her lips, wishing she had never made this silly

deal with Neville. In the afternoon, the White House doors were thrown open to ordinary people who wished to wait in a crushing line to file inside and shake the president's hand. Anna had never mustered the courage to do so, even though last year she'd waited in line for an hour before losing her nerve at the last moment. She always lost her voice when she got nervous, and what if she stared at the president like a mute dolt?

This year Neville promised to let her have the prototype of a battery-operated torch if she found the courage to shake the president's hand. The Ever Ready Company had just received their patent on the portable torches, and the company planned on calling them *flashlights* when they went to market in a few months' time.

"You're going to shake the president's hand or you're not getting the new torch," Neville said.

"You go ahead," she urged. "What would I do with it anyway?" A line of visitors was already forming outside the White House, and she really didn't want to put herself through the misery of waiting just to embarrass herself like last year.

"Don't be such a sissy," Neville said in exasperation. "Let's go."

She folded her arms. "Calling me names won't change my mind. I don't need to go tromping through the White House or mingling with fancy people to feel good about myself." She had long ago quit trying to be someone she was not. Her life was fine just the way it was, and she didn't need to shake the president's hand for some fleeting brush with fame.

Luke had teased her about never daring to venture outside the library walls. There might be some truth to it. It was easy to mistake complacency for contentment. On some level, she did want more out of life, and would never get it by staying safely ensconced inside her library.

She looked at the line, then back at Neville. "Oh, all right," she said.

The afternoon's crush of people waiting to get into the White House was different from this morning. Instead of carriages, hundreds of people arrived by foot, wearing commonplace coats and shoes. Anna wore her dark wool coat, quite a change from the fur coats she'd seen earlier in the day. Rather than a diamond hair clip, she had a red bow tied to the side of her head. The ribbon came from the wrapping on the present Aunt Ruth gave her and was the only festive item she could think of to wear.

Anna adjusted the ribbon. Had she been silly to wear it? Her toes were frozen by the time the line delivered her to the front door, and it wasn't much warmer inside. Whatever heating system the White House used wasn't adequate to offset the front door hanging open for three solid hours.

President McKinley stood at the far end of the lobby, wearing an overcoat and gloves and looking almost as chilly as the throngs of people there to shake his hand. But, oh, what a man! He had stern features and deep-set blue eyes that looked like they could see all the way to Europe. She shouldn't have come. She'd never have the nerve to shake his hand.

Neville bumped her from behind, nudging her forward and blocking her opportunity to bolt out the door like she wanted to. There was no escape. Neville kept propelling her forward along the red carpet. At last it was her turn, and she stepped forward to meet the president.

"Happy New Year, sir," Anna said, staring at the stickpin in the middle of his satin tie.

"And to you, ma'am," President McKinley said, his handshake firm and dignified.

Ma'am! The president of the United States had called her ma'am! A buzzing rang in her ears, and she was so excited that she couldn't even hear what Neville said to the president. They were then moved along quickly by the Secret Service men lining the halls, who pointed them toward a side exit.

She'd done it. Neville elbowed her in the side as they walked out the side door of the White House.

"Well done, *ma'am*," Neville teased.

She elbowed him back with a reluctant smile. Maybe she didn't have any family to speak of, or a husband or children to share the holidays with, but she had the world's best friend, who would never let her down. If it wasn't as exhilarating as her short-lived flirtation with a dashing congressman from Maine . . . well, that was okay. Loneliness was something she was accustomed to, yet as long as she had Neville, she'd never be truly alone.

Luke arrived back in Washington the second week of January, Philip in tow. It had been an ugly scene getting him to leave. Philip wanted to escape the rules and restrictions of city life. Both Gabe and his mother concurred, while Luke was adamant that he could do better by the boy in Washington. Luke dismissed his mother's vote. She'd never had the backbone to stand up to their father when he was drunk and driving their family over a cliff; what made him think she could stand up to Gabe?

Only Julia was undecided. She loved her son, but during the years while most mothers formed deep bonds with their children, Julia had lived in a fog of alcohol and depression. Luke had watched her closely for the entire month he'd been in Maine. He saw no indication she'd returned to drinking, and the way in which she oversaw the tourmaline mines indicated she had a sound head on her shoulders, but he still couldn't be certain she could handle Philip. Gabe was going to be a bad influence, and he doubted Julia could insulate Philip from their audacious older brother. Worse, Philip was becoming increasingly dazzled by Gabe. Luke was bland and boring in comparison.

In the end it was Julia's decision, and she decided to send Philip back to Washington with Luke.

His first day back at the Capitol was depressing. Normally, Luke was deluged with work when he returned to town, but not this time. His suspension from the Fisheries committee still held, and he'd been left with no official duties or responsibilities. He spent a dull day at his desk in the nearly empty House chamber, reading the newspaper and trying to think of some way to resurrect his political career.

Luke took the long way home, walking down Constitution Avenue and up Fourteenth Street, passing acres of shiny black lampposts, their glass orbs glowing in the night sky. These avenues were lined with stately white marble buildings that mimicked the order and rationality of ancient Greece. It seemed like a completely different universe from the deep woods of Maine.

A uniformed doorman snapped to attention as Luke mounted the stairs outside the Willard Hotel. Inside the lobby, there was a subtle difference in the way people looked at him. Their glances slid away when they spotted him, as though he carried a contagious disease that could be transmitted by looking at him. Luke's climb to power had been dramatic, but so had the swift way Cornelius Jones kicked him into the gutter. Ignoring the looks, Luke passed the ornate elevators and headed to the staircase. He never took the elevator unless he was with Philip, who was fascinated with new technology and never missed an opportunity to use it.

The hallway of the fifth floor was covered by burgundy carpet, its walls lit by electric sconces. As Luke moved to unlock the door to his home, he smelled something odd. Something burning.

He hurried inside. "Philip, have you got a fire going?" He hurried into the parlor to see Philip sitting before the modest tile-lined fireplace.

"The fireplace isn't built for a blaze that big," Luke said. "What's gotten into you?"

Philip kept staring at the fire, the light casting shadows onto the planes of his face. "Those men must have really loved Uncle Jason," he said wistfully. "One of them threw a beaver-skin coat into the bonfire."

"They were drunk." Only a boy who'd never worked for a dollar would think destroying a perfectly good coat was an admirable sign of affection. Then he stilled, his eyes fixed on the base of the fire, widening in shock. Fueling the fire was the unmistakable spine of a book.

"What are you burning?" he demanded. He strode to the fireplace, squatting down to see better. The remnants of at least three books lay blackened and curling in the flames. One of them was Philip's algebra book.

He pivoted to glare at the boy, who refused to answer.

"Your schoolbooks? You're burning the schoolbooks I paid good money for?"

"I wanted to have my own bonfire for Uncle Jason," Philip said. "Besides, I hate school. I want to go back to Maine and live with Uncle Gabriel. I want to be a painter, and Uncle Gabriel can show me how."

Luke shot to his feet, so angry he couldn't tolerate looking at the boy who spit on every advantage that had been given him. Gabriel had already left for the mountains to pursue whatever stupid impulse had taken his fancy this month. He wouldn't return until the next payment from the mines was due. Coming home for that quarterly handout was the limit of Gabe's ability to support himself.

Luke barged into Philip's bedroom and grabbed a fistful of his paintbrushes, then stormed back into the parlor. Without thinking, he threw the paintbrushes on top of the ruined schoolbooks, the flames burning brighter as they consumed the turpentine and linseed oil coating the bristles.

"Why stop at the books? Are those paintbrushes a fitting sacrifice for your drunken uncle?" he shouted. Black smoke sputtered from the flames, and the acrid scent of turpentine filled the room.

But Luke remembered the stench of hickory-smoked bacon.

He stepped back, bracing a hand against the wall. He was no better than his father. He was a brutal bully who'd found the one thing this boy loved more than anything and destroyed it before his eyes. He turned his horrified expression to Philip, whose face had gone white.

Luke reached a hand out. "I'm sorry . . ."

Philip scooted back, falling onto his backside and staring at him with the wide-eyed look of a cornered dog. Luke sensed that if he reached out again, Philip would bite his hand.

He backed away, breathing heavily and withdrawing to the far side of the room. "I'm sorry," he said again. "I'll buy you new paintbrushes." He retreated until the back of his knees bumped into the sofa and he collapsed onto it, never breaking eye contact with Philip. "I'm sorry. We'll talk about this, and what we can do—"

Philip stood and dashed to his bedroom, slamming the door so loud that the glass in the window frames rattled.

Luke bowed his head. What was happening to him? For so long he'd been toeing the line and restraining these base impulses, and now the worst side of him was snarling and clawing to the surface. He'd even sounded like his father, the tenor of his voice cracking when he yelled. Shame washed over him as the fire continued to snap and sputter.

He didn't even have the excuse that he'd been drinking—just the bottomless shame that he was as vicious as his father had been. He swallowed back the volatile emotions, stuffing them deep inside, where they would die from lack of oxygen if he just didn't think about it. Ignoring his darker side had always worked in the past, and he'd make it work again.

17

Something's going on," Gertrude said as she walked into the map room, two other female librarians behind her. "Mr. Young has called a meeting for all the librarians in the great hall. He has an announcement."

It was the first day following the holidays. Workmen were already taking down the Christmas tree and it was still a half hour until the library opened. In the past, Mr. Spofford had allowed the greenery to stay throughout January, but this was a new administration. A more formal and less friendly one.

"Did he say what the meeting is about?" Anna asked.

Gertrude shook her head, but her face was white with anxiety, and the other women didn't look any happier. Mr. Young was indeed a cold fish, no doubt about it, more businessman than booklover like Mr. Spofford. He was so busy on Capitol Hill, he was rarely in the building. But everyone knew he had spies out to watch the operations of the new library, biding his time until he could put his own stamp on everything.

"He's going to fire us," one of the women said in a shaky whisper. "He's probably figured out that women have always been on probationary status and can't wait to get rid of us."

"We don't know that yet," Gertrude said, though it was obvious by the grim set of her jaw and clenched fists that she thought so as well.

The male librarians looked just as concerned as they filtered into the great hall, their footsteps echoing off the cold marble. It seemed as if everyone was intimidated by the new director.

At last Mr. Young appeared, looking dapper in his starched collar and formal vest. He strode to the front of the group.

"I know you are all eager to return to your duties after the long Christmas holiday, so I'll make this brief," he said. "It has come to my attention that there is heavy sentiment regarding the previous library director, who has the esteem of almost everyone on Capitol Hill. Not wishing to stand in the way of people's long-standing affection for Mr. Spofford, I have made the decision to offer him the role of chief assistant librarian. His duties will evolve according to his own interests."

Murmurs of astonishment swept through the assembled librarians.

"An office has been designated for Mr. Spofford on the third floor. He will be rejoining our ranks immediately. Thank you. You are all dismissed."

Anna smiled. It seemed perhaps even the chilly Mr. Young recognized the injustice done to Mr. Spofford and was wise enough to welcome him back into the fold. It made her feel proud that her government had the decency to correct a wrong that had been done to a loyal employee.

Later in the day, Mr. Spofford visited every office in the building. "I understand you had something to do with organizing the grand send-off on my final day," Mr. Spofford said, standing in the doorway of the map room. Wearing a tweed coat and no tie, he looked like a college professor.

Anna set down her pencil. "All I did was spread the word.

Everyone wanted to be there. Tell me, what exactly does a chief assistant librarian do?"

"Be on hand to help the new director, if he so chooses. Mr. Young is a political appointment and has never worked in a library before." Mr. Spofford's eyes twinkled. "It was an astute move on Mr. Young's part to buy a little goodwill on Capitol Hill. Mostly my job will be to settle in and finally take the time to work on the books I've always wanted to write."

After the older librarian left, Anna settled in to work on cataloging a new batch of maps just sent in from the Indian territories, but a corner of her mind kept drifting to Mr. Spofford's plans to start writing. Was she going to be old and gray before she ever dared write the story about the cartographers?

"Pssst . . . Miss O'Brien!"

Anna looked up to see Jack Wilkerson grinning at her from the open doorway. Jack was the most rambunctious of all the congressional pages, always underfoot to cause a little mischief in the library. It was unusual for him to try being quiet, so she appreciated his shouted whisper, even as the two people studying in the map room pretended to ignore the boy.

"What can I do for you, Jack?"

The boy flung himself into the chair beside Anna's desk, leaning forward to whisper in a conspiratorial voice, "Did you know if you hide in the electrical closet on the first floor, you can hear everything they say in the director's office? There's an open air vent, and you can hear plain as day."

"You were eavesdropping on the library director?" Really, this was too much, even for Jack.

"A couple of fancy officers from the navy came to see him, so I scooted into the closet to listen in. They were talking about you, Miss O'Brien."

"Me? Who was talking about me?"

"The new library director and the navy officers. You should have seen their uniforms, Miss O'Brien. They had those fancy epaulets and buttons that looked like real gold."

"Never mind what they were wearing. What did they say?"

"The naval officer wanted to know if you had any legitimate reason to be looking into the Yukon Territory."

Anna's mouth went dry. She clenched the arms of her chair, dreading the next words out of Jack's mouth.

"Mr. Young said he couldn't imagine any reason you'd be dealing with the Yukon. You know how he insists on reviewing all the requests that get funneled to the librarians. He asked the men to wait while he reviewed his records, and I overheard the two navy men talking to each other. One of them said he was heading back to the Capitol to send a telegram to someone in the Yukon to be on the lookout for you."

Her breath came fast now, and she was feeling light-headed. "Then what did they say?"

"Nothing. Mr. Young came back with a list of the research questions you've been working on for the past month and confirmed you have no reason to be looking into the Yukon. That was the end of the meeting. I ran right over to tell you about it. Isn't this exciting?"

Jack's voice was rising again. Anna urged him to speak quietly, then glanced nervously at the two men sitting at the nearby tables. They appeared harmless enough, but if the navy was spying on her, they wouldn't use someone in uniform. They'd pick someone plain-looking, like that elderly gentleman supposedly searching through property records.

She braced her forehead on her hand. She was either the most irrational, paranoid person on the planet, or the navy was spying on her closely enough to know about her interest in the Yukon.

Why were they sending telegrams to the Yukon? To warn the Zanettis? To harm them?

Anna didn't understand much about how telegraph wires worked, but maybe there was a way to trace messages. Or even tap into the wires and learn what had been sent. Neville would know if such technological eavesdropping was possible.

The moment the workday was over, she ran all the way to Neville's boardinghouse. She darted up the front steps and pounded on the door.

There was no answer.

The landlady was usually home, so she kept banging, hoping to leave a message for Neville, but there was still no answer.

She wouldn't put it past Mrs. Norquist to have spotted Anna through the peephole and refuse to answer her knock. For some inexplicable reason, that woman always seemed to hate Anna, but this was too important to let a hostile landlady stand in her way.

She kept pounding. After several minutes, still no answer. It was so odd. This was the second time in a week that Neville wasn't where he was supposed to be. She'd have to wait for him. He was the only person she could trust to answer her question, and quite frankly she was terrified. The navy was spying on her and there could be repercussions for this. Big ones.

She crossed the street to the small park opposite the boardinghouse. The metal bench was cold beneath her skirts, chilling her blood even more. She cupped icy fingers over her mouth, blowing on them.

A lamplighter walked down the sidewalk, using his long pole to light the gas globes until warm circles of light glowed from each lamppost. Most of the passersby on the street were men returning from their workday, but there were a few couples and families too. Wasn't it odd that watching men holding their wives' hands made her feel so lonely? The women looked warm and content as they walked along in the shelter of a man's embrace. It made her miss Luke Callahan. They'd been good friends, and even though she was the one to shy away from him, at times like these she longed for his company.

Where on earth was Neville? He had been behaving so odd lately, meeting with her less and less, and rarely telling her where he had been.

She stared gloomily at another happy couple as they strolled down the street. It seemed that everyone had a partner in the world but her. Snowflakes began swirling in the air, floating down softly and adding a sense of peace to the scene, but inside she ached with anxiety and loneliness.

Her eyes widened when the couple mounted the front steps of Mrs. Norquist's boardinghouse. It was Neville! She hadn't recognized him because his heavy overcoat disguised his skinny frame, yet there was no mistaking his sandy-blond hair when he removed his cap. She dashed across the street.

"Neville!"

He swiveled around, surprise on his features. "Hello, Anna. What brings you here?"

Mrs. Norquist was with him. The landlady shot Anna a glare and then quickly twisted the key in the doorknob. "Dinner in twenty minutes," she barked before slipping inside and shutting the door. It was appalling the way Mrs. Norquist treated her boarders like truant children.

Neville didn't seem to mind as he turned to look at her. "Well?" he asked.

"I don't know why you let that battle-ax speak to you like that."

Neville shoved his hands into his pockets, his face looking flushed with cold. "She's not that bad. If you quit calling her a battle-ax, she might treat you a little better."

Anna didn't want to waste time arguing over Mrs. Norquist. "I need your advice about telegraph wires." She explained what Jack had told her about men from the navy sending a message to someone in the Yukon to be on the lookout for her. She desperately needed to know who that message had been sent to, and why. "Is there any way to tap into the wires and figure out what the original message said?"

Neville shook his head. "Telegrams are sent with quick electrical pulses. Once they've been sent, they are gone forever."

She'd been afraid of that. What was she supposed to do now? She was tired, it looked like the navy was one step ahead of her, and Luke seemed to have lost all interest in her. She was in desperate need of a friend, and Mrs. Norquist's porch was small, cold, and cramped.

"I'm starving," she said. "Can we go to a café and talk? I really need a friend right now."

Neville shifted, glancing inside the warmly lit dining room, then back at her. "I can't. Mrs. Norquist is making dinner."

"Don't tell me you're afraid of her too. Come on. Let's go get something to eat."

"Anna . . . I can't."

His gaze shifted away, and his ticks and twitches became so bad that he began bumping into her on the narrow front landing. He was never this twitchy unless really upset over something.

"What's going on?" she asked quietly.

He drew a ragged breath, his eyes painfully serious. "You're not going to like it."

She wanted to weep. She'd been out of her mind with anxiety for hours, and now her best friend was harboring some horrible secret. "Just tell me."

He nodded to the park across the street. "Let's head over there."

She followed him, struggling to keep up with his long-legged strides. Even from beneath his coat, she could see his muscles jerking.

A terrible thought struck. Neville had been to countless doctors over the years and none of them had any explanation for his strange condition. Had it been getting worse and she was too self-absorbed to notice? She couldn't bear it if something happened to Neville. His spasms were so strong, and he looked miserable waiting for her beneath the streetlamp. She'd stand in front of a speeding train to protect Neville, but she was helpless against this disease.

"Have a seat," he said, gesturing to the bench where she'd spent the past hour waiting.

"I'll hear it standing up."

His face softened with a combination of fondness and concern. Never in her life had she been so terrified of the next words out of a man's mouth.

"Anna, I'm getting married."

A bubble of laughter broke from her throat. "What?" She could not have heard him properly.

"Mrs. Norquist. Margaret is her given name. I love her and we're getting married."

She stood mutely before him, watching snowflakes land and dissolve on his face. She tried to speak, but her voice had evaporated. Only an ungainly croak emerged. Neville winced in sympathy, reaching out to lead her to the bench. His arm surrounded her shoulders as he guided her down. She sat with a thump and finally found her voice.

"She's so old!"

"No she's not. She is five years older than me and has been a widow for ten years. We've cared for each other for a long time, but I didn't know how to tell you."

"But she's such an angry person. I've never seen her without a scowl on her face. How could you marry a person like that?"

Neville's lips compressed into a thin line. He shifted on the bench and looked her in the eyes. "That's enough, Anna. Margaret is jealous of you. She always has been. But she's a different person when you're not around. She's funny and curious. She's got the world's most generous laugh, and I love her very much. I can't keep spending all my time with you now that she and I have confessed our feelings for each other."

Anna recoiled. "Well . . . I'm happy for you," she stammered. She was losing her best friend to a woman who hated her. Without warning, she burst into tears.

"Anna," Neville whispered, pulling her into an awkward hug on the cold metal bench. She tried to hold back the sobs, but they gushed out and she wasn't a pretty crier. It was sloppy and loud and embarrassing as she blubbered on his shoulder. It wasn't that she liked Neville in that way; she just didn't want to lose him. Never *thought* she would lose him. They'd always been two peas in a pod. This wasn't supposed to happen.

She pushed back out of his arms. "Okay," she babbled, wiping her nose on her sleeve and swiping away tears. "I've been a real idiot and I wish you the best. Of course I do."

"You can join us for dinner if you'd like," Neville offered. "I've always wanted the two of you to be friends. There's no reason you can't be."

Except Mrs. Norquist would see Anna's swollen eyes and runny nose and probably jump to all sorts of conclusions. She grabbed her handkerchief and dabbed at the tears dampening Neville's coat. "I'll get dinner at home," she said with a sniffle. "Who can resist dining with a group of twenty nattering women?"

"Are you sure?"

If she wanted to remain friends with Neville, she was going to have to accept Mrs. Norquist into the equation. Besides, it seemed mean-spirited to resent a woman who wanted to be kind to Neville. Hadn't she always wanted the rest of the world to see the extraordinary, caring man buried beneath Neville's gangly exterior? It seemed Mrs. Norquist had done exactly that, and Anna ought to be singing the woman's praises, not blubbering on a park bench like an infant who'd lost her baby rattle.

"I'm sorry I called Mrs. Norquist a battle-ax," she said, wiping the last of her tears away. "She's actually a fine-looking woman. She looks a little bit like the Statue of Liberty, you know?"

Neville grinned. "I always thought so too."

They both broke into laughter, but then sobered quickly. Anna had reconciled herself to a life of spinsterhood long ago, but Neville clearly needed more from life than their platonic friendship. He wanted a wife and marriage and all that came with it, and she'd been too blind to notice. Perhaps her friendship with Neville had made the prospect of being alone seem not so lonely. Maybe it had even smothered her ability to see another man.

Neville tried one more time to persuade her to come to dinner, but she was too sick at heart to join them. "I'd like to, but perhaps another night," she said. She'd do her best to befriend Mrs. Norquist. Any woman who saw Neville's true value was someone who should be easy to like.

Neville retreated inside the warm boardinghouse, while Anna faced a long, frigid walk home. She'd walked home from this spot hundreds of times over the years, but she'd never felt quite so lonely before.

Saturday morning dawned with an icy mist drizzling from the sky. Normally on a day like today, Anna and Neville would tour a museum, or find a library to prowl, or a cozy pub to get some decent food. But he'd made it clear he intended to spend more time with Mrs. Norquist.

Without Neville, she had no one. Sitting at the breakfast table, Anna picked at her bowl of oatmeal. She wasn't hungry, but she needed to eat. The food felt like a heavy lump in her stomach. She could go back to her room and read, but Mrs. Horton was knitting, and the clicking of her needles was distracting. And going to a museum by herself would only make her feel lonelier.

Why shouldn't she feel lonely? She *was* alone! She had only one real friend in the whole world, and he was getting married and leaving her truly on her own.

There was always Aunt Ruth. They had never had the best relationship, although this past Christmas was the nicest holiday they'd ever shared together. Anna knew the signs of loneliness well enough to be able to recognize them in another person, and her aunt was lonely. And Ruth's birthday was coming up in a few weeks. The shop where Anna had bought the lace had dozens of offerings. Perhaps a few more feet of lace might serve as a peace offering. At the very least, the visit to the sewing shop would give her something to do on this dreary day.

Anna didn't think her spirits could sink any lower until she walked into the shop and saw Eliza Sharpe, her old nemesis and the object of Neville's adolescent adoration. Eliza stood at the counter, surveying buttons beneath the glass. As usual, she was dressed spectacularly, in emerald velvet with a frothy lace jabot spilling from her throat.

Eliza looked up when the little bell over the door announced Anna's arrival. "Why, Anna O'Brien," she cooed, "fancy seeing you here. Please tell me you've come to buy something that isn't in a shade of brown."

Eliza's smiling face had no malice, and Anna doubted she was aware of the rudeness carried in her words.

"I'm here to pick out something for my aunt's birthday," she said, and tried to step around Eliza to see the spools of lace farther down on the counter, but Eliza blocked her.

"Come help me pick some new buttons," Eliza suggested. "Look, they've got glass buttons from Portugal, but these enameled ones are simply precious. I don't know which to pick. Buttons can be so confusing."

Oh dear, this was going to be a trying conversation. Though Anna had little interest in fashion, she joined Eliza at the counter to look at the display of buttons. Apparently, Eliza had cracked a Hungarian crystal button on her riding habit and couldn't find anything close enough to substitute, so the remaining ten buttons would all have to be replaced. It was surely a sign of how low Anna felt that she actually welcomed Eliza Sharpe's company.

"Minnie Carlyle said I should get ivory buttons, but I just don't know," Eliza babbled.

Anna winced at the mention of Minnie Carlyle. Minnie was the most vicious of all the bullies at school, a fearless girl who could round up followers to lead the attack whenever the mood struck her.

Eliza noticed. "Oh, you and Minnie never got along too well. Sorry!"

"No," Anna said slowly. "Minnie and I were never very friendly."

Eliza chewed on her lower lip and fidgeted, her lily-white hands clenched into fists. "I've always felt bad about the way people treated you in school. And Minnie could be pretty mean, even to me. But it seemed like she always saved the worst of it for you."

Heat flooded Anna's cheeks. She needed no reminder of her status as the target of Minnie Carlyle's poisonous attacks. "Why was that?" she asked. "You and Minnie and the other girls had everything. Why did you all pick on me?"

Eliza thought for a moment. "I think Minnie was jealous of you."

"Jealous of *me*?"

"You were always so smart. Minnie couldn't even *read*—did you know that? She hated every minute of school. I don't know why it made her feel better to tease you, but it did." Eliza stopped, her mouth screwing up as she continued looking over Anna's shoulder—at the ceiling, at the bolts of fabric. Finally she met Anna's gaze. "I wish I hadn't gone along with her. I don't know why I did. Some days Minnie was the nicest person in the world, and on others she treated me like a leper. It was stupid. Anyway, I liked the way you and Neville always stuck together, no matter what. The two of you were so smart. Where is he, anyway?"

"I'm not sure," Anna said, though she'd bet he was staring raptly into Mrs. Norquist's love-besotted eyes.

"Tell me honestly," Eliza said as she set a button back on the velvet tray. "When are the two of you going to get married?"

Anna gave a humorless laugh. "We're not. He's engaged to marry his landlady."

"Oh." Eliza wilted a little, and there was a flash of pain in her eyes. With a heavy sigh, she turned back to the buttons, tracing her finger along the rim of the tray. "It was kind of nice, the way he had a crush on me that one year. To be the object of that kind of adoration, you know? I've never really forgotten it."

Her voice trailed away, and Anna stood in amazement at the look of regret tingeing Eliza's features. Eliza always seemed to be the most frivolous and privileged girl on the planet, and yet even she harbored regrets stemming from those school years.

Eliza straightened, an artificially bright tone in her voice. "Of course, I'm very happy with Walter. Did you know he'll probably be postmaster general someday? I'm very lucky."

It was clear from Anna's brief meeting in the pub last October that Eliza and her husband were a terrible match. The way he cringed at his wife's ramblings made his lack of respect obvious for all to see. Eliza appeared to be empty-headed, but she surely sensed her husband's disdain or she wouldn't be silently mourning the loss of Neville's youthful adoration.

Eliza slid back behind the mask of a lovely, confident woman who didn't have a care in the world as she helped Anna select a swath of lace suitable for Aunt Ruth, and the two parted ways. As Anna watched Eliza walk down the street in her tailored suit and matching cap, it was plain to see that the elegant trappings masked a deeply insecure woman.

The conversation swirled in her mind as she walked home. She had misjudged Eliza, just as she'd once misjudged Luke Callahan merely because he had gemstone cuff links and an easy charm that attracted friends and success with ease.

Anna never pretended to be other than exactly who she was, and Luke Callahan still seemed to be fascinated with her. Would she someday regret turning him down, the way Eliza regretted treating Neville so carelessly?

She was cold and dispirited by the time she arrived home. It was only one o'clock in the afternoon and she had nothing to do with the rest of her day. Was this what the rest of her life was going to be like? Waiting for Monday morning so she could have something meaningful to do with her talents?

She drifted upstairs, where Mrs. Horton was still busily knitting.

"A telegram arrived for you," Mrs. Horton said. "The delivery boy said it came all the way from the Yukon Territory."

Anna sucked in a breath, surprised that Mrs. Zanetti had sent a telegram rather than a letter. She snatched the card and turned away, her fingers shaking as she broke the seal of the envelope. The note was brief.

> *You have no relatives, only enemies in Cuba. Stop looking and don't trust anybody. We fear you are in danger.*
>
> *Your dear friends,*
> *Maria and John Smith*

She crumpled the note in her hand. What on earth was she supposed to do now?

"Well?" Mrs. Horton asked. "I didn't know you had any relations in Canada. Who's it from?"

"Nobody," she said through bloodless lips. The fact that Mrs. Zanetti used her fake name indicated she was too afraid to use her real name. Had the government spied on this message? She had to see Neville. She didn't care that she was intruding on his and Mrs. Norquist's privacy. She needed his help.

Neville wasn't home. She waited all afternoon, but still there was no sign of him or the imposing Mrs. Norquist. And waiting on the bench across from his boardinghouse made her paranoia escalate. She hadn't noticed anyone following her, but the portly man on the neighboring bench didn't seem to have any apparent purpose for being there. Or what about the girl pushing a cart of cheeses for sale? Could she be the one who'd been sent to spy on her this evening?

Mrs. Zanetti said that Anna was in danger and she shouldn't

trust anyone. Anna knew she could trust Neville, yet he was nowhere to be found and she was afraid.

She could trust Luke Callahan. Luke was the most honest man in the world. And he was strong. Well connected.

She stood and began running toward the Willard Hotel.

The dinner hour was winding down, and men began filtering into the lobby of the Willard to enjoy cigars and the informal conversations that fueled so much of Washington's political engine. There was a time when Luke's company was eagerly sought during such gatherings. Now he had to invite himself to join the clusters of men while they congregated to talk business and politics. The shift was subtle. A slightly turned shoulder or a glance in the other direction was all it took to send a clear message.

Luke didn't care. If he couldn't regain his political footing, he was going to lose the next election, and that was unthinkable. Besides, if he returned upstairs to his hotel room, he'd be treated to an arctic blast from Philip, who still hadn't forgiven him for the paintbrushes.

Luke spotted Representative Steiner standing before the fireplace, talking to a group of congressmen. There was a time when Steiner had fervently courted Luke's time and attention. Now he barely met Luke's eyes before turning back to the men to recount the tale of a rogue wood quail that had built a nest on Farragut Square. There was great debate in the neighborhood about what was to be done about their new resident.

"I was for making a meal out of it, but she kept laying eggs. Four, six, eight . . ."

It would be nice if these men cared more about tariffs and the poor rather than a single quail, but Steiner held the group spellbound.

"That bird ended up laying sixteen eggs!" Steiner chortled, still keeping his shoulder to Luke.

"Perhaps we should notify the Smithsonian," Luke said. "Anything that can seize the attention of half a dozen congressmen is worthy of note."

"All very well for you, Callahan," a congressman from Philadelphia said. "The wilds of Maine are probably flooded with quail eggs ripe for the picking, and fruit growing on every tree. A veritable Eden on earth."

Not quite. Because of this new tariff, it was full of logging companies that would be scaling back production, and lumberjacks without enough work to earn a living.

A movement from the corner of his eye caught his attention. Amid the silk dresses and fine black dinner jackets was a woman draped in a plain brown coat. He couldn't see her face, but her narrow frame and the way she flitted through the crowd reminded him of Anna O'Brien. He leaned back, cocking his head to peer through the crowd, following the diminutive figure as she headed toward the front desk.

It was Anna. No doubt. Without a backward glance he left the discussion of Steiner's prolific wood quail and strode to the front desk.

"I understand he lives here," Anna was saying. "Can I send a message to him?"

Luke clenched his teeth. For an unmarried woman to approach a hotel clerk and inquire about a male guest at this hour of the night wasn't seemly.

"I'll take care of this, Mr. Grenville," Luke said to the desk clerk. Anna whirled around, relief shining in her eyes.

"Luke! Thank heavens . . ."

When she looked at him like that, every logical thought left his brain. It had been several weeks since he'd laid eyes on her, but now every ounce of those inconvenient emotions shot to the surface. He grasped both her elbows, looking deeply into her face. He had to fight the impulse not to drag her into his arms.

"What's wrong?" he asked.

"I need help."

He didn't care if she asked him to fetch pearls from the bottom of the sea. Whatever she needed, he was going to do it for her. By heaven, he missed her. He hadn't realized how much until he heard that warm, throaty voice and saw the kindness in her eyes.

"You look like you're freezing," he said. "Come on, let's get out of here." The breakfast room was closed, but he'd never been very good about following rules. No one paid them any mind as he guided Anna inside. The tables were covered in white linen and set for the next morning's meal, with china and water goblets glimmering softly in the darkness. Only a little moonlight filtered through the tall windows, and the potted palms loomed over them like silent sentinels.

"Are we allowed to be in here?" Anna whispered.

"It's all right," he assured her. He guided Anna to a chair, then stepped outside to summon a waiter. "Bring us something to drink and a few candles, please," he said quietly. If nothing else, it would give him something to concentrate on rather than look at the gratitude in her eyes. In the wake of his grief over Jason's death, he'd tried to let his feelings for Anna lie dormant while he healed, but everything had come roaring back to life the moment he was in her presence again.

He returned to sit beside her at the table, noticing a strange brass contraption clenched in her hands.

"What in heaven's name is *that*?"

Anna picked up the slim tube, a grin dissolving the worry on her face. She pressed a button, and a beam of bright light cut through the darkness. He almost fell off his chair.

"It's called a flashlight," she said. "Neville just signed off on the patent, and he let me have the prototype. It runs on a dry-cell battery. Neville says it's a unique invention because it holds a steady beam of light and can operate when held at any angle. Watch this." She twirled the brass tube around, the light bouncing off the ceiling, the plants, and the windows.

"For pity's sake," he muttered. Would Anna's bizarre fascination with technology forever prompt her to latch on to silly machines of no practical value?

"Wait, you have to see this!" She propped the flashlight beneath her chin, rolled her eyes, and contorted her face as the beam of light cast ghoulish shadows upward on her face.

"I'm doomed," he said.

She turned the flashlight off. "You don't really think that, do you?"

Looking into her eyes, hearing her alluring voice . . . oh yes, he was doomed. He wanted to pull her into his arms and shower her face with kisses, but the waiter returned with a pitcher of water and a couple of candles.

"Put that monstrosity away," he said as soon as the waiter left. He lit the candles, trying not to smile at the memory of her ridiculous face playing in the beam of light. "Isn't this nicer than your fancy mechanical light?" he asked. The warmth of candlelight illuminated the room with a soothing glow.

"It's old-fashioned, but yes, much nicer," Anna agreed.

Just the sight of her was enough to send Luke plummeting into hopeless infatuation, and that was the last thing he needed. He needed to solve Anna's problem and send her away before she broke his heart again. Unless her craving for a safe and predictable life had changed, they were destined to repeat the same difficulties as last autumn.

"Now," he said, "tell me how I can help."

"I've heard back from the Zanettis," she began, handing him the telegram.

In the cascade of tragedies over the past month, her farfetched quest had entirely slipped his mind. "And?"

"The signature indicates they are my dear friends, but I've never met a John or Maria Smith in my life. It was a very carefully worded telegram, and it confirms that Silas Zanetti is still alive and hiding under a fake name."

Luke read the wrinkled telegram, baffled by the terse message.

Could she have been right all along? It seemed impossible, yet it appeared Silas Zanetti had miraculously survived whatever happened to the *Culpeper*. Maybe his theory about a mutiny wasn't so outlandish after all.

Luke clutched the arms of his chair but kept his expression neutral. The memory of the old diplomat's words rang in his ears. Jeremiah Hammond had been certain he saw the *Culpeper* two years after it supposedly sank, repainted and renamed, in the bay of Manila. Luke had dismissed it. It was easy to claim he was trying to protect Anna from the failing memory of a ninety-year-old man, but he should have told her. She deserved to know what he'd found, and he covered it up because he thought she'd be better off consigning this to her past.

A headache began pounding, and Luke rubbed the skin between his eyes. This was the last thing he needed. He had no formal power in Congress anymore and a dwindling list of people who owed him a favor. Did he really want to expend his paltry political capital helping a woman who wanted nothing to do with him? For whatever reason, the navy wanted to keep this quiet. The thin ice he was standing on was likely to crack wide open if he dared to take on the navy.

He hadn't actually lied to Anna, though he did commit the sin of omission when he withheld the ramblings of the diplomat who swore the *Culpeper* still sailed. That sin of omission plagued him. Honesty came in shades of black and white, and he'd never had problems distinguishing them before.

However awkward, he owed her the truth. "I have something to confess, Anna."

He couldn't look at her as he recounted his meeting with the diplomat. She listened silently, not moving a muscle as he spoke in the deserted breakfast room.

"I'm sorry," Luke said after he'd finished delivering the story, bracing himself for a hearty crack of her hand across his cheek. He deserved no less.

"It's okay," she said.

He blinked, not quite certain she understood the magnitude of what he'd hidden from her.

She smiled as she continued, "In light of Mr. Hammond's dinner with Thomas Jefferson, most logical people would have done the same. Who could have possibly guessed the *Culpeper* was still sailing? I can't blame you for guessing wrong."

Relief he didn't deserve trickled through him. "I missed you," he said.

She nodded, then asked, "Why?"

Because he needed her good sense and kindness, her boundless optimism. He needed to be inspired by her soaring dreams and amused by her eccentricities. He wanted to babble about literature and poetry until the sun rose in the morning. Instead, he looked her in the eye and told her the truth. "Because I love you and I made a mistake by walking away last December."

She opened her mouth, but no sound came . . . only a squeak.

"Does that surprise you?" he asked.

"Yes," she stammered. "Actually, it does." She reached for a glass of water and took a long drink. Even after setting the glass down, she kept her eyes averted from him, twirling the glass with nervous fingers. "I thought you hated me," she finally said. "For what I did to your brother. If we had never met—"

"Anna, no. Jason did it to himself. You tried to show him compassion, nothing less. I love you for it." It humbled him to see the relief and joy that lit her face. He reached across the table to take her hands in his. "You've always shied away from me in the past, but Anna . . . I wish I had the words to explain what you mean to me."

"Try," Anna said, a hint of mischief lighting her eyes. "I've always wanted to hear a little of your poetry."

Was she finally ready to welcome his suit? He'd shout and swing from the rafters if that were true.

He pulled his chair closer, until their knees bumped and their noses were only inches from each other. "My dearest Anna," he whispered tenderly as he cupped the side of her face. "If you read my poetry, you'd howl and flee to the other side of the country to escape it." A soft smile hovered on his mouth as he leaned down to kiss her.

She kissed him back.

"Do you still have my key ring?" he murmured against her lips.

She nodded, pointing to her hip, where the precious gemstone lay beneath the folds of her skirt.

"Good," he said.

The next few hours would be forever branded on his soul as they clasped each other's hands and talked about everything from music to ancient mythology to the meals served in the Capitol's lunchroom. She told him about Mr. Spofford's return to the library and of Neville's impending marriage. He told of his sister, Julia, and the terrific scandal she had caused by giving birth out of wedlock. Luke confessed his shameful loss of temper when he burned Philip's paintbrushes.

"I sounded exactly like my father that night," he said. "I've never been ashamed of anything so much as when I flung those paintbrushes into the fire. I had once been battered and abused, and now I had become the batterer. In that instant I was truly Edgar Callahan's son."

The words were thick and bitter in his mouth, and Anna said nothing as she leaned in to place a gentle kiss on his forehead. Her lips were cool on his heated skin, her face gentle when she broke the kiss and leaned back.

"You need to forgive your father," she said.

"He doesn't deserve it. He was never sorry for anything—"

"Then don't forgive him because he deserves it, but because *you can*." Her voice was tender but firm as she held his hands. "Luke, your father was broken. He didn't have the strength or the wisdom to overcome his weaknesses, but you do. Don't let him defeat you. Unresolved anger will poison your body and soul, unless you quit giving it the power to hurt you. Jesus asked us to forgive our enemies, and that alone is a good enough reason to try, even if your father doesn't deserve it."

With their hands still clasped, she leaned down to kiss his fingers. "Try, Luke. Trust that Jesus was giving us wise counsel when He bid us to love one another, even those who have sinned against you. When your anger wells up, try to remember the loving forgiveness that has been extended to us all, and follow His example."

She staggered him. From the moment he'd met her and she'd whispered that clever reprimand in his ear, Anna had amused, dazzled, and humbled him. And he knew in that instant that he wanted to marry her. No matter what it took to convince her they belonged together, he wanted this woman in his life.

Anna felt like she was living in a dream. She had just spent the most magical few hours of her life with a man who had managed to slip beneath every one of her defenses and imprint himself on her soul.

The candles had burned down to nubs hours ago, finally sputtering out with wisps of smoke curling through the air. Moonlight streamed in through the Palladian windows, illuminating the room in a silvery glow. She teased Luke by threatening to turn on her portable flashlight, but didn't really mean it. The moonlight was too beautiful to spoil with the glare of man-made light.

It was almost four o'clock in the morning and she still hadn't gotten around to asking Luke for the favor she needed. Pressure built inside her chest. She wasn't used to asking for help, yet at this moment—this perfect moonlit moment—she felt like she had a friend whose strength of character would help her face down whatever dark forces were gathering against her.

"I need help," she finally said. "I don't understand Mrs. Zanetti's warning or what I've gotten myself into, but I can't turn back now. I need to know what happened to my father. Is there anything you can do?"

"I would do anything in the world for you," he said. He leaned closer until his forehead touched hers. "I'm glad you came to me. I want to be the one you lean on when you need help. The one you can trust."

He kissed her again, and joy surged through her, for she *did* trust him, flashy cuff links and all. They were as mismatched as a diamond and a lump of coal, but regardless they were perfect together. She had never, not for a single moment, pretended to be anyone other than exactly who she was, and this stunning man still adored her.

He broke the kiss. "First thing in the morning I'll start calling in whatever favors I have left to figure out what happened to that ship."

"Thank you," she whispered.

Luke reached over to tuck a strand of hair behind her ear. "I don't want this evening to end."

She agreed. At this precise moment, everything in her life seemed perfect. She wished it were possible to freeze this moment in time and live in it forever.

"I should probably get home," she said slowly.

Luke seemed reluctant, but nodded.

She waited in the empty breakfast room while he made the arrangements for a carriage to drive her home. Without his warmth, the room was cold and vacant. Even the ordinary noises of the building settling were worrisome, but it must just be her paranoia setting in again. The sun would be rising soon, and exhaustion would set in quickly without Luke there to electrify her world.

Luke returned and helped her into her coat. "The carriage is being brought around now. It would be best for your reputation if you weren't seen walking out with me, so we need to say goodbye here."

She nodded, already feeling the magic of the evening slipping away. "What happens now?"

His teeth flashed white in the dimness. "That's up to you, O'Brien. The whole *coup de foudre* that clobbered me last autumn . . ."

The strike of lightning. Love at first sight. Was such a thing really possible? Her hands tightened around his. "Still there?"

"Still there," he confirmed.

His voice sounded confident, but she saw hesitation in his eyes. They had already walked away from the attraction that hummed between them once before, which now seemed like a lifetime ago.

"I think I glimpsed a flash of lightning this evening," she whispered.

His eyes gleamed, and he stepped closer, pulling her against him. "Anna, there's *nothing* standing between us. I know you worry that you won't fit into my world, but I will make a place for you. Whatever you want. If you want to keep working at the Library of Congress, I'll browbeat the director into changing that stupid rule about married women. If you want to quit and write your book, I'll do everything humanly possible to help you. If you want to stay home and knit booties like the president's wife, that's fine too. All I know is that I want you by my side. Shoulder to shoulder. We belong together."

As she curled into the velvet-lined carriage, she replayed the memories of the past few hours. It was time to stop defining herself by the taunts of her childhood that made her believe she didn't deserve a man like Luke Callahan. His opinion mattered far more than the cruel girls who'd tried to convince her she would never amount to much.

Because whatever her flaws—and they were numerous—she fit like a puzzle piece alongside Luke Callahan. For the first time in her life, remaining safely ensconced in the upper floors of the library was not as appealing as stepping out into the world alongside a man who sparkled with gemstones and laughed in the face of danger.

After a morning of pounding on doors at the Capitol, Luke headed to the Library of Congress on Monday to tell Anna of his plans. For once, the sight of the solid bronze doors and gold-leaf ornamentation didn't irk him as he vaulted up the stairs. His heart picked up speed when he saw Anna bent over a six-foot map, taking notes on a pad of paper.

"I'm meeting with the secretary of the navy at four o'clock," he said.

She nearly dropped the notepad as his voice broke the silence in the map room, but the smile that blazed across her face could have ignited the room. It made him feel like a hero out of the old legends.

"How did you get an appointment so quickly?"

"I'm a very powerful man," he said, sauntering forward and tugging her into an embrace. "You should be glad I'm on your side," he whispered into her ear.

"I *am* grateful," she said with a smothered laugh, "but that door is open, and your hands are traveling in an unseemly direction. Stop that . . ." She swatted at his hands, but was laughing and didn't try very hard.

"What would happen if I pulled you behind that row of bookshelves and kissed you silly?"

"I'd get fired if anyone saw us."

"What if I told them we were getting married?"

"I'd say you were rushing things." But she was still smiling and didn't try to pull away from him. He pulled her behind the aisle of books anyway. The moment they were out of sight, he cupped her face in his hands and kissed her.

"I'm glad you came to me the other night," he whispered.

Her eyes twinkled. "That sounded a little naughtier than it actually was."

"I suppose it did." He was still smiling like an idiot as he kissed her again. "No matter what I find out this afternoon, I want to marry you, Anna. We're stronger together than apart. You know that, don't you?"

In response, she stood on tiptoe and kissed him back.

"I'll meet you here at five o'clock," he said, holding her hands to his chest. "Maybe a little later if the streetcars are packed, but wait for me here." It was hard to drag himself away.

Soon he was approaching the ornate office outside the navy's wing in the War Building. The secretary's man of business informed him of the bad news.

"I'm sorry, sir, but Secretary Long is unable to meet with you. However, the assistant secretary of the navy is ready to accept the appointment."

Luke sighed, but then thought maybe this was for the best. Rumor claimed Secretary Long was merely a figurehead and the real power in the navy rested with his ambitious assistant. Nevertheless, Luke wouldn't allow the assistant secretary to pawn off the ridiculous smoke screen about Admiral Channing's reputation.

Luke entered the assistant secretary's richly appointed office, noting the young man's strong build, his broad smile and white teeth. He rose from behind the polished mahogany desk, offering his hand.

"Thank you for seeing me, Mr. Roosevelt," Luke said.

Theodore Roosevelt was brand-new in Washington. After a brief whirlwind career in New York, he'd been appointed the assistant secretary of the navy only a year ago, but was already putting his stamp on the navy.

"Glad to be of service," Mr. Roosevelt said, then gestured to the chairs behind Luke. "I've asked a few others to attend the meeting."

Luke turned and was stunned to see the thin, withered figure of the Speaker of the House perched in the corner, a curl of smoke rising from his ever-present cigarette.

"Speaker Jones," Luke said tightly. The skin around Cornelius Jones's mouth tightened, and there was the strangest expression in his eyes, almost as though he were afraid.

To the left of Speaker Jones, a tall man with a cleft chin and perfect posture rose and offered his hand. "Admiral James Channing," he said, introducing himself. "I'm pleased to make your acquaintance, and I hope we can make progress on this whole *Culpeper* business."

Were they really going to trot the admiral out to accept responsibility for a shoddy report? Something much bigger was going on here.

There was a knock on the door, and the clerk stepped inside. "The president has arrived, sir."

Luke held his breath as William McKinley, followed by a few men of his guard, stepped into the office. Luke looked around at the men in the room in bewilderment. Despite the grin on the assistant secretary's face, the air crackled with tension.

"Close the door, Mr. Callahan," Theodore Roosevelt said. "We've got business to discuss."

18

The first thing Anna saw when she entered the map room following her lunch break was Jack Wilkerson slumped in the chair beside her desk. It looked as if the fifteen-year-old boy had been crying. "What's wrong, Jack?" she asked, settling into her chair.

"I got caught putting a derby hat on the Neptune statue outside. I didn't hurt anything, but Mr. Young is snapping mad about it."

"Oh my," Anna said, trying not to smile. The fountain in front of the library had a large sculpture of Neptune at its center. It would have required a healthy dose of courage for Jack to navigate through the spectacular fountain with its shooting streams of water to reach Neptune's head, and Anna secretly wished she could have seen the mighty Roman god wearing the derby.

"I've never been yelled at like that before," Jack said, his lower lip starting to wobble.

"I've groused at you dozens of times," Anna said. "It never seemed to bother you much."

"Yeah, but I'm not afraid of you. Mr. Young is a different

story. He yelled so loud it echoed all over the building, and he said I'm banned from the library for good. I shouldn't even be here, but I needed someone to talk to."

There was nothing Anna loathed more than shouting voices, but sometimes a man's bark was worse than his bite. "The man who owns the boardinghouse where I live is famous for his outbursts. I remember when Mr. O'Grady hollered at his wife because she overpaid for a crate of rhubarb. He yelled until he was blue in the face, but his wife wouldn't back down. She went right ahead and made a dozen rhubarb pies, and then wouldn't let him have any until he apologized. By the end of the day they were friends again." She paused a moment, allowing space for her words to sink in before continuing. "Wait a few days for Mr. Young's ire to simmer down. He's more likely to forgive you if he believes you're truly sorry. Only you can convince him if you deserve a second chance."

Although she doubted it would happen. Mr. Young seemed so formal and stiff, and nothing was quite the same since he'd taken over administration of the library.

After Jack left, Anna tried to concentrate on the railroad maps, but the extraordinary events of her evening with Luke kept distracting her. It made her realize how lonely she'd been all these years. Her friendship with Neville had helped to mask her isolation, though it was no replacement for the warmth and intimacy of what she had with Luke.

She'd never seriously considered the possibility that she would get married and share her life with a man. Now she could think of nothing else. She would have to leave the library, but Luke would be worth it. Maybe there would even be children. Her heart sped up at the prospect.

Luke would be an amazing father—passionate and gregarious and fun. She would have to be the sensible one. But between the two of them, they would be the finest of parents. She wished five o'clock would hurry and get here so she could see him again. Of course, she wanted to learn about the *Culpeper*, but she was just as anxious to savor his easy grin and maybe let him kiss her again.

Five o'clock came and went. She spent the extra time making a list of cartographers who deserved to be included in her biography. If she got married, she'd have a chance to finally begin her book.

By six o'clock she was getting hungry, but she didn't dare leave in case she missed Luke. After all, the meeting could have run late or the streetcars could be slow due to icy conditions. It was almost half past six when a congressional page stepped into the map room, an envelope in his hand.

"Mr. Callahan said he can't come today, but he sent this."

Anna tried not to let the disappointment show as she popped the seal on the envelope and read the brief note inside.

Anna: After this afternoon's meeting, I believe the navy's actions all stem from the need to cover up Admiral Channing's careless report of 1882, nothing more.

Luke

The letter fell from her hands.

Unbelievable. How could Luke write this message in light of what he knew about Silas Zanetti? And what the old diplomat said? Perhaps he didn't feel comfortable putting anything more insightful in a letter, so she would simply have to be patient and await further information. There was no point lingering at the library any longer.

The first thing the next morning, she rushed to the Willard Hotel to intercept Luke before he left for work. The clerk at the front desk told her that Mr. Callahan had left for Capitol Hill before dawn. Not to be deterred, Anna sent a message to Luke at the Capitol, asking that he visit her at the library as soon as possible.

She reported to the map room, breathless and only a few minutes late. Each time someone walked past the open door, she whirled around like an idiot, yet lunchtime came and went and still there was no sign of Luke. She spent the afternoon trying to answer questions about shipping lanes along the Saint Lawrence River, her concentration all but shattered. Why hadn't Luke at least sent another note if he couldn't come in person? At the end of the workday she remained in the map room for an hour in case he came. For a man who had been stripped of his congressional responsibilities, he seemed quite busy all of a sudden.

No message was waiting for her at the boardinghouse, and the next day passed without her hearing anything from Luke. Twice she had succumbed to curiosity and went to the Capitol to see him in person, but those annoying guards never let her near the congressional retiring rooms. One would think they were guarding the crown jewels the way they jerked to attention the moment a peasant like her tried to communicate with a congressman. She sent additional messages to Luke, but received no response back. It was bewildering.

And a little hurtful. She had no experience with romantic relationships, so perhaps her expectations of Luke were too high, but something didn't feel right and she didn't know what to make of it.

On Thursday, a large envelope was delivered to her in the map room. Her breath caught, certain it was a reply from Luke, until she noticed the return address printed in the upper corner.

Neville.

She tamped down her disappointment and opened the envelope, only to find a section of the *Washington Post* inside. Neville always teased her for never reading the current news, and she wondered what he wanted her to read now. She squinted at the note he'd written in the margin: *See the bottom of page 3.*

She flipped the pages, then sucked in a breath when her eyes landed on the story on page three. The headline read *Lucas Callahan of Maine Reappointed to House Budget Committee.*

A smile spread across her face as her chest swelled with pride. He did it! No wonder Luke had been too busy to see her. Somehow he'd either mended fences with the Speaker of the House or figured out a way to win his old appointment back. Either way, this was a huge boon to Luke's career. She skimmed the short article quickly. No additional details were given about why Luke had been reappointed to the most prestigious committee in Washington; it merely noted that his service was to begin immediately.

It would have been nice to hear the news from Luke himself. He'd shared so much with her that it seemed strangely impersonal to read about this in the newspaper.

She folded the page, sliding it into her top desk drawer. Perhaps now that he'd regained his leverage in the House, he would have time to see her. Memory of his moonlit face, carved in shadow, rose before her.

"I would do anything in the world for you," he'd said in a voice full of longing.

She had to believe that. Luke Callahan might be the only truly honest politician in Washington, and she trusted he would come through for her.

Anna finally received a note from Luke on Friday. It was a hastily scribbled paragraph, acknowledging that he'd gotten her messages and apologizing for being too busy to see her. He suggested his calendar would permit him more free time by early April and asked for her patience.

April? It was only the beginning of February! He needed two months before he could spare a few minutes for her? She wanted to be understanding, but this note was a slap in the face. After their night in the moonlit breakfast room, it felt like he'd leap across oceans to see her.

Anna didn't care if she was risking her job. She needed to see him. Congress was in session today, and the only way she'd see Luke was from a seat in the gallery above the House chambers, but it was better than nothing.

The session had already begun. Anna tried to be quiet as she slid into one of the squeaky seats in the gallery overlooking the floor of Congress. She braced her arms on the railing to look down at the hundreds of men milling about. In the front, three tiers led up to where the Speaker of the House sat. Cornelius Jones looked bored while a congressman droned on about the endangered white ibis bird. She scanned the crowd looking for Luke among the hundreds of men seated in the semicircle below her, not quite certain what she'd do when she spotted him. She could hardly call out to him, but if he saw her here, at least he might stop ignoring her.

A door opened on the opposite side of the room, and she was relieved to see Luke finally arrive, striding down an aisle with the self-confidence she always found so attractive. He darted up the steps toward the Speaker's rostrum, and Anna held her breath. There was no love lost between these two men, and she worried Luke was about to do something rash.

Instead, he hunkered down beside Speaker Jones to confer in a relaxed, casual demeanor. Speaker Jones didn't seem surprised as he leaned in to listen to whatever Luke was whispering.

The two of them seemed quite cozy up there, ignoring the business on the floor, swapping stories. A fleeting smile passed Speaker Jones's lips, and he clapped Luke on the back. Luke smiled back.

Anna leaned forward over the balcony to gain a better view. The tight camaraderie between Luke and his sworn enemy was simply stunning. Luke had a spring in his step as he walked back to his seat on the House floor.

"Luke!" she blurted, surprising even herself. He glanced up and saw her.

His smile vanished, and the color drained from his face. He looked away, swiveling so she could no longer see his face. He took a seat at his desk, his back to her.

Speaker Jones banged his gavel and called the House to order. "I have an announcement before adjourning for lunch. President McKinley has appointed me to chair a special committee on matters of pressing international affairs. I have selected Mr. Callahan of Maine to co-chair. A list of additional members will be posted in the *Congressional Record*. We will report directly to the president." He banged the gavel again. "No further business."

Anna bolted from her chair, angling sideways to move ahead of other spectators. She had to get down two flights of stairs to intercept Luke before he could flee to the safety of the congressional retiring rooms.

Luke's star certainly seemed to be rising on Capitol Hill, and perhaps he no longer had time for the librarian he'd been friendly with during his political exile. But he'd promised her an honest effort to discover what had happened to the *Culpeper*, and he hadn't delivered on that promise yet.

She nudged through the crowd, weaving around the broad-shouldered men as she hurried toward the hall of representatives. She spotted him as he left the chamber.

"Luke!" His step quickened as he headed toward the east wing. She reached out to grab his elbow just before he passed into the private corridor. The guards stepped forward and began pushing her back.

She wouldn't let go. "Luke, what happened to the *Culpeper*?"

"Stop it," Luke ordered firmly. She couldn't tell if he was speaking to her or to the guards. The guards paused and looked to Luke for instruction. "Let her through," he said.

The guards stepped back, and Luke directed her down the gold and ivory corridor. His demeanor was baffling . . . he'd never been so cold to her before. How was she supposed to respond to this terse, aloof man?

Luke's back was stiff as she trailed after him, and he stared straight ahead. The halls back here were almost empty. Anna had worked in the Capitol for six years, but had never been in the private wings for elected officials.

At last he opened a door and gestured her inside a dimly lit cloakroom, with rows of coats and hats and scarves dominating the space. An elderly clerk behind the coat-check counter looked up the moment they stepped inside.

"If you don't mind, Jacob," Luke said, "I need a few minutes of privacy."

"Certainly, sir." The man stepped around the counter, exiting the cloakroom and quietly closing the door behind him.

Luke peered down the four rows of coats to be certain they were alone.

"Well?" Anna said. "Were you planning on telling me anything more than the little note you sent the other day?"

"Anna, I'm sorry, but I've been very busy. I tried to get more information about the *Culpeper*, but didn't learn anything different from before." It was warm in the small room, and Luke tugged on the collar of his shirt, careful to avoid looking at her in the eyes. He glanced at the coats, the room's single window, anywhere but at her face.

"I don't believe you," she said.

"It's the truth."

"Why were you put back on the House Budget Committee? Cornelius Jones hates you."

He shrugged. "It's just politics, Anna. Stranger things have happened."

"Yes, like the *Culpeper*'s chief petty officer turning up alive and well in Canada."

A flush stained Luke's cheeks, and he took a step back. "Anna, I didn't want to tell you this, but Admiral Channing was at the meeting the other day, and he said Silas Zanetti had been ordered off the ship for insubordination one week before the hurricane. It was either that or face a court-martial back home."

"Insubordination? Silas Zanetti was an easygoing man, not a hothead who couldn't follow orders."

"You were only twelve years old. You didn't really know him. It turned out that being put off the ship was what saved Silas Zanetti's life. The ship sank, Anna."

Something was wrong. Four months ago, Luke had been stripped of political power and ritually humiliated by Speaker Jones. Now that same archenemy gave Luke his seat back on the House Budget Committee, plus an appointment on a special committee reporting directly to the president?

"What about what the old diplomat said?" she challenged.

"You mean the one who had dinner with Thomas Jefferson? That old diplomat?"

"You're lying to me."

His eyes turned flinty. "Anna, you don't know what you're talking about."

"I know that you've despised Cornelius Jones from the moment you arrived in Washington. Now you're sprinkling rose petals in his path."

His jaw clenched, and he turned away and began pacing in the cramped cloakroom. "I sent you a note asking for your patience," he said tightly. "I'm sorry we can't spend more time together, but I'm serving on a demanding committee and I'm asking for a little time. I have important responsibilities to deal with right now, and it would be selfish to get distracted by a romantic relationship. In a few months' time, perhaps that can change. Please try to understand."

"I understand that you know what happened to the *Culpeper* and are covering it up."

He stopped pacing and turned to look at her. "Are you ever going to be able to get the *Culpeper* out of your head? I want us to have a future someday, but that's impossible if you keep up with this obsession."

"I'll never give up until you tell me what you know."

He closed his eyes, and the way his shoulders sagged made him look twenty years older in the space of a few seconds. He swallowed and gathered a breath. "Anna, it's ancient history. It doesn't matter anymore. Please, just let this go. I've told you what I know and I don't see how we can ever be together if you keep accusing me of lying."

"But you *are* lying. You sold your soul to get back on that committee, and for what? To lick the boots of Cornelius Jones? Tell me what happened to the *Culpeper.*"

He moved closer, and she instinctively backed up, bumping into a row of coats. "I'm fighting for the most important cause of my life," he bit out. "If that means cooperating with Cornelius Jones to get things done, that's what I'll do. And I don't have to answer to you about that." His hands were balled into fists, and he struggled to control his breathing. "I'll ask you again.

Are you going to be able to forget the *Culpeper* and move on with the rest of your life? I need to know."

"I won't ever forget it. It taught me a lesson about who you really are, and how am I supposed to forget *that*? The man who couldn't become the world's greatest poet decided to crawl to the top by becoming the world's best bootlicker."

The barb struck home. Luke whirled around and gave the wall a good hard kick.

Anna flinched, but tried to keep her voice steady in response. "Charming, Luke," she said, her tone dripping with scorn. "The whole nation is safer because such a fine, rational man has won his precious appointment back."

She retreated closer to the door. She would only flee if he dared to raise a hand to her, for she had quit running from bullies long ago. "Look me in the eyes and tell me the *Culpeper* sank just like the navy said. You can't."

Luke met her eyes. They were smoldering with anger, and something else she couldn't place. She blinked back tears. The man who swore he would never lie, no matter what the cost, was now a lying bully.

"Anna, your father died in 1882. If you believe nothing else, believe that."

"You're just saying that so I'll give up. I know that report is wrong and I want it corrected."

"That will never happen." His voice lashed out like a whip, and it frightened her. "You have no idea what you're dealing with, and if you don't stop this, they will squash you like a bug beneath their heel. Do you understand me? You need to stop this."

He brushed past her and out of the cloakroom, but she followed him into the hallway.

"What about my father's letter?" she called.

He froze, then spun to look at her. "What letter?"

She walked to him, maintaining eye contact until she stood only inches away. "My father sent me a letter the week before the hurricane. He was in Cuba. I've still got that letter, and it's proof the navy is lying."

His jaw tightened. Voices and footsteps from the rotunda echoed down the hallway, yet it seemed as if they were the only two people in the world. "I see," he finally said.

How could she have let herself get close to a man who could flip on her like this? "I've been alone most of my life because I'm the only person in the world I can rely on. For a few days I deluded myself into thinking you were someone I could believe in. That I could trust you and lean on you, that you would never lie to me. What a mistake I made."

Luke turned away from her, but the longing that flashed across his face nearly drove the strength from her knees.

"Come with me," he said.

Anticipation built as she followed him down the corridor toward the rotunda. She prayed he had some reasonable explanation for his behavior and would hold her and tell her how foolish she'd been for doubting him even for a second. The voices from the rotunda grew louder as they approached the main hall, where the guards standing at attention in the doorway looked to Luke for instructions.

"Please escort Miss O'Brien back to the Library of Congress," he said. "And don't let her back here again."

Luke was shaking as he walked away from Anna. He hated liars. He hated bullies. And now he was both, and to a woman who deserved only his admiration and protection.

When he'd arrived in Washington, he'd vowed he would always tell the truth, but that was before he'd walked into a private meeting with the highest officials in the nation and learned that things weren't always so simple. That the truth shouldn't always be paraded for the world to see. That some secrets needed to stay safely hidden and consigned to the past.

He'd been richly rewarded for agreeing to keep one of those secrets, just as Anna had accused. Luke would have kept quiet about the *Culpeper* even without the reappointment to the committee, but when it was offered, he took it.

Cornelius Jones waited for him around a corner near the alcove, his face calm. "It had to be done," Jones said. "Come on, let's go have a smoke."

Luke followed Speaker Jones into the congressional retiring room, which was packed with men lounging between sessions. Curious eyes scrutinized him and the Speaker as they walked through the double French doors onto a private balcony. Anna wasn't the only person bewildered by the sudden turn in his relationship with the Speaker. Everyone was commenting on the strange alliance, but Luke had no intention of shedding any light on it.

It was chilly on the balcony overlooking the manicured grounds of the Capitol, now crisp and yellow in the bleak February light. Jones reached into his coat pocket for some wrapping papers, a sack of tobacco, and a box of matches.

"Cigarette?" he asked. Luke shook his head. Jones moved to the balustrade to set out the wrapping paper and tap a narrow line of loose tobacco onto the paper.

"I disliked you from the moment you arrived in Washington," Jones said in a casual voice as he methodically rolled the cigarette with practiced tobacco-stained fingers. "I thought you were hotheaded, arrogant, and stubborn. And an insufferable prude about smoking and drinking."

Luke said nothing but struck a match as Cornelius leaned forward to accept the light. He took a long pull on the cigarette, then tilted his head to release the smoke into the air.

"Now I believe that hostility was a blessing," the Speaker continued. "If two men from different sides of the House, total opposites in all things, can come together for a higher cause, perhaps we will be able to persuade others to follow us. It's our only hope."

Luke nodded, praying this unlikely alliance would work. What an odd twist of fate that the man he'd despised for so many years was now his tightest ally. After agreeing to drop the petty squabbles that separated them, Cornelius Jones was rapidly proving to be a mentor, a friend, and the father Luke had always wished he had.

Luke stepped forward and looked out at the horizon, the Washington Monument rising proudly at the far end of the Mall. While it'd been a privilege to serve in Washington, the truth was he'd run for Congress as an excuse to escape his family troubles at home, not for any noble reason. All that had changed. He now understood his life's mission, and it was more important than political squabbles or personal glory.

Or heaven help him, more important even than Anna O'Brien. Lying to her was a horrible thing to do, but he would take whatever action was necessary to steer his cause through to completion.

And that meant he had to stop Anna from ever learning what really happened to the *Culpeper*.

Anna would have broken down in tears if she wasn't so furious. For the first time since she was twelve years old, she wanted to curse and scream and hit another person. How could Luke betray her like this? Whatever happened to the *Culpeper* had to be important or he wouldn't have been showered with such high positions to keep silent. She spent the rest of the afternoon working on mundane questions in the map room. It looked like she was going to be a librarian for the rest of her life, and she would waste no more time daydreaming about marriage with Luke Callahan.

The scent of beef stew greeted her when she returned to the boardinghouse. She wasn't hungry, nor was she in the mood to make small talk with the women around the dining table. Walking down the dim corridor toward her room, she clutched Luke's tourmaline key ring, trying to ignore the squeezing in her heart. Women like her had no business with flashy gemstones. She'd get rid of it tonight and go back to her plain iron key ring.

Something was wrong with the doorknob to her room. Her key didn't insert into the lock properly. She pushed harder, and a bolt fell out of the knob, screws and pins scattering on the floor. She pushed the door open.

Oh, sweet heaven . . . It looked like a tornado had blown through her room. Her clothing was piled on the floor, books tossed about and splayed open, her bedding peeled back. The room had been ransacked.

She walked on shaky legs to her bed, sank down on her knees, and pulled the box from underneath the bed. It was so light she didn't even need to lift the lid to reveal the truth, but she did anyway. It was empty.

Luke had stolen her father's letters.

All the women at the boardinghouse expressed outrage at the plundering of her room. They came running when Anna staggered downstairs to alert Mrs. Horton that their room had been robbed. Most of the women went dashing to their own rooms to see if they had suffered a burglary as well, but they soon returned. Anna and Mrs. Horton's room was the only room plundered.

"We shall take a complete inventory of what has been stolen," Gertrude said, propping a pencil over a pad of paper. Despite their close scrutiny of the room, it appeared her father's letters were the only things missing. Mrs. Horton folded the clothes and restored the room to order while Anna sat limply on the bed, feeling like Luke had slapped her.

Had Luke personally ransacked her room or had he sent some anonymous henchman to do his dirty work? Not that it mattered. He had been the one to order it done, and that was all that ultimately mattered.

"Why would someone want your father's old letters?" Mrs. Horton asked.

All Anna could do was shrug. She couldn't tell anyone about her suspicions, for Luke's warning still echoed in her mind. *"If you don't stop this, they will squash you like a bug beneath their heel."* Everyone concluded it must have been young hoodlums out to make mischief. Mrs. Horton took it all in stride, but Anna was too upset to stay the night in her room. Grabbing what little cash she had, she fled to Neville's house.

She wasn't going to let Luke stomp on her. Mrs. Zanetti knew the truth, and if it took traveling up to the Yukon to drag it out of her, that's what Anna would do.

When Neville responded to her knock, she pled for the chance to speak with him privately. "It's about the *Culpeper*," she whispered. "It's important."

"Come on inside," Neville said. "I've already told Margaret everything about it."

Anna was appalled, while Neville only shrugged. "We're getting married," he explained. "Margaret and I don't hold secrets from each other. Married people tell each other everything."

"You're not married yet."

"We're going to be," he said. "And I can't wait."

The joy on Neville's face made Anna feel even lonelier. Still, the fact that he'd already blabbered about the *Culpeper* to Mrs. Norquist made it easier to sit in the kitchen and recount the recent events as the landlady prepared dinner. Neville sat beside Anna at the small table, slicing carrots and onions while Mrs. Norquist stood at the stove stirring a pot of Brunswick stew.

"If I go to Canada, I know Mrs. Zanetti will tell me what really happened," Anna said. "It's probably the only way I'll learn the truth."

"Be logical," Neville cautioned. "You'd have to quit your job to travel that far. You'll never find another position to compare with the Library of Congress."

"Probably not, but I'll lose my mind if I don't figure out what happened. I think there's a chance my father is still alive. I can't go through the rest of my life without knowing."

"How much will it cost to get there?" Mrs. Norquist asked, not looking up from her stew. Anna didn't know, but anticipation quickened her heartbeat when Neville and Mrs. Norquist exchanged looks.

"We've got the money, if you need it," Mrs. Norquist offered.

Anna's eyes widened in surprise. She didn't doubt that Mrs. Norquist wanted to see the back of her, but train fare to Canada would be steep and it wouldn't be a permanent solution to removing Anna from Neville's life. Anna would return to Washington in short order.

"I want to know the end of this story too," Mrs. Norquist admitted. She set the wooden spoon down to stare out the kitchen window, her stern features softening a bit. "It's like getting near the end of a great novel and not being able to read the last few pages."

And for the first time since learning of Neville's marriage, Anna caught a glimpse of why he was attracted to Mrs. Norquist. The woman's eyes shone in a way that was reminiscent of Neville himself. The same quirky humor, the same relentless curiosity.

"Let us know if you decide to go," Neville said. "We'll figure something out."

It was a tough decision. For six years Anna had defined herself as the map librarian at the Library of Congress. If that was lost . . . well, what else was there? She'd never be Luke Callahan's wife, or probably any other man's wife. Her one foray into a romantic relationship had showed her to be a disastrous judge of character.

That night she moved into a hotel. She couldn't bear to sleep in the room plundered by either Luke or one of the navy's thugs. Over the following days she wrestled endlessly with how to proceed. Quit her job and venture into the wilds of Canada? Or stay in the safety of her room on the top floor of the library and never learn the answer to the greatest mystery of her life. Through it all, a grinding sense of loss haunted her.

It was a physical ache that weighed on her heart, making it hard to breathe. She'd opened a piece of her soul and shared it with a man she thought she loved, and nothing would ever be quite the same. How could she have misjudged Luke so profoundly?

She visited the library's grand reading room each day to scan the Washington newspapers, looking for any mention of Luke Callahan. She skipped over the tedious stories about the unending squabbles between Spain and Cuba and went straight to the social pages, which made a regular feast of political high society. Apparently, Luke was flying with a very exalted crowd these days. He'd been to dinner at the White House. He'd dined at the home of his former archenemy, Speaker Cornelius Jones. He'd even escorted Speaker Jones's unmarried granddaughter to the opera.

Charming. Absolutely, positively charming. Anna wondered if steam was coming out of her ears. It wasn't that she was jealous. No, she was just furious and hurt, and she hoped Cornelius Jones's granddaughter was as homely as a mule.

Luke never visited the Library of Congress anymore. The man who had once whiled away his lunch hour with books of romantic poetry now had better things to do with his time. She stomped all the way back upstairs to the map room.

She had to know what had happened to the *Culpeper*. This howling ache could no longer be ignored. There was a chance her father was still alive, and she needed to find him. At the very least, she would make contact with Mrs. Zanetti and learn the truth of what happened, and she didn't trust the US Postal Service or the telegraph system to allow that contact to happen. That meant she had to go to the Yukon.

She used her lunch hour to trek to the Potomac train station. The clerk was a little put out at being asked to figure out the price of a ticket to the Yukon Territory, but Anna assured him she would wait while he calculated the cost. The train station wasn't heated, and she tugged the flaps of her coat together while the clerk paged through a series of schedules, making notes on a pad of paper as he calculated the fare. Her toes were freezing by the time he pushed the paper beneath the window to her.

She gasped at the figure. No matter, for she would find the money somehow. All her life Anna had sought out the answers to questions, and this was the biggest unsolved question of her life. She was going to find the answer, even if it meant traveling all the way to the Yukon Territory.

19

The pounding on her hotel room door awakened Anna from a deep slumber and made her shoot upright in bed. Someone was trying to break in to her room! She clutched the sheets to her chest, looking frantically in the dark for an escape. The flimsy doorknob twisted and shook as someone tried to force the door open, but thankfully the lock held.

"Anna, open the blasted door!"

It was Luke. She ought to be relieved, except that he sounded furious and it frightened her. He jerked the doorknob again, following it with more pounding.

"Anna! Open this door or I'm getting the Capitol police to haul you out of there."

Could he do that? She sidled up to the door, still flustered from the rude awakening. "Calm down," she said, trying not to let her voice tremble as badly as the rest of her body.

"Anna, I need you to open this door so I can talk some sense into that stubborn skull of yours. Apparently it's gotten so thick that common sense can't penetrate it, so I'm here to help you with that sorry condition."

Curiosity began to ease her nerves. She pulled on a dressing robe, clutching it to her throat, than yanked the door open. He glared daggers at her. Without asking permission he pushed his way inside and kicked the door shut.

"The Yukon Territory?" he bellowed, towering over her with scorn glittering in his eyes.

She raised her chin a notch. "I gather someone has been eavesdropping on me again."

"Someone has been eavesdropping on you since last October, when you sent that first letter to the navy."

In a strange way, it was comforting to know it hadn't all been her imagination. "It's none of your business if I want to travel to Canada. I haven't done anything wrong."

Luke grabbed her elbows, lifting her until her face was only inches from his. "You're playing with fire and you need to *stop*," he said, giving her a shake before letting her go.

She rubbed her arms and took a few quick steps back. "Yelling at me won't solve anything."

Luke drew a steadying breath. "If you don't stop, you're going to awaken a sleeping dragon, and I won't be able to protect you. You don't know what you're dealing with here."

"Then tell me."

"I can't."

Anna glared at him. "You lied to me about the *Culpeper*."

"Yes."

That surprised her, but she couldn't stop digging now. Not after she caught that hint of regret in his voice. "Why?"

"I can't tell you that."

"It appears Speaker Jones is very grateful for your newfound loyalty. Dinner at the White House, fancy committee appointments. Tell me, is his granddaughter pretty?"

"She's eight years old," he said flatly. He stalked over to the window to look outside with a stony expression. He braced his hand against the window frame, tension making the cords in his neck stand out. She waited for him to speak, but all she could hear was the rasp of his breathing.

"Cornelius Jones and I disagree on many things, but beneath the political disagreements, he's a good man. He's fighting for a noble cause, and I am his ally now." He turned to face her. "Do you understand? He and I are *united* now. This is the most important battle of my life and I can't let you interfere."

"Even if it means lying to my face."

"Yes." His eyes darkened, sympathy radiating from them. "I'm sorry, but yes." He leaned against the wall, crossing his arms and forcing himself to look her in the eye. "I wish I had never agreed to help you with the *Culpeper*. I wish I had never learned the truth. But, Anna, please believe me, the one thing I have not lied about is your father. He died in 1882."

His voice became soft as he spoke the words. Tears blurred her vision, because she believed him. The tiny flame of hope that her father might still be alive flickered out and died. Her bold, courageous father was never coming home. Her face crumpled, but she refused to give in to tears. This conversation was too important for her to lose her composure now.

"Tell me," she begged.

"Anna, you don't want to know. Please trust me on this."

"Too bad. I *need* to know."

He shook his head. "I was brought into confidence because the government wanted me to persuade you to let the *Culpeper* and her sailors rest in peace. Only harm can come from resurrecting the truth of what happened. And I wanted to protect you from the truth. But maybe once you know, you will agree to leave the story alone. Forget it for all time."

"Tell me," she repeated.

He glanced around her room—the rumpled bed, the stack of books on her bedside table. He crossed the room and turned the spines of the books toward him. He spotted a Bible at the bottom of the stack and pulled it free.

"Put your hand on this Bible and swear to me, and swear to God, that you will never tell another living soul what I am about to say."

Her eyes went wide, sensing she was on the verge of finally learning what had happened to her father.

"Anna, I'm warning you, this isn't an easy secret to carry. It will drag on your heart, and you'll want to shout it out to the world, but you can't. You can't tell *anyone*. Not Neville. Not your aunt. You can't write it in a book for posterity. This secret needs to be carried to your grave or I can't tell you."

She set her palm against the grainy leather cover of the Bible and looked him in the eyes. "I swear it."

For once, her voice sounded firm and clear, but Luke winced as though he'd hoped she wouldn't take him up on the offer. With great care he set the Bible back on the bedside table. He guided her to sit on the bed, then took both her hands within his own as he sat beside her.

"I wish there was something I could say to make this easier," he said as he gripped her hands. "The men of the *Culpeper* were executed by the Spanish army after they were caught running guns to rebels in Cuba."

The blood drained from Anna's face. "*No . . .*"

Over the next few minutes he filled her in on the tragic details. The *Culpeper*'s primary mission was to map the Caribbean Sea, but every few months they also delivered a shipload of guns to Cuban rebels. The United States quietly encouraged the revolutionary sentiment brewing in Cuba, hoping it would oust Spain from their last major foothold in this hemisphere.

The *Culpeper* made numerous drops of guns and ammunition, until they were finally caught in 1882 and brought to the port city of Santiago. A rogue Spanish official named Enrique Banales charged the crew of the *Culpeper* with inciting rebellion. The sailors were found guilty in a sham trial, and Banales ordered the entire crew to be executed by firing squad the next morning.

There had been a few British scientists aboard the *Culpeper*, and British diplomats in Havana caught wind of the planned executions. They raced to Santiago to intervene, but the executions were already under way. By the time the British diplomats arrived, only three crew members were still alive. Silas Zanetti was one of them.

Anna couldn't move, couldn't think. All she could see was a ghastly image of her father, lined up and shot like a common criminal. The numbness wore off, and the shaking began in her hands and traveled up her arms.

"Oh no," she whispered. "Please, God, no." Luke pulled her into an embrace, gently rocking her as she felt the pieces of her world start to crumble.

"It happened fifteen years ago," he whispered against her cheek. "Your father is in heaven, looking down on you right now. He's not suffering anymore." He rocked her, but it couldn't blot the image from her mind. Her father lined up to be shot . . . Did they give him a blindfold? Was he alone or did they shoot them as a group? She pushed Luke away and staggered to the window. It hurt too much to let him see her face.

"It was a diplomatic nightmare," Luke continued. "Spanish officials in Madrid were horrified by what had happened and were desperate to make amends. Our government wanted peace too. We'd barely recovered from the Civil War and we couldn't win a war against Spain. Both sides wanted to keep the affair quiet, because this sort of thing would inflame the American public, who might demand blood for blood. The hurricane was used as an excuse to explain the *Culpeper*'s disappearance. The ship was turned over to Spain, and they paid us millions of dollars in reparations. A portion of that money went to the three surviving sailors on the condition they never return to the United States, and never spread the story of what happened. Two of the survivors were brothers from Ireland. They were happy to leave the country. But Silas Zanetti was different. He hated the situation, yet understood the need to keep the peace. He changed his name, moved to Canada, and ultimately made contact with his wife, who joined him in exile."

She squeezed her eyes closed. Mrs. Zanetti's terse message made more sense now. *"You have no relatives, only enemies in Cuba,"* she had written. How terrible that the Zanettis had to live in exile because of the actions of one brutal colonial official.

"What happened to Banales?" Anna asked through clenched teeth.

"He was sent back to Spain in disgrace. Stripped of power, but they couldn't do more without endangering the fabricated story. I gather he is still living in Madrid."

"I want him punished," Anna said. She began pacing the room, which was too small to contain the anger radiating from her soul. "He killed fifty-three men! Murdered them!"

"Anna, hush." Luke pressed his hand over her mouth. Gently, but the message was plain. He'd warned her that this would be a hard secret to carry, but she had no idea what she'd agreed to. She was supposed to pretend she didn't know the truth? That a rogue Spanish official went unpunished for the murder of fifty-three Americans? It was unthinkable!

It was also what she had just sworn on the Bible to do. "Why are you so friendly with Speaker Jones all of a sudden?"

"He's a pacifist," Luke explained. "He's been trying to keep the peace with Spain for decades. Cuba is a hair's breadth away from revolution, and if that happens, the United States will probably be dragged into a war with Spain. Most of the men in Congress are eager for a war. They think Spain is weak and this is our chance to take their colonies. Last month the War Department sent a battleship to hover off the coast of Cuba. Spain is spitting fire over it and threatening war if we don't call the ship home. All it will take is a tiny spark to set off this powder keg. We can't get dragged into this war, Anna. The hawks in Congress will use any excuse to start a war. If they learn about the *Culpeper*, they'll trot it out to fuel the public's sentiment for war."

"I want Enrique Banales and every man who participated in that execution to be punished."

"Anna . . ." His voice was low with warning.

"You can't ask this of me," she said. "I can't just ignore it."

"Anna, we *can't* go to war. The machines of modern warfare would make your blood run cold. Do you know what a Gatling gun can do? I saw a demonstration my first year in Congress. A single soldier with a machine gun stood before a cornfield and blasted it to pieces. It took less than a minute to mow the entire field down, until not a single stalk of corn was left standing. Can you imagine what that gun would do to a field of men? Do you want that on your conscience? Because that's what we are dealing with, Anna. We can't go to war."

He grasped her shoulders, turning her to face him. "There must be a better way for us to settle disputes. Men of honor can't rush toward guns and bloodshed when reason and goodwill can triumph. I've spent my whole life believing in the power of the mind over the fist. That the lion can lie down beside the lamb. I couldn't let my feelings for you interfere with the quest for peace. I wish I hadn't lied to you about the *Culpeper*, but I didn't know how else to silence you."

"You trampled on me," she said, her voice vibrating with the memory of his betrayal. "You stole my father's letters. Do you know what that felt like? My last link to my father has been severed and is gone for good."

"Your link to your father will never be severed," Luke said. "That man's memory will burn like a beacon for as long as you live."

"How could you do that to me? I was falling in love with you."

He winced. "Anna, I wanted you more than my next breath of air, but I had a duty to my country. To the thousands, maybe hundreds of thousands of soldiers who could be ordered to fight a senseless war. Every nerve in my body wanted to tell you the truth, but I couldn't."

"So you lied."

He looked like a weary and beaten man as he looked at her. "Yes, I lied. I wish I'd found a better way to handle the situation, but I'd do it again if it means keeping us out of a pointless war. Half a million men died in the Civil War, and the technology of warfare has exploded since then. We are trying to fend off a bloodbath."

Her head ached and her stomach felt sick, but perhaps he was right. She drew a ragged breath. "I want my father's letters back. I know I can't tell anybody what happened, but I want those letters back."

Luke nodded. "I can deliver them to you tomorrow."

At least he was willing to grant her that much. Her heart had been trampled, and she wished she'd never seen the snarling, ironhard man Luke Callahan could turn into. She felt small and cold as she leaned against the wall, clutching her arms across her chest.

"Are you sorry at all?" she asked. "For what you've done? For what you've done to *us*?"

He looked as drained as she felt. "There are regrets I will carry until my dying day. This is one of them."

The door clicked quietly when he left the room.

FEBRUARY 15, 1898

Anna trudged into the library the next morning. For the first time since becoming a librarian, she hated stepping inside the map room. Across one wall of the room stretched a huge full-color map of the world, but all she could see were Spain and Cuba. And the expanse of deep blue ocean where her father's body had been buried at sea, along with all the other executed sailors of the *Culpeper*. She had always loved looking at maps of the ocean. Now she hated it.

She forced herself to begin cataloging a map of coal deposits in the Appalachian Mountains. She ascribed the proper terms and created unique catalog cards so that each map could be easily found in the future.

Her entire life had been dedicated to organizing information, preserving it, and helping people discover whatever piece of knowledge they wished to find. She loved the challenge of trying to guess how people would look for information in the future and never tired of creating access points to help lead them to the proper map.

Secrets didn't sit well with her. Now she knew a secret she longed to blurt out to the world, but she was struck mute. Just like in the old days, no matter how badly she wanted to speak, she was going to be forever silenced.

"Such a long face."

Anna glanced up to see Luke standing in the open doorway, the bundle of her father's letters in his hand. He set them on the worktable in front of her.

"I'm sorry the man who searched your room made such a mess," he said. "He intended to restore the room to order, but the women began returning home, so he grabbed the letters and fled."

The invasion of her private room still rankled her, but at least now she understood why it had happened. And why her father had written her that cryptic letter. He knew about the covert activities of the *Culpeper* and wanted to document their presence at the island. She was glad she'd been able to piece together his final message, even though she'd never be able to carry out his wishes and document it for posterity.

"I'm moving back home tonight," she said. "The hotel is a little isolated, even for a hermit like me."

Luke touched the side of her cheek. "I hate to see you looking so sad."

She leaned into his hand. Luke was the only other person who would ever understand the terrible secret she carried. Just for a moment she savored the comfort as she turned her face into his hand, but then she stepped back, retreating behind her desk, where she found space for the letters in a desk drawer.

She remained in her chair, facing away from him and uncertain what to say.

"Anna . . . am I forgiven?"

She blanched, not knowing how to answer. She could forgive him for lying to her. She didn't agree with his actions, but they weren't rooted in an evil or selfish motive. She loved him, she forgave him, yet she didn't know if she'd ever be able to forget what she had learned about him in the past few days.

"We may not be right for each other after all," she said softly, and the regret that clouded his face made her want to weep. She wanted to assure him all would be well, but the memory of him towering above her, shouting at the top of his lungs while she cringed, was going to be difficult to overcome.

"I need to feel safe," she said. "That means more than a roof over my head or money in the bank. It means trusting that the man I choose to spend my life with won't explode in rage when I upset him. You're stronger than I am. You have a temper I don't trust. I forgave my uncle for what he did to me, but I won't ever place myself in a situation where I'm helpless. Never again."

"Anna, I would never hurt you."

She lifted an eyebrow. "You threw your nephew's paintbrushes in the fireplace and watched them burn. You kicked a wall in front of me when you were angry in that cloakroom. I never thought you would stand above me and shout until the cords in your neck stood out—"

"Anna, don't," he begged. "Don't end it this way."

She didn't want to. More than anything, she wanted to rush into his arms and tell him all was forgiven and let him comfort her with tender words. It would be so easy, but it would be the wrong thing to do.

"Your explosive anger is more than I can handle, Luke. You need to convince me that you've tamed that dragon living inside you."

For the first time since he'd entered the map room, a gleam of hope lit his eyes. "I'll find a way," he vowed. "If we have to be old and gray before we walk down the aisle, I will find a way to earn your trust again."

A commotion stirred in the lobby downstairs, and a man began shouting in a commanding voice, "All members of Congress need to report to the Capitol immediately!"

"What in the world?" Anna said.

Libraries weren't the kinds of places where people bellowed at the top of their lungs. She darted outside, Luke close on her heels. Dozens of people filtered out of the offices and research rooms, looking equally confused. From her position on the balcony, Anna had a bird's-eye view as a single Capitol policeman stood in the middle of the great hall, shouting his commands again.

"All members of the House and Senate! You need to report to the Capitol immediately." The policeman turned and left the building.

"I'm leaving," Luke said.

"What's going on?"

"I have no idea, but it doesn't look good." He headed toward the staircase, then swiveled and returned to her, grabbing her roughly around the shoulders and pressing a kiss to her lips. Then he was gone.

The map room had the best view of the Capitol of any room in the Library of Congress. Dozens of librarians crammed into the room, squeezing around the single window to watch the commotion across the street. Carriages came racing down the street, careering to a halt before the Capitol and unloading frazzled-looking men, who quickly vaulted up the stairs.

Mr. Spofford stood to the side of the window, apprehension darkening his eyes. "I haven't seen this kind of uproar since the Civil War."

His concern was contagious. Anna couldn't imagine what sort of emergency had caused the members of the House and Senate to be summoned so abruptly. Things usually moved at a glacial pace in Washington, so this sort of panic was indeed disturbing.

"Look, there's the president's carriage," Gertrude said.

Sure enough, the black landau, with armed members of the Secret Service posted on the running boards, pulled up to the front of the Capitol. President McKinley stepped from the carriage and strode inside, not bothering to greet any of the hundreds of people milling on the steps to watch the hubbub.

"I'm going over to see what's happening," Mr. Spofford said, fastening the buttons on his vest. Before he could leave, a congressional page came bounding into the room, breathless and flushed.

"The Spanish have blown up an American battleship in the port of Havana," the boy said. "Hundreds of sailors have been killed."

Anna blinked. Luke had mentioned that a battleship had been sent to Cuba. Was this the one the Spanish sank? A stunned silence settled over the room.

Mr. Spofford was the first to break the silence. He looked pale and shaky as he sank into a chair. "This means war."

Urgent requests from Congress soon flooded the library, and the librarians dispersed to their proper offices. Anna was ordered to pull all their maps of Cuba and every port in the Caribbean. Other librarians began compiling information on the USS *Maine*, the battleship that had been blown to smithereens a few hours earlier. Demands were made for the current location of all US naval ships, army units, and the state of readiness for fully deployable units. More ominously, they wanted estimates of all Spanish naval and land-based forces in the hemisphere.

After the initial flurry of requests, there was little for Anna to do, but she dared not leave the library. A glance out the window revealed a steady stream of people coming and going from the

Capitol. She kept studying their faces, looking for Luke. She never saw him. He was on the new Foreign Affairs Committee, reporting directly to the president, so surely they would be at the forefront of the decision making. The responsibility must be overwhelming. She clenched her hands together, twisting so hard it made the bones ache.

"I thought you could use some company." She turned to see Neville at the door, holding aloft a brown paper bag. "And perhaps a little dinner."

"Bless you! I'm starving, but I couldn't leave in case more requests came in. You've heard what happened?"

"It's all people are talking about," Neville said. "Some reports say all the sailors are dead; others say no casualties at all. The real question is whether the Spanish hit the ship with a torpedo or if it was an accident in the boiler room."

"What do you think?" She began unwrapping the sandwich he handed her.

"I have no idea. Reports say the ship sank in less than an hour. That sounds like a torpedo to me, but I'm no expert."

It felt good to have something to eat. She bit into the sandwich, a tasty pile of seasoned roast beef with horseradish sauce. It was much better than the typical fare sold in the local vendors' carts. She eyed it with suspicion. "Did Mrs. Norquist make this sandwich?"

"Will you quit eating if I say she did?"

"No, I just want to know if I can expect to be poisoned."

He kicked her under the table. "The two of you don't need to be enemies."

"I know," she admitted. "When will I hear wedding bells? And am I going to be invited to the ceremony?"

"Of course you are. We don't want to wait very long, so probably sometime this spring." He rolled the ball of paper in his hands, took careful aim, and lobbed it into the wastebasket, where it landed with a thud. "So, any plans on purchasing that ticket to the Yukon Territory?"

She looked up in surprise. So much had happened since she'd last seen Neville, and she realized he was still burning with curiosity about what caused the Zanettis to turn up alive and well in Canada.

And she could never tell him.

"No," she said, scrambling for some explanation to account for her abrupt change of heart, but came up empty. This was a secret she would have to carry forever, and it wasn't going to be easy. "No, I'm not going to the Yukon."

"Why not? Why do you look so skittish?"

Her mouth went dry, and she began fanning herself to cool the rush of heat flooding her body. She couldn't tell Neville the truth, but she couldn't lie to him either. She'd been wounded to the quick when Luke lied to her. His motives had been good, but she still wished he'd found another way.

"You found out what happened to the *Culpeper*!" Neville's voice was triumphant. He could always read her so easily, and his face glowed with excitement as he leaned forward and waited for her answer. "Well?"

She looked away from the anticipation on his face. "I can't tell you about it."

"What do you mean you can't tell me about it?" he hollered. Anna dashed to slam the door, anxious to avoid even a word of this conversation from being overheard.

"Please don't yell in the library," she said, still unable to meet his eyes.

"Anna, what happened? You've *got* to tell me."

"I can't," she said. "Please don't ask me. I wish I'd never seen that error in the *Culpeper*'s report. I wish I'd never started prowling around all this ancient history, because nothing good will ever come of it."

Neville looked at her as though she'd grown a second head. From the time they were children, they had foraged through libraries on treasure hunts for arcane knowledge and answers to their incessant questions. The *Culpeper*'s fate was the most fascinating quest they'd ever embarked upon, and he naturally wanted an explanation.

"That's all I can tell you. Please don't ask me about it again."

Neville stared at her, dumbfounded. The waiting was endless, but she couldn't say anything. She'd sworn on the Bible to keep her silence, and the political situation with Spain was more precarious than ever before. And still Neville waited . . .

At last he closed his mouth, shifting in his chair and crossing his arms in frustration. "Okay, I'll back off."

"*Thank you*," she gushed, almost doubling over in relief. What a magnificent man Neville was. He respected her wishes, even though he was about to split at the seams with curiosity. She hadn't let Luke off the hook so easily. She'd hounded him relentlessly, pestering him with notes, following him down hallways and shouting questions at him. Thank heavens Neville was more respectful than she had been.

"Can I walk you home?" Neville asked.

She shook her head. "The lights are still on in the Capitol. I'd better stay in case they send over more requests for information."

Neville finally left, and by eight o'clock the lights were beginning to dim at the Capitol. It was chilly and damp outside, and she pulled her coat tighter across her chest before heading to the streetcar stop on Second Avenue. Just ahead of her was St. Joseph's, the old red church standing in the shadow of the Capitol. It wasn't where Anna attended, but the doors were open and lights glowed inside. Tonight, more than ever, she needed the simple spiritual comfort of falling to her knees in prayer.

Aside from a man kneeling in the front row, the church was empty. Just being inside the timeless sanctuary lent her a sense of comfort. The last few days had been full of anxiety, confusion, and despair, but peace descended on her as she slipped into a pew at the back of the church. She prayed for the leaders in both Spain and America. She prayed for the sailors of the USS *Maine* whose lives had just been lost, and for their wives and orphaned children who would soon be getting the news. She prayed for Luke.

The man on the front row rose and started walking down the aisle. Anna looked up and flinched. Lieutenant Rowland, the snarling naval officer who had first hounded her over the *Culpeper*, had never been a friend to her.

He caught her eye and paused. "Ma'am," he said, then continued down the aisle. He was in full uniform and looked exhausted. In all likelihood he'd been in those tense Capitol meetings all day. She stood and intercepted him.

"Do you know anything?" she asked. "Is there going to be a war?"

"I'm not at liberty to share any information." He tried to step around her, but then paused. "I'm sorry for the circumstances of our previous meetings. I didn't enjoy them any more than you did, but I understand that you've been fully apprised of the situation and have agreed to silence."

He spoke softly, though his voice still echoed in the quiet of the church. Anna clenched her fists. Everything about keeping silent seemed wrong and disloyal, but she'd sworn on a Bible, and Luke had risked his career bringing her into a trusted circle of people capable of keeping the secret.

"Yes, I have."

"I wish I could have been kinder, yet we couldn't risk the real story getting out. No one wants peace more than the men in uniform."

He didn't wait for a reply. After he left the church, Anna slipped back into the pew and said a prayer for Lieutenant Rowland and for all the soldiers who might soon be called to duty.

But a small part of her wanted this war. It would mean revenge for her father and for the other men of the *Culpeper* and the *Maine*. And from what she'd learned over the past few hours about the strength of the Spanish military relative to the United States, she knew America would win.

And that small, hard piece of her wanted this war.

20

In the days that followed, the newspapers printed numerous lurid stories about the sinking of the *Maine*. Luke held his breath each day as William Hearst and Joseph Pulitzer waged a war in their respective newspapers to outdo each other reporting the grisly details of charred American bodies floating in the Bay of Havana. The *Maine* had a crew of 327 men, 260 of whom were killed in the initial blast. Speculation was rampant as to whether the explosion had been caused by a torpedo, an underwater mine, or sabotage, but all the newspapers agreed on one thing: Spain was to blame.

Luke was a member of the committee charged with drafting the government's official response to the attack, and additional members from the State Department and War Department were added, with dozens of support staff recruited to attend the meetings. They needed military counsel, language experts, note takers, and research support.

Luke intended to ask Anna's advice about a decent research librarian to attend their meetings. It was too much to hope that she'd be willing to serve, but he trusted her recommendation more than one from a brand-new library director.

The freezing drizzle was a perfect reflection of his gloomy mood as he crossed the street to the new library. People from his district had been flooding him with cablegrams, letters, even telephone calls urging him to stand up for the downtrodden Cubans by supporting their rebellion against Spain. He listened, yet had no intention of moving toward armed conflict. Reason and logic were going to triumph over war and lawlessness. If he worked hard enough, the lion would lie down with the lamb. They lived in an era in which men of goodwill and honor would help build a world of rules and order and prosperity, but it would take courage to face down the war hawks.

He arrived at the map room to see Anna looking impossibly lovely in her prim white blouse and narrow black tie. She hadn't noticed him enter the room, which gave him a chance to savor the view as she scribbled notes at her desk.

"I see you found a new home for my dragon map," he said, nodding to the antique map he gave her all those months ago. It hung right beside her desk, the whimsical dragon and frost monsters oddly incongruent among the scientific order in the rest of the map room.

"I can see it better from here." Anna gave a fleeting smile of welcome, but didn't rise from behind her desk. There was still a distance between them, a sense of reserve he hadn't been able to crack. The fact that she'd hung the dragon map so close to her desk indicated she hadn't rejected him altogether, although she was hardly running to him with open arms. Not like that moonlit night in the breakfast room, when they held hands all night long. Had it only been a month ago? That magical night seemed like another lifetime now. A much better one.

He strode into the room. There were people studying at most

of the worktables, so he'd have to behave himself. He slid a chair over to sit beside her desk.

"I gave that map to *you*," he said quietly. "The last thing I wanted was for you to donate it to a library that just spent more money on ostentatious displays of art than the Louvre."

Anna fixed him with a polite smile. "How can I be of service today, sir?"

He glanced at the patrons a few yards away. They weren't paying any attention, so he leaned in closer to whisper, "You should know that I get a charge when you act all prim and efficient. Very fetching, O'Brien."

She tried not to smile, but her eyes danced with humor. "If by *charge* you are referring to the interaction between negative and positive ions, I am surprised but pleased by your knowledge of electricity. If you are referring to lowly male impulses, I'm sadly disappointed."

This razor-sharp intelligence and good humor were the reason he adored her. "Brace yourself for disappointment, Anna. My references are so lowly they're in a puddle at your feet. They also soar into the heavens. My feelings for you are to the depth and breadth and height my soul can reach."

She cocked her head. "Are you plagiarizing Elizabeth Barrett Browning?"

"Shamelessly. She's a better poet than I."

"How would I know?" she asked. "You've never shown me anything you wrote."

"I respect you too much to inflict it on you."

Now she was trying not to laugh. "Are you ever going to tell me why you've come? I'm hanging in breathless anticipation to hear something sensible from you."

"Even if it relates to boring politics?"

"I've been enduring it all my professional career. Let's hear it."

"The Foreign Affairs Committee needs a research consultant." He explained how the committee was gathering support staff and their need for a librarian to attend the meetings. That librarian would record questions and forward them to the appropriate person at the library for additional research. "Can you recommend someone willing to sit through tedious meetings and who can be trusted not to blabber with journalists? We need complete confidentiality."

Anna set her pen down, studying her hands clasped in her lap. At first he thought she was contemplating his question, but the longer he waited, it seemed as though she might actually be praying. He shifted a bit uncomfortably.

"The committee will need someone with cartographic expertise," she finally said. "I'm the best person for that, and I've also got a sound head for general research. I'm your best bet."

The last thing in the world he'd expected was for Anna to volunteer. "I thought you hated these things."

"I do, but I don't want to be a coward about this. I want to do my part, so if you think I'm qualified, I'd be happy to serve." Perspiration glistened on her skin, and she rubbed her throat. Luke knew what this was costing her, and it made him love her all the more.

"Thank you," he said. "Just knowing you'll be in the room is going to make things a little easier."

Anna couldn't sleep the night before her first meeting at the Foreign Affairs Committee. What foolish impulse prompted her to volunteer for this assignment? One moment Luke was outlining the most tedious and stressful tasks imaginable, and the next she had volunteered for service.

Her nerves were frayed as she walked down the marble corridor toward the meeting room, certain she'd be the most agitated, nervous, and uptight person in the room.

She was wrong. The air crackled with tension as senators, generals, congressmen, and diplomats filed into the chamber, taking their seats at an imposing table dominating the center of the room. Luke sat at the tightly packed table, papers and files mounded before him. There were shadows under his eyes, and the spark of energy that normally powered his every moment was missing. It was as if the stress of this assignment had aged him two decades. Briefly he made eye contact with her when she entered. His nod of greeting was swift as he turned his attention back to the general sitting beside him. Anna sat alongside other staff members in the chairs along the perimeter of the room.

Cornelius Jones called the meeting to order, and then the debate began. It immediately became clear that the committee was split down the middle as to support for the war. Anna took notes throughout the meeting, jotting down a huge range of research requests, and funneled the messages to congressional pages, who carried them across the street to be answered by librarians standing by to receive them. Throughout the day, the answers would be sent back to Anna, who then passed the information to the committee member who first asked the question.

The chair was hard and uncomfortable as the hours progressed, but Anna was too engrossed in the debate to care. The men around the table were all so well-spoken, and her opinion swayed with each new speaker. Luke proposed direct negotiations with Spanish officials, insisting that war should be a last resort. It was hard to see how anyone could disagree, until a general countered that the longer they delayed, the more time Spain had to strengthen their defenses in Cuba, and in the interest of sparing American lives they needed to move quickly.

As the day wore on, Anna's spirits began to wilt. Luke warned her that these meetings would last for a minimum of ten hours each day. There were a few breaks, but even during the reprieves the politicians broke into smaller groups and the negotiations continued. Anna stepped outside to take in a bit of sunlight and fresh air before going back into the windowless chamber for another round.

A book was sitting on her chair when she returned. Had one of the pages arrived with an answer to another research request? But when she picked up the thick volume, the title indicated it was an anthology of poetry. Flipping to the marked page, she read the underlined passage.

> Come live with me, and be my love,
> And we will some new pleasures prove
> Of golden sands, and crystal brooks,
> With silken lines, and silver hooks.
>
> John Donne, 1610

Her gaze flew to Luke at the main table, who winked at her. The whimsical passage was a fleeting glimpse of the beauty of the world, and it fueled Anna for the rest of the afternoon.

It was dark by the time the meeting adjourned for the night. The streetcars had stopped running, and Luke insisted on hiring a private carriage to take Anna directly home. She didn't quibble with him. The soft leather and scent of lemon wax was soothing as she climbed inside the carriage. Sitting opposite him on the gently rocking carriage, she passed the fat volume of poetry back to him.

"Thank you for the John Donne," she said. "I marked a little Emily Dickinson in reply."

"You did?" Luke grinned as he flipped the book open to the page she had marked. He had to tilt it to the window for the streetlamps to illuminate the page. He must have already been familiar with the passage, for he nodded and smiled broadly the moment he saw it. For the first time that day, Anna saw a spark of energy galvanize Luke's body, driving out the day's tension.

"She had a way with words, didn't she?" Luke said as he closed the book. It had taken Anna her entire afternoon break to find the perfect passage, but she was glad she had. It had given Luke his only smile of the day.

That day set the tone for the next week. The meetings were filled with tension, frayed nerves, and tedium, while the periodic exchange of poems was a perfect way to quickly communicate. Luke's vast command of poetry helped him identify the perfect passage within moments. Anna took much greater care, usually spending her lunch hour flipping through the book until she landed on precisely the right passage. The verses Luke chose were typical Luke: flamboyant, reckless, and burning with the force of the sun. Anna's passages were cautious, more likely to speak of hope rather than the blaze of love.

She was particularly proud of the passage she found at the end of the committee's first week. She'd already taken her seat after the noontime break when Luke arrived at the table and saw the slim pamphlet by John Keats. He flipped it open to the marked passage: *The problems of the world cannot possibly be solved by skeptics or cynics whose horizons are limited by the obvious realities. We need men who can dream of things that never were.*

Luke stared at it so long that she thought he must have lost track of time, but when he looked up at her, he covered his heart with his hand, gratitude shining from his eyes. *Thank you*, he mouthed to her before turning his attention back to the meeting.

The only thing anchoring Luke's sanity during the tension-filled weeks following the sinking of the *Maine* was Anna. Or more accurately, the *hope* for Anna.

She still kept him at arm's length, not even letting him touch her on their carriage rides home, which made sitting opposite her a unique sort of enjoyable torture. Nevertheless, he needed those few moments with her each evening, for he feared he was waging a losing battle in Congress that was beginning to take its toll. The tide turned against him as sentiment for war gathered strength, and the golden dream of peace seemed further away.

"Blessed are the peacemakers: for they shall be called the children of God." He clung to that passage like a lifeline, holding firm as tensions ratcheted higher and the drumbeat for war grew louder. By the end of each day, every bone in his body ached with exhaustion, but Anna's gentle smile was a balm on his flagging spirit.

It couldn't change the fact that the pressure for war was gathering momentum. This morning's straw poll in the House showed the war hawks winning by a vote of 280 to 37, and even the support of those 37 men was shaky. Anyone voting for peace risked his political career, yet Luke still dreamed of a world where the lion lay down with the lamb. While it was tempting to abandon what seemed a hopeless cause, he was haunted by the memory of that cornfield, mowed down by a single machine gun, only wisps of straw and dust swirling in the air as the gun fell silent. He couldn't give up the fight.

Echoes of that machine gun haunted Luke as he walked down the hall to his hotel room. At this time of night, Philip was usually sprawled on his bed, drawing charcoal sketches on an oversized pad of paper.

But not tonight. The door to Philip's bedroom stood open,

and he was tossing clothing into a traveling bag. Luke drifted to the open door.

"What are you doing?"

"Packing. I'm going home."

The contents of the bag revealed only a couple of shirts, although Philip was moving at full steam, hauling stacks of clothing from the drawers to shove into the bag. The boy had clearly sprung into action the moment he heard Luke's key in the front door.

"Why are you going home?"

Philip grabbed a section of the newspaper and flung it at his chest. "*That's* why I want to leave." Luke didn't even need to glance at the paper to know what had set Philip off. The political cartoonists had been savage, drawing pictures of Luke and Cornelius Jones on bended knee and offering flowers like lovesick suitors to the king of Spain.

"Uncle Gabe wouldn't be afraid of a fight," Philip said. "I don't want to live with a coward."

Luke stiffened. He'd been hearing the insult for the past week from others on Capitol Hill, but he'd never expected to be attacked from within his own home.

"And you think trying to find a peaceful solution with Spain makes me a coward?"

Philip tossed a pair of socks in a high arc that landed in the bag. "I saw photographs of the dead sailors floating in the harbor. They were charred *black*. I'm going to live with Uncle Gabriel. He's a real man."

Luke didn't want to argue with a fourteen-year-old boy about the war. Philip's dissatisfaction in Washington wasn't rooted in political convictions; it stemmed from Bangor and all its temptations. The boy had been wanting to return to Bangor ever since Jason's funeral, but this was the first time he'd launched a personal attack to get his way.

His limbs felt heavy as he sat on the bed beside the half-filled traveling bag. "Philip, I want you to close your eyes and tell me everything you remember about the main room of the Bangor house."

After a moment's hesitation, Philip slammed a drawer shut and listed the room's features. "The big stone fireplace. Wood beams across the ceiling. An Indian wall hanging to keep the draft out in the winter. Grandma's rocking chair and Uncle Gabe's spiral staircase."

"The infamous staircase to nowhere," Luke said. "Begun with such promise, but never finished, and it never will be."

"You don't know that—"

"Yes, I do," Luke said. "I love your uncle Gabe. He was a hero, and I doubt I would have survived if he hadn't been there to look out for me while I was growing up. But that staircase, that beautifully engineered staircase with inlaid wood and handmade nails . . . Gabe never got close to finishing that staircase. As soon as something else took his fancy, he abandoned it."

At last he had Philip's attention. The boy leaned against the wall, arms folded across his chest, and waited.

"I'm not perfect," Luke continued. "Neither is Gabe, and neither is your mother. We all want what is best for you, and the time is coming when you will need to make a choice. You've got such fire inside. I don't want to dampen that fire. I want to teach you to harness and control it so you can do something more useful with your talent than building a staircase to nowhere."

It was an effort to push himself to his feet. He didn't know what to do about Philip. Or Spain. All he really wanted to do was run to Anna and listen to her easy, gentle counsel, but even she was keeping him at a distance. And he needed to take care of business here. Luke sent a pointed glare at the traveling bag.

"The only place you are going tomorrow is school," he said.

"If you still can't bear to live with a coward at the end of the school year, let me know and I will accompany you back to Maine. But I'd rather you'd stay."

He closed the door quietly as he left. Instead of collapsing into bed like he longed to do, Luke trudged to the end of the hallway. Too tired to even walk down the stairs, he pulled the lever for the elevator and let the enclosed metal box carry him down the four flights to the lobby. He summoned a carriage and returned to the Capitol, where the telegraph office was operating around the clock. He sent a simple one-line message to Julia.

Please come to Washington. I need you.

21

As Anna walked to the Capitol, she felt a growing pressure for war against Spain. With each day that passed, more American flags were erected all over the city and on every street corner. Tailors began making uniforms, women rolled bandages, and pledge drives collected donations for the war cause. One morning as she walked into the committee room, she was stunned to learn that Cornelius Jones had called an end to the special committee, insisting on direct negotiations with Spain.

He banged a gavel to call the meeting into session. "The first order of business is selecting the men to negotiate with Spain." Given Jones's sympathies, everyone knew he would attempt to stack the delegation with men predisposed toward peace, and Luke was his first choice.

Pride surged through her as Luke nodded to accept the nomination, but even from across the room, Anna could sense he was tired, his heart losing hope for peace. Five more men were appointed to the delegation. Most of the men wanted peace, though Anna spotted a few hawks among them. The meeting would take place in Saint Augustine, Florida, and the outcome was entirely uncertain. Spain had angrily denied sabotaging the *Maine* and was reluctant to engage in direct negotiations until the United States withdrew the accusation. Nevertheless, a few Spanish diplomats had been selected to discuss compromise, and the covert meeting in Saint Augustine was the best chance for peace.

It wasn't that Anna wanted war, but she wouldn't mind if it happened either, as vengeance for the *Culpeper.* If her father hadn't been executed by the Spanish, would she still be this conflicted? The men of the *Maine* deserved justice as much as her father did. She'd even pressured Luke about it on the carriage ride home that evening. "No one on the committee can talk about the *Culpeper*, but Spain has already gotten away with a lot over the years. Maybe it's time to act. After all, don't you think—"

He stopped her in mid-sentence. "Anna, please. For a blessed few minutes I need to talk to someone who isn't consumed with anger or revenge or scheming for political gain. You're my safe harbor, Anna. Please don't change."

His face was lined with fatigue, and shadows darkened his eyes. He was becoming ground down as he swam upstream against the deluge of sentiment for war, and she felt guilty for adding her voice to that drumbeat. It was unsettling to witness this dynamic man who normally sparked with energy turn into a drained, disillusioned person. When the carriage drew to a halt outside her boardinghouse, Luke stepped down to bid her farewell. He would leave for Florida in the morning, and she didn't know when she would see him again.

It was past midnight and Philip had long since gone to bed. Luke sat with Julia in the modest parlor of his hotel suite, lit only by the glow from the fireplace. Julia had arrived two days ago, and he was grateful she would be here to look after Philip while he was in Florida.

She sat curled in the upholstered chair, her face framed by a trail of smoke from the tip of her cigarette. Julia had taken up smoking after she quit drinking, and Luke didn't try to stop her. It was a bit scandalous for a woman to smoke, yet it was a mild vice in comparison with the others Julia had consigned to her past.

Tonight, Julia needed the cigarettes to help cope with her anxiety about being in charge of Philip. She'd seen her son plenty in the years since Luke had taken custody, but there were always other relatives nearby whom she could lean on. While he was in Florida, she would have sole responsibility and it worried her. Philip was moving into his impressionable years, evidenced by the sudden charge of cowardice he'd flung at Luke the other night.

Julia drew on her cigarette. "Imagine what Father's reaction would have been if one of us had accused him of being a coward," she said.

"We'd have been taken out and shot at dawn," Luke said wryly.

"You may be underestimating him," Julia said. "Did I ever tell you what he did after I announced I was pregnant with Philip?"

"I know what he did. He flipped over the china cabinet and broke the entire set of Mother's new porcelain."

"After that."

He looked up in surprise. He didn't recall much of anything after Edgar's tantrum that long-ago afternoon. But the way Julia had averted her eyes and ground out the cigarette made him want to hear the rest of the story.

"He asked me to follow him outside to the barn," Julia said slowly. "I had no idea what to expect. I thought maybe he'd beat me within an inch of my life or shove a wad of bills in my hand

and banish me from his sight, but that's not what happened. As soon as we stepped inside the barn, he pulled me into his arms and wept. He cried so hard I feared he couldn't keep breathing. When he finally got control again, he blamed himself. He said if he'd been a better father, I would never have been out running around with Vincent Hanover in the first place."

Luke was stunned. Of all the sides he'd seen of Edgar Callahan—the rage, the joy, the brilliance—he had never seen any weakness.

"He wasn't all bad, Luke. On the day Philip was born, when everyone else in the family was embarrassed by me, Dad took out an announcement in the newspaper."

It shamed Luke to remember the way they'd all treated Julia at that time. He'd been furious that she'd brought another wave of scandal into their home and destroyed her prospects for a respectable marriage, but like all things, he'd stuffed the anger deep inside, never letting a hint of it show. His icy silence surely hadn't been much comfort, and yet he'd prided himself on not lashing out. How mortifying that his father had showed Julia more human decency and compassion than he had.

Julia hadn't finished speaking. "For a while he was the father I'd always wished we'd had. It didn't last. After Philip was born, Dad went back to raging when he didn't get his way or couldn't control every waking action of his children. He died alone because he couldn't force those he loved to be exactly how he wanted to mold them. It was mostly the rum that unleashed his demons, and I understand that temptation. When I was drinking, for a few hours each day I wasn't a failure. I wasn't the girl who let herself get seduced and abandoned. And when I walked down the streets of Bangor, rum gave me the courage to hold my head up when respectable ladies pulled their skirts aside as I walked past."

A log in the fireplace fell, releasing a shower of sparks and the scent of pine. He stared at the sparks swirling in the gust of heat, anything rather than look at the remembered pain on Julia's face. All his life he'd striven to accomplish and achieve, to prove that he was better than his drunken, reckless father. He'd refused to let the sin of anger corrode him as it had Edgar. Anger was a failing, something to be stifled and repressed.

"I forgave Dad a long time ago," Julia said. "In any event, I never expect people to be perfect. Not Dad. Not Philip. Not even you, Representative Callahan."

Luke kept staring into the fire. It seemed as if he was growing more like his father with every passing month. He was starting to snap and lose his temper. Ignoring the anger was no longer working. When he tried, the pressure built up inside, and then a minor offense could cause the dam to break. He'd inherited his father's impulsiveness and passion, a magnificent gift from God, but a terrible compass. He'd probably wrestle with the rash streak for the rest of his life. But if he quit pretending that he could ignore the anger, perhaps he could learn to tame it.

Anna's words from long ago came back to him. *"We are all beautiful but broken people. Jesus forgives us, even when we don't deserve it. That's a pretty good reason to be forgiving."*

He bowed his head, acknowledging the truth of her words. God sent His only begotten Son so that the world might witness a pure form of love and forgiveness. It was a gift, a grace, and a blessing beyond all measure. It wasn't a sin to feel anger, but it must be tempered by love and compassion. And until he could follow the loving example of Jesus in handling these truly human emotions, he wasn't worthy of having Anna or Philip or anyone else depend upon him.

That week seemed like the longest in Anna's life. The negotiations in Saint Augustine were being held in secret, and nothing was reported in the press, so it was impossible to know if the diplomats were making progress or if war was closer than ever. There were no meetings of the special committee during the Florida negotiations, and Anna was grateful to return to her normal role in the map room.

On the Friday following Luke's departure, she had the most unusual reference request in all her years at the library. A stunning woman with a young man beside her strolled into the map room, her willowy figure dressed entirely in black that matched the ebony upsweep of her hair.

"You must be Anna, the librarian," the woman said. "I'm Julia Callahan, Luke's sister."

Anna gaped. Julia didn't look like a scarlet woman. She looked as refined and elegant as the cameo pinned to her high-throated blouse.

"Our questions aren't related to government business, but I was hoping you could lend your assistance as a personal favor," Julia said. "My son believes you can help with a project he wishes to complete."

Anna was still struck mute by the beauty whose ostracism put the taunting Anna had endured to shame. Philip stepped forward.

"I need to know how to paint a fresco," Philip said. "A *real* fresco. The one time I tried, I messed it up pretty bad."

Luke had told her about his nephew's infamous midnight experiment in fresco painting, so she was sympathetic as Philip outlined his problem.

"I want to prove to my uncle Luke that I can tackle a job and finish it. I've already gotten permission from the hotel manager to try again on a wall in the laundry room. The manager wants a garden scene that the women who work in the laundry will like, but I don't know how to go about it."

Anna finally found her voice. "You've come to the right place."

Over the next hour they visited with the art librarian, who pulled books on modern techniques for replicating the ancient process. All it would take was a thin veneer of fresh plaster laid atop the existing wall. It would be cheaper, easier, and far less likely to fall like it did when Philip experimented last autumn.

Julia stood by Philip as he wrote down the process for mixing the plaster and preparing the wall. Anna fetched art books with examples of famous landscapes Philip could draw upon for inspiration. The boy's enthusiasm was contagious.

"When are you planning the grand event?" Anna asked.

"Tomorrow," Philip said. "I want it finished before Uncle Luke returns from Florida. He's supposed to be back on Monday, so I have to move fast."

"Can I help?" Anna asked impulsively, then almost bit her tongue. Just because she was lonely didn't mean she ought to barge in and invite herself to spend time with Luke's family when she was still a stranger to them.

"Would you?" Philip almost sounded relieved at her suggestion. "Just don't tell Uncle Luke. I want it to be a surprise."

She and Julia spent the weekend helping Philip mix plaster, carry water, and clean brushes while a garden scene of amazing beauty was quickly painted onto the fresh plaster. How wonderful to watch a boy so young and full of talent as he transformed the blank wall into a transcendent work of art.

Even as the country struggled beneath the threat of war, God still graced them with glimpses of beauty, new friendship, and happiness.

Anna was startled to see Neville waiting for her when she arrived at the map room on Monday morning. He hadn't come around so much since announcing his engagement, and he must have arrived very early given the way he was slumped over a newspaper spread open on a worktable.

"Hello, stranger," she said.

"Anna!" Neville folded the newspaper and pushed to his feet, swallowing hard. His ticks were out in full force, and he looked pale. "I'm so sorry."

"Sorry about what?"

"Haven't you seen the newspapers?"

"You know I never read the newspapers. Especially now, when all they report is bad news about Cuba."

His shoulders sagged. "You don't know then."

Now he was starting to frighten her. She glanced at the newspaper folded under his arm. With trembling fingers she held her hand out. Neville unfolded the paper so she could see the headline. "I'm so sorry," he repeated. "I didn't know."

The headline blared in two-inch type: *Spain Murders Crew of the USS* Culpeper.

"Oh no," she breathed. The strength drained from her legs, and she sank toward the floor, Neville catching her just before she landed.

"You knew?" he asked.

"Luke told me," she said through bloodless lips. Neville guided her into a chair, but she felt too sick to look up as she curled over. "He swore me to secrecy. He knew if it got out, it would be like pouring kerosene on a fire." Could there have been a worse time for this to hit the newspapers than while Luke was trying to walk a delicate balancing act with the Spanish diplomats?

Although perhaps it shouldn't be surprising this story had

been leaked to the press. With tensions so high, all it took was a single person who wanted to fan the flames of war by releasing the story to the press. There were dozens of people in the government who knew the secret of the *Culpeper*, and it looked like one of them was anxious to tip the scales toward war.

Neville offered her the paper, but she turned her head away. She didn't want to know the terrible details of her father's execution. All she knew was that the only thing to stop the country from plunging into war was a handful of pacifists desperately trying to stave off the vote for war until tempers cooled. This news made that even more unlikely.

"All the newspapers are coming out with late editions with more details," Neville said. "The war hawks are delighting in the story. It's fifteen years old, but they're shouting their outrage from the mountaintops. This is going to be bad."

And Anna knew it was true.

Anna was squeezed between chattering women on the bench at the boardinghouse dinner table. As usual, the volume in the room was deafening. One of the girls was caught wearing lip rouge to work and was ordered by her supervisor to stop. The other women at the table were outraged and discussed techniques for wearing cosmetics that could escape detection.

Anna stared at the cooling plate of mutton stew, the predictable meal served every Monday evening. She wished her only problem was the surreptitious use of cosmetics. Politics were almost never discussed at this table, and no one brought up the subject of the *Culpeper*, even though the news had triggered a flurry of outrage in the afternoon newspapers. No one here knew her father or his role on the *Culpeper*, and she wanted to keep it that way.

One of the girls produced the illicit pot of lip rouge, and another girl lunged across the table to grab it, almost knocking Anna's water glass over. Anna pursed her lips as she moved the glass to safety, wondering if she should take her plate of stew upstairs to escape this inane conversation.

A booming voice sliced through the chatter. "Anna!"

It was Luke, bellowing down the hall. He burst into the dining room, Mrs. O'Grady close on his heels.

"You can't come in here, sir. This is a women's house!"

Luke ignored the landlady as he held out a rolled-up newspaper, glaring at Anna. "Did you do it?" he asked, his voice vibrating with barely leashed anger. "Did you spill the news of the *Culpeper* to a journalist?"

Every muscle in her body tensed, and she fought the temptation to run away. The old Luke was back. The snarling, angry man with rage in his eyes. Shocked silence descended on the room. Anna stood, bracing her hands on the table to keep them from shaking.

"What do you think?" she challenged.

A muscle bunched in his jaw, and he struggled to contain his breathing, but he didn't break eye contact as he held the paper aloft. "I'm asking you, Anna. Politely and clearly. Did you talk to a journalist?"

He was barely in control of his temper, and she could put his mind at ease with a simple word, but then what? There would come a time when she would disappoint him for real, and would he then feel entitled to let his temper have free rein? She would never willingly put herself in the hands of a man who used violence to control those around him, and she needed to know if Luke was such a man.

"You knew I wanted the world to know the truth about the *Culpeper*" was all she said.

He flinched as if he'd been struck. The newspaper fell to the floor. He hung his head. Everyone waited, holding their collective breath as though a bomb were about to explode.

"Okay," he finally said, his voice heavy with disappointment but drained of rage. He kept his eyes averted. "Okay," he said again, "we'll figure this out. It will be all right."

He'd never sounded so defeated, his voice choked with regret. Anna climbed out from the bench and rushed to his side. "Let's take this outside," she said quietly.

He nodded and followed her from the room. He clasped her hand as she led him down the hall toward the alley behind the boardinghouse, where they could be alone. She tugged the door closed.

Luke looked beaten down and discouraged as he stared sightlessly at the empty vegetable crates mounded by the wastebins. "Oh, Anna, I wish you hadn't done this," he said, his voice ragged. "You let us both down, and there are going to be consequences. We'll figure a way to deal with them and find a path toward forgiveness, but I wish you hadn't done it."

"I didn't," she said softly. Luke's head shot up, and he looked at her with the beginnings of hope in his eyes. She placed a hand on his arm. "I swore I wouldn't tell, and I would never betray you like . . ."

Her voice choked off as he dragged her into his arms. "Thank God," he breathed.

She tightened her arms around his back, the tension draining from his body. If ever he had cause to vent his rage against her, she had just handed it to him on a golden platter, and he didn't rise to the bait. She'd never been so proud of him.

"When did you get back from Florida?"

"About twenty minutes ago." His voice was muffled, yet exhaustion weighed on every syllable.

"How did it go?"

His arms dropped away, and he lowered himself to sit on the back stoop. "Badly," he said. "The little hope we had going into the negotiations has now burned out."

Her heart squeezed. She still felt conflicted about this war, but she hated seeing him so defeated. "What happens now?"

"Spain has broken diplomatic relations with us. Cornelius Jones will try to delay the war vote until tempers have cooled, but there's not much left we can do. The House will vote for war in a landslide. So I failed." His voice was hollow, his eyes haunted. She joined him on the stoop, sitting and taking his hand between hers.

"I have no doubt you worked to the very best of your abilities," she said, "and that's all God asks of us."

"All my life I've had this idealistic image of a lion lying down beside a lamb. They're in a green pasture by a stream, and it's a perfect, cloudless day. I wanted to believe it could be real and held that image in my mind every day, hoping to find a path to that peaceable kingdom." He traced a pattern on the back of her hand, his blunt fingers weathered and darkened by the sun, while hers were smooth and white. "Now it will never happen."

She laid her hand over his. "I'm not so sure about that," she whispered. Maybe Luke couldn't solve peace between the nations, but he had tamed the wildness inside him. Trying to pretend his stormy passion did not exist would be hopeless and a waste of one of his greatest strengths. But he could tame it and turn it toward worthy goals.

"I'm sorry I barged in on you like that," he said. "You deserved better than to have me tear into you the second I got back."

It hadn't escaped her notice that when she let him believe the worst of her, still he vowed to stand beside her and work toward forgiveness. This time he'd wrestled with his temper and had won the battle.

"Have you had a chance to go to the Willard yet?" she asked.

"No, I came straight here after I saw that headline. What a thing to see the minute I stepped off the train."

"Because Philip has been eagerly awaiting your return."

He looked at her quizzically. "How did you meet Philip?"

She explained how Julia came to her with a reference question, but refused to supply any details. The fresco wasn't her surprise to share.

"I know you're exhausted, but Philip is going to want to show you something. Tonight probably. It would be good if you could find the energy to indulge him."

He sighed, but nodded his assent. He was so worn out, she had to help him stand. She walked him to the streetcar stop and waited on the bench beside him.

"I almost forgot," Luke said, reaching into the breast pocket of his coat. He pulled out a twig laden with extravagant fuchsia blossoms, a few of the limp petals scattering onto the pavement. "It's bougainvillea. From Florida. I stole it from the breakfast table at the hotel."

"You *stole* it?"

"They throw them out each morning, but I knew it would look better on you." He gently tucked the stem of the flower into her hair.

She reached up and touched the velvety petals. "I'm not the type to wear flowers in my hair."

"You ought to, O'Brien. The world can be a tough and gritty place. We need to seize beauty wherever we can find it."

"You mean *steal* beauty?"

He smiled and nodded. "If you'd like. Those blooms were so spectacular I couldn't resist bringing one to you. It's not going to last much longer, maybe not even till morning."

It was a chilly evening, and a gust of wind knocked a few

more of the fuchsia petals to the pavement, but she was glad Luke had brought this spectacular, outrageous bloom to her. She'd try to appreciate its beauty for as long as it lasted.

Luke stared at the wall of the laundry room in amazement. On a day that began as an unmitigated disaster, topped off by shouting at Anna like a rabid dog, he soaked in this glimpse of paradise. The garden fresco Philip painted had transformed the dreary laundry room, breathing color and life into the space. Firs, cypress, and flowering pomegranate trees filled the garden, all beneath an idyllic sky.

"I added a dove with a laurel twig in its beak," Philip said. "That's because I painted it while you were in peace talks with the Spanish."

The pride in Philip's voice startled him, and Luke stared at the dove perched on a low-hanging branch as it overlooked the garden. The dove was perfect in form and shading, its alabaster feathers in serene contrast to the azure sky. It made him feel like a failure.

"I thought you were embarrassed that I wanted peace with Spain."

Philip fidgeted. "Ma nearly bit my head off when I told her about that," he admitted. "I was just mad. And everyone else seems to want the war, so I did too, but she explained some things. About my grandfather and why you always want to settle things with words instead of fighting."

Luke's muscles were so worn out he could barely stand, and it was an effort to keep his eyelids open, but none of that mattered. "I'm proud of you, Philip."

And he was. Even after the catastrophe in the storage closet last October, the boy hadn't let defeat slow him down. After paying his debt for that bit of folly, Philip had studied, practiced, and produced this stunning mural that rivaled the art in the Smithsonian.

Philip reached up to point at some wispy clouds on the horizon. "Look how I painted the clouds so they add depth to the picture. See how I angled them so it looks like they're miles away? Miss O'Brien said that's how the Renaissance painters captured a three-dimensional effect in their art. I think mine are as good as the examples I saw in the art books."

"Let's not get carried away with your brilliance yet, Michelangelo," Julia said from behind them, a smile on her face.

Luke sent Julia a fleeting look of gratitude. Philip had a right to be proud, but he still needed to learn to temper his talent with humility.

Still, the beauty of this fresco made Luke's heart expand and ache. Was he delirious with happiness or about to break down and weep from exhaustion and defeat? He didn't know. All he knew was that he loved Philip more than he thought humanly possible, and that this laundry room was surely the most beautiful in the nation. His nephew's wild, reckless streak had been tamed but not stamped out.

Luke coughed to clear away the lump in his throat. "I hope this mural stays here for the next hundred years," he said. "When you and I are both long in our graves, I hope that painting will still shed a little bit of grace and beauty for the people who toil in this room."

Philip's eyes grew wide, and he swallowed hard. "I hope that too."

"Come on, let's go home," Luke said, having to summon the energy to get his legs moving.

Philip drew alongside him. "Um, I wanted to talk to you about something."

"Can it wait until morning?"

Philip and Julia exchanged glances. "He's been working up the courage to talk with you all day," Julia said. "Have mercy on the poor boy."

Come to think of it, Philip did look a little weak around the gills. All Luke wanted to do was collapse into bed and scrub this day from his memory, but he had a responsibility to the boy.

"Let's see if we can find a quiet spot in the breakfast room. It's usually empty at this time of night." He started heading back to the public area, Philip alongside him, then turned back around. "Aren't you coming too?"

Julia shook her head. "I think it's best for the two of you to talk alone."

The tension on Julia's face didn't bode well for whatever Philip had to say. He pushed through the door that led to the Willard's lobby, feeling grubby and rumpled compared to the starched formality of the guests in the reception area. As hoped, the breakfast room was empty and dark. He left the door open to allow a patch of light to illuminate the room. The tables were already draped in white linen and set for breakfast service. Luke pulled two chairs out from a table so they could sit and talk.

Philip picked at a hangnail and fidgeted in his seat, looking as if he were waiting for the executioner's ax to fall.

"I'm not going to start this conversation," Luke prompted.

Philip nodded and took a heavy breath. "You know that spiral staircase in the Bangor house, the one that leads to nowhere?"

"Of course."

"I decided I'm going to ask Grandma what she wants done with it. If she wants it to stay, I'll design a loft and get it built. I want to do the work myself, even if I have to hire a carpenter to show me how."

Luke quirked a brow. "And if she doesn't want a loft added to the main room?"

"Then I'll tear the staircase down. Mother hates it, and you're right that it's dangerous."

A thread of alarm began forming in the pit of Luke's belly, fearing where this conversation was headed. "What prompted this sudden desire to address that staircase?"

"I want to move back home."

It was as he'd feared. The boy was old enough to make this decision for himself, and Julia was no longer drinking and unable to care for her son. She had done everything Luke had asked of her. She was now a sober, responsible woman capable of looking after her boy, and Luke had no justification for insisting Philip remain in Washington.

"I understand what you said about Uncle Gabe and the way he never finishes things," Philip said. "I'll take care of that staircase. I'll get an education and quit fighting with the others at school, no matter what they say about me or my mother. And I'll finish things. I want to be an artist too badly to fail."

"Then why not stay here?" Luke asked. He tried to block the bewilderment from seeping into his voice, but failed. "I can give you everything. Museums, art lessons, introductions to all the right people . . ."

"But I'm an outsider here, and I miss the rest of my family." Philip scrubbed his palms against the fabric of his trousers, his face screwed up with anxiety. "Deep down, I think you're the only person who really understands me. I've always wished that you were my real father, but you're not, and it's time for me to learn how to get along with Ma just as well. I've heard everything you've tried to teach me over the years, but I don't belong here anymore and it's time for me to go home. Please . . . it's cost all I've got to admit that."

Luke's heart turned over. He didn't want to lose Philip, but it was time. He reached up to rub the ache in his chest. He hadn't expected this to hurt so much. An old instinctual impulse rose up to refuse Philip's request, to declare that he knew what was best for the family and force everyone to accept it.

But he didn't. If nothing else, Luke had learned the lesson of humility in these past few months.

Luke was right. The bougainvillea blossom didn't survive the night. By morning its spectacular fuchsia petals were limp, and Anna carried them to the rubbish bin outside.

On her way to the library she grabbed the latest issue of the morning newspaper to skim while packed into the streetcar. The outraged reaction to the *Culpeper* scandal was still on the front page, but it had slipped to a smaller story at the bottom. Nevertheless, it seemed the headline was all anyone could talk about.

The House and Senate would vote on a war with Spain today. Everyone expected the House to vote for war, while the Senate, always more insulated from the demands of public opinion, was more evenly divided.

This must be killing Luke. She'd seen the desperation and despair in his eyes, heard it bleeding into his voice. Sometimes wanting something desperately wasn't enough to make it happen, and it looked like today would be his crowning defeat. There was still a chance that the men of the House might change their minds when they actually proceeded to the vote. Saber rattling was easy when there were no lives on the line, but today's vote could send young men from across the nation to fight on an island most of them couldn't even find on a map.

She wanted to be in the gallery for the vote. Hadn't Luke

once said that merely having her in the room gave him strength? There was nowhere else in the city she'd rather be.

The crush to get inside the Capitol was unlike anything she'd ever experienced. Crowds of people gathered on the steps and made forward movement almost impossible. Flags snapped in the breeze, a band played music in the distance, and newsboys hawked the latest edition of newspapers. Some men handed out leaflets in support of the war, while others urged peace. Those daring enough to voice support for peace were taunted and heckled.

Anna ducked to get around the broad-shouldered men and nudge her way up the Capitol steps, but as she drew near the top, the source of the congestion became obvious. Members of the Capitol police guarded the doors, turning away all but elected officials and a handful of authorized visitors.

She'd resigned to waiting with everyone else to hear the result of the vote when she spotted Jack Wilkerson. He was busy carrying messages to the police.

"Jack!" she shouted. It was impossible to be heard over the band and a crowd of hecklers taunting a protester at the top of the steps.

Wadding up the morning newspaper into a tight ball, Anna took aim and lobbed it directly at the congressional page.

"Hey!" Jack shouted as he grabbed the missile that had brushed his head. He swiveled to see who threw it at him, then broke into a grin when he saw Anna.

"Miss O'Brien!" he called as he loped over to her.

"Have you been able to get inside?"

"No one's getting in today," Jack said. "I'm just here to run errands if the Capitol police need anything."

"Do you know what's going on inside?"

"The House is voting right now. The Senate will start as soon as the House finishes."

Anna sucked in a breath. Even now, Luke was hearing the roll call as hundreds of men stood up to vote for or against the war. "And how's it going?"

"Last I heard, it was eighty votes for war, two for peace. But there's a long way to go still." She blanched, and Jack must have noticed her expression. "What's the matter? Don't you support the cause, Miss O'Brien? They killed our sailors."

She knew he was referring to the men of the *Maine*, but all Anna could think about was her father. She looked up, not a cloud in the blue sky. Would her father have wanted this? Did *she* want this? All she knew was that she didn't want to be alone right now. Jack took a position beside her as they leaned against one of the cold granite columns. She reached out to hold his hand, and he grinned in excitement. Jack Wilkerson had been the bane of her existence since his first day on the job, but for today he was just a boy as desperately curious as she to learn the outcome of the vote.

Twenty minutes later, it was over. The House's sergeant at arms stepped onto the portico, carrying the ceremonial mace, which he banged on the ground. The people in the vicinity quieted, but the roar coming from the crowds made it hard to hear. He shouted the outcome of the vote.

"The joint resolution to declare war on Spain has cleared the House," he bellowed over the din. "The vote was 311 to 6. The resolution now heads to the Senate."

Never in her wildest dreams did Anna imagine the vote would be so lopsided. It was a brutal and humiliating defeat for Luke. Aside from him and Cornelius Jones, only four other brave men stood for peace. She bowed her head, Luke's chosen passage from the Sermon on the Mount coming to mind.

"Blessed are the peacemakers: for they shall be called the children of God. Blessed are they who are persecuted for righteousness' sake: for theirs is the kingdom of heaven."

Luke's political career was probably over. He'd tried so valiantly to work toward peace, and there were going to be consequences in next year's election. She hoped Luke would be able to put this defeat into proper perspective. He'd stayed true to his convictions, despite the overwhelming pressure to capitulate. What an irony that he and Cornelius Jones would both go down in flames together.

The war was now in the hands of the Senate. Rumors began to fly as they awaited results of the vote. Cornelius Jones, Speaker of the House for more than ten years, had resigned his leadership position in acknowledgment of the resounding defeat. People wondered if he would even run for Congress next year.

"The vote won't take nearly so long in the Senate," Jack said, chomping on a strand of licorice. "They've got better manners over there and don't argue so much."

It turned out not to matter. An hour later, the Senate's sergeant at arms stepped out onto the portico to make the announcement. The vote had passed by a margin of 42 to 35. The nation would be going to war.

The crowd cheered. Caps were tossed into the air, flags waved, and a band struck up a rousing tune. People started to rush the Capitol steps, pushing forward in their exuberance to shout victory.

She needed to find Luke. The Capitol police were still barring the door, and trying to get past security would likely be hopeless. Yet he'd turn up at the Willard sooner or later. Trying to get off the Capitol steps was like swimming upstream. She was buffeted by elbows, and her hair came tumbling out of its bun before she escaped the crowds.

She took the streetcar to Fourteenth Street, where there were no cheering people and everything seemed strangely normal. A nun bought an apple from a vendor's cart while a man in a bowler hat got his shoes shined. Word of the vote hadn't yet trickled to this part of town, and Anna wished the simple normalcy of this sight would last forever. The news would arrive here shortly, however, and then this heartbreakingly ordinary scene would pass.

She stepped inside the hotel and walked to the front desk. "I'd like to leave a message for Lucas Callahan. When he arrives, will you let him know that Miss O'Brien is here?"

The clerk looked at her over the rim of his spectacles. "He's already left, ma'am."

She blinked. "Left?"

"He left for the Potomac train station about fifteen minutes ago. We had to arrange for a special carriage to transport all the trunks and traveling bags."

Could Luke really be leaving Washington so abruptly? His political career was surely doomed, but she hadn't expected him to leave the city without finishing his term.

Memory of his haggard face made her doubt. How different he was from the laughing, confident man she saw striding into that Fisheries committee all those months ago, when he'd been filled with energy and optimism. That man had been beaten down in the most important battle of his life, and even she had lined up to join the opposition by complaining about keeping the true fate of the *Culpeper*'s crew a secret.

Luke was an impulsive man. If he didn't feel like he belonged in Washington, he would follow his heart and leave. After all, Speaker Jones had already resigned his leadership position, and it was in Luke's character to indulge in an extravagant gesture like resigning in protest. Would she ever see him again if he quit and returned to Maine? Would she be nothing more to him than a fond memory of a fleeting love like Violet Desjardins?

She wouldn't stand idly by, waiting to find out. If nothing

else, these past few months had taught her that she needed to step outside her cozy world and fight for what she wanted. It didn't take long to get to the Potomac train station, and she steeled her resolve for the battle ahead. She'd been willing to go to the Yukon Territory or to Cuba to find the answers about the *Culpeper*. She would be equally willing to go to Maine to hunt down Luke. Running after him might be an expensive and humiliating gamble, but she would risk it. She loved him too much to let him go without a fight.

The station was hectic and noisy as the powerful locomotives came to a stop, releasing gusts of steam and smoke. Three different railroad lines all converged there, and Anna had never realized how loud a locomotive could be until one pulled alongside the depot, its pistons and cylinders squealing to a halt, steam hissing as the hydraulic brakes released.

She headed to the ticket office, where she inquired after the next train that could get her to Maine.

"Sorry, ma'am. The last northbound train of the day has already boarded. It will be leaving shortly." He nodded to a long passenger train on the other side of the station. She longed to dash across the platform and climb aboard, only she didn't have any money with her, and no clothes other than what she was wearing.

"When's the next train?" she asked. The man at the ticket office consulted the schedule on the wall tacked behind him and told her she'd need to return the next afternoon at four o'clock.

She couldn't wait until tomorrow. Right now Luke was reeling from the worst defeat of his life. He needed comfort and support, and she wanted to be the one to provide it. She wanted Luke to know that she loved him and was proud of him for undertaking such a valiant cause, even though it hadn't worked out.

Without thinking, she turned and ran toward the train. Her boots thudded on the wood planking of the platform, her breath growing short as she hurried down a hundred yards toward the train. It was much taller than she and it was hard to see inside the windows, but the people sitting next to each window were clearly visible. She ran along the length of the train, looking for Luke's distinctive profile in one of the windows. The pressure building in the steam valves raised in pitch as the train prepared to depart. She hadn't even searched half the length of the train when the lead engine gave a mighty gust, and the pistons began their cranking.

"Oh, please . . ." Anna muttered, running faster now as the train pulled away. The faces in the windows slid away from her, the train gaining momentum as it pulled out of the station.

At last, Anna watched it disappear around a bend. Why couldn't Luke have stayed and said a proper goodbye? Now he was gone, and she hadn't even told him that she loved him. She wanted to fling herself down onto the platform and weep.

"Anna? What are you doing here?"

She gasped. Luke was standing before her, looking dashing and windblown, a curious light in his eyes.

"I thought you left!"

"I just came to help my sister and nephew with their luggage. I asked Julia to come for a week, and she brought two trunks. Two trunks! That woman must be the best-dressed female on the East Coast." He paused, then looked her in the eyes. "What, did you think I was fleeing back to Maine with my tail between my legs?"

"Well, yes, a little." How could she find the words? He was still here and he didn't look beaten down and defeated. He looked tired but . . . happy? Luke sent her one of those sideways smiles that always sent her heart into double time.

"I confess to being a sore loser, but I'm not a quitter. Why are you here?"

Because she loved him. Because she wanted to spend the rest of her life with him, while all she had ever done was push him away because she was afraid she wasn't good enough for him.

Another train came barreling toward the station, the chugging of its engine sending a deafening wall of noise rolling across the platform. But her heart swelled with a love so overpowering she couldn't contain it. She cleared her throat, drew a deep breath, and hollered with every ounce of strength she could muster.

"Because I love you!" she shouted.

Luke shook his head. "I can't hear you." He leaned in, cupping a hand to his ear. The locomotive roared into the station, yet she'd already summoned her courage and it wasn't going to wait.

She tried again. "I love you! I want to marry you!"

The train squealed to a halt, the high-pitched whine and clouds of steam causing the expression on Luke's face to turn tense and frustrated. He grabbed her elbow and walked her away from the newly arrived train.

"Anna, I couldn't hear a word you just said, but I think I understood the gist of it. I may be suffering from temporary insanity . . . but did you just ask me to marry you?"

Her momentary burst of courage evaporated, and her throat constricted. All she could do was nod.

The smile that broke across his face was like the sun emerging from behind the clouds. He lifted her off the ground and swung her in a circle. His laughter echoed across the train station and filled her with joy.

"I'd be honored," he whispered in her ear after he set her down. He cupped her face between his palms and looked at her with all the warmth and radiance in the world shining in his eyes. "Let's go out and celebrate."

His mood seemed odd to her. "I thought you'd be upset," she said. "About the war . . ."

He smiled and shook his head. "I tried with everything I had to avoid this war, but it's coming and there's nothing I can do about it now. I don't know if it will last a week, a year, or a decade, but I do know that I love you. That we are both stronger together than apart, and I want you by my side, Anna, no matter what the future holds."

It was true they were as different as could be. He was hard where she was soft. Flashy and flamboyant where she was plain. He had the ability to harness his impulses and passion into a political career, while she preferred to work quietly in the seclusion of a library.

She would have to quit her job and that was going to hurt, but she'd find something else to do with her talents. Now that the secret of the *Culpeper* was known, there was nothing to stop her from writing about her father's contributions to the field of cartography. Depending on the outcome of the election in November, she might have to leave Washington and follow Luke to his home in Maine. It would mean leaving Neville and the city she loved behind to walk into an entirely unknown world, but it would be all right. She had finally found her place in the world, and it wasn't inside a library. It was going to be new, different, and sometimes a little frightening, but she was ready.

Epilogue

THREE MONTHS LATER

Anna dreaded being the center of attention, although she'd have to endure it if she ever wanted to become Mrs. Lucas Callahan. The church was full and Luke was already standing before the minister at the altar. She fiddled with her veil one final time, and then Neville stepped beside her.

"Hey, Anna," he whispered, holding an arm out toward her. "It looks like we're finally heading down the aisle together after all."

She smiled as the music started and Neville walked her down the aisle to give her away to Luke, who had never looked flashier with his lavender silk vest and pink tourmaline tie clip. Only two weeks earlier they'd celebrated Neville's marriage to Mrs. Norquist, who had warmed up to Anna immediately upon hearing of her engagement to Luke. Now the four of them, each as different as the four seasons, had formed a tight friendship Anna knew would endure for decades.

Luke's brother, Gabriel, served as his best man, with Cornelius Jones watching from the front pew of the church. Jones had resigned as Speaker of the House in protest against the war, but he still served as a member of Congress. He and Luke renewed their outspoken disagreements over tariffs, the budget, and almost every other issue in Congress. During the day they were fierce political rivals, but after hours their friendship remained solid. It was proof that men of good character could disagree with one another and yet still respect the fundamental human decency in their opponent.

As they knelt before the altar, Anna listened to Luke's confident voice vow to be her faithful husband in sickness and in health, in joy and in sorrow, in times of plenty and in times of failure. He promised to love, protect, comfort, and cherish her for all eternity. For a girl who'd been alone most of her life, Luke's promise was overwhelming.

At first Anna had been reluctant to get married while the nation was at war, but Luke had disagreed. "What better time to celebrate the joys of life than in the midst of war?" he'd said.

Hundreds of people came to the wedding. It seemed that Washington society was eager for a chance to escape the grim news of the hostilities with Spain. The war was in full swing now, with American forces mobilized in the Caribbean and the Far East. The Americans had already seized Guam and the islands of the Philippines from Spain, and it was likely Puerto Rico would be next. Spain was gasping for breath and was unlikely to hold on much longer, yet thousands of lives on both sides had already been lost.

They held the wedding reception in an outdoor garden. It was a perfect summer day, and the garden had been draped with white bunting and bridal flowers. Anna had convinced Mrs. Zanetti to sing for them. Now that the secret of the *Culpeper* was laid bare, there was nothing to keep the Zanettis trapped in frozen exile, so last month they had returned to Washington to resume leading a normal life. Mrs. Zanetti sang with her joyous soprano voice while Silas accompanied her on the cello.

Aunt Ruth had initially declined the wedding invitation, claiming she had nothing suitable to wear. But after Luke paid a visit to her, a new dress magically appeared and Ruth eagerly agreed to attend. After that, Ruth had been almost like a mother in helping Anna plan the luncheon menu and select the floral arrangements. They might never be as close as a real mother and daughter, but they were on their way toward mending a long-simmering rift.

"The waiters have brought in the wedding cake," Luke said. "Your final task is to help me with the cutting before you slip back into a life of quiet anonymity."

She smiled in relief. True to Luke's word, he had no plans to pressure her into any sort of public role as a congressman's wife. She'd had to resign her position at the Library of Congress, but she still visited the library almost daily as she began research on the monumental biography of the world's great cartographers. She had a brand-new typewriter and was learning how to use it. They had no idea if Luke would win the reelection in November, so she was doing as much preliminary research as possible in case they ended up moving to Bangor in a few months.

No matter what happened, though, the past year had taught Anna that she was no delicate bougainvillea blossom, for she'd finally found the courage to venture out into the world beyond the safe walls of the library. She had embarked on a new quest to write a book that would someday be added to those wonderful library shelves all over the nation.

Luke helped Anna to her feet, and they walked to the table holding the cake. She sent a secretive nod to Neville, who lifted the cloth from a boxy contraption sitting atop a tripod a few yards away. Mercifully, Luke didn't notice until they were standing before the tiered wedding cake, ready to begin cutting, when Neville squinted into the eyepiece.

"Slide closer to Luke so I can get both of you in the frame," he called out.

Luke recoiled as soon as he realized what was happening. "Don't," he said, pulling aside to get out of the camera's view. "Can't we just enjoy the moment without spoiling it with that monstrosity?"

"Quick, get back in the frame!" Anna laughed. "It's a motion-picture camera, and Neville is already rolling the film. You look like a bear."

"You'll thank me for this someday," Neville said while rotating the crank on the side of the camera, and Anna knew he was right. So long as she didn't have to speak, she was delighted to have these few jubilant moments of her wedding day captured on film forever. She beamed and waved at the camera, and then nudged Luke in the ribs, trying to get him to do the same.

"I bought you a typewriter," he grumbled. "That's the limit of my tolerance for modern contraptions. Make Neville stop cranking that thing." He folded his arms, lowered his brow, and scowled at the camera.

"Our children are going to love this someday," she said, which caused Luke to plant a whopper of a kiss on her laughing mouth. Mrs. Zanetti stood up and cheered. Neville finally stopped turning the film.

"Perfect!" he called. "Fifteen seconds of film immortalized for all time."

"I should have known you were trouble the first day we met and you tried to foist that newfangled pen on me," Luke muttered as he sliced into the cake, although he was smiling as he said it.

For all his blinding self-confidence, Luke still struggled with the coming flood of technology. She could help him with that, even if she thought his old-fashioned romanticism of the past was rather charming. After all, wasn't it their differences that made things so interesting? God had sent her someone who was exactly right to inspire her to make full use of the talents she'd been blessed with. Luke had helped her learn the truth about the *Culpeper* and encouraged her to write a book about mapmakers, no matter how impractical it might be. By joining their lives together, they had what it took to weather the storms ahead and reach beyond all their dreams.

Historical Note

The Spanish-American War was fought from April to December of 1898. Cuba had been agitating for independence from Spain for decades, and the US government quietly supported their cause throughout most of that time. Tensions boiled over in February 1898 when the USS *Maine* exploded in Havana Harbor, a tragedy that has yet to be fully explained. American casualties from combat during the war were low, while deaths from disease were shockingly high on both sides. An estimated 5,000 Americans and 60,000 Spanish soldiers died during the brief war.

Although the *Culpeper* is a fictional ship, it was loosely based on the *Virginius*, an American ship caught smuggling guns to Cuban rebels in 1873. Cuba was in the midst of a decade-long revolt against Spanish rule, and the American government had been covertly supplying arms to the rebels. The crew of the *Virginius* was put on trial, found guilty, and ordered to be executed. When the British government in Jamaica heard of the incident, a team of diplomats raced to the island to stop the killings, but by the time they arrived, fifty-three crew members had already been executed. President Grant had no desire to plunge into another war and downplayed the incident by accepting huge reparations from Spain to quietly settle the matter. In the weeks leading up to the vote to declare war against Spain, the scandal of the *Virginius* was resurrected to stoke anti-Spanish sentiment among a population still divided on the war.

Theodore Roosevelt made his reputation during the Spanish-American War. After resigning his position as assistant secretary of the navy, he formed the first US Volunteer Cavalry regiment, better known as the Rough Riders. His leadership during the Battle of San Juan Hill was widely celebrated, leading to his election as governor of New York later that year. His popularity was so great that he was selected to be President McKinley's running mate in 1900. Only a few months after the election, McKinley was assassinated, and at the age of forty-two, Theodore Roosevelt became the youngest man ever to serve as president of the United States.

Discussion Questions

1. Is love at first sight possible? Luke's experience with the opera singer taught him about infatuation, so he was already suspicious of the feeling when he met Anna. How can one determine if one is in love or merely infatuated?
2. Anna and Neville had such a long and enduring friendship that most people assumed they would eventually get married. Do you believe such an entirely platonic friendship between a man and a woman is possible? What are some of the advantages of being friends before becoming romantically involved?
3. Luke grew up with an abusive father and feared becoming an abuser himself. Why does this pattern of destructive behavior often get handed down from parents to their children? What patterns of behavior, both positive and negative, have you inherited from your own parents?
4. Throughout the novel, Anna is able to forgive those who have sinned against her, while Luke is not. What power has Luke surrendered to his enemies by continuing to hold grudges? Are there some sins that can't be forgiven?
5. Both Luke and Julia loved their father, even though they feared him. What accounts for this?

6. Is war always wrong?
7. Both Anna and Neville carry scars from their painful years in school, but so does their sometimes-tormentor Eliza Sharpe. Why do so many people look back on their school years as a difficult time in their lives?
8. Why was Neville reluctant to tell Anna of his relationship with Mrs. Norquist? Have you ever been in a platonic relationship and felt "left behind" when your friend became romantically involved with someone?
9. At one point, Luke tells his nephew that the boy's passion for art is a gift from God, "even though we don't know yet what form it will take. If you don't make it as a painter, perhaps you'll be a great teacher. Or a museum curator. Maybe you'll become a rich industrialist and fund a museum. Just don't limit yourself by thinking you already know God's purpose for you." Did you have any childhood dreams that later didn't come true but were funneled toward another worthy goal?
10. Anna and Luke are a case of "opposites attract." What are the advantages and challenges of such a relationship? Would Anna have been better off married to Neville?
11. Political rivalries are nothing new in Washington, D.C. Luke and the Speaker of the House genuinely loathe each other for years before they unite to work toward a common cause. Is it possible to have serious disagreements about policy or social matters without demonizing one another? How might this be accomplished?

Elizabeth Camden is the award-winning author of six novels, including the highly acclaimed *With Every Breath* and *Against the Tide*, winner of a RITA Award, Christy Award, and Daphne du Maurier Award. With master's degrees in both history and library science, she is a research librarian by day while scribbling away on her next novel by night. Elizabeth lives with her husband in Florida. Learn more at ElizabethCamden.com.

More From Elizabeth Camden

To learn more about Elizabeth and her books, visit elizabethcamden.com.

United in a quest to cure tuberculosis, can physician Trevor McDonough and statistician Kate Livingston overcome past secrets and current threats to find hope for a future together?

With Every Breath

After a fire destroys her city, Mollie Knox struggles to rebuild her business while two men vie for her affection. Can Mollie rise from the ashes with both her company and her heart intact?

Into the Whirlwind

When Lydia's translation skills land her in the middle of a secret campaign against dangerous criminals, who can she trust when both her life and her heart are in jeopardy?

Against the Tide

BETHANYHOUSE

Stay up-to-date on your favorite books and authors with our free e-newsletters. Sign up today at bethanyhouse.com.

Find us on Facebook. facebook.com/bethanyhousepublishers

Free exclusive resources for your book group! bethanyhouse.com/anopenbook

You May Also Like . . .

Charlotte wants nothing more than to continue working as an assistant to her father, an eminent English botanist, but he feels it is time for her to marry. Will she find a way to fulfill her dreams and her family's expectations?

Like a Flower in Bloom by Siri Mitchell
sirimitchell.com

As secrets come to light at the abandoned manor house, Pembrooke Park, will Abigail Foster find the rumored treasure and the love she seeks…or very real danger?

The Secret of Pembrooke Park by Julie Klassen
julieklassen.com

A Bible story brought to life! After she is forcibly taken to the palace of the king, a beautiful young Jewish woman, known to the Persians as Esther, wins a queen's crown and then must risk everything in order to save her people . . . and bind her husband's heart.

Esther by Angela Hunt
A Dangerous Beauty Novel
angelahuntbooks.com

BETHANYHOUSE

Stay up-to-date on your favorite books and authors with our free e-newsletters. Sign up today at bethanyhouse.com.

Find us on Facebook. facebook.com/bethanyhousepublishers

Free exclusive resources for your book group! bethanyhouse.com/anopenbook